InterstellarNet: Enigma

Books by Edward M. Lerner

InterstellarNet series
InterstellarNet: Origins (*)
InterstellarNet: New Order (*)
InterstellarNet: Enigma (*)

Fleet of Worlds series (with Larry Niven)
Fleet of Worlds
Juggler of Worlds
Destroyer of Worlds
Betrayer of Worlds
Fate of Worlds

Other Books
Probe (*)
Moonstruck (*)
Creative Destruction (collection)
Fools' Experiments
Small Miracles
Countdown to Armageddon / A Stranger in Paradise (collection)
Frontiers of Space, Time, and Thought (collection) (*)
Energized
A Time Foreclosed (chapbook) (*)

(*) Available from FoxAcre Press

InterstellarNet: Enigma

by

Edward M. Lerner

InterstellarNet: Enigma

FoxAcre
Press
www.foxacre.com

For Ben

May your future always be this big (but never as problematic)

Contents

PROLOGUE

From pole to pole, from one shoreline to the next, from mountaintop to deepest valley, the land was barren. Nothing crept over the ground, nor burrowed beneath, nor flapped its wings overhead. Except for the crack of thunder and the occasional seismic event, only the whistle of the wind and the patter of the rain ever disturbed the silence.

And yet the world's lakes and oceans teemed with life. Single-celled forms, in a bewildering variety. Fungal cell clusters. Vast bacterial mats, afloat on the storm-wracked waves. Jellyfish, more or less. Sponges, of a sort.

For eons, the few changes that transpired came slowly. But unlike the ceaseless sleet of the cosmic rays, the drift of the continents, the uplift of the mountains and their weathering into dust, the advance and retreat of glaciers, the stately dance of the planets, and the ages-long rotation of the galaxy itself, *life* was about to dramatically transform ....

THE MATTHEWS CONUNDRUM

CHAPTER 1

"It ain't a fit night out for man or beast," the autocab said. The words had a pretentious tone to them, as though it were quoting someone. Or maybe this was just AI wit.

Either way, the effort was wasted. From the garlic-smelling interior of the passenger compartment, Joshua Matthews grunted indifferently. He sensed the dawn through the twin filters of heavy rainfall and a pleasant buzz. The buzz he understood. He didn't recall the downpour starting. He didn't remember the hour being so late. Or, rather, so early.

He had evidently nodded off.

A peal of thunder rolled on and on. The drumbeat of rain on the cab intensified. A summer thunderstorm was hardly out of the ordinary in Charleston. But a downpour like this? Unannounced? How had the forecasters missed it?

Joshua subvocalized a weather query to the net. His neural implant returned only an intracranial, mind's-ear hiss.

"Driver." Hmm. His tongue felt too large in his mouth. He tried again. "Cab!"

"How may I be of service?" the vehicle replied.

"Do you have infosphere connectivity?"

"There's a localized outage, sir." Lightning flashed. The in-ceiling speaker crackled with static. "Probably the storm."

"How far?" It came to Joshua that he did not feel well. His bed would be much more comfortable than the autocab.

"Ten minutes to the address you gave me, sir. That is, if traffic and the weather don't get worse. Without net access, who can say?"

In the cab window, Joshua's reflection was pasty. It *had* been a hell of a party. Who better to indulge than the guest of honor?

Still, he had overdone the munchies, and perhaps more alco-hide nanomeds would have been prudent.

His stomach rumbled ominously. His tongue felt larger still. His lips tingled. "As fastht as you can."

At last the cab turned into the canopied semicircular driveway of his condominium. "Thankth," Joshua managed. His door swung open: however weird his voice had become, his implanted ID chip evidently sufficed for authenticating his payment.

He stumbled out just in time, vomiting explosively onto the brick-paved entryway. A cacophony of shrieks, bleeps and discordant warbles flooded his mind's ear. He had no sooner rerouted one alarm to voicemail than another replaced it. And another. And the next. He stumbled against the side of the cab.

The liveried doorman stared. In disapproval at Joshua's obvious drunkenness? In distaste at the mess? Joshua cringed. Within his head, sirens continued to blare. "Th-orry about that, Alan."

Alan unfroze and scurried over. "Dr. Matthews. It *is* you. My lord, it *is* you." He offered a handkerchief. We've been so worried."

"Worried?" Joshua repeated. "Why?"

It was Alan's turn to be confused. "You've been missing for weeks, sir."

• • • •

Lalande Implosion: the global economic crisis that began in 2006. Unlike many historical turning points, the collapse of Earth's petroleum economy had an unambiguous cause—electrical cars had become practical almost overnight. The revolutionary fuel-cell technology for those cars originated in the interstellar radio message with whose receipt in 2002 we mark the start of modern human history. (See related entry, *First Contact*.)

On balance, reduced energy costs were a boon for the world economy. In the short term, however, plunging demand for petroleum impoverished the major oil-producing countries. In response, the United Nations in 2010 enacted the Protocol on Interstellar Technology Commerce. The protocol established the Interstellar Commerce Union (ICU) and gave it authority over all aspects of the human side of trans-species technology import and export.

The epochal message came from Lalande 21185, transmitted by the species popularly known as the Leos (after the constellation, Leo Minor, in which their star can be seen). The message revealed to human analysts that the Leos still used vacuum tubes and analog computing. Earth's reply included primers on quantum mechanics, transistors, and digital computing. Due to light-speed delay, it was not known until seventeen years later that Earth's message had unintentionally triggered a reciprocal economic crisis and technology upheaval among the Leos.

—Internetopedia

• • • •

Groveling, like partying, worked best in person.

Joshua assumed he had been summoned to Geneva, more than seven thousand kilometers, to grovel. Now he waited on a sofa, trying not to squirm or stare.

Dr. Robyn Tanaka Astor, secretary-general of the Interstellar Commerce Union, glided expressionlessly from one exercise apparatus to the next. She seemed indifferent to her workout, the panoramic view from her penthouse office windows, and Joshua. The gym equipment was first-rate; the furniture and bare walls were entirely utilitarian.

The Augmented trained like normal people fidgeted, only more systematically. An AI submind constantly supervised every element of health maintenance: exercise, neural and hormonal biofeedback loops, and armadas of nanomeds and nanosensors. It kept the Augmented wiry and thin almost to the point of gauntness. The regimen was joyless and pragmatic, its sole purpose to postpone the inevitable next phase: uploading.

Her features were finely chiseled, her widely spaced eyes an astonishing green, and her jet-black hair flowed to her shoulders. Augmentation gave her an imposing, charismatic presence. The overall effect was of unapproachable androgynous beauty. She was seventy-five, twenty years older than Joshua. She could have passed for half her age.

"Ir am displeased," she began abruptly in the Augmented first person. Returned from an unknown task on the infosphere, her eyes finally found him. Immobilized him. Impaled him. "You have disgraced the ICU."

Was that her human side speaking or her AI side? Had the latter, the erstwhile Astor 2215, taken its name from John Jacob Astor, or Mary Astor, or—?

Did it matter?

Augmentation was new; the Augmented population was still tiny. The symbiotic brilliance of the composite mind suited them to positions of authority and responsibility far outside the circles in which Joshua moved. She was the only Augmented he knew—if two stressful interviews during the vetting process qualified as knowledge.

This situation was stressful, if not surreal. Perhaps that was why his mind kept jumping to other things. Whether all the Augmented were like her. Whether Robyn Tanaka had been aloof to begin with. Whether her/its/their present iciness had something to do with the Augmentation procedure. What decanting an AI into a human brain had done to, well, both of them.

Did it matter?

And while his mind refused to come to grips with present problems, the professional opportunity—the career coup—of a lifetime was slipping between his fingers. "I'm very sorry," Joshua said. "Truly, I am. I wish I could explain my disappearance."

"Your absence is explained." All inflection had vanished. *That* was the AI side, coldly rephrasing Joshua's wording.

"The police can't explain it," he countered hesitantly.

"Permit mir to summarize," she/it/they said. "You departed the party at the Ritz-Trump by autocab. Two days ago—call it a month later—you arrived home. Between those events, we know nothing.

"Your family filed a missing-person report, but the police found no trace of you. There were no ransom requests. Only obvious crooks and cranks answered your parents' reward offer. With no signs of foul play, the police lost interest in the matter after you reappeared."

Joshua studied his shoes. "The police believe I was off on a drunk the whole time."

"Why wouldn't they?" she asked atonally.

A mind's ear trill made him start. Her netted message linked to a 3-V clip. Hotel security system? Public-safety spy eye? Random passerby with a smartphone?

How hardly mattered.

Time froze for Joshua as the scene looped. There he was: staggering from the autocab. Retching convulsively. Staring like a deer caught in headlights. Wiping vomit and thick strings of saliva from his face. Falling back against the taxi. The ambulance racing away, its sirens keening, with him inside.

"But don't you find any of this … incongruous?" *Because I'm not a drunk, damn it!* "If you would just *look* at the police files you'd see that—"

"Access the non-public case file of a police investigation? You imagine that because Ir *could* probably hack into a police database, that Ir will? If so, you are mistaken. It suffices to know the authorities see no crime here."

Just for a moment, Joshua toyed with getting the police to

drop the investigation. Suppose he indicated that he wouldn't press charges. Maybe then, armed with a copy of their findings (but would they release the file to him even then? He'd better find that out first), he could get Tanaka Astor to consider the anomalies of his long absence. Maybe then he could save his appointment.

As quickly, the temptation passed. He *had* lost a month from his life. He wanted to know why. And whom to blame. And for them to pay for what they'd done. For any of that to happen, he needed to get the cops reengaged.

Somehow.

He stood, shoulders squared. "Madame Secretary-General, I understand how irresponsible this looks. Yes, I had been drinking, but please hear me out.

"Wherever I disappeared to was off the net. Family, friends, the police, your office—*many* people kept trying, at higher and higher levels of priority, to reach me. All those undelivered messages remained queued on comm servers. Suddenly, I reappeared on the net. You're seeing me inundated by alarms and crash-priority messages. *That's* why I appear so confused."

His digital doppelgänger dry-heaved again. Joshua winced. The vid was *not* pretty. "For the rest, somehow I had eaten some crab. I'm massively allergic. The hospital confirmed an allergic reaction."

Tanaka Astor never broke her rhythm on the elliptical trainer. "Dr. Matthews, your dietary indiscretions are of no concern to the ICU. Your month-long absence from work on a binge is."

Stepping outside her circuit of exercise equipment, she fixed her gaze on Joshua. The undivided attention of an Augmented was a terrifying thing. His heart pounded.

She said, "You had friends and supporters in the organization, but you also have detractors. Your critics think only family connections got you into the ICU. Despite the skeptics, Ir endorsed your recommendation for an official ICU history. Despite the skeptics, Ir considered your application, one of many, for appointment as our official historian."

Had friends? Joshua suddenly wanted to be anywhere else. How much had his very public humiliation injured an institution he loved?

"For purposes of compiling the 175th anniversary history, Ir considered your family ties, if anything, a plus. Ir presumed your family background offered a unique resource for the task. And so Ir entrusted to you the duties of ICU historian.

"The Augmented make very few mistakes, Dr. Matthews. Here, it is clear, Ir made one. It seems that the cynics had it right. You were *not* up to the task.

"*In vino veritas*, Dr. Matthews. In wine is truth. Your friends gave you a party to celebrate your good fortune. There, you had some wine. There, you confronted your inadequacies. You realized you were in over your head.

"The mystery, Dr. Matthews, is not your as-yet undisclosed hideaway. The mystery is your shameful, very public return."

It's not true! I don't know *where I was!* Joshua somehow held the scream inside. In their consensual net vision, the damning video clip started over. "I recognize that these events have embarrassed the organization. For that I apologize."

Despite Tanaka Astor's beliefs, Joshua felt as qualified—and eager—as ever to serve. But did feelings matter to an Augmented? Facts alone might sway her, and Joshua had none. That left only one thing to say. "To spare the ICU further embarrassment, I resign as historian. I'll resume my former duties."

"Correction." The inflectionless precision of the AI facet was unmistakable. "The historian serves at the pleasure of the secretary-general. Civil-service protections do not apply. Effective immediately, you have no affiliation with the ICU."

CHAPTER 2

Corinne Elman thrashed in her sleep, knowing that she dreamed, helpless to wake herself. Her recurring nightmare took many forms. The God's-eye view was the worst: too vast, too fast, too horrible.

Only God's eye could encompass this much deception.

She woke screaming, and Denise stopped shaking her. Absent the worried expression, Denise's sleep-tousled appearance might have been comical. "Nightmare?"

Corinne nodded, her hands trembling. "Sorry for disturbing you. Go back to sleep."

"Will you be okay?"

"A dream hasn't hurt me yet," Corinne lied. Sunlight peeked between the bedroom curtains. Her neural implant said 5:34. She would never fall back asleep. "I'll be fine, hon."

She tucked Denise in, then padded barefoot to the living room. She drew back the drapes, seeking serenity in the view.

Your average reporter didn't own a penthouse overlooking Central Park, but she was hardly the average newsie. Twenty years before, she had broken the story of the oncoming starship. That got her the first interview with the ship's Foremost. That got her the pool-reporter seat on the lifeboat orientation cruise, hobnobbing with United Planets bigwigs and the top scientists from Himalia.

That got her almost killed, and twenty years of nightmares. And counting …

Corinne's memoir, 3-V specials, and interviews with less articulate principals had made her rich. She had assigned most of the royalties to victims' families so she could live with herself. Then another talk-show offer would come in, or another anniversary of the Himalia Incident would roll around, and she would convince herself to milk it one last time.

The park looked pleasantly uncrowded this early. Something she couldn't make out was going on near the lake. She resisted netting for the information. Instead Corinne dressed for a jog and rode down the express elevator. She would *see* what was happening.

How had she devolved from investigative reporter to celebrity? She had turned into a one-trick pony—in an age when gengineered ponies learned many tricks. Corinne managed a "Morning, Charles," to the doorman on her way outside.

She dodged the still light traffic, crossing Central Park West into the park. The morning breeze felt great. The smart-tar path was resilient beneath her feet. She tried to concentrate on her breathing and maintaining a steady pace.

And failed.

"Walt," she subvocalized.

"You're up early," Walt answered instantly. "What's the story?"

In her mind's eye, Walt's avatar sat behind a battered wooden desk. He was an AI; the hour didn't matter to him. His suit, two centuries out of style, and a bristly mustache honored Walter Cronkite. The cigarette was an homage to Edward R. Murrow.

It saddened Corinne that Walt considered what she did journalism. She hoped he was only being polite.

"Any updates to my calendar?" Corinne asked. Her schedule showed nothing for days but more of the depressing same.

"A few more 'twenty years after' interview opportunities. Some talk-show appearances in the works. Nothing definite, Corinne."

"Thanks, anyway, Walt." Her last impression as he dropped the link was of a centimeters-long ash being tapped off his virtual cigarette. What a curious affectation.

She picked up the pace, angling toward the activity near the lake. Twenty years … *that* was the problem. These anniversaries always reminded her of where her life had gone awry.

New Beginnings was now well on its way to Alpha Centauri. Centaurs too long away from home comprised much of its crew; humans the rest. And she could have been aboard.

She knew many who were: ICU specialists. Her fellow abductees on the ill-fated lifeboat cruise. Those who like her had survived ….

Seven years ago, she had come to a crossroads. She could have gone on *New Beginnings*, on the adventure of a lifetime. Instead she had chosen to remain behind. Staying home made Corinne the highest profile witness still available to the Himalia Incident and the destruction of the Centaur starship, *Harmony*. Famous. Sought-after. Transformed from journalist to celebrity.

Once again, she hated herself for that moment of weakness. For surrendering to the fear of another adventure.

Huffing now, Corinne neared whatever she had glimpsed from ninety stories above. Cars with strobing light bars encircled the lake. Inside the ring, behind a barrier of sawhorses, a skirmish line of flamethrower-wielding figures in hazmat suits, advancing slowly, were sweeping the ground with jets of fire. Just as she caught a whiff of something nasty, a cop wearing a breather mask waved her off.

A puddle of shadow hinted at a ditch lased through the access paths, isolating the perimeter road. Beyond the gap, smart-tar shimmered and seethed. It was not supposed to do that.

The nanites that autonomously resurfaced the roadway supposedly couldn't hurt living things. The grass alongside the rogue pavement looked normal—

And the workers doing battle with the road all wore hazmat gear.

Corinne veered from the path to jog uphill on the lawn. Something tickled the back of her mind. That this incident was news, and she ought to be reporting it? Nope. Nanotech flare-ups were boringly common: a local-interest story, at most. She was better than that.

Then what? What else had she been musing about? *New Beginnings*. Centaurs. Himalia survivors. None of those felt right, either.

The ICU members of the crew? That wasn't quite it, either.

She reached the crest winded, and slowed to a cool-down gait. *Something about the ICU*, she thought. *Not* anyone who was starship crew. Not anyone she knew from the long-derelict *Harmony*. Something more recent about the ICU.

Breathing heavily, Corinne plopped onto a park bench. It finally came to her. *Two* high-visibility anniversaries fell this year. The twentieth anniversary of the Himalia Incident. And later in the year, the 175th anniversary of the ICU.

A tie-in? She could manage that. It would give a fresh spin to the old rehash. Maybe that was all. Something about the ICU anniversary had been all over the net of late, though she didn't recall the details. There were days she couldn't stand to follow the news anymore. Real news only reminded her of everything she had lost. Abandoned. Squandered.

She queried the infosphere for recent stories about the ICU.

And after skimming the headlines, Corinne knew what kept nagging at her. A warmth suffused her, and not because the breeze had faded and sunlight now streamed between two towers east of the park. She formulated a task, a true journalistic research assignment, for Walt.

Maybe, Corinne decided, *I have one more real story in me.*

CHAPTER 3

"You need a job," Aaron blurted out.

No one on Earth needed *a job*, Joshua thought. Ubiquitous nanotech synthesis, nearly lossless recycling, and literal oceans of fusion fuel provided a comfortable standard of living to everyone on Earth essentially for free. Automated factories provided most of the few things people couldn't synth for themselves. When recycling fell short, AI-operated probes delivered raw material from the limitless reserves of the main Belt, the Kuiper Belt, and the Oort Cloud. Much less did anyone in the Matthews clan need a job. The family trust fund had seen to that.

Many more people *wished* to work than could serve any productive purpose. Or even unproductive purposes like concierge. Most people with the vocational urge moved off-world. Joshua didn't see the point. Modern tech would catch up with them soon enough.

Wanting work or needing it. Perhaps only historians still drew any distinction. And ex-historians.

Joshua knew his little brother meant well. Aaron was among those with the compulsion to work. He operated an interior-design boutique, mostly custom programming of holo sculptures and digital wallpaper. For decades now, AI art had been indistinguishable from human efforts. Double-blind experiments reconfirmed that regularly. Some people nonetheless paid for human designs.

Joshua admired the view, only partially as a delaying tactic. They stood on a graceful, cantilevered balcony that projected from the cliff face in a remote part of the Grand Canyon. Layer upon layer of red rock, eons congealed in stone, stretched as far as the eye could see. The Colorado River, far below, was a trickle. The canyon floor must have been brutally hot; convection currents upwelling from

24

the gorge blurred the opposite wall.

Behind Joshua, living quarters burrowed into the rock. Aaron's lodge was hand-built with supplies flown in on hovercraft. His getaway went far beyond anyone's slice of the family trust fund. Some people paid *very* well for human designs.

"Joshua!" Aaron rapped the railing. "Did you even hear me?" And more softly, "Are you okay, Bro?"

Joshua's young nephews shrieked inside, oblivious to maternal shushing. Tina's whispering skills needed practice: the boys had to be quiet so Daddy could have some "special alone time" with Uncle Joshua. Scenery changed, but never the treatment. Parents, friends, sisters, and now his brother—everyone felt the need to express concern, scope out his presumed instability, and nudge him back toward respectability.

Rather than "helpful" hints, he wanted support. He wanted *belief.* A girlfriend might have given him that, but he'd been between girlfriends when—whatever—had happened.

Joshua suspected he would be a long time between girlfriends.

Friends, parents, and sibs, but not yet Grandma Matthews. Somehow, he had let her down the most. He couldn't imagine what he would say to her. And he couldn't duck her calls and messages forever.

"Joshua!"

"I'm fine, Aaron, if still confused."

Aaron waited.

There was no mystery what everyone wanted to discuss, over and over. "It's the damnedest thing, Aaron. It's as though those weeks never happened."

"The police found no sign of you," Aaron said.

By every account, his brother had pestered them enough to be authoritative on that point. And, assuming Joshua possessed *any* aptitude at reading body language, had pestered them enough to piss them off. That was one theory, anyway, for Joshua's case ending up on the bottom of the stack even before his reappearance.

He meant well, Joshua kept telling himself.

Aaron was suddenly shocked to discover the cold beer in his own hand. He bustled indoors to set the glass on a table in the living area. "Sorry about that." Awkward silence. "And your doctor?"

It always came to that question. Comprehensive testing said that Joshua had had a bit too much liquor and, mostly, an allergic reaction to crab.

Joshua knew as much going in. Crab (the natural stuff, far worse than the common synthed version) always got to him. He had to be soused not to avoid crab. So he knew one thing about where he had been—it was someplace with upscale hors d'oeuvres.

"I'm *fine*, Aaron. There's nothing wrong with me. There's no evidence I was held against my wishes. And Bro, there was also no sign of alcoholism"—no matter what most people seemed to believe—"just, obviously, some alcohol. Reclaim your beer. Better yet, find one for me."

Aaron ignored the suggestion. "And the … other kind of doctor?"

And then it always came to *that* question, couched in sympathetic hesitance. "I've been analyzed and hypnotized. It's strange. My memories weren't repressed and they weren't damaged. I simply have no memory of that time. Not even my neural implant has data between the party and my reappearance." Had he turned off the implant, its audit log should have recorded the shutdown event. Not that anyone had access to the inside of his skull, but *Joshua* knew: there was no such annotation.

Suppression fields kept neural interfaces from functioning. Police and prisons used suppressors legally, keeping prisoners from conspiring over the infosphere. As for anyone else …

Officially, the police considered his disappearance a cold case. In practice that status differed from closed only as a matter of semantics. What should he do next? What could he do? The only idea that ever came to Joshua's mind was hiring a private investigator. That approach seemed more melodramatic than useful.

"I feel for you, Joshua. It's just so weird." Aaron studied the remote depths of the canyon. "We have to move you past this. So about that job?"

Aaron had to work. *Joshua* had to know things. He had worked because some things couldn't be found on the net. Not the public net, anyway. The subjects that most fascinated Joshua were best explored at the ICU. The salary that came with the job supported a nice home, but doormen and concierges did not motivate him. Few of their relatives grasped the distinction. Was it worth getting into now?

But maybe he could postpone that discussion. The mind's ear trill that only Joshua could hear signaled an incoming call. "Accept," he subvocalized.

A famous visage popped into his mind's eye. Round face. Tight brunette curls. Dark, lively eyes. Engaging smile.

Corinne Elman opened the conversation with three simple words that overwhelmed Joshua: "I believe you."

• • • •

The concierge netted precisely on the hour to announce a visitor.

Joshua Matthews's punctuality did not surprise Corinne. Mid-level bureaucrats and middle children: two breeds that followed all the rules. Her guest was both.

She was an only child. Of the people Corinne knew who weren't also only children, most had just one brother or sister. It verged on child abuse in this era to make someone a middle child.

Corinne's grandfather had a favorite proverb. The nail that sticks up gets pounded down. Whether or not Joshua Matthews knew the adage, the public record showed he lived by it.

Until very recently. And then he had gotten hammered. In every possible sense of the word.

Matthews had leapt from obscurity directly to notoriety. He was without credibility now: a laughingstock. The video clip of his reappearance was everywhere on the net. Dazed. Puking his guts out—ad nauseam, as it were.

It wasn't like the vid itself was noteworthy. People did stupid things every day, after all, often enough in public. What didn't get caught on camera every day was the scion of a prominent family publicly losing it. The rich and famous enjoyed many advantages—but the opportunity to screw up in obscurity wasn't among them. As of the evening before, the last time she had checked, Matthews's vid had topped ten million hits. Not even cute kittens could compete. For two days after his reappearance, not even hacked celebrity selfie porn could compete.

She was almost certainly kidding herself that anything useful could come of this meeting—and desperate to prove herself wrong. Desperate to be a reporter again.

There was a tentative knock at Corinne's door. She picked up a full wineglass before opening it. "Dr. Matthews, thank you for coming."

"Just call me Joshua," he said. "And I was happy to get out of Charleston."

I'll bet you were, she thought.

"And call me Corinne." She waggled her glass. "Something for you?"

"Ice water, if you don't mind."

Corinne filled his glass at her minibar, allowing him to reconsider. He didn't. *First test passed*, she thought.

Matthews was more than a head taller than she, easily 185 centimeters. He was stocky but soft-looking. *Bureaucrat*, she thought again. His face was all lines and planes: broad forehead, straight nose, thin lips, and square jaw. Clean shaven. His eyes were an unexceptional blue—and his gaze guarded. His blond hair was close-cropped with long sideburns. His nanornaments offered a trace of tan and no personalized design that she could see. His shirt and slacks fabrics were programmed in uninteresting grays. His avatar and net bio had previewed all that, of course. He seemed *way* too healthy for someone supposedly just back from a month-long debauch.

Happy to get out of town, was he? Corinne could imagine the sidelong glances and furtive whispers as he moved around his neighborhood. She would want to be elsewhere, too.

She opened the French doors onto the rooftop terrace. Potted plants—dwarf Japanese red maples and staked Centaur bluefruit vines—lined the balustrade. He followed her outside into warm afternoon sun. She said, "Let's start at the party, Joshua."

He studied the park far below and the Manhattan skyline, quiet for a long while. "It began, at least for humans, nearly one and three-quarters centuries ago."

Something about him (the brooding gaze? the careful selection of every word?) conveyed great intelligence. His 175 years presumably referred back to the founding of the ICU. This was going to be a *long* conversation if his speech was always this oblique.

"The party?" she tried again.

His brow furrowed in mock concentration. Never mind that Joshua was in his mid fifties, he had a boyish charm. She sensed he had it to a fault. He struck her as an underachiever.

Data diving had shown considerable family money. Riches to rags in three generations: that was the rule of thumb. Joshua wasn't impoverished, but neither was he distinguished. Still, maybe she could cut him some slack. Despite the trust fund, he had chosen gainful employment.

"Joshua, I'll save us both some time. I know it was a happy-promotion party. I know this was somehow—or so you believe—about the ICU. I know this, too." She netted a complex graphic, a lopsided, multicolored data tree, into their consensual space. Each main bough was a timeline, a concise summary of dealings with a particular InterstellarNet species. Color-coded leaves clustered and clumped on the branches: dialogue milestones; AI trade-agent version upgrades; technology announcements, auctions, and publicly disclosed transactions; rumored commercial conflicts. Only the branches for Alpha Centauri and Barnard's Star showed a red leaf, representing physical contact. "I did my homework before netting you." Her point made, she dropped back to reality.

"I see you've discovered the family ties," he said.

Walt had annotated the "leaves" with IDs of key participants. The Matthews name appeared all over, back to the Leo contact, predating even the founding of the ICU with Joshua's umpty-great-grandmother as secretary-general. Another past secretary-general, his grandmother. Three former chief technology officers. Many mid-level bureaucrats. Entrepreneurs working interstellar trade from the private side. Throw in some kin not named Matthews, and there was even an interstellar journalist in the family two generations back. Data Jockey to the Stars, that one had called himself.

Corinne swirled the wine in her glass. "It's not a deep secret."

"I guess not." He exhaled sharply. "Since you researched the ICU so thoroughly, you've doubtless researched me. You know what I've been going through. You'll understand I'm in no mood for games. I want to hear, no holds barred, what *you* think happened.

"I don't know where I was. I don't know what I was doing. But I do know myself, Corinne. Whatever anyone else may think, I was not drinking myself into oblivion. And however much they sugarcoat it, my own family doesn't believe me. Why would you?"

"Reporters have connections."

And police, as much as anybody, often got a kick out of doing favors for celebrities. This was hardly the first time a cop had let her peek at the file from an active investigation—however nominally, in this instance, the label *active* applied. And with Joshua's reappearance, her source admitted, they had bigger fish to fry. Including minnows and tadpoles.

She continued, "The cops are sure you panicked after winning the new job. That you found yourself in over your head. And that disappearance and faked amnesia are your cover. It's an easy explanation."

Joshua coughed. "I asked what *you* thought."

So he had. "The police confirmed they found no signs of you. Not an access to your financial accounts. Not one encounter with a friend, relative, neighbor, colleague, or acquaintance. Not a single appearance on a public-safety camera. Not one digital trace anywhere on the net. All the while, infosphere messages, no matter their urgency, piled up undelivered on servers.

"I find all that intriguing. A month-long bender without ever touching your money? A nonstop binge without as much as a mention on a police blotter for a bar brawl?" Corinne patted her right arm where her personal ID chip was implanted. Stores, restaurants, cabs, elevators: they polled her chip—everyone's chip—countless times each day. Such chips made it all but impossible to go unnoticed in the modern world—and Joshua had. And yet, he hardly seemed the type to find an identity launderer, or to have diverted enough untraceable wealth to hire one. "Even if you were on a drunken spree, something more was involved."

She took Joshua's hand. "All that said, there's a chance the police have it almost right. That you vanished on purpose, maybe living off someone else's money, and then, somehow, truly got amnesia. Are you *certain* you want to find out?"

"I'm terrified to find out," Joshua said. "But regardless, I have to know."

CHAPTER 4

Joshua feigned sleep, the better to ignore his fellow passengers aboard the packed lunar shuttle. The problem was, he wasn't tired. And closed eyes did nothing to vanquish laughter.

You're not the universe's lone source of amusement, Joshua told himself. *Don't be paranoid.* The chiding did nothing to erase memories of the winks, nudges, and knowing grins that had pursued him through the Charleston spaceport concourse. And for every obvious gawker, how many more had watched discreetly through the public-safety monitors, sharing a good chortle by net?

Passers-by seemed to recognize him wherever he went. Oh, not everyone. He knew that. It only felt that way. Yet somehow no one could find a trace of him for four entire weeks. How could that be?

Meanwhile, the motion-sickness meds had yet to kick in, and the roiling in his gut did nothing for his mood. Neither did memories of the stewardess, floating down the cabin at mid-flight bearing a mesh bag of drink bulbs. Approaching his row, her eyes had studiously avoided his. Her enumeration of beverage choices—the list he had heard a dozen times as she'd made her way aft—suddenly lacked adult options. For all he'd felt like a beer, he had asked for water. On the space line's infosphere site, in very fine print, the alcoholic beverage policy read *Management has the right to refuse service at any time.*

Choosing his battles? Or chickening out? Maybe he was angrier with himself than with the stewardess.

Here and there about the cabin, the sniggers grew louder. Opening his eyes and craning his neck, Joshua saw the infamous vid playing on a seatback display across the aisle. He watched long enough to see the vid had been improved. Now, at the point where Joshua exited the taxi, his face had been digitally rendered a Wicked

Witch of the West green.

Two rows away, a passenger was looked back. Staring. Staring at *him*. When Joshua caught her eye, the woman turned away. She didn't even have the decency to shrug.

Almost an hour left till Tycho City Spaceport. Joshua let his eyes full shut and filled his mind's ear with Beethoven.

Two symphony movements later, he still didn't know what he would say. He hadn't told Grandma Matthews that he was coming. He could always hole up in a bar or hotel while he found the words. Even without the chuckles drowning out a pianissimo passage, he knew that was a stupid idea.

Did the words matter? Nothing he said could make things right.

He had failed the whole family, but Joyce Matthews most of all. Grandma had been secretary-general of the ICU. Much of a century later, she remained legendary in the organization. Now *he* was a joke there.

Grandma's stories were why he had become an historian. Had he ever told her?

She told such great stories. About alien AI trade agents. About misunderstandings large and small, often momentous, on occasion hilarious. About how the InterstellarNet took shape. For almost two centuries, ICU history and the Matthews family annals had been entwined.

The tech of it all sometimes went over his head, but never the scope. The sheer scale of InterstellarNet had captured his imagination. With its members all light-years apart, every communication cycle took years. Even a trade deal negotiated overnight with a local AI agent relied upon programming and instructions from years earlier.

He remembered the day—it was at a party for Aaron's ninth birthday, which made Joshua twelve—when the LED of enlightenment had lit. Grandma (and Grandpa, still healthy) had not yet relocated to the Moon. Thunderstorms had driven everyone inside the house. His brother, sisters, and cousins were watching some 3-V toon. The adults were in another room discussing adult stuff. Grandma began telling stories and he had sat at her feet, rapt.

Every incoming interstellar message was a communication from the past. Every communication that humanity transmitted was a missive to the future. And so, the passage of the years complicated even the most basic of exchanges. Did a question or its reply still have meaning? Between asking and answering, how had circumstances changed? When talking to the Centaurs, nine years separated question and answer. When dealing with the fringes of the InterstellarNet community, the Dragons of far-off Alrakis, the cycle took thirty-seven years.

A pause between movements. Scattered chortles filled the gap.

It took more than techies to phrase and parse InterstellarNet messages. Whatever they chose to call themselves, it took historians. To reconstruct years-old contexts. To imagine what a distant society might be like when a Sol system message would be received years later.

And yet, what had seemed so clear to Joshua eluded others, even within the ICU. If they could not grasp the role of historical analysis in the InterstellarNet process, then what, besides nepotism, could he expect them to believe?

When the lunar shuttle landed with a soft thump, Joshua still had no idea what he would say.

. . . .

Grandma was as tiny as Joshua remembered and even frailer. Fair enough: she was 110 years old, and even Earth-side she wouldn't have weighed fifty kilos. Still, she leapt, easily wrapping her arms around his neck. "It's good to see you, boy!"

Earth retirees were a growth industry on the Moon. Joshua could see why. "Hi, Grandma. May I come in?"

"Of course." She gave a final squeeze, and let go. In slow motion, she settled to the floor. "What can I get you?"

"Nothing, thanks." He followed her inside. Tiny woman, tiny furniture, tiny apartment. Giant spirit.

"You look awfully glum, Josh," she said. She perched on the

edge of the sofa, patting a spot beside her.

He sat. Grandma was the *only* one who still called him Josh. He didn't mind it from her. "I've had a rough couple weeks, Grandma. You know why, of course. I've embarrassed everyone in the family. You cannot imagine how sorry I am. Most of all, I let you down."

Grabbing his chin, she turned his face toward hers. "How, possibly, could you let me down?" She squeezed hard when he opened his mouth. "Still talking here, Josh.

"Of course I know about your disappearance. I worried about you the whole time. I netted your parents practically daily. And no one was happier than I when you returned home.

"Being away isn't an embarrassment. Being ill isn't an embarrassment. How can you imagine you've let me down?" After a final pinch, she released his chin.

"Our family had this wonderful legacy at the ICU. Now, when people hear the name Matthews, they think about drunkenness and nepotism. I am so sorry, Grandma." It was hard not to shout: haven't you *heard* the mockery?

And it was precisely because the clan had accomplished so much at the ICU, Grandma more than most, that his supposed indiscretion refused to fade away.

"I'm telling you something in confidence," Grandma said. "Of all my grandchildren, I'm the proudest of you. Am. Present tense. Your grandfather, if he were still with us, would feel the same.

"Both your sisters and their husbands are content to live on their trust funds and public allotments. There's nothing wrong with that. They're good people and I love them all, but they're hardly ambitious. Your brother is a successful businessman and I respect him for that. What Aaron does, however, is mostly frivolous.

"Now you"—she reached up again, this time to pat Joshua's cheek—"you took a hard road. You chose to do something useful and difficult. You did it despite the complication that so many in the family preceded you there."

Why tell him this now? "You're very kind, Grandma. It doesn't alter—"

"*One* question for you, Josh. Were you hiding away, drunk or stoned?"

"No!" He steepled his fingers. "I don't know where I was, but no. Absolutely not."

"That's good enough for me," Grandma said. "It should be good enough for you. Don't *ever* let other people tell you how to think about yourself." She stood. "I'm getting myself a beer. Can I get you one?" It was ten in the morning local time; he must have looked shocked. She cackled, her eyes twinkling. "Josh, lad, did you look out the view ports on approach? It'll be night here for another standard week."

What a simple pleasure: to be trusted with a beer. He grinned. "Good enough for me."

She started the synthesizer. "Can I give you some advice?"

"Always."

"Lighten up. Decide what *you* want to do next, and then go do it. Don't worry what anyone else thinks. Not your parents, or your pushy little brother, as much as I love the dear, or me." The synthesizer beeped. She handed him a foaming glass, then clinked it with her own. "Expect the world to be confusing as hell. That's *its* job.

"Did I ever tell you about the time the Centaur trade agent applied for political asylum? That was almost seventy years ago. Your Dad was a baby. The AI emancipation movement was first beginning. I'd just become S-G. Looking back, I didn't know *what* I was doing. The United Planets were in a redistricting uproar over the latest census ..."

Had she? At least ten times. Joshua would happily hear her retell it ten more. When she finished, he said, "Thank you, Grandma." For listening. For believing in me. "Clearly age brings wisdom."

She downed the last of her beer. "Sometimes. Other times it just brings on new mistakes. The Snakes have been civilized a lot longer than humans, and I don't see that the ages have made them any wiser."

And with that, Grandma launched into more reminiscing, this time involving the AI trade agent from Barnard's Star.

CHAPTER 5

Corinne's suborbital hop from Long Island to Geneva diverted, minutes before landing, to Basel. The pilot's announcement said only that there had been a glitch in terminal ground control. The net offered no immediate explanation, although AI hiccups had become common enough of late that Corinne had her suspicions. She was too preoccupied to run down the details.

A maglev train brought her to downtown Geneva just before one p.m. local. The depot's main exit tunnel, lined with boutiques and eateries, led to ICU headquarters. VR and netheading went only so far; Joshua had found himself in Geneva several times every month. She sauntered into a café he had mentioned. Where he had often eaten, his ex-cronies might still.

"Beyond" digital walls, slowly "turning," snow-covered slopes plunged toward a distant timberline. Snow devils swirled. An alpine hare hopped past, winter-white. The place was packed, diners lingering over coffee and desserts. She had downloaded an ICU staff directory into her implant. She scanned the room now, searching for facial matches.

Four translucent icons, three men and a woman, popped over her real-world view. Tags beneath gave names and titles. All were in the trade-policy bureau where Joshua had worked before his ill-fated promotion. An org-chart fragment showed different immediate bosses than any Joshua had had. Perfect.

Joshua was on the Moon, on personal business. That was fine with Corinne. She hadn't yet mentioned this expedition to him. Depending what she learned, she might never.

She strolled to the booth where her unwitting sources sat, their table cleared but for coffee cups. "Excuse me." They looked up, two seeming to recognize her. "Do you work at the ICU?" The woman nodded. "Good. I'm a reporter researching a story for the upcoming 175th anniversary. I'm asking people about their impressions. Background stuff."

Eyes on both sides of the booth glazed for a moment: a netted consultation. Perhaps some of the four did a quick infosphere lookup of her. If they were checking her out, well, fair enough. "Sure, Ms. Elman," the woman said. She slid closer to a coworker. "Have a seat."

"Corinne. Thanks." She sat.

"I'm Becky," the woman answered. She had floral nanornamented cheeks and a weightlifter's upper body. Becky pointed to her companions. "Fred, Juan, and Travis." Carrot top; bald with wings-of-Mercury cranial tattoos; blond with puppy-dog eyes.

Old habits kicked in. Step one: put your subjects at ease. "How long have you been at the ICU?" Corinne began.

"Eight years," Fred and Juan said in unison. Travis raised a hand, fingers extended, thumb folded.

"Ten years," Becky answered, indicating by her tone that she was establishing seniority.

They net-swapped bio files. Corinne commended the ICU. She inquired about their duties, nodding encouragement as they spoke. She lamented how the public failed to appreciate the beneath-the-hood complexities. She bought espressos and plates of sacher torte all round.

On to step two: circle the real topic. "One hundred seventy-five years. That's quite an accomplishment." The observation got Corinne only nods. A touchy subject, it would seem. That might be Joshua's doing. "I'd expect so, anyway."

"A hundred seventy-five years *is* a big deal." A glazed-eye flicker, more consultation, and then—

Ping! Corinne took the netted call, smiling inside. Déjà vu: Corinne "sat" with the foursome at a virtual café table. "You want confidentiality, obviously. That's fine."

"I begin to doubt we'll see much of an anniversary," Becky netted. "At first I thought an ICU commemorative history was a great idea. No more. It's made us a laughingstock."

"I always thought it was a dumb idea," Fred said. "Too diffuse a story to tell. So much of what we do happens in interstellar slow motion."

Juan and Travis jumped in, championing particular ICU highlights. First-contact moments. Historic trade deals. The rise of the modern InterstellarNet. A distant relative of Joshua's had invented the mechanisms behind swapping AI trade agents, and the AI quarantine mechanism so quaintly called the sandbox.

Corinne let them chatter. It conditioned them to say things that perhaps they shouldn't.

Some journalists still claimed they produced the first draft of history. Not Corinne. Had worldliness or cynicism first changed her mind? Maybe there was no difference. She struggled to remember something Joshua had told her about history, miffed she had let her mental filing get behind. Ah: nothing might happen for millennia on end, beyond, perhaps, a marginally better method for chipping rock—and the next day, a genius might tame fire.

Some days changed everything. Columbus reaches the Americas. Mobs storm the Bastille. 9/11. First Contact.

The Snake trade agent, secure in his sandbox, data-mining his way to discovery of the undisclosed human antimatter factory on Himalia. The discovery that motivated a hijacking that ...

The memories washed over her: of *Harmony* shutting down, coming apart, hurtling into the cold and dark. Of corpses adrift in the corridors. With a shiver, she buried those images—until her next nightmare.

The four had sufficiently agitated themselves, Corinne decided. She had best go on before, contrary to appearances, one found an interest in returning to work. And so, step three: sidle toward the real topic. "Someone mentioned a laughingstock. What's that about?"

"Joshua bleeping Matthews," Becky snapped. "I'm so *sick* of hearing about him. He's made the ICU a joke." Virtual heads nodded agreement.

Step four: ask the real questions—oh, so casually. "Do you know him?" Corinne asked.

"For years, although not very well. He's the quiet type." Becky glowered. "If only he had stayed that way."

Travis mock-retched. Everyone laughed. "The shame of it is, now no one will take the historian job."

Oh? "No one?" Corinne repeated.

"Who wants to become known as second choice to Joshua?" Travis mock-retched again. "It would be the kiss of death for a reputable historian."

Juan nodded. "I predict there'll be no formal cancellation of the history project. It will fade away, never again mentioned. History killed by an historian: another Matthews conundrum."

"It's clearly nepotism," Fred said. "The ICU professional staff are technical specialists, whether in trade or economics or InterstellarNet plumbing. Why, except nepotism, bring in an historian? If Matthews hadn't already been on-staff, no *way* would he have gotten the appointment that panicked him." And with a sympathetic expression, "Whoever pulled strings to get Joshua his historian gig did him no favor."

"No Matthews has been high-ranking for years," Juan said. "Joshua was in the most senior post."

The four of them debated nepotism, hypothesized ancient obligations, speculated about professional courtesy, and generally belabored every possible explanation—other than talent and enthusiasm—for Joshua's appointment. The longer they went on, the more Corinne thought: Joshua's dismissal was a real loss to the ICU. *What a shame no one here understood that.*

Somewhere in reality, chairs scraped against the floor. Travis glanced at the café's wall clock. "Guys, I need to get back to work. Corinne, it was a pleasure to meet you."

Within minutes, Corinne had the restaurant almost to herself. Most other tables had also emptied out. A robot with a clattering tread moved about, clearing and cleaning. Sipping coffee, two thoughts chased around her head. First, it felt *good* to work on something new again. It made her feel, for the first time in a long

time, like a real reporter. And second—
Another Matthews conundrum?

CHAPTER 6

Joshua waited on the couch in his condo lobby, enjoying an actual fire of actual logs. Neighbors streamed past, dispensing sniffs of disapproval and oblique glances. He ignored them all. Maybe it was Grandma's pep talk, maybe a stubborn streak he had not known he had in him. Whatever the reason, he was not about to accept ostracism.

And waited some more. Corinne was late.

Until the outdoor security cameras finally caught her scurrying beneath the front-entrance canopy for cover, he had started to worry. She folded an oversized umbrella. Dismissing the netted view, he stood, stretched, and turned toward the doors.

Rain was coming down in buckets. Corinne, despite her umbrella, was soaked. Dark hair wet-plastered to her head made her face seem even rounder than usual. Her stomping feet sent water drops flying.

The doorman was too distracted by this celebrity arrival to notice Joshua approaching from behind. "It's all right, Alan. Ms. Elman is with me."

Corinne beamed when she saw Joshua. Not even a drenching could diminish her aura of energetic chaos.

Heads turned as he escorted her into the vestibule. He asked, "Downstairs by the fire or upstairs for dry clothes?"

"Definitely up." She left a soggy trail across the carpet and a small puddle in the elevator.

He shut her in his closet to find something to wear. "It's tough to catch a cab in the rain."

"To tell the truth, Joshua, I didn't look for a cab." The door opened a crack. A hand emerged dangling a terrycloth robe by its hanger. "Mind if I wear this?"

"Whatever you want." He scratched his head. The nearest maglev station was a good klick away. "*Why* did you walk through this?"

Corinne came out, lost in his robe. She rubbed her hair vigorously with the towel he offered. The sea-anemone look worked surprisingly well for her.

"There's no record of the cab that dropped you here that night," she said. "Odd, don't you think?"

"I remember paying for the ride," Joshua protested. "Well, I remember leaning up to the backseat chip reader and the door unlatching."

"Trust me." She blotted a trickle running down her neck. "There's no record of any payment. When I bugged them, the police checked."

Joshua accessed his bank account. Sure enough: he had never been debited for that ride. "I remember leaving the party. The waiter at the Ritz Trump put me into the cab."

"The waiter. Didn't that strike you as odd? Hell, didn't it strike you as odd that there *was* a waiter? I don't recall anyone named Gates or Rockefeller hosting your soiree."

He had been surprised, too. "In fact, I did ask. The waiter told my friends"—that night, in any event, Danny and Frank were still his friends—"his services had been arranged through the caterer by some high muck-a-muck at my employer. Chipping in, in honor of my promotion."

"Per my police source, the ICU did no such thing." Corinne raised a hand, cutting Joshua off before he could find the words to argue. "Which, I'm told, only means the waiter was an off-the-books moonlighter. The caterers, for their part, deny there even *was* a waiter. Of course admitting to having used one temp would only open them up to questions about how many more workers they've paid in cash."

He asked, bitterly, "So why didn't the police find any of this?"

"Till you reappeared, they had no reason to suppose you'd left the party in a cab. And once you were back"—she paused, looking embarrassed on his behalf—"well, you know."

All too well. "They had more pressing things to spend time on than a drunk with the ludicrous story of a lost month."

"Afraid so," she said.

With a sour look on his face, he changed the subject. "What's any of this have to do with you swimming here from the station?"

"Patience. Getting back to your mysterious reappearance, here are your choices. Option one: someone put you into the cab and prepaid the fare. It sounds benign. The problem is, we know the cab company from the famous vid clip. They have no record of a drop-off here at the right time. I know.

"Option two: someone arranged your return off the books. Maybe the vehicle only looked like a cab. That's more sinister sounding, don't you think?"

He did. "Can the cab company identify the AI who drove that cab?"

"As it happens, no." She handed Joshua her very wet towel. "Check the vid. Mud or something obscures the ID."

"It was raining hard that night," Joshua remembered. Like today. "Why wouldn't mud wash off?"

"Mud would. Paint, on the other hand …" She studied him, her eyes narrowed. "Now do you see why I was leery about coming here in a cab?

• • • •

Corinne figured she looked like a drowned rat. Joshua's robe hung on her. Still, the condo was cozy. He was a nice enough guy. She had been in far worse fixes.

He was giving her a quick tour of his unit. "My brother designed that," and he pointed to the fireplace. Flames danced. Logs crackled and hissed. Smoke curled, never straying far from the blaze. After the soaking she had had, the fire's warmth felt wonderful. Only the lack of odor convinced Corinne the fire was virtual. Clever: the digital wallpaper masked electrical heating elements.

With reluctance, she followed Joshua from the living room.

"Here's my rare-book room." He laughed. "That phrase alone labels me an historian. For anyone else, 'book room' would suffice. By normal standards, what paper book isn't rare?"

Corinne turned, taking it all in. "You have a Gutenberg Bible in here?"

He made a show of scanning the shelves. "I must have lent it out."

Ah, the boyish charm. Have that, and once the world turned on you, it was all *anyone thought you brought to the table.* "We need to talk," she said.

"Sit." He took one leather wingchair, leaving the other for her. The chair, like his robe, was too big for her. "I assumed as much when you mentioned stopping in. Charleston isn't exactly down the block from Central Park."

Keeping a straight face on one's avatar was, for the most part, a matter of programming—and, for the most part, that was some expert's programming. Controlling one's physical face required personal skill. "I kept poking around while you were away."

"And?"

"No matter where I look, there's no sign of you for those four weeks. It's frustrating."

He grimaced. "*You* think it's frustrating? Try being me."

"So, Joshua, I looked at the problem a different way. No financial trace of you during those weeks means one of two things—kind of like the cab payment. One, you hid money so well no one can find it, and that's what you spent. Two, someone else supported you."

Some red, leather-bound tome sat on a walnut end table beside him. He began leafing through the pages. "No one ever called me a financial genius. I wouldn't know where to begin hiding money untraceably."

All he would have needed was a cash stash, easily accumulated by withdrawing more money than needed for routine purposes. He honestly looked baffled. Good.

Corinne chose her next words with care. "The obvious question is: why would someone pay your way for all that time? Did their reasons relate to your invisibility? To your inexplicable and very public return?"

He shrugged.

People do nothing without a reason, Joshua. "Who benefited from your absence?"

"Who?" Joshua frowned. "No one. Maybe supporting me was an act of random kindness."

Kindness would have been bringing him home, or to a hospital, or to the police. And mere random behavior would not keep anyone below the radar for four weeks. "I don't know who, Joshua. I suspect I know why."

"Why would someone benefit?" he asked, perplexed.

"The incident has had only one real consequence. You lost the historian post at the ICU. So who benefited from that? Someone opposed to your appointment."

His brow furrowed. "You mean another historian? Someone who might get the post if I became discredited?" Joshua shook his head. "You don't know historians. We're hardly cloak-and-daggerish."

Either Joshua was one hell of an actor, or this angle had never occurred to him.

"Have you spoken with my successor?" The question clearly pained him.

"Here's what's so interesting, Joshua. You have no successor." She watched him closely. Eyes don't lie. "It's too embarrassing to be seen as runner-up to you."

Wince. "I didn't know."

She believed him. "Maybe *that's* what your disappearing act is about. Suppose someone didn't want you compiling an anniversary history for the ICU. That begs a question, Joshua.

"Exactly what is the Matthews conundrum?"

• • • •

Fermi Paradox: the famous riddle posed by twentieth-century physicist and Nobelist Enrico Fermi, rebutting speculation that—despite the lack of evidence—technologically capable, intelligent alien life must exist. Responding to popular conjecture that the immensity and great age of the universe made the alternative inconceivable, Fermi is said to have asked, simply, "Where are they?"

Radio contact with several intelligent species, commencing within a half century of Fermi's death, definitively answered his question: they are all around. The InterstellarNet community (see related entry) presently includes species from eleven solar systems.

This once unanswerable question became emblematic of a naïve bygone era.

—*Internetopedia*

• • • •

Joshua flinched. "So you've been in touch with my coworkers. Ex-coworkers. And the skeptics among them, at that. For whatever it's worth, I'm not so immodest. I call it the InterstellarNet enigma."

What's in a name? Corinne wondered. "Either way, what is it?"

"Are you familiar with the Fermi Paradox?"

He *had* to be kidding. "Doesn't chatting with the folks around ten other stars discredit the paradox rather dramatically? Not to mention aliens paying us a visit?"

"Yes and no." Joshua gestured expansively, but his hands didn't help him get his point across. "Meet me online."

His proffered consensual space was blackness. Where was this going?

Speckles emerged from the dark. Scattered dots brightened one by one, as Joshua recited, "The Sun, Alpha Centauri, Barnard's Star, Tau Ceti, Epsilon Eridani …."

Brighter lights among dim ones. Was contrast the *no* part of his answer? "We're encircled by intelligent aliens, Joshua. What's your point?"

"That *is* my point. Humans are surrounded by intelligent aliens. Now consider our neighbors' perspectives. A few are likewise surrounded. Most are on the periphery of the community. Why aren't *they* surrounded by intelligent neighbors?"

Corinne permitted her avatar to shrug. "Subpar comm gear?"

"Comm technology is always among the first things traded. It's hard to trade other stuff unless everyone can communicate. Hence InterstellarNet members all have equivalent comm capability."

She dealt with ambiguity all the time—but not like this. Interstellar puzzles made her head hurt. "I guess you're questioning why, say, the Dragons can't talk with a sphere of their near neighbors. That's the 'no' part of your answer about the discrediting of the Fermi Paradox?"

One star brightened still further. "The Sun. We're near the center of this set of privileged stars. Look outward twenty light-years in any direction and, as far as I can tell, Fermi's paradox starts taking hold again."

"The Matthews conundrum," Corinne supplied.

"So my colleagues—former colleagues—refer to it. I just call it 'the puzzle.' Or, when the situation calls for formality, 'the InterstellarNet enigma.'

"Not that long ago, we believed Earth was the center of everything. Then we believed the same of the Sun. That was just as mistaken. For a while, it looked like humans might be alone. Wrong again. Time after time, humanity's circumstances have proven to be unremarkable. The reminder to be cosmologically modest has its own label: the Mediocrity Principle."

Paradox. Conundrum. Principle. Corinne's headache throbbed. "Then your puzzle is: if Earth, the Sun, and humans aren't special, why are they at the center of a small region of communicating intelligent species?"

"Exactly." Joshua let her absorb it all for a while. "Now please answer *my* question. What can the puzzle possibly have to do with my disappearance?"

Maybe nothing, Corinne thought. *If so, she was out of ideas.* "Here's the snag, Joshua. You vanished just long enough for it to cost you your job. And your former colleagues are pretty snide about 'the Matthews conundrum.' "

He sighed. "Yes, the puzzle would surely have featured in whatever history I compiled. Regardless, I'm not going to stop talking about it."

"I don't doubt it," Corinne said. "But someone has gone to a *great* deal of effort to ensure that no one will take you seriously."

CHAPTER 7

Being three was wonderful.

The twins, Joshua's six-year-old sisters, had just gotten their implants. That put Joshua, years too young for his own implant—what one would do for him remained quite mysterious—mostly beneath their notice. Aaron, on the other hand, was an infant. He needed constant parental supervision. Joshua had the run of the house, often with only Worthington, the house AI, watching him through residence sensors.

All too soon Aaron became mobile enough to wander, still eager to cram everything he found into his mouth. Mom or Dad followed Aaron. The golden age ended.

The year between explained much about Joshua as an adult.

He remembered roaming the house and the fenced backyard. Worthington seldom cared what Joshua touched unless it could be dangerous. The AI even covered up Joshua's frequent slip-ups, synthing a replacement knickknack whenever Joshua handled and broke one. "They were synthed in the first place," Worthington explained. "I see no difference."

But the hobby room remained off limits unless Dad was there. Dad's model train setup couldn't compare to Grandpa's, but Grandpa had worked on his forever. Dad had the train bug, too—and he had passed it along to his son.

Joshua knew he could run the train. There wasn't much to it, really, and he had watched Dad closely. An engineer's cap. The throttle to make the train go fast or slow (though Joshua had no use for slow). Levers that made the train change tracks. The button to toot the locomotive's horn—only not while unsupervised, if he didn't want to get caught.

Joshua explained it all patiently to Worthington—at least as patiently as an almost-four-year-old could. That didn't work. Joshua tried fussing. He working himself up until great tears ran down his cheeks. Worthington said something silly about crocodile tears. "Why *won't* you let me in?" Joshua had finally cried, stomping his foot. "I won't break anything. And if I do, you can fix it."

"Maybe I could," Worthington had said. "That's not the point. Whatever I synthed would not be a proper replacement for something your dad made himself, by hand. Do you understand?"

"Yes," Joshua had lied. High up, in Dad's arms, the little models were wonderful: an entire village nestled in a forest. But up close, standing on his own feet, Joshua's eyes weren't far above tabletop level. Up close, the models were all toothpicks and colored cotton balls and papier-mâché boxes with brush marks. All fake. What he really understood was that Worthington would tattle on him if he went alone into the hobby room.

So he built a fort of family-room sofa cushions, inside which Worthington could not see him. The cushion-fort became a spaceship, a submarine, and then the cab of an old steam locomotive. He laughed when Worthington asked anxiously, "Are you all right in there? What are you doing?" If Worthington was so intelligent, why couldn't he recognize a train?

Making chug-a-chug noises to himself, having forgotten he was mad at the world, Joshua sensed he had learned something important about AIs and parents and how the world really worked.

• • • •

"Fortunately for you," Tacitus netted, "I am of the patient sort."

"Fortunately for you," Joshua answered, "I'm of the paying sort."

Maybe money would change hands, in a manner of speaking. Maybe not. Tacitus was an AI and didn't need patience, not with the whole infosphere to amuse himself. Nor did he need money, the trickle of power that kept him going insignificantly cheap. Joshua sometimes wondered what the AI did with his consulting income.

Once upon a time, theirs had been a strictly business relationship. They had long since become fast friends. Joshua had had too few of those, even before the recent debacle. It was disturbing how notoriety turned supposedly close friends very distant.

Tacitus shared Joshua's fascination with history. People had long looked to the past for an understanding of the present. AIs were no different—and their roots lay in humanity's past. Many AIs showed their respect through their choice of names. Those who had shaped human institutions, technology, and literature lived again, in a manner of speaking, in humanity's descendants.

Tacitus 352, as was his wont, had manifested a tunic, toga, and sandals. One hairy arm clutched a bunch of fat papyrus scrolls. Many AIs with an interest in history registered as Herodotus; when Joshua last checked, the rolls listed more than ten thousand. Tacitus, when asked about *his* election, had said, "Herodotus? It's been done to death."

The Roman persona had once amused Joshua. Nothing amused him any more—not after weeks of disapproving looks and muffled titters.

Laughter or pity? Joshua couldn't decide which he hated more.

Corinne's theorizing had not helped. It seemed bizarre that anyone could want to suppress Joshua's speculations. More than bizarre. Fantastical. Ludicrous. No other explanation presented itself, and *still* he couldn't bring himself to believe. If there were the slightest chance Corinne was correct, though—he would be *damned* if he'd drop it. "Okay, Tacitus," he finally responded. "What have you got for me today?"

"Less than I would like," Tacitus netted. "Someone got around to revoking my access to ICU archives."

That saddened Joshua further, but it didn't surprise him. He had gotten Tacitus access in the first place. "Then what's in all your scrolls?"

"Diversion." Tacitus snapped open a scroll. "Some thoughts. Why after millions of years hunting and gathering did farming suddenly begin? Why did the Native Americans never domesticate bison? Why, among all the writing systems in the world, was the alphabet invented only once?"

Joshua didn't want diversion, whether offered by way of friendship or commerce. He still couldn't help asking, "One alphabet? Roman, Cyrillic, Hebrew, Arabic—"

"That could be a very long list," Tacitus interrupted. "Of course there are many alphabets. They all trace back, though, whether by explicit adaptation or conceptual influence, to a primitive Semitic alphabet. One original alphabet. Unlike, say, syllabaries or pictographic systems, which have been invented several times."

Huh, Joshua thought. That was news to him. "Play historical parlor games on your own time, Tacitus. Can you find alternatives for the off-limits archives?"

As a flourish of unseen trumpets rang out, images flashed: the Library of Congress, the British Museum, Roman catacombs, the Valley of the Kings, an unidentifiable grass-covered plain.

"I'm not following you today," Joshua netted.

What must be the Roman Senate appeared. Tacitus sat, setting the scrolls beside himself on the stone bench. "You wanted more data about the Matthews conundrum, right? About the incredible circumstance that puts the only known intelligences within easy radio reach of each other, at about the same technology levels."

"I know what I asked." Joshua sensed a great cosmic shoe waiting to drop. First, whatever had happened that night on his ride home from the Ritz-Trump. Now … what?

"History." Tacitus patted the pile of scrolls. "Human existence, depending how you define human, a few million years. Recorded human history, a few thousand years. And human radios? Scarcely three hundred years."

The metaphorical shoe loomed ever larger in Joshua's imagination. He *almost* saw what Tacitus was driving at. Almost.

"Joshua, you've made a very astute observation. A cluster of solar systems, a tiny bubble of intelligence, huddles in an otherwise silent galaxy. Eleven stars among billions." Tacitus leaned forward. "My point is that proximity captures only one part of the improbability. Sol is a bit under five billion years old. Alpha Centauri is six billion. Barnard's Star is at least ten billion. Yet humans, Centaurs, and Snakes—all the InterstellarNet members—are in technological terms quite similar. If any were only a bit less advanced, they could not communicate at all. If they were only a bit more advanced—we'd be communicating in person. That's already begun."

A physical glass of iced tea slipped from physical Joshua's hand. The metaphorical shoe had fallen. Eleven stars out of billions—somehow all nearby. A few hundred years out of billions—and somehow the neighboring species were technologically synched.

The puzzle was far stranger than even Joshua had imagined.

• • • •

The potted trees of the penthouse garden twittered with birdsong. The sounds were recorded, Joshua decided, but pleasant nonetheless. While Corinne focused on a fist-sized muffin, dropping crumbs all around her plate, he took in the panoramic view of Central Park.

Denise Chang, as trim and blond as her wife was plump and dark, flitted about being hostess. She set a fresh carafe of coffee and a wholly unnecessary second plate of muffins on the patio table. "How's it been going?" Denise asked.

"Rough," he admitted. "I forced myself to take a cab from the maglev station. The cab said, 'You puke; you clean up.' "

Denise smothered a chuckle. "Sorry. I'll leave you both to your work." Bursts of random noise from indoors suggested where she had settled down. Maybe he would have sensed a melody if he had been gene-tweaked to hear ultrasound. Access to broad-spectrum music never struck him as sufficient reason to be rewired.

"Let's do this," Corinne said. "You said you have new information."

"The Sun is about 4.6 billion years old," Joshua began. He grinned at her horrified expression. "Not to worry, I'll skip over most of that time. In fact, permit me a metaphor. Call the Sun's age one day. All right?"

"Where are you going with this?" she asked.

"I'll give you a hint. Remember the Mediocrity Principle." She didn't comment further, so Joshua continued. "Midnight, the Sun coalesces out of some primordial nebula. Four minutes later, the planets have formed. The first microbes appear on Earth around three a.m."

Corinne topped off his mug of coffee. "And one of them had it in for you?"

"Believe it or not, I'm going somewhere with this. Okay, life, but not oxygen-producing. We don't see *that* until about ten-thirty in the morning, still single celled. Skipping a few steps—and you're welcome—it's not until about nine in the evening that we see multicellular life more complex than sponges or jellyfish. Extinction of the dinosaurs at about twenty before midnight."

"Whoa. Whiplash," she said.

"Primitive humans, if you're inclusive in your definition of human, show up at about three minutes to midnight. For most of our three minutes, humans are hunters and gatherers. Agriculture and writing are inventions of the last second before midnight. Marconi and Tesla experiment with radio starting about six milliseconds before midnight."

He stopped his recitation. For a time, birdsong and the audible portion of Denise's broad-spectrum "music" were the only sounds.

Corinne stared into space. Finally, she said, "By the Mediocrity Principle, we're to doubt that our place in space is anything special. I guess you're saying we should question our place in *time* being special. I don't see the extension to time, though. I don't understand what planetary history has to do with anything. We're in the time we're in. That's all."

He shook his head. "Agreed, we only see the moment in which we find ourselves. Here's the puzzle. Eleven intelligent species clustered into InterstellarNet. They're all technologically synchronized within, in my simple metaphor, milliseconds of the one-day clock. Only it's *not* always one day. Barnard's Star is more than twice our Sun's age. Epsilon Eridani is scarcely one billion years old. Or if you prefer, a bit over two 'days' at one extreme, and just over five 'hours' at the other.

"So why are we all at the same tech level?"

• • • •

Rising temperatures drove Corinne and Joshua inside. *That's okay*, Corinne decided. *We can be befuddled as readily indoors as out.*

Denise rejoined them for lunch. She quickly caught up with Corinne's confusion. "So *this* is the latest thinking? Someone kidnapped Joshua, made him a laughingstock, and gave him amnesia—all to discredit his publicizing an astronomical oddity. And now you're both excited about a second astronomical anomaly."

Joshua poked at his chicken salad. "You don't sound convinced. The way you tell it, I wouldn't be either, only I have nothing else to offer."

Denise wasn't buying it. "So who, exactly, is out to discredit you? The Inquisition? The Kansas Board of Education? No, wait. They advocated reasons Earth and humans *were* special. Now that the orthodoxy is this Mediocrity Principle, that we live in a typical galactic backwater, you're claiming we *are* special. So I guess the Secret Order of Mediocrities is after you."

Corinne felt herself blush.

Joshua didn't rise to the bait. "The facts are what they are. We *don't* know why only these neighboring stars are special. I'm open to a better explanation why whatever happened to me happened. And that our era is also special makes me even more curious."

As Denise, with pursed lips, sat watching, Corinne had to concede: all this *did* seem absurd. A secretive bender was far more plausible than any Secret Order of Mediocrities.

Her professional comeback depended upon breaking just the right story. The wrong story would only turn her into a joke by association—

And those doubts must have shown on her face.

"Don't lose faith in me," Joshua said. "Of all people, Corinne, *you* should be open-minded. You were kidnapped by Snakes and you fought alongside Centaurs—as a result of scheming that spanned years and light-years. How likely was any of that?

"I can't say what, or who, or why, but something very strange is happening. Somehow it relates to InterstellarNet. I'm sure of it. Show me my error, and I'll walk away quietly."

CHAPTER 8

Gaia Hypothesis: the collective term for several interpretations of an unremarkable observation— the life forms and environments of Earth interact to sustain livable conditions. The name gives homage to the Earth goddess of ancient Greek mythology.

In its weakest form, the hypothesis merely encapsulates the fact that organisms alter their environment. Plants take in carbon dioxide and emit oxygen. In its intermediate forms, the hypothesis acknowledges the many interdependencies among living populations. Plants take in carbon dioxide and produce oxygen. Animals breathe in the oxygen and exhale carbon dioxide. In its strongest—and most metaphorical—sense, the hypothesis views the world as a unified organism that consciously maintains and fosters conditions favorable for all life. In this view, the planetary entity actively guides its own evolution, inter-species balance, and climate.

Despite its widespread popularity, no evidence exists to substantiate the Gaia Hypothesis in its strongest form.

—Internetopedia

. . . .

Joshua's neighbors gradually responded to weeks of public sobriety. The thaw wasn't much, in the main just nods of greeting in the lobby, but at least they again acknowledged his presence. No one brought up what, in overheard conversations, he had learned most residents of the building referred to as "the episode." He told himself that the trend was positive.

AI friends kept him going. Drinking was a vice only experience made explicable: his presumed lapse and any possible relapse held no interest for software. Joshua was just happy for their companionship.

Not so his family's. Their recurrent checkups, by net and in person, grew ever more tedious. Cousins, an uncle, and the sister who had never before found their way to Charleston had suddenly, one by one, been "in the area." Aaron was due at any moment, "just passing through."

Alan the doorman netted in. "Dr. Matthews, your brother is here to see you."

Neighborhood sensors showed Joshua a balmy evening. "Please take Aaron's bags and tell him I'm coming down."

"Yes, sir."

They did the fraternal backslapping hug thing. "You up for a walk, Aaron?"

"Sure. I've been sitting all day: scramjet, maglev, cab." Aaron pretended not to notice Joshua flinch at "cab." Body language said Aaron wanted to collapse into a massage chair. His eyes said, resignedly, he would follow wherever Joshua led.

Joshua was sick of the walking-on-eggshells treatment. "Then off we go." They ambled downhill toward the harbor, into a salt-smelling breeze. The night sky was clear. Space stations and orbiting habitats slid by overhead. Between the cusps of the crescent Moon, cities gleamed like diamonds.

Lesser lights crept through the harbor shallows: tourists on ghost tours of the old, sunken city. Off Patriot Island, red lights blinked atop the flight-control tower of the long-submerged carrier *USS Yorktown*.

Aaron plodded beside him, oblivious to everything. "Tina says hi." It was his first attempt at conversation for three city blocks.

"Hi, back," Joshua said. "How are she and the boys?"

"They're good."

Would the family's surprise inspections ever end? Given Aaron's exhaustion, Joshua managed to credit good intentions. He could hold his frustration in abeyance till Aaron pushed a new job at him.

Joshua said, "Let me tell you what I've been doing."

His narration accomplished one thing: it revved up Aaron.

"Damnation, Joshua. You had esoteric-enough interests to start. That has-been reporter is only making things worse."

Corinne had accomplished far more than he and Aaron combined. Letting the slap pass, Joshua pointed skyward. "Still, it's fascinating. I—"

"I've got to say something here," Aaron snapped. "You're being absurd. So our solar system is younger than some, and older than others. Why wouldn't you expect that? Now, for all your prattling about some Mediocrity Principle, it offends you that Earth's age *isn't* special."

Joshua shook his head. "You misunderstand me. What surprises me is that, disparate as are our stars' ages, the InterstellarNet species have converged to the same technological level."

"Billion of consumers and millions of businesses make their individual decisions. Stuff gets made, distributed, bought and sold, recycled. No one knows in detail what's happening. We anthropomorphize the process, call it 'the market' and move on." Aaron's voice shook with frustration. "Plankton and grass and cows and koalas and pandas and and and somehow add up to an ecosystem. No one pretends to entirely understand how *that* works. We call it nature or evolution or Gaia, and let *that* go.

"So maybe there's another mysterious mechanism out there. Different order emerging from chaos viewed on a yet bigger scale. Some kind of interstellar feedback loop. Before InterstellarNet, we couldn't have known. What does it matter to me?"

Seagulls wheeled overhead. A ship's bell tolled. Joshua waited.

On Aaron's forehead a vein gradually slowed its pulsing. In a softer voice, he tried again. "Joshua, there are a thousand things I don't understand. A million. The universe doesn't care. The difference between you and me is, I accept that. I don't ..."

"Don't what?" Joshua demanded. "You don't obsess?"

"Your word," Aaron said. "And if I do, I don't allow my obsessions to hurt the family. For most people, an incident like yours would have blown over by now, and a fixation like yours would embarrass only you. That's for most people. If the Matthewses aren't Kennedys, Gateses, or Coopersmiths, neither are we 'most people.' You *know* that, or at least you ought to.

"My boys are still taunted now and again about you. So are your niece and other nephews. Mom gets crap at her work and Dad takes not so good-natured ribbing from his so-called buddies. I'm willing to bet I've lost a couple of customers, through snickering by association. Oh, not everyone knows or cares about your ... indiscretion, but more than enough do.

"Joshua, we all love you. We support you. We'd do anything for you. The question is: when will you start thinking about us?"

"Damn it! Those four weeks of my life were stolen!"

Aaron jerked to a stop and grabbed Joshua's arm. "I believe neither you nor the police know where you were. To me, that sounds like amnesia and a good samaritan. But you? You're constructing an ever more elaborate conspiracy theory involving, well, I'm not sure what. Every InterstellarNet species? The billions of years of evolution that made them? Joshua, admit it. You need *help*."

They stood face to face, glaring. Joshua's mind spun. His gut churned. Denise and his brother, in their very separate ways, were *so* down to earth. So pragmatic. So sensible.

Buoys rolled in the swell, their bells clanging. Waves slapped the shore. Couples strolled, hand in hand, along the boardwalk. In an alley, unseen, cats hissed and yowled.

Why *couldn't* he accept that there were things he didn't know? *I do need help*, Joshua thought. "Let's get some dinner," he said at last.

In the awkwardly silent walk back home, he wondered how

close the family was to having him committed. If they were to try, he didn't know that he could blame them.

Or that they would be wrong.

CHAPTER 9

Antebellum Charleston scarcely existed anymore. Most of the old city lay submerged or in rubble or both. At the mouth of the harbor, little remained of Fort Sumter but underwater gravel. Calvin had been a Cat Five hurricane, and Charleston had taken a direct hit. Still, more and more historic reproductions lined the streets. Palmettos and crepe myrtles, however young and spindly, again grew everywhere.

Joshua had to admire the civic tenacity. He projected stately full-grown magnolias over the wide boulevard on which he strode. His inner vision also tinted the gray sky blue and the drought-withered grass a vibrant green.

This should be poker night. Another regular had brought a friend—to fill in—to the third weekly game during Joshua's absence. Two months after his reappearance, Temp Guy was still sitting in. Joshua couldn't bring himself to object. He didn't see why he should have to object.

No job and fair-weather friends had left him with too much time on his hands. Today that had meant a quick jaunt by maglev to and then home from DC. Now, as the familiar streets of Charleston emptied, he netted with Tacitus as he walked, more about the Smithsonian's Museum of Natural History than anything else. The bug zoo. Trilobites and coelacanths. Mastodons. Dinosaurs.

"None of which," Tacitus netted, "tells us anything useful." His recent notion of *useful* was all too often limited to matters of InterstellarNet and the Matthews conundrum.

"You have to admit this was great," Joshua replied. *This* was a netcam pointer to a favorite exhibit, of Tyrannosaurus and Alberto-saurus skeletons locked in battle. He refused to be drawn into those supposedly useful topics.

"You doubtless rooted for the Albertosaurus," Tacitus answered.

True enough. Joshua usually rooted for the underdog. But why did his friend seem disapproving? "Am I to understand you rooted for the T-Rex?"

Tacitus primly straightened his toga. "I rooted for the meteor."

Joshua snorted. An elderly passerby gave him a dirty look. There was no recognition in her expression—Joshua might have been any errant whippersnapper. He had long since exceeded his allotted fifteen minutes of fame; perhaps the worst had passed. The possibility lifted his spirits, just a tad.

Tacitus began net-texting mastodon recipes he had encountered somewhere online. Joshua deleted the information—esoteric even by his lofty standards—as soon as it struck his mind's eye. His thoughts, wandering, had found their way to Corinne.

Doubtless he was better off apart from her.

As she must have come to the reciprocal conclusion. When last they connected, she had mentioned pursuit of several possible stories. Boredom within the Upload community. Statistics among hunters and gengineered tigers (the tigers were winning). Growth rates in the Augmented population (all by conversion, of course—Augmented minds disdained sex as a distraction).

Her recent interests suggested only one organizing principle: they could scarcely be further removed from Joshua.

How grandiosely paranoid he and Corinne made each other! Happily, Aaron had brought him to his senses. Denise, apparently, had done the same for Corinne.

He missed Corinne anyway.

Tacitus had moved on to pontificating about primitive man hunting various Ice Age megafauna to extinction. Back Joshua went, by fly's-eye views, to reexamine a museum exhibit.

Overcast day faded into ominous night with little visible sunset between. The streets emptied. A cab passed, two blocks ahead on a cross street, and Joshua cringed. Would he never be over this?

A golf-ball-sized lump of rock lay in his path. With a well-placed kick, he sent the stone skittering along the sidewalk.

Tacitus, meanwhile, had segued to human evolution. Joshua dutifully revisited the Neanderthal burial diorama. "That hand axe is at least ten thousand years too advanced," Tacitus netted. "Notice the delicate flaking on the working edge. It would not hurt to update these displays on occasion."

"Stone flaking." Joshua caught up with *his* stone and gave it another punt. "You see the exhibit that clearly?"

"You can, too." Tacitus briefly vanished, his avatar replaced for those seconds by a zoomed view from inside the museum. "I do not get why you went physically. Between guards keeping you back and crowds blocking your view, how did you expect to see anything?"

Joshua had made the day trip to DC precisely because of the crowds. Especially on weekdays, museums teemed with schoolchildren; his residual infamy registered mostly with adults. The legions of kids paid him no attention. The teachers and chaperones were too frazzled, if they even recognized him, to care. He had basked in their indifference.

That was then. Now, Joshua felt anxious. Not from roaming deserted streets—he was only a few blocks from home. Not about the foreboding sky. He couldn't decide why. As Tacitus tried to engage him in a discussion of prehistoric trade routes for flint, Joshua polled nearby public-safety cameras.

He banished the pedantic lecture from his thoughts. Cycling views from the sensors atop the historical district's faux gas lamps revealed nothing of interest. Although a few faces *did* strike Joshua as familiar ....

This was stupid. He often walked in this neighborhood. The familiar faces would be people who did the same. *Quit being paranoid.* Images flickered as Joshua continued cycling through the real-time feeds.

A burly man in a broad-brimmed black hat had been strolling a block behind Joshua. Black Hat had turned down a side street. Now a tall woman in a tan overcoat trailed behind Joshua. She wandered off, replaced by a man clutching a furled umbrella.

Cameras one block over showed Tan Raincoat had turned

to parallel him. Black Hat paralleled him from the opposite side. Alarmed, Joshua downloaded buffers from the public-safety cameras along his perambulating path. Each buffer kept thirty minutes of vid.

These people had taken turns following him!

His neural link dissolved in a hiss of static. A cab careened around a corner, its brakes squealing. A passenger leapt out, weapon in hand. A Taser?

Joshua's jaw dropped. He *knew* that face. Brush-cut gray hair; dark, piercing gaze; aquiline nose, cleft chin—

The waiter from his ill-fated party!

Joshua whirled to run, only to see Umbrella Man dashing straight at him—

Until a honking, speeding black van, jumping the curb, sent Umbrella Man diving between two parked cars.

The waiter looked wildly about, then leapt back through his still-open cab door. The van swerved, clipping the cab's rear bumper, bouncing the cab into a lamppost.

Umbrella Man and now Black Hat came racing at Joshua.

The van's back door slid open. "Get in!" shouted a familiar voice. "Quick!"

It was Corinne.

• • • •

Corinne kept checking her rearview mirror. Too soon, the cab shuddered to life.

She thought she'd smacked it thoroughly, but she waited to see that it wasn't keeping up before turning down a cross street and speeding away.

Her van had a nasty shimmy from the collision.

"Th-thanks," Joshua managed. "What just happened?"

"Hold that thought," she said. The nearby public-safety cameras showed nothing significant on the all but empty streets. More interesting was the slowly moving region in which cameras failed to respond. Somewhere in that blanked-out area was the battered cab. What did a little illegal jamming matter, after all, compared to attempted kidnapping? "Are you all right?"

"Rattled, but okay." He coughed. "Terrified and relieved all at once."

Relieved? "Did you recognize them?" she asked.

"The man from the cab." Joshua squirmed in his seat. "He was the waiter that night at my party." His voice turned wistful. "I wish I could prove that."

She cruised a seedy neighborhood until she found a block without public-safety cameras. Shot out, not jammed. They would walk to the maglev station and take their chances on a mugging. She pulled to the curb. "Joshua, the van stays here. Your waiter and his friends will be looking for it." He stared as Corinne wiped the controls and door latches. "Our story is the van was stolen." If the rental company disbelieved her, the wiped-off areas would suggest a thief erasing his fingerprints. She had no intention of admitting to having disabled autodrive, much less having rammed the cab.

"What about DNA?" he asked. "I mean mine. Shed skin. Hair."

"You were in the van before it was stolen. We'll work out details later."

Would anyone ask? Corinne doubted it. Public-safety cameras had been suppressed at the crash site. Joshua's assailants wouldn't report the incident. Had they meant to involve the police, they would have left behind their mangled vehicle. Instead, they had driven off in it.

"Now we talk online," Corinne netted. "Heavy encryption. We don't want anyone to overhear." She set a brisk pace toward the maglev station.

"Why are you even in Charleston? How did you know?" Joshua's avatar shrugged, somehow plaintively. "What is going on?"

"Why?" she echoed. *I'm stubborn* was an inadequate response. "Despite everything"—including Denise's skepticism—"your situation gnawed at me. I got to data mining, and I turned up something interesting. Joshua, you're not the first to see InterstellarNet coincidences."

"I never assumed I was."

"The thing is, Joshua, bad things happen to those who notice. Two cases involved media projects on the topic, timed for the centennial of the ICU." *Was he up to this?* "People died. Others disappeared—permanently."

The neighborhood improved as they approached the station. He looked around for the first time at their surroundings. "Where are we going?"

"New York," she netted. "Joshua, there's an obvious question ...."

"Uh-huh. Why am I still here? Maybe I'm too conspicuous to harm overtly. Someone decided discrediting me was better." In the real world, Joshua punted another stone with feeling. It clattered along the sidewalk. "Who *are* they? No, that can wait. How did you happen to turn up in the nick of time?"

They plunged into the station, on whose platform dozens of people milled about. A train was just pulling in. Corinne relaxed, if only a little, for the first time since arriving in Charleston. "After uncovering those earlier incidents, I came to watch you. I was *worried* about you." She admitted, "It wasn't happenstance that I pulled up when I did. I'd been following you for several hours."

He gave her a hard stare, but didn't comment on her using him as bait. "I've gone from infamous to amusing to old news. Everyone 'knows' I'm a world-class drunk. *Now* I can be safely vanished. Or maybe this time I'll come back dead, seemingly from alcohol poisoning or some other kind of overdose. Same old, same old, people will say. That's why, this time, they didn't care if I saw them coming."

Time to change the subject. "I didn't forget your other question: what's going on? I only wish I knew." Corinne used cash to buy two access chips from the kiosk, and they boarded the maglev. An hour to home. They took seats in a mostly empty passenger car. Half their fellow riders were glassy-eyed, off somewhere in the infosphere. The rest looked asleep.

Joshua sat stiffly, hands clasped. "Something is going on. Someone is after me. You've seen it, too, but we have no proof."

True, Corinne thought, *but now we've both seen it. That's one hell of an improvement.*

· · · ·

A soft trill returned Joshua's thoughts to the present. No one in their maglev car seemed to be paying him any attention. He bookmarked his files and connected.

"You're back online, I see," Tacitus netted. "Good. I decided you're right."

Joshua had been surveying Corinne's latest research. The disappearances and untimely deaths went back almost to First Contact with the Leos. For such a wide-ranging and long-lived conspiracy, it had remarkably limited resources. A cab and four people? None of which could be on Tacitus' mind. "Of course I am. Right about what?"

"Mass extinctions," Tacitus answered. "That's the key."

If so, Joshua didn't recognize the lock. Corinne snored softly beside him, making this conversation all the more surreal. "Mass extinctions?"

"Dinosaurs. Trilobites. Mastodons. Isn't that what you went to the Smithsonian to study?"

"Mass extinctions." Maybe, subconsciously, that was how he picked exhibits. Maybe he just liked dinosaurs. "Go on."

The virtual sky darkened. Virtual stars twinkled above the avatar. "I checked with all the agents. Every InterstellarNet species reports mass extinctions."

So asteroid strikes and ice ages happened elsewhere. "That's not surprising."

In the imaginary night, his imaginary face pale and shadowed, Tacitus nodded. "Agreed. Still, allow me an observation. It's odd that the InterstellarNet species are so well matched in capability. So closely ... synchronized."

"Right," Joshua netted. "Very odd."

"Then you will find this at least as weird." Tacitus banished the stars. "Occasionally two or even three worlds had mass extinctions at about the same time. And then there's this—

"All eleven home worlds experienced a radical, biosphere-altering event at the same time, about 550 million years ago."

CHAPTER 10

Cambrian Explosion: the rapid appearance on Earth, about 550 million years ago, of complex multicellular life forms. Duration estimates generally range from 10-40 million years. Even the long end of that range would ordinarily be an evolutionary eye-blink.

The Cambrian Explosion is noteworthy for both its biological innovation and concurrent mass extinctions. Many new animal species emerged in a variety of novel body plans. In marked contrast, no new phylum of animal life has appeared since the Cambrian bout of evolutionary creativity (although many phyla and classes from this era disappeared in later extinctions).

Unlike most evolutionary turning points—such as, for example, the better known Cretaceous/Tertiary asteroid strike that doomed the dinosaurs—scientists cannot point to any conclusive cause(s) for the Cambrian occurrences.

Only the origin of life is a more dramatic biological event.

—Internetopedia

• • • •

Corinne had paid their way to New York. Suddenly, Joshua had other ideas. He led her off the maglev during its brief stop in Richmond, onto a local subway to Arthur Ashe Memorial Spaceport, and aboard a commercial scramjet flight to the other side of the world. So why Australia? Her questions about their new destination got her only an enigmatic smile.

Joshua's harness could scarcely keep him in his acceleration couch. He brimmed with newfound energy. Adrenaline from their narrow escape? Uncertainty banished by a second incident—this time stone-sober, with her present as a witness? New data? *Maybe all three*, she thought. *In any event, he was a changed man.*

She sort of missed the middle child, underachiever, trust-fund dilettante. This take-charge Joshua reminded her too much of … her.

In the run-up to launch, Joshua hit her with a massive info dump. Mid-speech, he linked in an AI colleague named Tacitus. Mass extinctions. Emergence of phyla. Divergence of species. The Cambrian Explosion. Netting meant never stopping to take a breath.

Being on the receiving end was like drinking from a fire hose.

The torrent did not abate until the final launch warning. It was a lot to take in.

Acceleration mashed Corinne into her seat. *Only a few minutes of this,* she told herself. A suborbital hop was mostly coasting.

As always, those were a long few minutes. When the engines cut off, she turned toward Joshua. He was gazing longingly at the blue-and-white globe receding beneath them. He looked pale. His hand felt clammy. Space sick?

Joshua seemed to have lost the will to communicate. *Poor guy.* "I need time to process all that information," Corinne said, yawning. She closed her eyes, the better to organize her thoughts. She yawned again. "And I have a call to make." They had more than an hour until reentry and comm blackout.

Let him conclude she was letting Denise know about their detour. She *should* do that, but Denise was accustomed—resigned—to no-notice jaunts. That Tanaka Astor would not take Joshua's calls did not mean the secretary-general wouldn't take Corinne's. At least once.

Celebrity had its perks.

Quit stalling, Corinne.

Tanaka Astor accepted the connection request, appearing as an iridescent sphere in a featureless space. "Ms. Elman," she acknowledged flatly.

Tacitus' Roman persona had been only mildly idiosyncratic. Most of Corinne's AI acquaintances, in fact, assumed human avatars. Some honored progenitors. Others possibly projected human forms as subtle reminders of their legal equality. Like Tanaka Astor, the Augmented almost exclusively manifested the opposite way: impersonal and austere. Because their human partner assured their citizenship, perhaps that austerity revealed true AI disdain.

It was only four a.m. in Geneva. Likely only Astor, the AI facet, was awake, and might be much easier to deal with than two personalities. More logical, too—or so, anyway, Corinne told herself. "Good morning, Doctor."

"You may call me Madame Secretary-General," Astor said. "What is this about?"

Corinne looked and felt bedraggled. She revealed none of that online. "I have new information about the Joshua Matthews situation. I would appreciate your reaction.

"To begin, my research has revealed similar cases. Knowing that, I followed him. That was fortunate, because tonight I rescued him from assailants. They jammed the local network, however, so there isn't any surveillance vid."

"How convenient." Even the shimmering of the sphere was somehow icy.

Of course the Augmented seldom exhibited emotion. AIs only feigned it. Corinne knew she was psyching herself out. "Nonetheless." She explained it all. Past disappearances among likeminded researchers. The cab. The waiter and his cronies. Only gradually did Corinne suspect Robyn Tanaka had joined the conversation. The seamlessness of that transition was creepy.

She/it/they netted, "You would have me believe in the persecution of historians of like persuasion to Joshua Matthews. You infer a conspiracy more than a century old, prosecuted by waiters and taxicabs.

"That you saved Matthews from a mugging, and that the muggers had stolen a cab, is far more plausible." Some nuance of delivery too subtle to pinpoint finally convinced Corinne that the Robyn Tanaka facet had taken charge. "Ms. Elman, one wonders if you share any of Dr. Matthews's habits."

Corinne would not have minded a stiff drink, even squeezed from a freefall bulb. What hard evidence could she offer? That the caterer denied assigning a waiter to Joshua's party. Even she hadn't found that assertion convincing. Nothing else was new, except—

"Madame Secretary-General, I expect you've heard mention of the Matthews conundrum. That is: why are a few nearby stars home to technological species? There is a second incongruity that Joshua can explain in more detail than I, and that seems as counterintuitive as the first. Epsilon Eridani is a billion years old; Barnard's Star more than ten billion. Both gave rise to species possessed of very similar capabilities. Yet a few hundred years ago, there were no radios with which to coordinate."

The glistening sphere radiated indifference. "We communicate with those species able to communicate. Any hypothetical intelligences in other solar systems by definition remain unknown to us."

Not indifference! Nothing. No cues. You're doing it to yourself! "Allow me a final observation. Our era is not the first synchronization. Are you familiar with the Cambrian Explosion?"

"I am Augmented, Ms. Elman." Tanaka might as well have said: I am now. "How is that relevant?"

"It's relevant, Madame Secretary-General, because eleven InterstellarNet species synchronized then, too."

Now, unchanged, the sphere somehow radiated impatience. "I assume you are in communication with Dr. Matthews."

Beside Corinne, oblivious to this conversation, Joshua looked ever paler. "Yes," Corinne netted. "Also his AI historian colleague, Tacitus 352."

"Mir advice, Ms. Elman, if you value your credibility, is that you break off those contacts. Of course the journalist's role is to ask questions, but those questions must be grounded in reality. These aren't.

"You speak of a time when, except for perhaps lichen—and, Dr. Matthews would have you believe, waiters—Earth's continents were bare. And at sea, what? A conspiracy of trilobites?

"Ir will accept no further communications from either of you."

The sphere vanished like a pricked soap bubble.

• • • •

A strident alarm interrupted Corinne's funk. Imminent reentry. She tightened her seat harness then double-checked Joshua's. He smiled wanly. On the ground would be soon enough to update him on her latest fiasco. Her failure.

Odd occurrences. An astronomical curiosity. Paleontological coincidence. Tanaka be damned, it meant *something*. Corinne had no idea what.

She hoped the newly assertive Joshua would have a suggestion what to try next.

CHAPTER 11

Shrieking children clambered in the trees. An evening breeze soughed through the leaves of those trees. The setting sun, fat and red, hung low over the horizon.

Squint, Joshua told himself, *and this will all seem normal.*

With a crackle, as of twigs snapping, leaves rained down. Joshua picked one of the leaf clusters off the ground. Each leaf was an undulating tube, the color of a mallard's head, softer and a bit thicker than a pine needle.

From some branch high overhead, a baritone voice called out, "Sohr-ree."

And fair enough, that he(?) struggled to pronounce the word. The eight-limbed child swinging through the trees knew at least one more word of English than Joshua could speak of any Centaur language.

Growing up, Joshua had had—back then, who hadn't?—a four-eyed, green, furry, and eight-limbed toy teddypod. No more: teddypods had become politically incorrect.

Even as he had slept hugging his teddypod, the first-ever Centaur starship had been well into its twenty-year unannounced journey to the star humans called Barnard's. One needn't be steeped in ICU lore—or Corinne's friend—to know what had ensued. A renegade Snake clan exiled to the outermost fringes of the Barnard's system captured *Harmony*, its Centaur crew still in suspended animation. Another twenty years traveling to Sol system, where Snakes presented their prize as the Snake starship *Victorious*, in a scheme to obtain the secrets of human antimatter production.

Trickery and subterfuge and battle, and the destruction of both humanity's sole antimatter factory and *Harmony/Victorious*. The Snake survivors settled into a new exile, this time on the remote

Uranian moon Ariel. Thirteen years for humans to stockpile more antimatter and build a starship based upon Centaur technology. *New Beginnings*, with its mixed human/Centaur crew, now halfway through its fourteen-year epic flight to Alpha Centauri. The Centaur colony established on Earth for those too old or too traumatized to undertake yet another marathon voyage—even to return home.

And now, in a remote corner of the Outback, Joshua marveled: *I'm going to meet the elders of that Centaur colony.* If all went well, that was. It was about time that something did.

Harmony's evacuees had rescued a few seeds and small animals. They now had this otherworldly grove to show for it.

Joshua sat on the leaf-strewn ground, leaning against the barkless bole of a sort-of-tree/sort-of-needle-free-cactus. The trunk yielded beneath his weight like a soggy carpet roll. A good twenty-five meters away, Corinne stood talking with two adult Centaurs. They towered over her. More Centaurs walked about, their many-limbed perambulations a wonder to behold. Tree-swinging, even for the gleefully shouting young ones, was a sometime thing.

Ping! "Okay," Corinne spoke into Joshua's mind's ear. "They've agreed to talk with you."

· · · ·

Five people occupied the small forest glade: two humans, two Centaurs, and an AI avatar manifested in holo form. Corinne knew everyone, and she made the introductions. "Joshua Matthews. Tacitus 352. K'tra Ko ka. T'Gwat Fru." The comm console that projected Tacitus also linked in a translator AI for the Centaurs.

K'tra Ko ka stiffly circled the clearing, dignified despite her advanced years. Age-faded fur only hinted at the teal-and-jade stripes Corinne so vividly remembered. "To be ka is an obligation," Ko explained, "more than a title. In a crisis, my judgment must substitute for consensus." A wave rippled from her almost-shoulders to the tips of her tentacles and reflected back: ironic laughter. "I hope never to experience another emergency."

Is this an emergency? Corinne wondered. Joshua had yet to reveal, beyond his desire to consult with Centaurs, why he had brought them to Australia. Until their landing in Perth, Joshua had let her think he was only putting distance between them and his stalkers.

T'Gwat Fru, the closest among the exiles to a Centaur historian, likewise circled the clearing. Corinne guessed the Centaurs were not as much pacing as keeping their old joints from seizing up. Fru was the taller of the aliens, a head taller even than Joshua. Scattered bold emerald streaks still highlighted his fur.

"Ka," Joshua began formally. "Thank you for seeing us."

"Just Ko," she said, her voice a deep bass. "And Fru for my colleague."

"Ko and Fru." Joshua gave up trying to maintain eye contact as the Centaurs circled in opposite directions. "I'm struggling to find a way to present this. For anything even half this complex, I am accustomed to using implants."

"We don't use neural implants." Ko kept circling. "We know most humans do, and those you call Snakes, and several other InterstellarNet species. It's just not attractive to us."

"Project what you need," Corinne netted Joshua. She held back a grin at his response: a Centaur laugh gesture superimposed onto his avatar's boneless shrug.

"Ko and Fru," Joshua began again. "It appears that we live in a very special corner of the galaxy." With admirable brevity and a few holographic projections, he explained all that troubled him. The Matthews conundrum. The Cambrian coincidence. Technologies uncannily synchronized across all the InterstellarNet species.

"Not identical, of course," Tacitus said. He interspersed comments without, Corinne thought, adding much. To be fair, *he* had first spotted the Cambrian coincidence. "There would not be trade otherwise."

No one spoke for a long time. Fru stopped walking, the better, it seemed, to poke and prod at the comp he had unhooked from his utility belt. "I cannot disagree," he finally said. If the translator had correctly applied inflection, Fru was unhappy. "Your facts appear correct."

"Can you add anything?" Corinne had no more reason than Joshua to expect the Centaurs would have insights to offer—just the desperate hope Joshua must feel.

"Details," Fru answered. "On Haven"—the Centaur home world—"the equivalent to your Cambrian Explosion proceeded a little faster. Life in Haven's oceans had evolved a bit further." He resumed his circling, but slowly, still manipulating his comp. "Of course, Haven is an older world. You would expect that."

Tacitus cleared his virtual throat. "Alpha Centauri is not much older than Sol. Tau Ceti is twice Sol's age, and Barnard's Star yet older. Epsilon Eridani is far younger. Microfossils show, or so we've been told, life emerging on every InterstellarNet home world within a few hundred million years of its formation. Then, suddenly—half a billion years ago—synchronization. Across eleven neighboring solar systems."

Asteroid impacts. Rampant volcanism. The onset or end of glaciations. Theories for epochal changes abounded—while hard evidence remained elusive at best. "Separate catastrophes, light-years apart, all at around the same time." Corinne shivered. "Somehow, it's why we're all here now."

● ● ● ●

Joshua sat on rocky ground, lobbing twigs into a small campfire. Its dancing flames were mesmerizing. The almost trees rustled in the breeze. Creatures unseen twittered and chirped in the underbrush.

He tried, and failed, to empty his mind, the thoughts and memories of this evening all too painful. Mysterious enemies. Prehistorical enigmas. A proud family legacy reduced to infosphere punch line.

What had he expected to find here? He had no clue. Something. Anything. It was so much wishful thinking.

Joshua leaned to gather a fresh handful of twigs. The night grew cold, and he didn't feel like going indoors. The smoke smelled of vanilla and dill.

InterstellarNet meant AI trade agents. An AI trade agent scoured its host society's infosphere and transmitted its findings home. Tacitus had already data-mined everything humanity's agents could find or buy about those other civilizations. He had found the Cambrian coincidence in the first place.

AIs can't know everything, Joshua told himself. Himself was unimpressed. They still knew more than he did, or ever could. *Should he now add jealousy to his list of failings?*

Model trains. More specifically, Dad's model train. Joshua poked the campfire with a stick, bemused by this latest synapse misfire.

Pop! A sap bubble exploded and Joshua twitched. Maybe there was no more to this trip than flight from his near-abduction. "Research" sounded better than fleeing. Maybe, at some level, he meant to hide where any human's arrival elicited comment. He tossed in another handful of twigs, and the scent of dill intensified.

Joshua stood, stretched, and kicked dirt over the campfire until, in a shower of sparks, the last flicker of flame went out. Cool lights and Corinne's easy laughter indicated the way to company. He walked in the opposite direction.

More and more stars twinkled overhead, Alpha Centauri among the brightest, as his eyes acclimated to the dark. The Moon shone above and sparkled in the nearby creek. He, in any event, considered it a creek; the map he had consulted on the flight here had called it a river. He didn't remember the river's name. He could have looked it up but didn't bother; net surfing had no part in his program of mind-emptying. Surely he could manage one evening without using his implant. The Centaurs spent their lives that way.

Suddenly curious why, Joshua turned toward the sound of Corinne's voice.

He found her in a far older wood, this one terrestrial, hugging the banks of the creek. Oh yeah, the Katherine River. She stood chatting with Fru and two Centaurs whom Joshua had yet to meet. Fru still towered over her. The strangers, though, were eye to eye with Corinne—because both hung upside down from an ancient boab tree. Their orientation didn't seem to phase her.

"Fru," Joshua said, "why don't Centaurs use neural implants?"

"I'm not sure," Fru answered. The three Centaurs consulted in bass rumbles. "Having thoughts put straight into one's head—it's too much like telepathy."

Corinne looked as puzzled as Joshua felt. "Would telepathy be a bad thing?"

"An eerie thing," one of the other Centaurs said. "Nepathian."

"That didn't translate," Corinne said.

"Nepathian," Fru repeated. "Nepath is a proper name. A character in an old story. Very influential."

Joshua leaned forward. "What's it about?"

More bass rumblings. "A mad-scientist story from the dawn of our scientific revolution. Close to four hundred Earth years ago. The 'science' was ludicrous, of course, but Nepath invented helmets that enabled mind reading. He promised telepathy would banish all misunderstanding. Instead, the helmets spread envy and distrust. Unfiltered emotion tore at the fabric of society."

Corinne laughed. "And a thousand angry villagers with torches and pitchforks attacked his castle."

Joshua had had the same thought. "It does sound like Frankenstein, doesn't it?"

"Frankenstein?" Fru blinked. Among Centaurs, blinking also denoted surprise, but they did it using only their inner eyelids. "That didn't translate for us."

"A mad-scientist story of Earth's," Corinne said. "As it happens, written around the same time. Frankenstein sought to create life. He assembled a creature from parts of stolen corpses, and then reanimated the creature with lightning."

All three Centaurs now blinked. "That truly is a coincidence," Fru said. "We have that old story, too."

CHAPTER 12

Not-quite-trees and the gentle green octopods who glided among them were the main evidence of an extraterrestrial presence. The few Centaur structures were gracefully curved and low to the ground, melding with the arid plains and native red-rock formations. It was all quite eco-friendly. Very subdued and understated.

Then there was indoors.

The colony's surface constructions were mostly antechambers to long tunnels, multitiered basements, and expansive caves. The heart of the community was a twenty-meter-high artificial cavern, its atrium bathed in sunlight.

Corinne supposed the enormous dome was a plasteel skylight, its exterior surface treated to mimic the sun-parched terrain. But maybe only a very large digital replica of a sunny sky hugged a rocky cavern ceiling. She was not about to climb up to investigate.

On the Commons floor, in no pattern she could discern, consorted: manicured gardens; clusters of round tables and backless stools in a riot of bold colors; hypnotic water sprays, part sprinkler and part dynamic sculpture; meandering graveled pedestrian paths; holo exhibits; decorative boulders; food synthesizers; and apparatuses to which Corinne could put no label. Three tiers of rails for swinging ringed the stone walls. Hooks for swinging dotted the ceiling and its few slender support columns. Singly and in groups, Centaurs threaded the cluttered floor and swung through the vast enclosed space. For the latter set, a few swoops of rope were the closest thing to a safety net.

Sighing, Corinne looked away. Again. The meeting grotto shared a clear wall with the Commons whose throngs kept catching her eye. Across the table, his back to the glass, Joshua helped Fru fiddle with a projected data graphic. Their unending tweaking made her nervous as hell.

Her nerves weren't entirely their fault. She had slept poorly the night before. It wasn't the usual *Harmony/Victorious* nightmare, in any of its variations, that kept her tossing and turning. She had survived that ordeal, and her subconscious knew it. Failure scared her more than danger. Fear of ridicule frightened her most of all.

Adrenaline and stims would substitute for lack of sleep, and she had taken plenty of stims. Nothing could make up for a loss of nerve.

Dr. Robyn Tanaka Astor and two aides must have come straight from Perth Spaceport to the Centaur colony, because suddenly, a good two hours earlier than Corinne had expected, Ko was escorting them through the Commons. Approaching the meeting grotto, Tanaka's aides started. The S-G's face remained impassive. Of course.

Ko and Fru began briefing the newcomers.

A mind's ear *ping* announced an incoming call: Tanaka Astor. In Corinne's mind's eye, a featureless sphere spun. Or did it spin? If it's featureless, how could she gauge spinning? *Never mind! Focus!* Joshua's avatar joined in an instant later.

Tanaka Astor netted, "K'tra Ko ka asked ur here to meet with a Centaur delegation. Ir did not expect to meet humans here."

You did not expect to see Joshua and me, Corinne translated. There was nothing to be gained by commenting.

That didn't stop Joshua. "My apologies if you feel misled, Madame Secretary-General. I've been consulting with the Centaurs."

"You should not have bothered the colonists. It is not helpful," the S-G netted. At the same time she conversed the old-fashioned way with the Centaurs.

Corinne had only the one mind. She couldn't process simultaneous conversations in real and cyberspace. Maybe that was Tanaka Astor's plan: keeping Joshua and her from the audible conversation.

The hell with that. Corinne dropped the net link.

Oblivious to the netted dialogue, Fru was wrapping up his summation. He, Joshua, and Tacitus had found several disturbing synchronizations between Earth and Haven history.

"Interesting coincidences, perhaps, but over a time span of eons," Tanaka Astor said. Joshua's red face suggested a second, more dismissive critique. "Ir do not see the urgency the ka indicated in requesting this gathering."

Once, Corinne thought, *I was a reporter. I uncovered news. I helped set the public agenda. Then fame went to my head. I turned into a journalist, more apt to present how I found or felt about a story than the story itself. And now, nearing bottom, I'm a* celebrity. *Now it's all about me. It's become an endless rehash of things I've already done.*

But the ladder had a final lower rung. Buffoon. It terrified Corinne. *Am I seriously considering this? Challenging one of the most powerful figures in the Solar System?*

"How do you explain two all but identical Frankenstein stories appearing on both worlds at almost the same time?" Joshua demanded.

"Ir don't explain it," Tanaka Astor said expressionlessly. "Nor do you. Neither humans nor Centaurs had radio, so you can't explain it."

"It *needs* explaining," Joshua insisted. "There are too many coincidences. Here's another. Both worlds share the RUR story."

(RUR? Joshua must not have slept last night, either. Corinne queried. Rossum's Universal Robots. *R.U.R.,* like *Frankenstein,* was a cautionary tale, this time with rebellious automatons exterminating their creators. Earth's version appeared in 1921, the Centaur equivalent ten years earlier. Humans and Centaurs had had radio by then, but very primitive and low-power. Neither could yet receive transmissions from the other.)

Tanaka Astor stood to leave. "With all due respect, ka, Dr. Matthews would exploit you to rehabilitate himself. He raises endless questions but offers not a single answer."

Corinne's thoughts raced. She had lain low since the ICU contingent arrived. Her presence remained plausibly in the service of newsgathering. Reporter, journalist, celebrity. She did *not* want to take the final step down. And yet, there were worse fates than being laughed at. Joshua had survived ridicule, still holding his head high. Abandon a friend over a little embarrassment? She had not yet sunk so low.

Nor would she.

What might give Tanaka Astor second thoughts? Not appeals to loyalty and trust. Those might be as foreign to an Augmented as amusement and jealousy, contentment and despair. How about the prospect of time lost to handling foolish human manias? A new popular obsession was something PR could achieve. Something Corinne could invoke.

Corinne cleared her throat. "Madame Secretary-General, I wouldn't be so quick to dismiss these parallels. In fact, I expect my viewers will find them most intriguing. Joshua, would you show the matrix?"

The S-G made no further move to leave.

Good enough, Corinne thought. *I'll take even small victories.*

Joshua coaxed a complex graphic from the unfamiliar Centaur projector. "The Frankenstein coincidence suggested a plan of study. *R.U.R.* confirmed it." He pointed into the holo. "InterstellarNet has several more fascinating literary coincidences. They've had similar consequences.

"Earth and Haven share the Frankenstein fable. The result? By InterstellarNet standards, humans and Centaurs were both slow to develop biotech. Humans licensed modern gengineering, eventually, from the Wolves. And we needed the help! Adapting proven methods to Earthly biology was faster and cheaper—and more acceptable to the public—than playing catch-up. The Wolves had nothing resembling the Frankenstein story until long after their biotech was well established."

"True," Tanaka Astor said. The usual flat delivery made the word sound grudging. "Ptask Syn Frnch"—the local AI representing Wolf 359 interests—"confirms that. It also appears plausible that Leo and Aquarian instances of the same fable discouraged their development of gengineering."

"Literary analysis as market research," one of the S-G's heretofore mute aides offered. "Useful, perhaps. What does it have to do with drunken disappearances or the Cambrian Explosion?"

Joshua ignored the gibe. "The pattern recurs in robotics. Those species with an early *R.U.R*-type legend were slow to develop robotics, or had to import it. Some still shun robots.

"It's not only human legends. Four InterstellarNet species have variations of the Nepath story. None developed, nor will any adopt, neural implants." He pointed elsewhere in the holo. "Neither humans nor Snakes have the Nepath legend. Snakes developed implant technology, and humans were quick to license it. Meanwhile Snakes dread nanotech, seemingly based on a fable of their own. *They* won't touch Centaur nanotech."

The lack of implants should strike close to home, Corinne thought. *No implants meant no Augmented.*

Eyes glazed on Tanaka Astor and her aides: an intense private consultation. "Ir confirm the analysis," Tanaka said. "Recurring myths. Technologies impeded or suppressed with strong correlation. Ir must consider this hitherto unsuspected pattern among InterstellarNet member species." Hints of wholly human frustration somehow managed to escape. "Ir do not understand what it can mean."

Friendship and gut instinct offered Corinne the same advice: give Tanaka Astor a final shove. Commit. "There is a deeper meaning here, Madame Secretary-General. Time and again, we see technologies discouraged by fables. The stories vary. The technologies differ. And yet these circumstances have something in common.

"Gengineering, nanotech, robotics, computing itself—these are the technologies that could render *people* extinct."

CHAPTER 13

Triple his normal weight pressed Joshua deep into his couch. He appreciated the free ride on the ICU courier ship as far as Geneva—but not the takeoff. Commercial flights took things much easier. Maybe the Augmented took no notice of acceleration.

Ping! Gasping, Joshua accepted the connection. It was Tanaka, from an adjacent seat. Piloting and three gees must have been insufficient to occupy her. "Yes, Madame Secre—"

"Robyn," she interrupted. "It's more efficient." She didn't wait for him to parse the sudden informality, or that Corinne, also aboard, remained unlinked. "Joshua, you discovered something very important. For that Ir thank you. The interstellar pattern of cautionary fables is significant—no matter that its meaning remains obscure."

"Thanks," Joshua managed. Even netting was a struggle, what with his brain trying to burst out the back of his skull. Still, he sensed that a very large "but" impended.

"The problem, Joshua, is that you see connections that don't exist. That can't exist. And what if they did? Shared fables don't prove there is a narrative, the Matthews conundrum, that anyone would want suppressed. Shared fables caused neither your disappearance nor the Cambrian Explosion. Shared fables cannot make credible a plot half a billion years old, or that any society, any species, could even survive that long. If somehow a civilization has, its resources are surely not limited to waiters and a taxi."

Acceleration ended abruptly.

Joshua's gorge rose. Somehow, he kept his breakfast down. Corinne's surprised yelp almost made him smile. His stomach lurched again, and he clutched the padded arms of his couch for whatever good that might do. He *refused* to puke in front of Tanaka Astor.

He would have seen it eventually—space sickness only brought everything together sooner. The question had been gnawing at him: why a waiter? "Of course," he said aloud.

"Of course, what?" Corinne snapped.

"The waiter is the key." As though in affirmation, Joshua's stomach rumbled again. "The doctors say I ate crab. The waiter supplied it."

Robyn swiveled to face him. "You ate crab before reappearing. Are you remembering seeing the waiter there—wherever *there* was?"

Joshua shook his head. In micro-gee, that was a big mistake. He tried to ignore the bubbling in his gut. "I'm going to ask you to think outside the box."

Robyn netted a question mark.

He remembered a long-ago pillow fort, and Worthington's confusion. Metaphor was a human skill. Perhaps a wholly human skill. "Imagine the goal is to discredit me. A bit of crab can make me almost instantly nauseous. It makes me violently ill within the hour. Hence, I *never* eat anything with crab. Living in Charleston, crab-stuffed dishes are everywhere. I learned long ago: always ask about crab. I don't take chances. I distinctly remember asking at the party what was in several of the hors d'oeuvres.

"The way to get crab into me—however briefly—is to lie. The caterer claims no record of a waiter, yet one *was* at the party. In that very specific context, he was an authority figure. So: feed me crab, hustle me into a cab when my face starts to puff up, and then disappear me."

Corinne squinted. "I don't see—"

The words tumbled out, unstoppable. "To Robyn's question: I don't believe there was a *there*. Everyone says I was gone for four weeks; my allergy says I was away for maybe an hour. Take your pick of improbabilities.

"One, I dropped off the grid so completely that no one can find a trace of me for four weeks. I slipped up and ate crab a second time. Entirely coincidentally, the Matthews conundrum points us to inexplicable interstellar synchronizations half a billion years ago and a few hundred years ago.

"Or two, these events *are* related. The enigmas share an explanation. Time travel." He waved off their questions. "Embody the mechanism in the backseat of a cab. Or drive the cab into the time machine. Shift me four weeks into the future—hence, my disappearance without a trace. The crab remains in my system.

"And on a larger scale, maybe only time travel can explain meddling that spans eons."

• • • •

In the crowded skies over Europe, reentry and terminal approach demanded even Robyn's full attention. Conversation halted until she landed the ship.

First metaphor blindness, now an upper bound on her abilities. A few failings could make even an Augmented seem human. Even one who still doubted him.

Joshua made no comment when Robyn summoned an ICU limo rather than take a cab from the spaceport, or when she dismissed the AI driver to operate the limo herself. Or when, as the limo wended its way to ICU headquarters, Robyn insisted upon a second layer of encryption over their net links.

"Time travel is not the answer," Robyn resumed the conversation without preamble. "Or rather, Ir am loath to accept it. There is no known theoretical basis. To the contrary, granting the hypothesis would raise countless cause-and-effect paradoxes. You could as well attribute everything to magic."

And yet, Robyn continued to discuss it. Corinne, in contrast, appeared numb. Joshua challenged, "Do you have another explanation?"

"Time dilation." Robyn peered out of the limo into the distance. "Special and general relativity alike would permit slowing the passage of time. Maybe there are other ways."

Joshua twitched. Her matter-of-fact manner somehow conveyed profound confidence. Had he been oblivious to a consultation among Augmenteds? "So time froze in the back of that cab. Or time braked to a crawl. Like time travel, that would explain why my neural implant has no memories of those weeks *and* no record of having shut down. It had become too slow to connect to the infosphere."

"Crab affects you within an hour," Robyn netted. She gave no indication of a subject change.

"As a rule." Joshua didn't see where she was going.

Corinne did. "You were missing a bit over four weeks. Call it seven hundred hours. The crab didn't bounce until you got home. Also, you remember parts of the cab ride. If slowed time was involved, the effect was active for just part of the trip. All in all, seven hundred hours elapsed in subjectively less than an hour. That's time retardation on the order of a thousand to one."

The limo stopped in front of the tallest office tower of the park-like ICU headquarters campus, in and out of whose main entrance people endlessly streamed. "Wait in the car," Robyn netted without explanation before sinking into an Augmented trance. And then, "A thousand to one. That ratio almost makes this believable. At that compression, the Cambrian Explosion was only a half-million years ago. Maybe Ir can believe a society lasting that long. And maybe they can slow time even more when they choose."

Only who were *they*?

Beyond the tinted limo windows, past a manicured lawn, yachts bobbed on Lake Geneva. Workers out for fresh air and sunshine wandered the grounds or lolled on the lakeside benches. Fat, honking geese waddled along the shore, demanding, and often getting, scraps from picnickers. It was all so … normal.

They.

An unknown force who wielded planetary disasters to drive evolutions. Who had meddled in at least eleven solar systems—and in the affairs of eleven intelligent species. Who worked in timeframes, as humans measured time, anyway, that exceeded a half-billion years. Who nonetheless took notice of *his* vaguest intimation of *their* existence.

"Maybe I am crazy," Joshua netted to Corinne. "Considering

the alternative, my insanity seems so much for the best."

Corinne shivered. "Such power. Such an inexplicable thirst for secrecy. And if we're not all delusional: the ability to pass as human, or, at least recently, human agents."

CHAPTER 14

Why are we sitting here? Corinne wondered as the minutes passed. People strolled by the limo, glancing in vain at its tinted windows. But Joshua seemed almost happy. Despite his protestations, it must be a relief to know he *wasn't* insane.

Corinne caught herself whistling tunelessly. It had been far too long, two decades ago, creeping sunward in an overcrowded lifeboat—but she *knew* this feeling. She was giddy with relief, with danger escaped—

With being a reporter again!

Vid specials took form in her mind. *Frankenstein* across the stars. Mysterious aliens whispering in the ear of a young Mary Shelley. Entire societies shaped by the myths imposed on them. She had a story, by God! An epic. The mother of all scoops. A certain second Pulitzer. And better still—

"Joshua," Corinne burst out. "It's over! Once this news is out, any further move against you would only intensify public interest. We'll lay low for a few days, while I make discreet arrangements before—"

"No."

A single syllable, but it made Corinne flinch. That was Astor speaking, no longer the briefly approachable Robyn. Timbre, subtle harmonics—something—about that short word resonated in Corinne's brain. It was no mere opinion or recommendation. This was a *command*, more intense even than the usual focused attention of an Augmented.

Did all Augmented have this power over normals? "I don't understand," Corinne managed to get out.

"There can be no story." Beneath Tanaka Astor's stare, Corinne felt like a bug under a microscope. "In a way, because you are correct.

92

They would take note. They would gain an inkling how much we have discovered. And that must not happen, for these others are no mere storytellers.

"Let them have a name: the Interveners. 'The Matthews conundrum' had been obscure. It appears all that has befallen Joshua revolves around suppressing that story. That being so, ask yourself: how did the Interveners learn of his interest? How did they come to know so much about him, down to his allergy to crab?"

"My family knows both," Joshua netted. "And the people I worked with …"

"Correct." Tanaka's emotionless delivery suddenly rang sinister. "Agents within the ICU itself. Where better? InterstellarNet allows trading of mature, proven technologies. The old cautionary tales lose their ability to frighten after all the dangerous experimentation has been done light-years away. Now every argument ever made in the ICU against a technology deal becomes suspect."

"And every untimely illness," Corinne added. "Every accident. Every death. Thousands of employees for nearly 175 years. That's a lot to investigate."

"Agreed," Robyn netted. "But first Ir must check out the two longtime aides, sworn to secrecy, Ir left doing busy work in Australia."

• • • •

In recent centuries, working across light-years, the Interveners had segregated intelligent species by technology. In an earlier—*much* earlier—epoch, the Interveners had shaped the many-times-removed ancestors of ancestors of ancestors of those same species. And between: made what other interventions, as yet unsuspected?

Perhaps more than bad luck had lobbed an asteroid at the dinosaurs.

"Tip of the iceberg" fell woefully short as a metaphor. The Interveners had set their plans into motion long before the first animals crawled onto the land, on Earth or Haven or nine other worlds. On Earth, before there were fish to attempt the ascent.

Plans to accomplish … what? Joshua's imagination failed him.

Robyn netted, "In time, this story will be told. Ir promise, Corinne, you will be the first to tell it. In time. For now, we dare not reveal to the Interveners that we have learned of them."

"That's why we're still in the car. You can't be seen with me." Joshua shrugged. For a moment, at least, it sufficed to be believed. "I must remain disgraced so that you can hunt unsuspected for moles."

"You deserve better." Tanaka Astor's voice hummed once again with that eerie power. She meant them to *believe* her. She reverted to the encrypted link. "Both of you. Regardless, discovering the Intervener agents comes first. We must do nothing to alert them. Even as we—very discreetly—find ways to work together. To do what? That, Ir do not yet know."

We. Not the Augmented first person. Joshua netted his private, heartfelt thanks.

Tanaka opened her door. "Once Ir am in the building, summon a driver to return you to the spaceport."

"The Interveners." Corinne trembled. "They raised us from the level of jellyfish."

"True." Joshua found his eyes drawn to Robyn, found confidence in her calm self-assurance. "And it's about time they learned we're not jellyfish anymore."

CHAMPIONSHIP B'TOK

CHAPTER 15

By the directed stimulation of neurons, virtual knight captured imaginary pawn.

"Crap," Lyle Logan netted. Many thousand championship games uploaded into his neural implant—and not one of them anticipated that gambit.

"Mate in five moves," Corrigan confirmed. "And, by the way, *Betty* will arrive before lunch."

Lyle banished the game from his mind's eye. Likewise, his opponent, with the perpetual devil-may-care smirk. Wearing a snug leather helmet, its chin straps dangling, and aviator goggles. Seated in the open cockpit of some dawn-of-flight biplane. As AI avatars went, that wasn't especially ironic. Corrigan might have been out walking on his virtual wing.

Lyle told himself, yet again, that there was no shame in losing at chess to an artificial intelligence. Even to an AI who specialized in piloting, not games of strategy. Even in losing over and over, more times than Lyle could remember.

Doubtless Corrigan remembered.

"Good game," Lyle said. The measure of his boredom was that he spoke aloud when neural interface would have been faster. One measure, in any event. Should anyone ever ask, he had spent the entire trip at two gees, without a break except the few minutes at turnover, for the miserable-duty pay.

Why did a roboship never break down within a billion klicks of civilization?

With a thought he retrieved the current view through the ship's telescope. 2182 DV189 finally presented a recognizable, if battered, profile. On that Phobos-sized, stippled snowball, one speck was the autonomous mining ship he had been sent to repair. He was close enough, at last, for sensors to detect its low-power, self-contained, traffic-control transponder. The mining ship was otherwise unresponsive, whether queried, commanded, or sent a master reset.

Of course, a multibillion-sol ship going mute was why Lyle had been dispatched into the outer darkness aboard a *very* fast ship.

"How soon can you set us down?" he asked Corrigan.

"Forty minutes."

He had wondered for days what could have gone wrong on the miner. Something unusual, for sure. Any AI had too many levels of redundancy, too many fail-safes and fallback modes, to have gone silent without warning. And yet this miner had. Rumor had it, others, too.

With nothing better to do, Lyle tried, once again, to make contact. Nada. For the hell of it, he cranked up the beam power from his comm laser. Still no response, but the vapors boiled off the snowball revealed water, oxygen, and lots of hydrocarbons. Even metals.

"I'll suit up," Lyle announced. Sooner started, sooner finished. And sooner on his way back to civilization. Or, though he hoped otherwise, sent across hell-and-gone on another service call. The Kuiper Belt was *big*, and no way, no how, could human crew accompany every ship.

"We have robots to make the initial survey."

Yes, they had. Perhaps he would even end up delegating the repairs to bots. But *he* would diagnose the problem faster, because the bots weren't all that bright. Had they been half as smart as Corrigan—

He wouldn't go near them, much less be alone with them. Who would?

AIs were colleagues, often friends. Certainly Corrigan was a friend, if not the sort of buddy with whom he could share a carouse.

So why not AI-smart robots?

Robots, somehow, were different. Because they would be … competitors? Possible successors? Maybe. That was only part of it. The reasoned part. The noncreepy part. He wasn't the type to imagine things going bump in the night—but neither did he see any reason to create them. Give enough smarts to robots, and would they be so different from zombies and vampires?

If dreading smart robots made him irrational, so be it.

Lyle waved vaguely, the gesture meant to encompass the claustrophobic bridge. The adjoining multipurpose "cabin," in which he slept, ate, exercised, and washed, was yet tinier. *Betty* was all legs. Apart from military couriers, he doubted any ship was faster or offered a greater cruising range. "I feel like a change of scenery."

In his mind's eye, Corrigan shrugged. Lyle took that as "okay." Or, maybe, as "wacky human."

On snowballs like the one *Betty* was approaching, one docked more so than one landed. He felt his ship shudder, just a bit, as Corrigan fired grapples. By then deceleration had ceased, and with it any semblance of gravity. He waited, already suited up, in the air lock.

As soon as Corrigan had winched them down to the snowball, almost before the AI could dispatch survey bots from a cargo hold, Lyle was through the outer hatch. With one gauntleted hand, he patted the larger-than-life figure painted on the hull beside the air lock. For luck. *Betty* had never failed him.

The distant Sun, although merely a spark, outshone the full Moon seen from Earth. With a bit of amplification by his visor, he could see fine. But that spark, so near the horizon, would soon set. Hills and rubble piles cast long, inky shadows across the pockmarked landscape. Wherever the Sun managed to reach, the surface glinted: a brittle, frozen froth of ice mottled with tarry streamers. His HUD declared the surface temperature to be a balmy fifty. In degrees absolute.

Mining ship 129 stood, looming, perhaps a hundred meters distant, almost midway to the freakishly close horizon. All struts and pipes and reagent tanks, MS129 was as much a factory/smeltery/refinery as a vessel. By comparison, his ship—no matter its thirty meters of fuel tank, reaction-mass tank, and muscular fusion drive—was a toy. Just a whole *lot* faster than the lumbering miner.

Dozens of robots, motionless, lay strewn across the landscape.

That couldn't be good.

Whatever had happened here had happened *fast*. The first thing a mining ship did was construct tanks to receive what it extracted. He saw only two storage tanks, neither complete.

Lyle's own bots, spiderlike, scuttled toward the miner, rolling out and staking safety cable for him and deploying work lights. On his HUD, status indicators glowed green. He gave the bots a fifty-meter head start before following, "climbing" hand over hand, his safety tethers clipped to the cable. Sans tethers, one careless twitch here could set him adrift in space.

By the time he reached the mining vessel, bots had already begun to encircle it with cable. Moving clockwise, he began a methodical survey. Dubbing where the main cable met the incomplete loop twelve o'clock, it was between two and three where he first spotted a problem.

A more-or-less oval expanse, about one meter by two, about six meters from the ground, looked … weird. Stuff had boiled/bubbled/spewed from MS129's hull, only to congeal into an amoeboid glob. In this meager gravity, the melt had frozen faster than anything like an icicle had had the chance to take shape.

Per the schematics on his HUD, a primary computing node was just beneath.

A meteoroid strike? Something internal overloaded, shorted out, or otherwise overheating? Maybe. Didn't matter. A single comp node gone bad would not disable the ship. It carried three more computing nodes just like this one.

"Ouch," Corrigan remarked. He was monitoring via Lyle's helmet camera and a radio link.

Lyle resumed his circuit around the inert vessel. At four o'clock on his imaginary clock face, he plunged into the mining ship's long, black shadow. Methodically he surveyed, as the bots directed work lights wherever he faced. Nothing seemed amiss until, between five and six: a *second* melted-and-recongealed mass. A second main computing node.

Had a meteoroid struck one node, drilled through the ship, to exit through a second node? That wasn't impossible—just damned improbable. He was surprised at Corrigan's failure to comment.

"Are you seeing this?" Lyle netted.

A static hiss was the only answer. Interference from all the metal in the mining ship's hull? Perhaps. Even so, the link should have been relayed around the ship from bot to bot.

With a shrug and a yank on his safety tether, Lyle resumed his survey.

Two comp nodes down, he mused, but the hull seemed otherwise intact. That should leave MS129 with a pair of functioning comp nodes. Unless those, too, had somehow—

Something jabbed Lyle in the back. Something *hard*. One of his damned robots?

On the emergency radio band, a synthed voice instructed, "Do not move."

CHAPTER 16

Hunters: the intelligent species native to the dim red-dwarf Barnard's Star system (see related entry). Hunters are commonly referred to as Snakes, after the constellation—Ophiuchus, "The Serpent Holder"—in which Barnard's Star can (with a telescope) be seen from Earth. In formal/diplomatic usage, for their native world of K'vith, they are known as K'vithians.

Hunters evolved from pack-hunting carnivores. Their early culture centered on clan structures, an apparent extension of pre-intelligence packs. From that genesis has developed an economic system of pure *laissez-faire, caveat-emptor* capitalism, centered on competing clan-based corporations. The dominant group dynamics are territoriality between clans—in modern times, the contested "territory" can be commercial rather than geographical in nature—and competition for status within and among clans. Usually of relevance only to the clans, these rivalries have on occasion impacted interstellar relations.

A Hunter enclave exists on the Uranian moon of Ariel, settled by survivors of an unsuccessful Solar System incursion (see related entries, "Himalia Incident" and "Ariel Colony"). Following eighteen years of intrusive United Planets supervision, the

Hunter settlement has been granted broader (but still limited) self-rule.

—*Internetopedia*

• • • •

The woman sat alone in the all but deserted cafeteria, picking indifferently at the tossed salad on her meal tray. At the soft *zip-zip* of shoes against grip strips, she glanced up. "Did I do something wrong?"

"No," Carl answered, arching an eyebrow. "Why would you ask that?"

"Because the warden made a beeline for me."

Beeline? Earther slang, he supposed. Warden, he understood. As someone had once noted, the most anxious man in a prison.

"UP liaison," Carl corrected. That was his job title, for the past couple of years, anyway, though the change had fooled no one. If Ariel was no longer a POW camp, if its residents had been granted new privileges, neither was this the typical United Planets protectorate.

Nor would it ever be. Not on his watch.

The young woman still eyed him skeptically. Only she was no more young than he was middle-aged.

"Let's try this again." Carl offered his hand. "Carl Rowland. We don't see many new faces here." Not human faces, anyway. The Snakes bred like rabbits. That was another thing he worried about, no matter that their population on Ariel barely topped twenty thousand. "I just stopped by to introduce myself and ask how civilization is faring."

"Grace DiMeara." She set down her fork to shake hands. Hardly anyone her age did that anymore. "Who says I'm from civilization?"

Truth was, he had known her name. He'd known her flight plan, the ship's registration, and her passenger's stated business here. He knew that Grace was thirty-five, though something (her eyes? The massive, antique bracelet? The facial nanornaments so understated he barely saw them?) made her seem much older. No ship landed on this rock without a thorough review first. Under his classified title, UPIA station chief, all that intel came through him.

"Simple process of elimination," he said. "You're not from around here."

She had a nice laugh. "If you're planning to chat me up, you may as well have a seat."

He sat. "So, routine flight?"

"That's how I like 'em." Grace reclaimed her fork and went back to pushing lettuce shreds around her bowl. "Anyway, as routine as it could be with the owner aboard."

"Corrine Elman. The worlds-famous reporter."

"That's her."

"Too bad. You had to keep everything shipshape."

"Mmm." Grace fixed her eyes on her salad. Not speaking ill of the boss.

He held in a grin. Grace wouldn't know it, but he and Corinne went *way* back. To call Corinne a slob would be too kind. But that was from another life, another era. When he had gone by a different name, had worn a different face. The year he'd spent as Corinne's personal pilot had been among the happiest in his life—up until the Snakes showed up.

In the crazy, desperate actions that had followed, he had caught the eye of some UPIA types. Who better to forever bury his past than the United Planet's premier spy agency? Where better to lie low than on this godforsaken, ass-end-of-nowhere rock?

And so, here he was. The warden. And Corinne, his supposed friend, whom he had not seen in years—the single person outside the UPIA who knew the old *and* the new him—hadn't bothered to message that she was coming.

"How long will you be on Ariel?" Carl asked.

Grace shrugged. "You'll have to ask the boss."

"You know? I might just do that."

CHAPTER 17

In a series of glides and hops, Corinne followed her escorts. Only her hops, as often as not, bounced her off the corridor's low ceiling. Too many of her glides did their best to become pratfalls.

While her Snake escorts moved with an understated elegance.

When had she last been farther from Earth than the zenith of a suborbital jaunt? Too long, clearly. She had just begun to reacquire micro-gee skills—and to keep down food—when her ship had reached low-grav little Ariel. Whereupon she discovered new ways to flounder.

That she still *owned* a long-range interplanetary ship was fairly ridiculous, no matter that renting it out made it a decent investment. But to sell *Odyssey* would mean admitting she no longer expected to launch on short notice, unconstrained by commercial flight schedules, to chase a Big Story. That she had ceased to be a journalist.

So you are *still a journalist? Then quit whining. Quit wallowing. Observe.*

At least act like a journalist lest anyone wonder why you're here.

What did she see? A windowless corridor. Without retinal enhancements things would have seemed dim. Other than off Earth, the passageway could have been most anywhere. Not so the Snakes, streaming both ways.

Snakes: two arms, two legs, and a head. Upright posture. And there any resemblance to humans ended. Whippet-thin. Nostrils set flat in the plane of the face—and a third, upward-gazing eye set near the apex of the skull. Hairless and iridescent-scaled. Glimpses of retractable talons in each fingertip (and, as they wore sandals, each toe). The tallest Snakes stood a quarter meter shorter than she—and she struggled to aspire to petite.

Not about you, Corinne chided herself.

Clumsily, she hopped/glided/careened after her minders.

Filter plugs irritated her nostrils without keeping out the smells of rotten eggs, freshly struck matches, and all manner of other sulfurous stinks. Collectively, *bouquet de Snake*. Aptly, fire and brimstone. Every whiff raised bad memories.

They traveled along a main "road." Lesser tunnels split off every ten or so meters, marked by wall plaques labeled (in English and, equally impenetrable for her, Mandarin and clan speak) for life support, power generation, and other basic services. To her right, beyond an arc of clear wall, stretched a vast underground farm. To her left, a few bounding paces later, a second plasteel wall looked over an ancient crater. In that hollow sprawled factories, pipelines, and a fusion reactor. Spacesuited workers teemed around a construction whose facade looked newly patched.

How many Snakes had she seen? Several dozen, at the least. Maybe hundreds. Adults and children. Workers. Families. The ones sporting nape-of-the-neck ridges were male. Clad, regardless of gender, in belted, one-piece jumpsuits. The variety in colors and adornments designated schools, civic groups, and utility workers.

But it was the uniforms of Snake officialdom that drew Corinne's eye, the black garb of the police that made her want to cringe. She had had too much experience with Snake warriors. In twenty years, she had not forgotten.

No matter how much she tried.

A clumsy hop sent her tumbling. "Sorry," she said.

"Careful," said an escort. And he was the talkative member of the pair.

She had visited Ariel before. Visited the Foremost before. It wasn't much farther to the clan leader's office, she remembered, not needing to access the map download in her implant.

And she had a job to do here, if not what the Foremost might imagine.

"Walt," Corinne netted. "I'm almost there."

In her mind's eye, seated behind a battered wooden desk, an

avatar appeared. As always, his suit was two centuries out of style.

"I'm ready," Walt said, tapping an imaginary cigarette out of a virtual box.

Turning a corner, she came upon a foyer offering human- and Snake-sized chairs. The Foremost's office was just beyond.

"Here," an escort said. His eyes glazed, telltale of an implant-mediated infosphere consultation.

Wait here, she supposed that meant. Clan-speak implied verbs. Only the more fluid English speakers managed to use verbs appropriately. Glithwah did.

The escort reconnected with the physical world. "Arblen Ems Firh Glithwah, Foremost, in acknowledgment of your arrival."

Definitely, *wait here.*

Corinne decided: *I don't think so.*

• • • •

I'm ready.

So, anyway, Glithwah supposed the message would indicate, in preemptory tone if perhaps not in precise wording. Her implant had shown only a sender ID. Glithwah dismissed the alert, the message unopened, staying focused on her labors. She didn't *have* to see this woman, even after agreeing to an interview, although to refuse now could raise suspicions.

None of which elevated the human's appointment to the importance of Glithwah's work.

I'm tired of waiting.

The second message might have said that. Or not. Glithwah dismissed it, too, unread, concentrating on the latest spate of industrial accidents. More than she could explain—other than by attribution to United Planets saboteurs. And, perhaps related: the pattern of attempts to penetrate the colony's secure networks. (Or, the experts told her, at least two patterns. One grouping of failed intrusions, almost certainly, was by their jailers. Other would-be intruders would be her rivals within the clan.)

And if a surge in accidents had not occupied her thoughts, other important matters would. The productivity of mines, factories, and farms. Demographic data. Staffing trends and labor shortages. Graduation rates and skills deficits. Macroeconomic statistics. Current events on Ariel and across this solar system …

The details seemed endless, and yet the torrent of data somehow kept managing to grow. It was too much to wrap her brain around. Even offloading much of the task to her implant. Even netting to trusted allies. Even delegating simulations and analyses to trusted AIs.

But maybe with an AI *in* her brain? Not netted and bandwidth-limited. Physically embedded, thoroughly integrated. Though they remained a tiny minority, more and more humans were doing that. The Augmented, the changelings called themselves. Two minds, one never sleeping, in one body. A temptation, every now and again, just for a moment ….

And if the notion *weren't* disgusting? It wouldn't have mattered. Glithwah's United Planets overlords would never allow the clan access to such advanced technology.

And so, summary graphs, tables, and animations covered her office walls. As for her aspirations for the clan and her progress toward achieving them, the walls gave no hints.

At a hesitant knock, Glithwah glanced at the door. "What?" she snapped.

Cluth Monar entered. The aide said, "Foremost, that woman in readiness for her interview."

Mind to mind, *that woman* would have been fine. Too kind, in fact: Corinne Elman merited no courtesy. Aloud, however, the phrase lacked discipline.

No matter that humans could not reproduce any Hunter language. (Absent the gene tweaks to grow an extra pair of vocal cords. A handful of diplomats had had the procedure done.) Plenty of humans *understood* clan-speak. Elman had never demonstrated that aptitude, but Glithwah had her suspicions. And if the woman didn't understand? Doubtless she had a translator AI netted in.

As Glithwah would link in Loshtof to interpret and analyze the journalist's every word and gesture. Her AI was but a netted command away.

(No matter that Glithwah had long ago trained herself to think in all major human languages, and even to intuit their often absurd units of measure. "Know your enemy" was clan protocol long before Sun Tzu scribbled *The Art of War*.)

"Respect for my guest," she growled at Monar.

Because she would *not* have that woman stirring up the human public over needless slights. A bit of waiting, though, to put the human in her place? To remind who was Foremost of the clan and who a mere gossipmonger? That was appropriate. Perhaps even expected.

In English this time, her voice pitched to carry to the anteroom, Glithwah ordered, "In five minutes, show in Ms. Elman."

With his head bowed and shoulders hunched, Cluth Monar turned to scamper away.

Glithwah netted to a nearby security cam. Her visitor squirmed in her chair. Jammed her hands into vest pockets, then removed them. Studied her nails. Curled a long tress around a finger. Once, twice, the woman's eyes glazed over in a netted consultation. Squirmed some more. Glithwah returned to her statistics on industrial accidents, satisfied she would not be matching wits this day with an Augmented.

Many of the recent incidents were true accidents, traceable to carelessness, bad luck, or honest equipment failures. A few of the incidents she hoped appeared to be more of the same. But some events, that her most trusted aides had failed to explain, had the feel of sabotage. Glithwah, without proof, *knew* whom to blame: Carl Rowland and his minions. Who else could it be? Starting with the latest gray-goo runaway in Nanofab Two. The presence of nanites, even half a (small) world away, made her skin crawl. But to have foregone a technology in such common use among the humans would have conceded an advantage, and that—

A mind's-ear chime reminded Glithwah that the five minutes were almost up. With a thought she blanked the floor-to-ceiling displays, then netted in Loshtof.

Turned a featureless slate gray, the office walls *looked* as though she hid something.

Setting both exterior walls transparent, crescent Uranus imbued her office with a wan, blue-green cast. The planet's rings, seen edge-on, were barely visible. Miranda was just past full phase; lesser inner moons were mere brilliant dots.

Much better, she decided.

A final inspection revealed her desk to be too orderly. It and everything on it were props. With the brush of a hand, she ruffled a neat stack of printouts. It had been a basic tenet of clan doctrine since the surrender: never appear organized to the humans.

• • • •

At Glithwah's door, another knock—this one self-assured.

Not waiting for permission, Corinne Elman strode into the office. Or tried, anyway, her entrance ungainly. But however awkward her gait, Corinne's *mind* had always been adroit. For a human, anyway.

Her hair was longer than Glithwah remembered, and shot through with more gray. Her face was rounder than when they had last met, five Earth years earlier. She was short for an Earthborn human—and nonetheless, even standing in the recessed entryway, she and Glithwah stood eye to eye. If Corinne should exhibit the egregious bad manners to step up onto the Hunter tier of the split-level office, the low ceiling would force her to crouch; they would remain eye to eye.

Corinne took a seat on the lower level. "Foremost, I am pleased to see you again."

Are you now? Glithwah thought. *You had the good fortune, for a journalist, anyway, to be in the wrong place at the wrong time. And having survived to tell—and sell—the tale, the experience made you wealthy. You've milked the one incident, exploited the clan, ever since. And maddening as that was, the human had done it very well.*

But Glithwah said only, "Welcome back to Ariel." And the visit *was* welcome, in the narrow sense of something long dreaded being at long last almost out of the way. What was it with humans and anniversaries?

Glithwah intended to be elsewhere before the next five-year "commemoration."

"Thank you, Foremost." Elman leaned forward in her chair. "And thanks for agreeing to meet. I'm sure you're busy. Shall we begin?"

"Are we waiting for a cameraman?"

"Not necessary. I have an A/V upgrade."

An implant to record everything the woman saw and heard. Yet one more technology denied to the clan.

Glithwah bided her time, contained her resentment.

Corinne squirmed, just a little, in her chair. "Shall we begin, then?"

To Glithwah's mind's eye, Loshtof texted unnecessarily: SOME EMBARRASSMENT.

"That will be fine," Glithwah said.

"Do you know what angle would interest my viewers?"

"I do not."

But Glithwah could guess: humans loved to gloat. Because while the United Planets leadership continued to suppress just how dicey matters had been, at some level, however intuitive, humans saw the big picture. That a few thousand Hunters had made fools of them.

Alas, the humans refused to stay beaten. If for little else, Glithwah respected the humans for their dogged determination. And so, worlds of them, billions of them, had absorbed one rout after another and kept coming. The endgame had left *Victorious* adrift and abandoned, the clan decimated, its leadership slaughtered. It had left the survivors marooned on this remote moon, to beg for resources and technology that should be theirs.

But that would change … *if* their captors remained clueless for just a little while longer. To which end, disinformation channeled through this persistent pest might contribute.

"No," Glithwah repeated. "What angle would interest your viewers?"

"Change. Progress." Corinne smiled. "When last I visited, this was still a frontier settlement. Ariel has become a civilized world. You did that."

If human authorities should ever learn *half* of what had been accomplished—much less how, or why—Glithwah's life was forfeit. Perhaps many lives. Did this troublesome woman suspect?

"What do you mean?" Glithwah asked.

"Such false modesty. I could not fail to notice the recent construction, least of all the colony's own spaceport."

A civilian spaceport, the human meant. A spaceport not controlled by United Planets personnel. With splayed fingers, Corinne swept wisps of hair from her forehead. There was a momentary frown that Loshtof annotated, SHE IS NERVOUS. POSSIBLY CONFLICTED.

ABOUT WHAT?

UNKNOWN, Loshtof admitted.

"We should have had ships earlier," Glithwah said. "The delay had consequences."

"How so?"

(FEIGNED INTEREST, Loshtof interpreted.)

Glithwah had picked up on that, too. Off a corner of the desk, from the hand-carved wooden chess set that had been a human's gift to her uncle, she picked up a castle. Rolled the piece between fingers and thumb. "Without practice, skills are lost. Such as piloting, to be sure. And such as the knack for keeping ships flying, when something goes amiss. Because something always does."

Corinne's face reddened. (EMBARRASSED, texted Loshtof.)

Taking the point—when, after so many years, the clan *had* been permitted to acquire a few lumbering, obsolete scoop ships—that two vessels and crews had been lost? For something as mundane as harvesting of Uranian atmosphere, the gathering of deuterium and helium-3 for the colony's energy needs? Corinne's periodic rehashing of the old conflict had played no small part in denying the clan autonomy—and its own ships—for so many years.

"I ... I see," the woman said. "If it's any consolation, I understand the authorities have been looking into a rash of unexplained mishaps across the outer system. It's not only your clan that has lost ships."

"How is that a consolation?"

Murmuring something apologetic, again red-faced, Corinne segued into a banal interview topic. What do you remember about the "incident" twenty years earlier?

Time and again Glithwah offered a contrite response—even, tersely, and with rigid circumspection, admitting to having regrets. She *did* regret the casualties, thousands among the humans, hundreds among the clan—but not for the reason Corinne might expect. In war, casualties were unavoidable. Any Foremost learned to accept them. What Glithwah could not accept, despite the years that had passed, was so many having died for naught.

Failure made the losses sting. Failure was what she would not permit to stand.

Inane questions kept coming. Do you appreciate the help the UP has given to build a new home? (Of course.) Has Ariel come to seem like home? (Yes.) Can humans and Hunters learn to get along? (But we already have. Look at the two of us.) And on, and on. And *on*.

The human had come a long way to ask general questions that she could as well have submitted by vidmail, to which Glithwah could have recorded answers. The only acceptable responses were obvious. She dared to believe that this pointless session must soon end. More and more, the questions seemed pro forma, the questioner disengaged.

And then Corinne surprised her. "One more thing …"

"Yes?"

"Let's move beyond past conflict and beyond the steady progress of the Ariel settlement. *Discovery* is all but complete. What are your thoughts about that?"

Discovery. Humanity's second starship. The first was seven years on its way, repatriating survivors of *Victorious*'s original crew—those not resettled on Earth, too old and feeble for the long voyage—to Alpha Centauri.

"A great accomplishment," Glithwah said. "From what we are told." That wasn't much.

"Nothing more, Foremost?"

Glithwah set down the chess piece. "I haven't thought much about it."

"Truly? *Discovery* could be used to send home your people."

"It could," Glithwah agreed.

It wouldn't, of course. The investment to build *Discovery*, to manufacture enough antimatter to fuel an interstellar voyage, had been, well, astronomical. And if the humans had been so inclined, regardless? Great Clan rivalries had exiled Arblen Ems to K'rath's comet belt in the first place. The exiles would not be welcome.

But Arblen Ems would be great again. Glithwah felt it. She believed it. More, she had sworn it.

Then would be the time for a return to K'rath. In triumph.

CHAPTER 18

InterstellarNet: the network that made possible and continues to bind the interstellar trading community. Radio-based commerce in intellectual property accelerated—and continues to bring into convergence—the technological repertoires of all member species.

A key milestone in InterstellarNet history was the development of, and cross-species agreement upon, artificially intelligent surrogates as local trade representatives for distant societies. Quarantine procedures govern the delivery and operational environment of each alien agent, protecting agents and their host networks from subversion by the other. Only once, soon after the earliest deployments of AI agents, has this security mechanism been breached. A trapdoor hidden within imported biocomputers, technology that had been licensed by Earth from the Hunters of Barnard's Star, was exploited by their trade agent. The attempt at extortion was foiled, the vulnerability within the adopted technology expunged, and the AI returned to its containment (see related article, "Snake Subterfuge").

What impact the dawning age of travel among the stars will have on the InterstellarNet community remains to be seen.

—*Internetopedia*

• • • •

From the spartan living room of his modest apartment, Carl consulted with the stern-faced, severely tailored woman who was going by the name Danica Chidambaram. As far as anyone else on this rock knew, Danica, arrived the week before as a passenger aboard a routine supply run, worked for Worldswide Insurance. Who better than a claims adjuster to poke around the sites of Snake industrial accidents?

In a glimpse across the Commons, the nearest they had come in person on this world, Danica seemed reserved but pleasant, with a mild manner and an averted gaze. But that reticent nature was an act, as contrived as her avatar. Among her fellow spooks, she was a flaming extrovert.

They were linked by the most robust and tightly controlled encryption software known to mankind. Across the entire solar system, perhaps a few dozen operatives, their names and exact numbers also classified, had access to the tech. (A few United Planets high officials doubtless had also gotten the biochip upgrade, though Carl *knew* that to be true only of the deputy director of UP Intelligence, having twice delivered especially sensitive reports to his boss on a COSMIC ULTRA link.) All the fancy tech notwithstanding, Carl would have preferred to debrief Danica in his office: behind *two* locked doors (inner and outer rooms alike swept every morning for bugs), within the most thoroughly shielded facility on Ariel.

Talented actor that Danica was, she might not have revealed any more face-to-face than over the link. He still wished they could have met in person. Espionage was a lonely business.

"So what do you think?" he asked her. "Let's start with the

deuterium refinery."

"Heavy hydrogen is still hydrogen. All it took was a spark." Danica shrugged. "Boom."

The Snake investigative report had surmised much the same.

"Uh-huh. And the cause of that spark?"

"We may never know. Between the blast itself and the dome blowout, evidence is, shall we say, scattered. As often as not, vaporized."

"Speculate," he netted.

"Carelessness? Sabotage? *I* don't know. I'll keep looking, but don't expect definitive answers."

"Can you confirm the headcount?" Snake media had reported twelve fatalities, including the missing and presumed dead, and three times as many injured.

"Not without running DNA screens, or the Snake equivalent, against many square klicks of Ariel's surface. Maybe not then. Stuff got blasted off-world."

He considered. "It could have been much worse, I suppose. An hour later, when a bunch of technician trainees were due …."

Danica turned her hands palms-up. For someone so loath to speculate, spy was an odd career choice.

"The meltdown at the plasteel mill?"

"Software glitch," she netted.

"And?"

Another shrug. "Of unclear provenance."

"And the gray-goo incident?"

"Puzzling. It was Centaur nanotech."

In other words, mature and reliable. "And did *it* exhibit any software glitches?"

"By inference, yes, though no one has found proof. Or is apt to."

Because the standard response to nanoassemblers run amok was flamethrowers.

Case by case, they reviewed the various recent Snake misfortunes. None related in any obvious way to Ariel's *other* run of bad luck, several months earlier, the scoop-ship losses. Bottom line: mayhem and destruction, all of unclear antecedents. A high toll, but seldom as bad as it might have been.

"Insurance fraud?" Carl eventually asked.

Shrug.

"Ever feel you were trapped in a game of b'tok?"

"What's that?"

"The traditional Snake game of strategy."

"Oh. Like chess."

"Kind of."

Except that b'tok was to chess as chess was to rock-paper-scissors. For starters, b'tok was four-dimensional and could only be played virtually. The offensive and defensive capabilities of a b'tok game icon depended on its 3-D coordinates, the time spent at that location, and interactions with nearby pieces both friendly and rival. Also unlike chess, with its unchanging board of sixty-four squares, the b'tok domain of play *evolved*. It varied turn by turn, and the view differed by side. A player saw only as far as his pieces had explored. Those dynamics tended to undo any equilibrium that might arise between rivals; it was a rare match that ended in a draw.

He could play, just a little. As a reason for unofficial face time with Glithwah, he tried to fit in a game with her at least once a month. Almost every match Carl did better—and yet he never won. He had come to believe that she played just well enough to beat him, imparting as little as possible about how experts played the game.

Carl's gut also told him the wave of accidents was sabotage. If so, if the Foremost *was* up to something, who was he kidding that he would win their game of cat-and-mouse?

Danica netted, "Tell me why you're thinking insurance fraud."

"The usual reason. For the money."

"Money for …?"

She didn't need to know Carl's source: Pashwah, the Snake's trade AI on Earth. Its latest allegations were scary, and he had confirmed bits and pieces. Someone new was buying alien tech. Someone canny, their transactions relayed from world to world, at each step disguised by an anonymizer service. But anonymized or not, huge cash flows couldn't entirely hide. Regulators had to know when banks made big bets with their own money, and when big bets were made on behalf of customers. Even the banks representing aliens' trade agents.

If Pashwah's inferences were to be believed—not a given, because the Great Clans to which it was beholden knew how to carry a grudge—that shadowy buyer was clan Arblen Ems. And that meant Glithwah.

"For?" Danica prompted again.

This time Carl shrugged. It indicated he didn't care to say, not that he couldn't. Raising an eyebrow, Danica acknowledged the distinction.

She was too smart not to involve.

"To acquire interstellar trade goods," he told her. "The transactions were too well obscured, too indirect, to reveal anything beyond that there's been a major, secretive InterstellarNet buy. I don't know by whom. I don't know from whom. I don't know of what."

"But you suspect the local Snakes."

"As does my sometimes reliable source."

Danica needed a moment to take it all in. "I gather that my supposed employer paid out on the earliest claims."

"Uh-huh."

"And you have a theory what the Snakes would buy."

"Yeah. Advanced industrial tech. The last couple years I've been ordered to supervise with a light hand, but I still get to oversee imports. Glithwah keeps asking for advanced robotics. I keep denying her requests."

"How advanced?"

"Boater tech." Boaters because their sun, Epsilon Eridani, appeared in the constellation Eridanus, the River.

"*We* haven't deployed much Boater robotics. Humans. Have we?"

None, in fact, and Carl approved. From what he had seen online, Boater bots were … creepy. Too lifelike. But if humans had been built like jellyfish—the nearest terrestrial analogue to a Boater—he conceded he might have seen the pluses. Whatever the reason, Boaters had embraced robotics early and wholeheartedly.

With a shiver Carl kept from his avatar, he answered her, curtly, "No."

"Why keep asking for your okay? So you won't suspect they already have the tech?"

"That's my guess." As he guessed that Glithwah *knew* he would turn her down. Given Ariel's ongoing labor shortage, not to have asked for such useful tech might also have made him suspicious. So who lied to him? The wily Snake, or the wily Snake AI?

Danica netted, "Suppose the locals did obtain Boater robotics. We're talking designs, nothing physical. Sure, the Snakes *could* smuggle the banned designs to this world. But why? You'd see if the Snakes built a new, modern factory. Which, I assume, you haven't seen."

"You're right," he conceded. "I gather that in your poking around, you haven't, either."

"Nope. So maybe we're barking up the wrong tree. Maybe the Snakes are working a different scam."

"Maybe." Or maybe, as whenever he sat down to b'tok with Glithwah, he was several moves behind.

CHAPTER 19

Amid the grove of miniature pines in the settlement's lone terrestrial park, Carl caught up with Corinne. Full access to the settlement's security cameras helped.

"Hey, stranger," he said. "Busy, I see."

"Hey, yourself." She kept glancing at the ceiling, at the unconvincing sky simulation he had, over the years, trained himself to ignore. Her left hand clutched a pinecone. With her right hand, scale by scale, she was picking apart the cone. "You're looking well."

"I look like someone's grandfather, but thanks for making the effort."

He didn't remember her as a fidgeter. Of course, he hadn't seen her in … five years. People changed. Witness that she hadn't radioed that she was coming. It made him sad.

"How's your better half?" he asked.

"Fine, thanks," Corinne said. "Though Denise is less than thrilled at me jaunting three billion klicks from home."

"Can you blame her?" But that sounded judgmental, as though he wasn't happy to see Corinne. He changed subjects. "I met Grace. She seems nice."

"Nice enough." Corinne shrugged. "Just a temp. My regular pilot caught a bug. I was lucky to find someone on short notice open to making the trek to Uranus. 'Maybe just this once,' Grace told me. Truth be told, her chief motivation seems to be bringing home a Banak. Without middlemen, without shipping costs, she ought to turn a tidy profit."

"This rock isn't a big tourist attraction," Carl agreed. As for Dolmar Banak's work, no matter how trendy the sculptures might have become in-system, they did nothing for Carl. Any Snake art was odd enough. As for Snake impressionism—

His implant pinged, sparing them both his impersonation of an art critic. He said, "Work calls. Give me a minute." Expecting within that minute to be offering his excuses—because the ping was COSMIC ULTRA.

"It's about time you made contact," said the avatar that appeared on the link. "I couldn't risk being seen to be looking for you."

It was Corinne.

• • • •

"It's complicated," the avatar netted. It wore the battered captain's hat he had favored back when he had worked for her. *Odyssey's* familiar, cluttered bridge provided the backdrop.

Only this *couldn't* be Corinne. He wondered what game Danica was playing.

"Life is complicated," he netted back. Aloud, gesturing at a park bench, he said, "Why don't we sit?"

Corinne tossed aside the tortured pinecone. Glancing around, admiring the park, she sat. "Reminds me of Nottingham. Ever been there?"

Nottingham? As in the Sheriff of? He couldn't imagine any resemblance, not unless Sherwood Forest had been reduced to a dozen trees.

Whoever it was on the link netted, "You don't believe I'm me, despite the encryption."

He didn't know what to think. COSMIC ULTRA crypto was seriously compute-intensive. To handle the load, a neural implant needed a *major* upgrade, and it did not suffice to know the top-secret algorithms. You had to get the code across the blood-brain barrier, then splice it, just so, into the implant. Accomplishing that required a fancy designer microbe, combining Snake microbiology with a terrestrial retrovirus. And lest, somehow, the tech get stolen—or recovered from a dead agent's brain—the transporter microbe incorporated elements of viral meningitis. Take the microbe without a dose of the matching, tightly controlled vaccine, and you died. Quickly. And badly.

"Convince me," he answered.

"I have a message for you," the avatar netted. "From someone I hope you *will* believe."

The Corinne avatar receded, its *Odyssey* bridge backdrop with it, to a corner of the consensual meeting space. In their place: an iridescent sphere afloat in a featureless mist. A padlock icon showed the sphere to be spinning—and also a recording secured with COSMIC ULTRA encryption.

"Ir am Robyn Tanaka Astor," the message began.

The pronoun. The avatar, devoid of personality. Both suggested an Augmented. (Not that he'd ever known one. The tech had yet to be invented when he had first hidden himself away on Ariel.) The voice, without emotion, without a trace of gender, pointed to the AI component as dominant when the recording was made. And Robyn Tanaka, secretary-general of the Interstellar Commerce Union, *was* among the senior UP officials apt to have COSMIC ULTRA clearance. Within the ICU, perhaps even the only one.

Nottingham, Corinne had said. Nottingham. Sherwood Forest. Robin Hood. Robyn Tanaka. He could connect the dots. But what could the ICU want with him?

"The United Planets faces a serious challenge," the sphere continued. "Security, at the highest levels, has been compromised. Ir cannot go through normal channels. Corinne is among the few outsiders enlisted to help. She nominated you as another. Ir hope you will accept, because worlds are in peril."

Left unstated: giving COSMIC ULTRA access to Corinne was itself a security breach at the highest level. That Tanaka Astor had been entrusted with this technology didn't give her the right to pass it along. That she *had*, somehow, so equipped Corinne signaled a scary amount of reverse engineering, or an unsuspected vulnerability within the COSMIC ULTRA implant tech, or both.

If he reported this, someone would go to prison for a long time. If he kept it to himself, *he* might end up in prison. But what if this undefined threat was for real?

The sphere faded. Corinne's avatar expanded to reclaim the entire consensual meeting space. "Just from me having high-level codes, you know I've made a friend in high places, whether or not you believe that friend is Robyn. So, where can we talk?"

His office? Get Corinne inside that shielded room and he would know at once whether she was the one on the secure link. But to have Corinne in "the warden's" office would not be keeping their encounter casual.

His ship, then? It, too, was well shielded. He just needed a pretext.

Carl netted, "Ask me about the rash of accidents in Snake industrial facilities."

"I was wondering," Corinne said aloud, "about this rash of industrial accidents. The Foremost doesn't care to volunteer much. Can you tell me anything?"

"Better than that. I was going to fly out tomorrow to see for myself what's left of the old deuterium refinery." Halfway around this little world. "Care to ride with me?"

"That'd be great," she said, standing.

"Thanks," her avatar added with a wink. And dropped the link.

• • • •

Carl radioed the tower to report an air-recirc fan had died and needed swapping out. Traffic Control bumped his shuttle to the end of the line for takeoff. As he sifted through hand tools in a drawer, he got a ping. COSMIC ULTRA.

"I imagine that little charade was for me," the avatar netted. Corinne.

"Now I know it *is* you." He closed the drawer and sat. "We're secure here to just speak. I figure we have fifteen minutes or so before anyone checks on us. Use them wisely."

She unbelted from her crash couch, stood, and stretched. She was short enough to manage despite the shuttle's cramped cockpit.

"This will take a few minutes to explain. You won't want to believe it. Neither did Robyn, at first."

"Why don't you begin at the beginning?"

"That's a half billion years ago."

"Talk fast, then," he suggested.

She laughed. "Here's the deal. Half a billion or so years ago, very quickly, life on Earth changed. Whole new phyla of life appeared. Pretty much every sort of animal life more complex than a bacterial colony. Paleontologists call that period the Cambrian Explosion."

"Not an obviously existential threat to the present world order," he said.

"Maybe not, but a bunch of worlds had similar experiences at around the same time." She waved off his objection. "Coincidence? Hard to swallow, even if that were the only eleven-of-a-kind concurrence. It's not." She rattled off others. "And if the known intelligent species—native to worlds differing in age by billions of years—hadn't all developed high-tech within a few years of one another. And if—"

"You mean the InterstellarNet members," he got in.

"Yeah." Rummaging beneath the copilot console in a tiny corner locker, she found a drink bulb of water. "Eleven species close together, in a galaxy that's otherwise silent. Quite the twist of fate—if it is. We call it the Matthews conundrum. And if ..."

Carl let the words wash over him. He could scarcely grasp the broad outlines, much less pore over the timelines and data files Corinne transferred as she spoke. So what did he think? That he sought out conspiracy for a living. But a conspiracy dating back to the Cambrian era? Seriously?

When he objected, Corinne said, "We think they have the technology to slow the passage of time. Slow it way down."

He just looked at her.

"That's another long story," she said.

Time they didn't have, if he planned to keep up appearances and take off soon. Something had to wait, and magic tech to slow time seemed like a good candidate.

"Talk to me." With stiffened fingers, Corinne jabbed his shoulder. "You look, shall we say, less than convinced."

"I'll say this for your bad guy. He's persistent. A half-billion years after conspiring with the trilobites, he's whispering in Mary Shelley's ear as she writes *Frankenstein*. And to some Czech playwright, as he writes about robots." Carl ended on a rising inflection, not remembering much about the play. He was pretty sure, though, that it ended with the robots rebelling against their human masters.

Corinne nodded. "*R.U.R.* Standing for Rossum's Universal Robots. And Karel Čapek didn't just write a play about robots, he invented the word. The thing is …"

"There's more?"

"Yeah. Literature like *Frankenstein* and *R.U.R.* crops up across InterstellarNet species. And everywhere the effect is the same. Whole lines of scientific inquiry were rendered untenable, at the least delayed, for many years."

Uh-huh. Maybe anxiety over new technology was normal. Maybe stories in which everything went smoothly didn't catch on. But if he turned around Corinne's suspicions ….

"Okay," he said. "Suppose that selected research was discouraged. How many lines of investigation got encouraged?"

"Huh." She gave him a sideways look. "No one has asked that question. See, this is why we need you."

Carl's console display showed they had been talking for about ten minutes. He called the tower. "*Tempest*, here. My fan problem is fixed."

"Roger that, *Tempest*," Traffic Control radioed back. "We'll have you on your way in a few minutes."

Corinne plopped back into her crash couch and buckled up. "Which part is hardest to swallow?"

"We're talking about aliens, right? Only not any we know. Someone from *waaaaay* back. Impossibly far back." She didn't comment so he plowed ahead. "What am I supposed to believe? That the aliens look like us? That they have robots or androids or whatever that do? Or that human agents serve these aliens for reasons we don't yet know?"

"Something like that. Pick one."

"Secret, starfaring aliens."

"Robyn named them the Interveners," Corinne said. "And I don't see starships as a big obstacle to belief. *We* have starships. As do the Centaurs."

As would the Snakes—instead, in fact, of humanity—if the hijacked Centaur ship hadn't been wrested away from them.

Helping to retake *Victorious* was one of the few true accomplishments in Carl's messy, muddled life. Not so much destroying the starship in the process. *That* was the stuff of nightmares. His other recurring nightmare was that the Snakes secretly had another starship under construction. They had had control of *Victorious* for decades. What if they had learned enough to copy it?

Awake, he told himself no one could hide an undertaking of that magnitude. Not even someone as devious as Glithwah.

"You okay, Carl?"

"Yeah." He could worry any time about the Snakes. "So *why*, exactly, would these Interveners do all this?" If they even exist. Her evidence, such as it was, seemed entirely circumstantial.

"Haven't a clue." Corinne sighed. "*Robyn* hasn't a clue. Neither half of her. Well, she believes *Frankenstein* and the like were intended to discourage tech developments, but she hasn't a guess why. As for the larger questions—why influence us at all, why interventions vary by solar system, why the meddling began so long ago—she's as in the dark as me."

Traffic Control interrupted. "*Tempest*, you're next up for takeoff."

"Roger that." Carl gave his console a final look-over. He radioed back, "Ready when you are, tower."

"One other thing …," Corinne said.

Nothing good, he guessed. "And that is?"

"Bad stuff happens to people who come too close to seeing the pattern. They disappear, suffer odd 'accidents,' have unexpected things befall them." She netted yet another file, and his quick skim turned up names in the ICU and the UP Secretariat. "I got into this mess by investigating an historian's strange disappearance."

Mess was an understatement. "Any more good cheer to share?"

"That's it." Corinne flashed a wan smile. "So, are you in?"

"To do what, now?"

"What you can. What's necessary. In your line of work, you'll know better than I what that might be."

The tower radioed again, clearing *Tempest* for immediate take-off. It was a relief to turn his attention to ship's instruments, to concentrate on the pitted and fractured landscape racing past a few klicks below. Flying over one of Ariel's sinuous canyons, hundreds of klicks long and in places ten deep, even the largest crater seemed puny.

How much punier, mere humans?

Was he in? And what would being in mean? Apart, by failing to report the compromise of COSMIC ULTRA tech, from being in league with traitors. Apart from, at least technically, becoming a traitor himself.

It all boiled down to Corinne. Was she insane, a traitor, or every bit as savvy and honest as he had always believed?

It wasn't even a contest.

He told her, "I'm in."

CHAPTER 20

Caliban (moon): a small outer satellite of Uranus, discovered in 1997. Caliban's irregular orbit—both retrograde and dramatically tipped from the planet's equatorial plane—suggests a captured asteroid rather than a moon that formed with the planet. Caliban's composition (as a codiscoverer had predicted, "A plum-pudding mixture of rocks and ice") and reddish hue imply an origin in the Kuiper Belt. Like most Uranian moons, this one is named for a character in the play *The Tempest*. Shakespeare's Caliban was the brutal and misshapen slave of the sorcerer Prospero.

Caliban's small size (80 kilometers in diameter), remoteness (mean orbital radius of 7.3 million kilometers) and irregular orbit render it unattractive for commercial exploitation. This tiny world has seldom been visited and remains unsettled.

—Internetopedia

• • • •

With hand and claw, tentacle and pincer, the warriors fought. Grappling, they smashed and slashed and tore out entrails. They struggled and they died. A short distance away, across a dim and rocky plain, others dueled with laser rifles and projectile weapons, shock devices and grenades.

Boaters designed their robotics for industry, not infantry. Re-optimizing for combat required testing and time.

Over the theretofore silent mind's-eye video, the narration began. "Progress substantial, faster than my forecast."

No matter the voiceover's redundancy, Glithwah found pleasure in that summation.

Each communication entailed a risk, however small, of interception. Encryption might safeguard content, but the UPIA had only to back-track an incoming message to uncover Caliban base. And so, besides robustly encrypted, reports were infrequent, sent at low power, and relayed through a string of scattered, stealthed comm buoys, those also few and far between.

As Pimal narrated, the visuals continued to speak for themselves. Combat robots, several octets of them, undergoing their final field trials. Weapons, of every sort from personal arms to MIRVed rockets. Secret factories humming, the Boater robotic designs instantly productive for *that* purpose. A deuterium refinery operating at full capacity. Vessels of the clan's reconstituted navy—the scoop ships reported lost and several of the captured vessels—armed, armored, and made stealthy. All concealed within roofed-over craters on the remote moon.

Over a reprise of robot duels, Rashk Pimal concluded, "Combat competitions informative. Finalization imminent of combat chassis design."

Though this was all welcome news, Glithwah permitted herself a moment of envy. Day after day, year after year, she was the clan's public face. She cooperated with her jailors. Projected contrition. Exhibited patience. Feigned assimilation. Was seen to enforce the UP's onerous rules. Complained only enough to maintain credibility, to allay suspicions—

All the while—in the privacy of her head, and with the anonymity only possible in the infosphere—planning and conspiring. While Pimal, her tactical officer, enjoyed the freedom to act. Being believed dead had its rewards.

Among Glithwah's secrets was that the clan *had* a tactical officer. Carl Rowland and his UPIA lackeys would not approve. Then again, if affairs would proceed according to plan for only a brief while longer, the days of caring what the UPIA thought, or suspected, or knew, were numbered.

That prospect made the upcoming game of b'tok with Carl a bit more palatable.

. . . .

"It has been too long since we played," Glithwah said. "Not since before your reporter friend came and left. She and I had a good meeting."

In the clamor and chaos of Ariel Commons surrounding shift change, Carl had to struggle to follow an out-loud conversation, much less to discipline his thoughts for b'tok. Given his supposed recent progress—defeat at a less embarrassing level?—Glithwah had proposed taking the competition up a notch. Championship b'tok was played amid distraction. It was yet another way that b'tok seemed Machiavellian.

Except that, to a Snake, Machiavelli was an adorable naïf and a rank amateur.

Crap. His thoughts already tugged in too many directions. More distraction was the last thing he needed. What had Glithwah commented on? Oh, right. Corinne's visit.

"She and I are more like old acquaintances," Carl answered, wondering whether the Interveners were as observant as Glithwah. If Interveners even existed. With each passing day, Corinne's assertions seemed more, well, fantastical. "Over the years, we've gone our separate ways. Apart from mooching a ride from me, we hardly overlapped this visit. Regardless, I'm glad your discussion went okay."

Glithwah sipped from a bulb of iced lovath, the Snake analogue to coffee, while, in their consensual space, a b'tok "board" took form. She asked, "Do you recognize the configuration?"

B'tok, despite its many rules, had no fixed starting point. Games used any layout and any deployment of opposing forces to which both players agreed. Often, as in this instance, players let the game-management software randomly choose an historical scenario from a library, then adjust parameters for parity between the sides. That fluidity was one more reason Carl struggled. With chess, at least, he could fall back upon standard openings.

Did he recognize anything? Boats. Primitive aircraft. A few specks of land in a vast ocean. Where his game icons lacked visibility, whole regions showed only as featureless gray. Given the stylized representation of b'tok, he wondered if the simulation was on K'vith, Earth, or a fictional world.

As he pondered, three diners, deep in high-pitched, guttural conversation, finished their meals and stood. Winding through the commons, making a path through closely grouped tables, the Snakes nodded deferentially to Glithwah. One trod on Carl's shoe. All part of championship-level play.

Focus. Carl shook his head. "What is this place?"

"A part of your Pacific Ocean. The Battle of Midway. A sea-and-air skirmish from your Second World War. It appears you have the side that won."

Carl, although he hadn't lived on Earth for ages, and had never set foot on an ocean-going ship, still ought to have an advantage over Glithwah. Her entire life had been spent aboard spaceships or on icy, lifeless worlds, like Ariel, in the outer reaches of one solar system or another. But it had been Glithwah, avid student of history—and humans—who identified the setting. That their match was in a terrestrial setting would only serve to make his inevitable loss that much more humiliating.

"Okay," Carl said. Assuming he had the right conflict in mind, that was more than two centuries earlier. He could not remember the sides, much less a particular battle.

Once the board was set, b'tok etiquette prohibited surfing for historical insight. And if he had had the bad manners to search anyway? Whatever background he might have retrieved would have been rendered subtly wrong in untold ways by the randomization process.

"Shall we begin?"

Her question was rhetorical, because in a corner of Carl's netted vision, the game clock had already begun to increment. "What's the latest word about the refinery accident?" He wanted to know anyway, and to ask might distract Glithwah.

He launched aircraft to surveil the unknown regions of the game map. He sent up a few more planes to patrol around his ships, to give warning of any attack. He adjusted the deployment of his ships, dithering whether while bunched up they protected one another or just put all his eggs in one too easily bombed basket. Except for enemy surveillance planes in the distance, Glithwah's forces had yet to make an appearance.

"Metal fatigue," Glithwah said. "Tubing ruptured in a cryogenic coolant loop. Our engineers suspect radiation embrittlement in the ..."

As Carl considered that diagnosis, and wondered whether embrittlement was a word or a coinage of Glithwah's, and as the definition popped into his mind's eye, within the game an enemy sortie burst from the clouds. Waves of planes darted toward one of the islands. He ordered more of his planes into the air, and was dismayed at how slowly they responded.

As his supply icons on the island disappeared in puffs of symbolic flame, as bomb-crater icons marked his runways unusable, he wondered: who's distracting whom?

Which suggested the possibility the surprise attack, so early in the game, might be intended to divert him from Glithwah's answer. She wouldn't lie—about things he could, and would, confirm. The deuterium refinery had had metal fatigue. That didn't preclude the bad tubing being there on purpose. But sacrificing a third of the colony's energy supply in an insurance scam? That would be no small thing! Not to mention the loss of life.

Had Glithwah wanted illicit tech *that* much?

Belatedly, as he launched shipboard aircraft to repel the attackers, one of his long-range surveillance planes radioed in the location of an enemy carrier group. His options and confusion expanded.

Should he attack at once, with his reserves? Wait till he could refuel the planes now flying defense? Hold back planes lest Glithwah attack with more aircraft? As he weighed his choices, fighter planes from Glithwah's carriers chased away his recon planes.

"… Specialized alloys in the tubing," Glithwah continued explaining. "After a freighter failed to appear, we had to postpone routine maintenance."

His position deteriorating rapidly, Carl reminded himself the *conversation* was his purpose here. What did one more embarrassing loss matter after so many?

"What's the prognosis for repairing or replacing the refinery?" Carl asked. "How long can the settlement operate with just two units before having to ration power? And can I pull a few strings for you regarding replacement parts?"

"Pull strings? I see: to expedite. Yes, that would be appreciated."

And in swooped more of Glithwah's planes, wave upon wave.

His aircraft scattered, his ships vulnerable, Carl relegated his play to reflex. As for the larger puzzle, there, too, he saw only unpalatable answers. One: with parts unavailable and maintenance overdue, the Snakes recklessly kept a critical facility in operation. Why not shut it down, at least while their reserve supplies lasted?

Two: Glithwah, playing a longer game, making a point about dependency, *wanted* the refinery to go boom. She had been pushing him to okay the settlement getting its own long-range ships. She wanted her people to handle at least some resupply runs on their own. The accident investigation would, without doubt, confirm metal fatigue. But maybe Glithwah had had old tubing reinstalled, kept from past maintenance.

(One of his aircraft carriers, its flight deck aflame, dead in the water, racked by explosions, began to sink. "Too bad," Glithwah netted. Carl scarcely noticed.)

Or, three: the Snakes needed money, lots of it. The disaster was simple insurance fraud.

Or, four. Four was the most intriguing. The most worrisome. The hardest to know how to handle. Four was sabotage, but not of

Glithwah's doing. Factions among the Snakes were nothing new, but rivalries had not yet (to Carl's knowledge) risen to major sabotage.

But there was yet another spin he could put on the sabotage scenario. Suppose Snakes were indeed trying to get their talons into Boater robotics—tech that *someone* had long tried to keep out of this solar system.

The sabotage might mean Corinne's Interveners had an agent right here on Ariel, among the Snakes.

CHAPTER 21

Alongside the banded and ringed magnificence that was Saturn, above the potato shaped, much cratered, icy moon Prometheus, against a field of diamond-sharp stars, hung Discovery: a featureless patch of black. Dark as pitch. Surface laser-ablated to a smooth finish. Details lost in the blur of its stately rotation. A dim and ghostly presence ....

And ghostly the starship would remain. Because scrolling across the bottom of the striking image, the repeating message from the project office on Prometheus began, *Media access revoked.*

It might have been nice to have been told that, oh, say, a half-billion klicks earlier.

"This is nonsense," Corinne snapped, turning her head this way and that, defying anyone and anything in *Odyssey*'s cramped bridge to contradict her. Posturing, all of it. She had included *Discovery* on her itinerary to make the trip less about Ariel. Less, if any Interveners should be watching, about her connecting with Carl.

If someone else chose to seem responsible for redirecting her home—great. With Saturn and Uranus on more or less opposite sides of the Sun, and Earth still lying ahead, she hadn't yet gone far out of her way. Back sooner with Denise had its charms.

Corinne kept glowering, to keep up appearances.

"It's pretty damn rude," Grace said. "I mean, this isn't a trip anyone would undertake on a whim. Aren't you offended?"

"I'm sure they have their reasons." Reaching into the holo—flicking through the verbiage, past the excuses, reading between the lines—Corinne came to their reason. "A shipboard accident. This close to scheduled departure, they'll be scurrying to clean up."

"How serious of an accident?"

"They don't say."

Nor did any of the hour-old broadcasts within reach of *Odyssey*'s high-gain antenna. So, most likely: no worlds had shattered this time. No innocents had been slaughtered. Nothing had as much as interrupted the transfer of fuel from the antimatter factory on Prometheus.

The glimpse of *Discovery*, so like the ship of her nightmares, still made Corinne queasy.

"I'd be hopping mad, too," Grace said. Misreading the grimace on Corinne's face? "I mean, you're a worlds-class reporter. Near-legendary. The voice and face of the Himalia Incident and of the raid to retake *Victorious*. If anyone has earned the right to cover a story about a starship, that's got to be you."

"Only *near*-legendary?" Deflecting the flattery with humor.

"Well?" Grace persisted. "Tell the truth. Don't you feel slighted?"

"A bit, maybe." Well, yes, actually. "Set aside the ship's tour and the interviews I had scheduled. Any accident aboard *Discovery* is news in its own right. The project office shouldn't be turning away the media."

"And it's a free solar system. Except for Snakes."

"Except for Snakes," Corinne agreed.

"So …?"

"Okay, I admit it. I *am* annoyed. And curious, too. But they've revoked my access."

"Are you sure?"

"What do you mean?" *More: what does your sly smile mean?*

"Who's to say we got their message?" Grace gestured at the main nav holo, in which nothing was anywhere close to this ship.

"So, just show up?" *Because after coming about four billion klicks, who could turn them away?*

"That's what I'm thinking." Grace grinned. "Have I mentioned? I haven't gotten around to acknowledging the message. It'd be easy enough to clear it from the ship's log."

"They know we're coming from Ariel. If we don't acknowledge, they'll simply relay the message through Ariel."

"Then we ignore messages from Ariel, too." Grace gestured again at the nav display. "We're well on our way. Considering the distance, no one will think a thing about us not responding."

"Maybe." Something didn't ring true to Corinne. "I'm surprised *you* care so much. Don't I remember you sneering at travel aboard a starship as a lifestyle choice, not flying?"

"That doesn't mean I wouldn't want to *see* a starship. It's a flying habitat. It's my taxes at work. It's a whole freaking manmade *world*."

"Uh-huh."

"Laying it on too thick? When I signed on, I was expecting a longer gig."

With a bigger payday at the end. So, okay, Corinne could see why cutting the trip short might disappoint her rent-a-pilot. That didn't make Grace wrong. Because, damn it, she was still journalist enough, or maybe just stubborn enough, to race straight to whatever people didn't want her to see.

"Okay," Corinne said. "My wife is bound to hear about the revoked access. She'll expect me home soon. I'll shoot Denise word to expect me when she sees me."

Grace shook her head. "You have to assume they'll be listening."

Because only a fool believed that the government never intercepted private communications, at least whenever they could convince themselves they had cause. *Odyssey* arriving disinvited at Prometheus might go a lot smoother if no one could show she had heard the wave-off. And just as she couldn't contact Denise, Corinne also couldn't bounce ideas off Walt. He had long ago returned to Earth, riding radio waves, just as he had traveled to Ariel. "No offense," he'd said, just before transmitting himself, "but I have more productive ways to spend *weeks* than cooped up, light-minutes from anywhere." Walt had promised to beam himself to Prometheus once, *finally*, she arrived.

So: forward or homeward?

It wasn't even a contest, because something had struck her. The UP had an interstellar drive only because Snakes had hijacked *Victorious* to this solar system. Given how the Interveners discouraged some kinds of tech, maybe they weren't big fans of human-built starships.

Maybe whatever had gone wrong aboard *Discovery* wasn't an accident.

CHAPTER 22

"I feel like a rat in a maze," Danica grumbled. Privately and silently, of course. Over a COSMIC ULTRA link.

In her real-time audio and video feed, collapsed into a corner of Carl's mind's eye, nothing seemed all that challenging. Then again, this world was his home. He had lived on Ariel longer than, well, anywhere else. To her, this warren of tunnels was all still new.

"Just souvenir shopping," he reminded her. Corinne's pilot had given him the idea. "If anyone asks, someone in the Commons mentioned Banak's work to you. So when you saw him on the street, you thought you'd ask about buying a piece."

The sculptor himself could be seen via public-safety cameras making his way down a pedestrian tunnel to the new Snake spaceport. While he retrieved his package, Carl might get fifteen minutes to plant bugs and make a quick search. Infamous recluse that Banak was, known to hole up in his gallery/workshop/apartment for days, even weeks, at a time, they had to make an opportunity.

"I know my cover story," Danica netted. "It doesn't make these corridors any less claustrophobic."

"And me being a head taller than you, it shouldn't be a mystery why you're over there and I'm here."

"Yeah, yeah." In her vid feed, two Snakes in rumpled jumpsuits, perhaps cargo handlers, glided down the corridor toward her. As they passed, Danica rated only the briefest of sidelong glances. Three minutes later she netted, "We're here."

In any event, Banak was there, brandishing a package claim, to be waved into a storeroom by the bored-looking Snake watchman. Danica's point of view indicated she had hung back, loitering at a window in the passenger terminal. From there she could waylay

Banak if he started home too soon.

"Be careful," Carl netted back.

"Yeah, yeah."

Ariel's entire population wouldn't fill a small town. Local security—originally, by UP insistence—was correspondingly relaxed. If Carl had known only what Danica knew, he'd have been as dismissive.

Whistling tunelessly, with one hand in his pants pocket, Carl sauntered up to Banak's gallery. The door's scrolling display, alternating among clan speak, English, and Mandarin, indicated Closed.

Along the left edge of his augmented vision, four red dots dimly glowed: alarm systems flagged by his gear. The low intensity denoted mere commercial-grade alarms, although to have four systems seemed excessive. Nothing his Agency gear couldn't handle with ease.

Uh-huh. And what did the Agency wizards know of Intervener tech?

Danica netted, "From what I can see through the doorway, Banak is wandering up and down the aisles of the receiving area. Maybe his package is misplaced?"

"Maybe." Or maybe Banak was also exploiting an opportunity. "Be careful."

"That's twice in two minutes. Something you want to tell me?"

"No." What he had already shared—that Banak might be behind some of the recent sabotage—should suffice. That the Snake might be blowing stuff up as part of an interstellar conspiracy spanning eons? That was on a need-to-know basis.

And if Danica already knew? He already suspected one Intervener agent. Why not two? All the more reason to treat today's op as routine.

Indicating success with a slight vibration, the device in his pocket overrode Banak's alarms and reset the electromagnetic lock. The door unlatched with a soft click.

Low on the hinge-side door jamb, a circle pulsed: an app in Carl's implant, highlighting something out of the ordinary. A filament of some kind, stretched across the crack. Old school. He captured an image, so that he could restore the filament as he had found it.

"I'm in," he advised Danica.

Her avatar smirked. "Be careful."

"I deserve that."

Banak had left the overhead light panel on in his gallery before leaving to retrieve his unexpected parcel. No reason, therefore, to work in the dark by the unnatural tint of amplified vision. Scouting around back, in the messy, congested, workshop area, Carl found he could dispense with hardwiring his bug. Inductively self-charging cordless tools lay everywhere; Banak would never notice the sip of power a bug would use to recharge. From a deep squat, ducking his head, Carl stuck a bug far back beneath a Snake-low workbench.

In the workshop, as in the main gallery, sculptures loomed: big metallic constructions welded, hammered, and twisted into eerie, contorted shapes. A tall, skinny pyramid giving birth to a mutant lobster. An upright coffin. (Obviously not. Snakes didn't bury their dead.) A chain-link fence/snake devouring its tail. A smushed giant cruller.

Nonrepresentational art, even of the human kind, eluded Carl. He hadn't a clue about Snake abstract art. Half the time, he couldn't even decide whether a particular sculpture was finished. The price tags on the gallery pieces suggested that *someone* appreciated Banak's talent. Then again, maybe the prices just reflected novelty. In the Snake home system, all metal, even iron, was precious.

"How are you coming?" Danica netted.

"Done," he answered. "What about Banak?"

"Still searching for his package. Pretending, anyway." Between sidelong glances, her relayed vision continued to take in the desolate, much churned landscape beyond the window. "Checking over everything on all the shelves. I guess you'll have time to look around, too."

"Turn a bit to your right," he netted. One of Danica's peeks had caught someone sliding past. The second look left him no doubt. After twenty years on this rock, he thought he knew most of the Snake counter-intel types. Glithwah and company, just as surely, knew who among the human workforce worked for him, which was why he had brought in Danica. "That's one of Glithwah's senior people. Not the sort to be sent on routine errands."

"We knew the Snake authorities are interested in Banak. Isn't that why we are?"

"Yeah." Carl wasn't even lying, just not being entirely truthful. Glithwah's people watching Banak *had* caught his eye.

But Carl didn't plan to share what kept him curious. Not with anyone but Corinne.

Twenty years earlier, in the shattered hulk of *Victorious*, the op had been billed as a final sweep for survivors. The search-and-rescue squad did, in fact, come across an injured Centaur. But that was serendipity; what the marines sought was any kind of records. Petabytes of scavenged data, personal files and clan records alike, were taken aboard the final evac ship to depart the dying starship.

By sixty years, a Snake—if he survived that long—was a senior citizen. And yet in more than a century, "Banak" had scarcely aged.

Sole survivors, without family and friends, were common enough among Ariel's settlers. The Snake who called himself Banak would not have stood out. Just as, two decades earlier still, fleeing the Barnard's Star system, a lone refugee reaching *Victorious* might have drawn sympathy, but no special attention. Just as, before that, cycles of clan warfare had time and again created opportunities to disappear. And then, under a new name, to reinvent oneself ....

In the purloined archives, the names changed. Faces changed, too, but not the bone structure beneath or the subcutaneous patterns of blood vessels. To recognize the same Snake in four separate guises took UPIA facial-recognition software that peered beyond the visible spectrum.

Perhaps before anything else, recognition took the right person looking. Someone who had had more than once to reinvent himself. So: Carl might have discovered an Intervener mole.

Or, more than likely, he emulated the proverbial drunk who searched for his lost keys where the light was brightest.

"Banak and the newcomer are arguing," Danica netted. "That's to judge from body language. The watchman doesn't seem happy, either. I'm going to sidle closer. Maybe I'll overhear something."

"Be—"

"Careful," she completed. "Yeah, yeah."

• • • •

Banak dawdled amid the crowded shelves. He had spotted his package—and left it, for the nonce—on the first shelf he checked, where the arrival notice suggested it would be. He wasn't expecting any package. What mattered was the excuse to survey the cargo area.

Something unusual was underway in the colony, and that something was approaching a climax. The Foremost herself revealed nothing, but several among her minions lacked Glithwah's discipline. Their preoccupation spoke to something major soon to occur.

Something, doubtless, of which their UP warden would disapprove.

If Glithwah connived only to evade United Planets rules, Banak would ignore it. He always did, still Hunter enough to savor such defiance. But what if Glithwah's scheming involved something he was duty-bound to resist? Until he discovered the nature of her plot, he would not rest.

And so, the notice to retrieve a package had been fortuitous. Cargos incoming to Ariel might offer clues. What unusual had been received? Were any of the typical imports present in unaccustomed quantity? Boxes and bins told *him* nothing—but to the subtle instruments he carried, even sealed cargo, even the trace chemicals in the very air, had already implied much.

Such as crates of ships' life-support components generically—some might say, misleadingly—labeled as heavy-industrial goods. Such as pilferage from the stocks of specialty alloys imported for rebuilding the shattered deuterium refinery, but with additional uses. Such as—

"You there."

Banak startled at the voice. A moment ago, he had been alone but for the watchman standing in the outer office. The nearby public-safety cameras into which Banak remained netted had shown no one else. They *still* showed no on else.

And yet here stood Cluth Monar, one of Glithwah's chief lieutenants. The public camera feeds had been overridden, making this a Security operation. It meant *he* had been followed—with his pockets full of instrumentation he could neither explain nor permit to fall into others' hands.

"Me?" Banak asked.

"You." Monar stepped closer, sharp talons peeking from his fingertips. "Reason for your extended presence in this area?"

"Here for a pickup." Banak held out his claim slip. "Location of my package uncertain."

"Or perhaps here with inappropriate curiosity."

What would Monar consider inappropriate? Banak wanted to know. But more, he wanted to escape that storeroom, to avoid becoming the object of *Monar's* curiosity—unless he was already too late for that. Banak said, "Search almost at completion."

With feigned nonchalance, Banak continued his methodical scan of the shelves. To retrace his steps and claim his package now would only confirm his dissembling. "Old eyes," he grumbled.

"Your thorough explanations necessary," Monar said. "In my office."

The spaceport watchman had become tense. Beyond the anteroom, from a hallway still vacant on the public-network view, Banak heard hurried footsteps. Many of them.

The future became all too clear to Banak. Taken into custody. His instruments found. Suspicions raised. His gallery and workshop searched.

Ancient secrets imperiled.

He had served the masters faithfully, devotedly, unquestioningly, for far too long to allow that outcome.

The consequences for him scarcely mattered.

• • • •

"Something's up," Danica netted. "I'm going to amble by the store-room door."

Be careful, Carl thought. At himself, too.

If Glithwah's operatives were bringing in Banak, others would be showing up—soon—to tear apart this gallery. Maybe he would overhear something before they found his bug. He permitted himself a last, quick look, with images from his entry overlaid on the real-time view. Where he had bumped against a workbench, the double vision revealed a welding torch out of its place. He nudged it to its original position. And over there—

On one sculpture, the sort-of coffin, a red spot glowed where all had been inert metal. "Run!" he netted to Danica. For good measure, he net-texted the warning, too.

He was out of the workshop, through the gallery, the door into the curving public corridor not quite shut behind him, when the blinding flash came. And the searing heat. And the palpable sound—for the instant before his eardrums burst.

The "coffin" had been rigged. Why *it*?

He flew through the air scarcely long enough for synapses to fire. To remember how Banak disappeared for days into his workshop. To intuit that in that "coffin" Banak slept, or hibernated, or slowed time. To realize that the coffin's open cavity was at least a meter taller than necessary to accommodate a Snake. And to marvel that, just maybe, he had his first clue to the physical nature of the Interveners.

Then, as a wall loomed to swat Carl, the world went dark.

CHAPTER 23

From boundless apathy, out of a deadening fog, sensation emerged. The scratchiness of stiff sheets. Soft, rhythmic beeping. An antiseptic smell. A dry, irritated throat. In his left arm, an odd twinge. A floating sensation …

Drugged! Forcing open gummy eyes, Carl saw the issue with his arm was an IV needle. The beeps came from bedside instruments. A hospital room, then. Because …

The memories flooded back. "Danica," he croaked.

"You're okay," a familiar voice said.

Bruce Wycliffe, the latest deputy to rotate through, sat beside the bed to Carl's right. Bruce looked like he hadn't slept in a while. The man was more bureaucrat than spy. They had never gotten along.

Carl found a control, elevated the head of the bed, before rasping, "How long?"

"Since the explosions? Almost two weeks. You were pretty banged up. The doctors had you in a medically induced coma."

"I hope …" Carl's wish lost itself for a time in a coughing fit, "I hope you haven't been sitting here that whole while."

Bruce offered a bulb of water. "I didn't have that luxury. Things have been busy."

"Anyone, besides me?"

"Twelve dead. Twice that injured."

He must have been the closest to the explosion. How had so many others …?

"Go back, Bruce. You said explosions, plural."

"Correct. Two. You got … caught by the smaller one."

The *smaller* one? The other explosion must have been horrendous. Then there was Bruce's hesitation, and his circumlocution, as

146

though the room might be bugged.

"I'm well enough to net," Carl sent. "Start explaining."

Bruce studied his shoes.

"That wasn't a suggestion," Carl prompted.

"All right." Bruce's avatar joined the link. "But lose the attitude. You're not the boss anymore. Even Snakes have rights, you know? And you were caught red-handed, at the very least burgling Banak's rooms. As soon as you're ambulatory, ideally before you're in any shape for Glithwah to speak with, I'm to put you on the first ship home."

Home? He'd lived on Ariel for twenty years. As Carl Rowland, he had never lived elsewhere. Even after softheaded policies demoted him to an all but powerless observer, he had stayed. Home? Hardly.

Recalled to Earth.

"Consider this as a request, then," Carl netted. "Or a parting favor."

The update was no favor. Banak's second bomb had been in ... Banak. No one would be questioning him *or* any of the five who had been about to take him into custody. Another five Snakes had died nearby, from explosive decompression. And Glithwah was more than a little curious why Carl happened to be at the terrorist's shuttered gallery when the bomb there went off. She anticipated "a chat" before Carl left.

His thoughts remained fuzzy: drugs not yet out of his system, he supposed. He could still add small numbers. The answer was obvious, but he needed to hear it. "*Twelve* dead?"

"Yeah. That insurance woman visiting from down-system. Decompression, too."

Because *he* had assigned Danica to keep an eye on Banak. Wearily, Carl dropped off the link. "Thanks for coming, Bruce. I think I need some sleep."

Bruce stood. "Get well soon."

Maybe, Carl heard a shred of human concern in the words. Mostly, he heard satisfaction at getting rid of him.

• • • •

Still unsteady on his feet, Carl made his way to the Foremost's office. The exterior walls had been set transparent, showing the stark landscape outside.

"You look terrible," Glithwah said. "Sit."

And you're gloating, Carl thought. *Glad to be rid of me. Glad to have stolid, unimaginative Bruce left in charge.*

Carl sat.

"You'll be leaving us tomorrow," Glithwah said.

"Yes." And a long, uncomfortable flight it would be, aboard the freighter that had been held over while he convalesced. Danica's sealed casket was already aboard.

"So," Glithwah said, "tell me about Banak. The truth."

The truth? It was tempting, if only to shake Glithwah's smug complacency. How much easier her scheming—whatever it was— would proceed without him. He settled for the partial truth he had shared with Danica. "I became interested in Banak because you were interested. Do *you* care to explain?"

She licked her lips: the Snake version of a smile. "I'll miss our game. Sincerely. You were learning."

B'tok? Or the larger game? Getting him sent away was a coup in the latter.

But he hadn't left yet. He asked, "What *was* Banak up to?"

"Why ask me? The listening device found in his gallery was not of clan manufacture."

"I know nothing about that."

"A pity." Lips licked once more. "And the dead woman?"

"An innocent bystander, in the wrong place at the wrong time. Like several of the victims."

"My medical people did autopsies." Glithwah fixed him with a stare. "The *clan's* bystanders did not exhibit abnormal brain chemistry."

He stared straight back. "I know nothing about that."

Nothing more than that an agent's implant dissolved when it

sensed an oxygen-level drop in the cerebrospinal fluid. You could not recover information, even in death, from an operative's implant. No more than—Carl had seen pictures from the explosion scene—anyone would be recovering information from the scattered stains that had once been Banak.

"To be sure," Glithwah said skeptically. "What can you tell me?"

"Nothing." Because apart from Corinne and—once he got back to Earth—Robyn Tanaka, he would not be discussing what he had learned with *anyone*.

"If not citizens, exactly, we of Arblen Ems are under the protection of the United Planets. We have rights, too. You violated them."

Her little speech had an air of dismissal. Despite Ariel's trivial gravity, he struggled to climb to his feet. He shuffled to the door and paused, out of breath.

Carl's valedictory was shorter. "Be good."

• • • •

Admiral, despite her grand name, was plodding, scruffy, and old. She moved lots of cargo cheaply, and her owners wanted nothing more. Accommodations for the occasional passenger? Dependable hot water? A decent galley, or even synthesizers that didn't impart to every meal an aftertaste of sweaty socks and days-old fish? The scow offered no such amenities, much less decent comm gear.

Leaving Carl, eager to get word to Corinne, frustrated almost out of his skull.

He could not trust this ancient comm gear to transmit anything securely. That ruled out sending anything specific. Not his evidence of an Intervener mole, deceased, among the Arblen Ems exiles. Not the imagery held in his implant of what might be an Intervener time retarder. And most certainly not his musings whether Robyn had the influence to postpone *Discovery*'s scheduled departure to the Mobie home world. The Mobies were hive minds, each a continent-sized swarm. Wherever the Interveners came from, it wasn't Tau Ceti.

Still, he would have liked *some* response to the short message he had sent Corinne: *That thing we discussed? I've seen it now, too.*

A day passed, then two. He tried relaying his message via Ariel's much more powerful transmitter. That attempt didn't get a response, either.

He told himself the absence of an acknowledgment meant nothing. So, *Odyssey* had deviated somewhat from its flight plan. So, what? It could mean space junk to be dodged, or a spot of unscheduled maintenance, or that Corinne, being Corinne, had simply changed her plans. Piloting for her, those many years ago, he'd experienced all three.

Only he wasn't flying *Odyssey*. Neither, due to mischance, was Corinne's customary pilot. Leaving Carl to wonder about the woman who *was* at the helm. And about something he devoutly hoped was a freakish coincidence.

Grace DiMeara had traveled to Ariel to meet with Banak.

CHAPTER 24

In a remote mining camp, deep within an abandoned shaft, without deputies or aides, Glithwah rendezvoused with her tactical officer. She desired his insight and candor.

He stood as she entered. "Foremost," he greeted her.

"Pimal," she acknowledged. "Welcome back to Ariel."

Tall and trim, martial in his bearing, Rashk Pimal was the very embodiment of a Hunter warrior. He even bore battle scars. A jagged slash crossed one cheek, from a melee in seizing one of the clan's new ships. A forearm bore a puckered burn scar, from putting down a human riot in the internment camp.

When had *she* last seen combat? As a young lieutenant, aboard *Victorious*, in the final struggle against UP commandos. Twenty interminable years ago ....

Pimal's composure assured her that their plans continued to advance. His posture wordlessly added that, sooner rather than later, he meant to challenge her. In his sandals—leading the return to independence and honor, while an aging Foremost begged favors from and affected subservience to the humans—she would aspire, too.

Of course, the scars he so proudly bore demonstrated carelessness more than courage, just as the human casualties during the short-lived resistance—clubs and shivs and homemade incendiaries against armored soldiers!—showed more courage than sense.

Almost certainly, the humans had had no chance from the outset. *Almost* certainly. But had they prevailed, it would have been catastrophic. For all that, Glithwah had to respect the humans' valor. She found herself glad that this Lyle Logan, instigator of the rebellion, had come through it alive.

In ordinary circumstances she would have demoted Pimal for

negligence, for having allowed matters, however briefly, to come to armed resistance. But circumstances were far from ordinary. At this moment the clan needed heroes more than a tutorial on the importance of proper crowd control. Only let her plan succeed and, if such should be the will of the clan, she would gladly step down. Even in favor of Pimal.

But not yet.

"Your conclusions," Glithwah asked directly. Weeks had had to pass after the explosions, after Carl Rowland's fortuitous and ignominious departure. Long enough to smuggle Pimal back to Ariel aboard a routine scoop-ship flight. Long enough for her to hazard the occasional hinterlands inspection tour without drawing unwelcome attention. Pimal had had more than ample opportunity to consider the evidence.

He did not hesitate. "A conspiracy against the clan."

"By whom? And to what purpose?"

"Intracranial bomb no random occurrence. So, Banak, of course."

"Of course." She waited for Pimal to expand his list, or to address her other question. He did neither. "How strange a thing: a conspiracy of just one."

"More than one, Foremost. But whom else? Long study in search of an answer. Detailed study of Banak."

"The conspirators? UPIA?"

"A strange thing about Banak." Pimal's eyes glittered. "Banak absent from clan records prior to *Victorious*."

Many of the clan's records had been lost or abandoned in the chaos of evacuation. "Not without precedent," she reminded.

"Banak unfamiliar also to other evacuees." A talon point flicked into sight and as quickly retracted, as though to dismiss the obvious rejoinder: sole survivors bereft of family *had* been all too common. "And yet not."

"Not the time for riddles," she growled.

"My pardon, Foremost. Among the elders, his art familiar. From earliest days aboard *Victorious*."

Too long ago for Banak to have created them. She said, "By a parent, then, or a mentor or"—what was that human term?—"a role model."

"Perhaps, though as parent doubtful. Earlier sculptor without any resemblance to Banak. And yet …?"

"The *other* conspirators?" Glithwah reminded.

"Almost there." Pimal's eyes glazed, whether marshalling facts in his implant or netting to an aide. "That earlier sculptor also without any youthful presence in clan records. A metallurgist, a supposed refugee of the clan wars."

"Not impossible," she said.

"Nor this impossible." He netted an image: a charred metal structure, much taller than a Hunter, the dominant feature its long central cavity. A twisted ruin from Banak's workshop. Ground zero of that explosion. "Except for the isotopic analysis. Metal origin on K'vith."

"A moment, Pimal." *While I think.*

Human organized their prehistory around metal tools: the Bronze Age, the Iron Age. K'vith, though, was almost without metal. The earliest Hunter eras marked stages in the development of ceramics. What very little metal a Hunter-built ship carried was in trace amounts within electronic devices.

Nor were only the humans so fortunate. She had been a cadet, little more than a child, but she remembered her first glimpses of *Victorious.* What a shock that had been! Metal walls. Metal shelves. The Centaurs had even squandered metal on mere toys and table utensils.

That cadet could never have foreseen commanding a metal army—but on Caliban, such a force grew stronger by the day. A fleet sheltered there, too, on which to transport her robot warriors. Thanks to Pimal's diligence. Thanks to *her* scheming.

None of that could explain the twisted metal sculpture.

To have possessed so much metal back home denoted incredible wealth and stature. *Someone* among the clan should have recognized Banak's mentor. And yet, no one admitted to.

"A longstanding conspiracy," Glithwah concluded. "No other option believable. Agents of another clan?" From among the accursed Great Clans that had driven Arblen Ems to exile among the comets?

"Perhaps," Pimal allowed.

Suppose that metallurgist was another clan's agent. Suppose he recruited and trained Banak. How better, light-years from home, to serve his clan than by spying on Arblen Ems? How better to misuse Arblen Ems than through sabotage and by revealing clan secrets to the UPIA?

Pieces of the puzzle still eluded her. "And Carl Rowland's near-death?"

"An accident, perhaps."

Such as had befallen the "insurance" woman? In the wrong place at the wrong time, Rowland had phrased it. Glithwah had not believed the warden, either. She didn't much like him, but she had grown to respect him. Hunters took their first lessons in b'tok as children. Coming to it when he had? The pace at which he had been mastering the game was impressive.

"No accident," Glithwah decided. Banak, knowing he had been caught, must have tried to clean up after himself. Likely he had summoned Rowland to a trap.

Pimal peered into distance, into the murky depths of the abandoned mine shaft. "No accident," he agreed.

• • • •

With Earth looming in the bridge view port, Carl was as ignorant as when he had first set foot aboard *Admiral*. About Corinne's location and well-being. About whether Grace DiMeara was an Intervener operative. About the goals of the Interveners. About where the Interveners came from, and whether *Discovery*—through Robyn's intercession—might yet carry a human mission to wherever it was they came from. And about, in contrast, an almost trivial matter: whatever plans the UPIA had for him.

Just let him get to Earth, and all that could change.

Any sec-gen of the ICU was a formidable figure. Robyn Tanaka Astor, besides, was an Augmented. With Augmented intelligence and the ICU resources at her command, surely together they could find Corinne.

If no better option presented itself, *Discovery* had been Corinne's last known destination. He'd take a ship to Prometheus and back-track. Any ICU ship would do. Or a ship he hired. Twenty years back pay ought to cover it. If need be, on a ship he stole.

"You want to sit?" *Admiral*'s pilot said. He was a scrawny guy, on the squirrelly side, but he'd been genial enough throughout the long flight. Mostly they had talked hockey, with Carl left to rely upon boyhood memories. Devon, the taciturn engineer and copilot, had mostly grunted. Devon had no use for sports.

Carl shrugged. "I'm fine, Brad."

"That wasn't really a question."

"Right." Carl buckled into the jump seat behind Devon.

Between exchanges with Traffic Control, Brad asked, "So who do you like in the playoffs? The Rangers or—"

"Whoa!" Devon interrupted. "Sorry. Not us; the ship's fine. It's something on the news."

Admiral was barely in range for Earth's commercial broadcasts. Carl had yet to link in. When he reached the ground had seemed soon enough to start catching up.

"What channel?" Brad asked.

"Any channel."

That sounded ominous. Carl let his implant choose among the available channels. And then he froze. The breaking news involved a car bombing.

Robyn Tanaka Astor was dead.

• • • •

"Your orders, Foremost?" Pimal asked.

Because, at last, their consultation was complete.

She commanded a robot army and a war fleet in which to

transport it. She commanded yet more ships, sufficient to evacuate everyone yearning to be free. Apart from a gargantuan ice miner, too lumbering to keep pace with the fleet, the clan retained every human vessel they had ever seized. Her crafty UPIA watchdog was discredited and banished. Of her Great Clan opponents, their saboteur was no more than smears on a wall. Across the solar system, *Discovery*'s outfitting would be almost complete.

The pieces were in place. The opportunity would never be better.

Her voice firm, her bearing proud, Glithwah directed, "Onward to capture of human starship."

THE XOOL EMERGENCE

CHAPTER 25

Carl was not under arrest—exactly. And yet, two somber men had met him at the spaceport. A courtesy, they said. Just expediting, they said. They whisked him around Passport Control, past Customs, straight to UPIA headquarters in Basel.

Where he wasn't interrogated—exactly. No bright lights shone on his face. No restraints held him in his chair. No one played good cop, bad cop.

But neither was any of this routine. Routine was a lot to expect after arriving with a colleague in a body bag. Maybe too much.

"Let's go over it again," McBride said, "this time from the top." The agent was a broad-shouldered, middle-aged guy with pig eyes and a phlegmatic manner.

"All right," Carl said.

What else could he say? What did McBride—and whoever observed from behind the wall of one-way glass—suppose yet more repetition would reveal? And how much further back was "the top?" The founding of the Snake settlement on the Uranian moon, Ariel? Snakes showing up unannounced in a hijacked starship they tried foisting off as their own? Carl's own, even earlier, shadowed past?

"Any time now," McBride prodded.

"Danica was loitering in the Snake spaceport terminal. Her job was to stall Dolmar Banak if he headed back too soon. I was planting a bug in his workshop."

"Banak, the Snake sculptor."

Was there another Dolmar Banak? "Right."

"And Banak is now ...?"

"Bloodstains." As Carl had almost become in the sculptor's workshop. If he had been even a few seconds slower in spotting the bomb arming itself . . .

"You okay?"

"Yeah," Carl lied.

Officially the inquest was into Danica's death. Not the doubtless self-serving comments on the incident offered up by Carl's ambitious weasel of a former deputy. Not Snake factions trying to blame Carl for their internecine rivalries. Not, he fervently hoped, curiosity about what he knew about Banak.

McBride rubbed his chin. "Why did you request Agent Chidambaram come to Ariel in the first place?"

"My CI"—confidential informant—"believes the local Snakes are making illicit tech buys through InterstellarNet. That takes serious money, and an insurance scam could've explained the spate of industrial accidents. I brought in Danica, posing as an insurance investigator. Maybe the incidents weren't accidents."

"Okay." McBride gave an earlobe a tug. "And did Danica find anything questionable?"

"Not the point." Carl had begun to wonder what *was*. Apart from Danica's death, of course.

"And why were you two investigating a sculptor? Art fraud?"

Carl made a sip of coffee last. Keeping secrets didn't make this debrief any easier, not with his almost certain knowledge the UPIA had been compromised. "Look, this is simple. After my many years on Ariel, I know most or all of the Snake counter-intel types. The Foremost had her agents watching Banak. I wondered why. Danica was helping me look into that."

All of which he had already explained—twice.

McBride leaned back in his chair, appearing comfortable. Appearing set for hours and hours more of this. "So tell me more about this insurance scam."

"Hold that thought." Carl turned toward the one-way glass. "How about a break, people? It was a long flight"—from wrong-side-of-nowhere Uranus!—"and this is about forty times the gravity I'm used to."

He had spent that flight in endless exercise, popping capsules of grav-adapt nanites, swilling calcium-laced protein shakes, and feeling old. Even the tenth gee at which, of a mercy, *Admiral* had begun the trek had been torture—but by the time they reached the Belt, he had been able to walk brisk laps through the ship's corridors under a half gee. He wondered how long Earth would take to feel normal, and if he would be here that long. He wondered whether the chalk-and-seaweed aftertaste of all those shakes would ever fade.

But mostly he wondered how much longer this not quite an interrogation would drag on.

McBride also turned to the mirrored wall.

A door opened. Carl didn't know the young, distinguished woman who entered. She was spacer-born, to judge from her height, at least two meters, and the hesitancy of her gait. Her tailored gray suit, tasteful facial nanornaments, and no-nonsense demeanor all screamed *boss*. "This will suffice for now, Agent Rowland. We appreciate your cooperation."

"Am I cleared for work?" Carl pressed. Without his clearance restored, without an official Agency task, he would not have access to Agency resources for what he really wanted: to search for Corinne and her mysterious Interveners. If he could pull off getting himself assigned to the investigation into Robyn Tanaka Astor's death …

Boss Lady shook her head. "Matters will take a while to sort out. Until that happens, consider yourself on administrative leave. And stay close."

• • • •

Among Earth's teeming billions, Carl did not know a soul. Well, he knew McBride, to stretch a point—but no one would expect them to hang out. As for the woman Carl *had* planned to seek out—

More bloodstains.

Banak's suicide by bomb on Ariel. Robyn Tanaka Astor's assassination by car bomb, here on Earth. Did anyone besides Carl see a connection?

Knowing no one, his Agency reactivation possible at any time, he had no reason to set down roots. No one should give a second thought to him wandering about, taking in the planet's sights. How not, then, to pass through Manhattan? And while in Manhattan, why wouldn't he call on the wife of a friend?

Because any such visit might get Denise killed. Or himself.

All Carl knew for certain was that Corinne Elman, worlds-famous investigative reporter, and Robyn Tanaka Astor, secretary-general of the Interstellar Commerce Union, had been in league. Now Robyn was dead. Corinne's ship could not be reached by radio. What were the chances someone *wasn't* watching Corinne's wife?

Corinne's best hope—refusing to believe it was too late for hope—was Carl.

That left him following up his one lead, also in New York City.

• • • •

Ten minutes by subway from LaGuardia, the apartment complex had only location to recommend it. A bit of data mining—no challenge for a seasoned operative; scarcely enough to count as an invasion of privacy—showed many of the tenants to be spacers. They weren't often in residence for spaceport noise to bother them. When they were on Earth, they had to appreciate the convenience.

Corinne's rent-a-pilot was one of those absentee tenants. Grace DiMeara, who, on her layover on Ariel, had met with Banak. *Odyssey* had departed Ariel with a Banak sculpture in its hold; that meeting may have been no more than an art purchase.

Or not. Carl, endlessly revisiting in his mind his encounter with Grace in an Ariel cafeteria, kept remembering little things. Turns of phrase. Mannerisms. Like something in her eyes, she seemed older—much older—than the age indicated by her records.

Like Banak?

When he spotted the strand of hair spanning the gap between jamb and door, he guessed he was on to something. He captured the image in his neural implant, pocketed the hair in a handkerchief to replace on his way out, bypassed the alarm systems, and entered her apartment.

The plainly furnished living room could have been anywhere. A loveseat and one chair. Wallpaper set to a simple rustic scene. Low coffee table with nothing on it. The bedroom (bed, dresser, night-stand) was as impersonal. In the kitchen, a few canned and frozen groceries and a mug in the dish drainer offered the only suggestion anyone had ever been here. Drawers and closets revealed nothing, nor did a deeper search turn up ... anything. Apart from the lack of fast-food cartoons, the ascetic rooms reminded him of every safe house he had ever seen.

Anyone choosing to fly billions of klicks to shop for a sculpture, even as an investment, ought to have *some* art in her apartment. Grace did not. In particular, she had nothing to resemble the coffinlike structure Banak had had in his workshop—and that the sculptor had taken such care to blast into shrapnel.

If Grace were an agent of the Interveners, she kept her exotic gear elsewhere.

Carl made certain he had left everything in the apartment as he had found it, rearmed the alarms, restored the hair to the crack of the door, and exited the building.

No wiser on how to proceed than when he had arrived.

CHAPTER 26

Augmentation: the blending of an artificial intelligence and a biological intelligence into a composite sapient. Those who have so combined commonly refer to themselves as Augmented.

The augmentation process migrates the AI member from a conventional computer to biochips implanted within the brain of the biological member. Approaching end of life, the composite mind can be uploaded to a computer, just as can a purely human mind—the synapse-by-synapse readout of the biological brain in each case being destructive and irreversible. At any time prior to upload, the AI component may offload data snapshots from its biochips as a precaution against the death of the human component (e.g., in a traffic accident).

Process overview: the human partner undergoes minor surgery (as needed) to upgrade their neural implant with expanded capacity. Program and data contents of the AI are then encoded into strands of artificial messenger RNA, which are spliced into a customized retrovirus for delivery. The retrovirus, designed to pass through the blood-brain barrier (mimicking microbial carriers of such neurological diseases as viral meningitis), is then administered with a simple injection. The retrovirus reproduces the AI's program and data as DNA incorporated into the implant's genome. Next, the upgraded implant stimulates synapse formation across the cerebral cortex (whereas a standard neural implant interfaces only with the visual and auditory cortices).

Final integration proceeds under the conscious guidance of both minds ....

—*Internetopedia*

• • • •

I DO NOT KNOW YOU, the curt dismissal read.

Rejection came as no surprise to Carl, but the personal pronoun threw him for a moment. He had expected *Ir*, the Augmented first person.

But Robyn Tanaka Astor was not Augmented. Not any more. She wasn't *alive* anymore. The spinning iridescent orb presented to his mind's eye was avatar only for Astor 2115. All that remained of a prospective powerful ally was a backup copy of her AI component.

"No, you don't," Carl agreed, subvocalizing. He felt netted speech was friendlier than netted text (though for all he knew AIs were of the opposite opinion). "A reporter I met off-world suggested I look you up. Of course, that was before."

BEFORE IR DIED.

"Well, yes."

Without comment, the shimmering globe spun. And spun.

Carl wondered, *Does it care that its host, partner, whatever, was murdered? That for all their digging, a horde of UPIA investigators had a hundred theories, a very few clues, and no suspects?*

At last, the AI responded, switching to mind's-ear speech. "Who is this reporter?"

"Corinne Elman."

"I only know *of* her. We have not met."

Huh? Either the AI lied, or Corinne had.

His neural implant still held the message Robyn had sent, via Corinne, to recruit *him*. The avatar in that vid was the same shimmering globe, the "voice" the same emotionless contralto. How would the AI react if he returned that recording to her?

Only he couldn't. Robyn Tanaka Astor had had a COSMIC ULTRA encryption upgrade to her neural implant. Her AI remnant no longer had an implant. Or neurons, for that matter.

A test, Carl decided. He summoned up a snippet of Corinne's conspiracy assertions. "Corinne said you'd be able to enlighten me about the Matthews conundrum."

"Matthews conundrum." The globe spun in silence. "I see. A Joshua Matthews used to work at the ICU. A drunkard. A disgrace to the organization. Apparently, I severed his relationship with the organization."

"Apparently?"

"As a matter of record, Robyn Tanaka *did* separate him from the Interstellar Commerce Union, but the actual occurrence is not within my memories."

"I don't understand."

"After Robyn's death, my more recent backup files were discovered to have been corrupted. I was initialized from an archival backup more than a year out of date."

"I'm sorry," Carl netted. Not to mention shocked. An AI was a *mind*. Its backups did not just *get* corrupted, and certainly not a year's worth of them, replicated across however many mirror archives. "Data corruption by whoever was behind the bombing?"

"Investigators are undecided if there is a connection. Mine were not the only backups found to be affected." The sphere whirled on. "From what I can glean about you, Mr. Rowland, *you* are the spy. Perhaps you can enlighten me."

"Sorry, no. I'm not involved in the investigation."

"Are we done, then?"

Had they finished? Corinne's referral had gotten him nowhere. But as fellow bombing victims, maybe he could establish rapport.

And any sec-gen of the ICU—even the retired, blown-to-pieces, memory-wiped AI vestiges of one—would care about Snake machinations. Maybe he could leverage shared interests to sometime later broach his true interests.

Uh-huh. And maybe whatever Intervener agent had trashed the AI's backups *didn't* still have backdoor network access to monitor what little remained of Robyn Tanaka. Would he bet his life on that?

"I guess we're done," Carl netted. He let the AI break the infosphere link. To himself he added, "And I am fast running out of options."

· · · ·

The entire way to Earth, Carl had counted on Robyn Tanaka Astor as an ally and, as a senior UP official, someone with great resources at her command. But she was neither, only, in every sense of the word, a dead end.

Leaving Corinne out in the cold.

Every fiber of his being ached to rent a ship—to steal one if need be—and go looking for Corinne. But running off alone would be a stupid move. Labeling his status "administrative leave" did not make his future with the Agency any less tenuous. He couldn't just gad off for, probably, months.

To help Corinne, he needed *information*. He needed the resources only the UPIA could provide. If he survived the inquest and managed to get himself reinstated. If he could tap those resources without drawing the wrong attention to himself.

Because recorded Robyn, the Robyn of Corinne's recruiting pitch, had warned of compromise at the highest levels of the United Planets.

CHAPTER 27

Standing at the center of an empty room, slowly turning, Joshua Matthews took in the floor-to-ceiling map that obscured the walls. Or, rather, maps: elevation detail and deep-radar scans. Resource surveys, both orbital and ground-based. Railway routes and utility easements. Population distributions from the latest census. Exploration reports back to the Soviet Lunokhod rovers.

The wealth of information, so far, had mocked rather than enlightened him.

At least—in lunar gravity, anyway—toting the living-room furnishings to another room had been within his abilities. Those shufflings, and the start to a goatee, were the sum total of his recent accomplishments.

"Too damned much data," he muttered.

The complex graphic stared back at him.

He was missing something; he *knew* it. But what?

Emptying out the room had accomplished one thing: he had ample space to pace. He made full use of it as his thoughts ran round and round in all too familiar ruts.

The Interveners—for reasons unfathomable—had, for eons, meddled with Earth. When they began, when sponges and bacterial mats were among Earth's most advanced native life forms, the Interveners could base their operations on the planet. But in recent times, as humanity spread across the globe, any terrestrial hideouts would have been discovered. Observation posts in Earth orbit would have gone undetected a bit longer, but that era, too, had passed. That left, as the only place nearby from which to secretly monitor Earth, as somewhere human settlement had yet to overrun: the Earth-facing side of the Moon.

And so he pondered lunar expanses not yet well explored, in regions blessed with the resources to sustain a hidden base. By process of elimination, he *would* find the lurking aliens. The logic was impeccable. Also, in practice, unworkable.

After two weeks of unproductive sorting and sifting, he had begun to doubt himself. The aliens' tech had to far exceed anything humans used, perhaps anything he could even imagine. How could he know the resources they would want nearby and in what concentrations?

After a month of fruitless immersion, he had begun to question whether the Interveners existed—to doubt his sanity. Maybe he *had*, simply, lost weeks of his life to a drunken spree. Even most of his family believed that.

Was the subsequent attempt to kidnap him an interstellar conspiracy? Maybe. More likely he had conflated an ordinary would-be mugging with his wild theorizing. Corinne had dropped out of touch. Did that signal foul play? Could be. And maybe Corinne, having returned to her senses, was screening her calls.

The logic that he was crazy became more compelling by the day—until the day Robyn was slaughtered.

"Where *are* you?" he asked of the wall displays, keeping his voice to a whisper.

Background static on his neural implant didn't help his fruitless reflections. He rebooted the biochips; after a few seconds the stuttering hiss returned to his mind's ear. The interference, whatever it was, was annoying. He made a mental note to look for software updates his implant might be missing, banishing as crazy, even for him, fleeting notions of Intervener jamming. A leaky door seal in a nearby microwave oven was surely more likely. Disabling his implant's audio mode, he went back to contemplating the map overlays.

Staccato rapping on the apartment door made him jump.

A few months earlier, pressed to describe the gray-haired gentleman captured by the hall camera, Joshua might have chosen words like affable and elderly. Certainly, he would have opened the door.

A few months earlier, he hadn't been abducted off the streets of Charleston, hadn't had his life turned upside down, hadn't made a secret ally at the highest levels of government—only to see her assassinated.

The apartment's security system offered no match for the newcomer's face. Whoever this was, he hadn't been seen before in the neighborhood.

Joshua pressed the intercom button. "May I help you?"

"Joshua Matthews?"

"Yes."

"My name's Carl. May I come in?"

Joshua was not hiding, per se, but neither was his presence here advertised. "May I ask what this is about?"

"I'd rather explain in private."

"Text me about it, then. If I'm interested, I'll get back to you."

Looking straight into the hall camera, Carl said, "Let's call my visit an … intervention."

His heart pounding, Joshua opened the door.

• • • •

"I thought I was alone in this," Joshua Matthews said. "I haven't heard from Corinne since soon after she left Earth. And then Robyn …" He shuddered.

Carl took a moment to size up the man. Matthews's net bio pegged him as fifty-five, but sunken, puffy eyes made him look a good ten years older. He was tall, stocky, and a bit stoop-shouldered, hiding behind a new, scruffy beard. Twitchy. All in all, he looked like crap.

As for the room's wraparound lunar map, layered with false-color overlays and festooned with symbols, Carl reserved judgment.

"Cheer up," he said. "I'm here to help."

Joshua cleared his throat. "How did you find me?"

"Bear with me for a minute, please."

A walkthrough confirmed what an IR scanner had shown from the hall: that Joshua was alone. The concurrent bug sweep found nothing. But here in the low-rent district, the walls were thin. For that, Carl had brought a music player. He selected a choral piece with many voices and cranked up the volume.

"First, how I got involved." There wasn't any furniture in the room, so Carl leaned against a wall. "Corinne and I go way back, and she came to Ariel to talk to me. She mentioned uncanny historical and cultural similarities across the InterstellarNet species, too many to seem credible as coincidences, from evolutionary milestones a half billion years or so ago to alien versions of *Frankenstein*. She attributed it all to hypothetical, behind-the-scenes manipulators."

"The Interveners," Joshua murmured.

Carl nodded. "How did I find you? Corinne called these historical anomalies collectively 'the Matthews conundrum.' She also said she'd gotten into this mess by investigating the abduction of an historian. The ICU had had a staff historian, much in the news, named Joshua Matthews. QED."

"The news?" Joshua studied his shoes for a while. "You're kind to call it that."

"Whoever grabbed me, they aren't hypothetical. Nor was returning me drunk and ill, after weeks at, well, I still haven't a clue where. And the way I came back …"

Carl had seen the vid: Joshua, drunk, staggering from a cab and then puking out his guts. Gone viral, that vid would *never* be off the net. Anything Matthews ever said—or ever would say—was discredited. Clever, those Interveners.

"Sorry," Carl said.

"How'd you find me *here*?"

"I find things out for a living."

"You're a UP diplomat of some sort?"

"Close enough. Look, could you find me a chair? This is better than Earth, but I'm still *way* heavier than what I'm accustomed to."

Joshua brought a spindly kitchen chair from the next room.

"Thanks." With a contented sigh, Carl sat. "Are you up to answering questions? There are things I'd like to know."

A *ping* hit Carl's neural interface, COSMIC ULTRA-encrypted. But

Joshua hadn't responded to Carl's pings. Without a proper implant, the pings would have seemed no more than static. So, who was this? "Hello?" he netted back, accepting the connection.

As a frail, white-haired woman manifested in his mind's eye, the doorbell rang.

When Joshua answered the door, the same woman, older and frailer than her avatar, all but lost in a much too large cardigan, shuffled into the apartment.

"Grandma!" Joshua said.

Grandma answered, "You've been holding out on me, Josh."

CHAPTER 28

Snake Subterfuge: the short-lived subversion by Pashwah, the Hunter (colloquially, Snake) AI trade agent to Earth, of the interstellar commerce mechanism. In 2102, that agent escaped from its infosphere quarantine through unsuspected trapdoors hidden within ubiquitous Hunter-licensed biocomputing technology. The emergency ended when, applying xeno-sociological insight, a United Planets crisis team convinced the AI to abandon its attempted extortion. After the Hunter agent revealed technical details of the original biocomp vulnerability, a UP-tailored biovirus was released to seal the trapdoors by mutating the biocomp genome.

While the breakout and its associated extortion attempt were foiled, modern civilization and humanity's viability as a member of the InterstellarNet community had been imperiled. The incident caused a decades-long crisis of confidence in Hunter biocomputers.

—*Internetopedia*

• • • •

"Grandma," Joshua said. "This isn't a good time."

It was, in fact, the middle of the night and, Carl thought, *an*

173

improbable time for a social call. He netted, "I doubt this is a casual drop-in."

"I've never encountered COSMIC ULTRA traffic in Tycho City," she netted back. "When I sensed a faint ping, I dashed—okay, more like I crept—from my home in case the signal repeated. It did, and I took a second bearing. When that rough triangulation put the source near Joshua's apartment, I had my suspicions. He's been more than a little evasive about why he's on the Moon. And now I find *you*. Here, with Josh. Whomever *you* are."

"Grandma, are you all right?" Joshua asked aloud.

"Give your friend and me a minute, Josh," she said.

In her day, Joyce Matthews had been a player. Chief technology officer of the Interstellar Commerce Union, then its secretary-general. Chief technology officer for the United Planets itself. Nor was it only her: for generations, even before the ICU's founding, members of the Matthews family had been prominent in interstellar trade. All very fortunate for Joshua: when anyone *not* a Matthews tried publicizing curious InterstellarNet coincidences, that person tended to end up dead, not merely discredited.

None of which knowledge had forewarned Carl that Joyce Matthews had COSMIC ULTRA capability. She must have been among the very first people to have received the biochip upgrade.

And *he* had Robyn Tanaka's report, COSMIC ULTRA-encrypted, on the Interveners.

"Do you want to know why a sec-gen at the ICU was just assassinated? Why your grandson was kidnapped?" he netted.

"Hell, yes," Joyce shot back.

Guiding her by the elbow, Carl led her to the room's lone chair.

In their secure consensual meeting space, his avatar receded. An iridescent sphere, spinning, afloat in a featureless mist, took its place. "Ir am Robyn Tanaka Astor …"

. . . .

Comparing notes took hours: Robyn's recorded message to Carl, then his conversations with Corinne. Joshua's lengthy collection of anomalies, from historians who had met untimely ends, to alien species—on worlds differing in age by billions of years, located light-years apart—currently using all but identical technologies. Carl's investigation of Banak. Corinne dropping out of touch. Joshua's futile quest for the Intervener base. Carl's unhelpful dialogue with Robyn's year-obsolete AI remnant.

And to Carl's surprise, Joyce had something to contribute. "I wouldn't call Robyn and me friends. She was without social graces, or at least indifferent to them, even before Augmentation. That said, living sec-gens of the ICU comprise a pretty exclusive club. She and I talked shop on occasion, commiserated about the petty annoyances of the office more often than that." Joyce scowled. "At least we *did* talk, till she dumped Joshua. Believe me when I tell you: Robyn was rigorous about, well, everything. Certainly, about personal backups. Weekly, as a rule. Never less often than monthly. A year's worth of corrupt backups? That was no accident."

"I wouldn't have thought otherwise," Carl said.

"Where do we go from here?" Joshua asked.

"Snakes," Joyce said, shaking her head. Maybe she hadn't heard her grandson. "I thought matters were scary the first time."

During the Snake Subterfuge, Carl decided. "You were at the ICU then? You must have been young."

"You've got that right," she said wistfully. "And naïve. I imagined compromised biochips were the worst Snakes could do to us. Then they showed up on our doorstep." She looked at Carl. "Anyone willing to ride herd on them all these years has my respect and admiration."

He nodded, embarrassed.

"Now this," Joyce continued. "Snakes are allied with these Interveners? Criminy."

"I'd guess not allied," Carl said. "Banak suicided to avoid capture by Snake authorities."

"Where do we go from here?" Joshua repeated.

"Good question." Carl gestured at the many-layered holo projection. "Talk us through this, Joshua. You made a good case the Interveners must have a base here."

"*Where* here?" Joyce said. "It's no Earth, but the Moon is still huge. The Earth-facing side alone is larger in area than South America."

"And no matter how I slice and dice the data," Joshua said, "I keep coming up with *way* too much territory to search."

"What are you looking for?" Carl prompted.

"Places not yet explored, and that rules out every ice-rich crater. Far from civilization, where there's little chance of being discovered by accident. Places with exploitable concentrations of subsurface water. Nearby mineral wealth, for stuff to build with."

"Makes sense," Joyce said. "But that still includes a lot of terrain."

Carl shook his head. "You're reasoning like colonists or engineers. But reasoning like a spy ...." He trailed off as something tickled the back of his brain.

"Unexplored, sure." He spoke to himself. Thinking aloud sometimes helped. "Near water? Maybe. We don't know that the Interveners need water—but if their human agents ever visit, *they* would. But far from civilization? I don't know about that. Maybe *just* far enough."

Joshua frowned. "What do you mean?"

"Hide your base in the hinterlands, and your only access is by flying in. Once upon a time, that would have worked fine. Now there's traffic-control radar, and satellites always watching, and human ships ever coming and going. To avoid attention, you'd want to fly to your base as seldom as possible." The more Carl thought about it, the more logical that seemed. "Near ground transportation seems more probable to me."

"Then why has no one seen the base?" Joyce asked. "Could advanced alien tech disguise an installation *that* well?"

"So it's not there at all," Joshua interpreted. "Dumb idea. Sorry."

"You misunderstand me," Carl said. "Close to ground transportation doesn't have to mean on top of a city. A base might be remote *and* just a few klicks from a train track or major road."

"Makes sense," Joshua conceded.

"Close enough to ice and ore veins to foresee that humans might in time build nearby." Carl pondered some more. "But for all that, someplace with immediate surroundings as worthless-seeming as possible."

Joshua's eyes glazed over, his attention elsewhere, refining his map. The candidate terrain receded to a tracery of ground corridors—still too extensive to search. Then uneven dashed lines replaced solid corridors. Some of the dashes shrank.

"What have we narrowed it down to?" Carl asked.

"Better than a hundred thousand square klicks," Joshua groused. "Call it Pennsylvania."

"Look near lava tubes," Joyce suggested. "Shelter that doesn't look like shelter, and that provides ample shielding from cosmic rays."

Lava tubes? Carl netted a look-up. A lava tube turned out to be an underground channel through which lava had once drained. Harder, higher-melting-point rock able to withstand comparatively cooler lava, he supposed. As dead geologically as the Moon seemed, its surface had once seethed with magma. Of *course* the Moon had lava tubes.

On the color-coded map display, the candidate area had shrunken further.

"South Carolina-sized," Joshua offered.

Carl pivoted, taking in the graphic. Inspiration did not strike. He pointed at random to a candidate area. "Zoom, please."

A half meter inward from the wall, another holo opened. The close-up told Carl nothing new. "Is this real-time data?" he asked.

"Composite historical data," Joshua said. "It does away with shadows."

And, for that matter, the composite data put the entire hemisphere in daylight. Three nights earlier, when Carl had left Earth, the Moon overhead had been waning, several days past full phase. "Show me the same region, with as close as public sats have to real time."

The pop-up sprouted long shadows.

"Hard to see much this way," Joshua said.

"Zoom in tighter," Carl answered. Still nothing. "Tighter still."

At full magnification, the real-time image encompassed a narrow swath of terrain, with a surface tramway running along the strip's center. Almost, he had … something. "Follow the rails."

"Which direction?"

"Doesn't matter," Carl said. Because his subconscious was still being coy.

Their view undulated along the railway, skirting craters and mountains, on occasion bridging a crevasse, twice "flying" over trams. The second tram was parked on a rail siding, offloading. An uneven thread—dark gray, almost charcoal, against lighter gray—led away from the rails. Churned-up regolith.

"Go back to that rail spur," Carl said. "Follow those boot prints."

Looking skeptical, Joshua complied.

"Just bear with me," Carl said.

In dots and dashes, the trail led to an inflatable shelter. The lunar regolith around the campground was churned.

"Prospecting or mining," Joyce surmised.

Carl puzzled over the many interruptions to the trail. Lost in shadow, sometimes. Ground too hard, or the regolith too thin, to show boot prints.

If there *were* Interveners on the Moon, they had evaded detection for a long time.

"Refine the search, Joshua," Carl said. "Find spots along the rail- and roadways that run right up against rough terrain."

"Define rough."

"Like the apparent gaps in this trail. Areas that won't take boot prints or vehicle tracks." Carl thought some more. "Especially any narrow passes."

Along the walls the candidate terrain shrank *way* back, to scattered pockets.

One by one, Carl examined them.

CHAPTER 29

In graceful arcs and long straight-aways, the maglev railway extended, seemingly without end, across the basaltic plain that was the Ocean of Storms. Fields of solar cells, black to absorb the unfiltered sunlight, ran alongside the guide walls and rails. Craters and hills, crevasses and railway, all dissolved into a blur as the tram tore across the stark lunar landscape.

Skimming the ground, a klick per second seemed faster than the fastest spaceship.

Nearing a pre-programmed waypoint, the tram began to brake. On the virtual map in Carl's mind's eye, a switch icon began to blink: the transfer from this main circumpolar route onto east-west tracks. "Two minutes," he said.

Joshua only grunted.

They had departed Tycho City with a list of twenty-four candidates. Ten site surveys later, given the Law of Averages, the surprise would have been having found something interesting. Carl kept the math to himself. Joshua was grumpy enough already.

They surveyed from east to west, staying ahead of the Sun. With Carl's usual luck, the Intervener base they sought would lie just east of the terminator when first they had set out: in darkness, impractical to search, for almost two weeks. With his more recent luck, there was no Intervener base to be found, or he had misjudged where to look.

Either way, he might not be searching in two weeks. In less than one, the Powers That Be expected him to appear for a second round of questioning in the ongoing inquest. At least this time the Agency had offered to hold the session at the main UPIA lunar station.

Inertia threw Carl against a wall, and Joshua against Carl, as the tram took the banking turn onto the intersecting tracks.

"Ten more minutes on this leg," Carl said.

Joshua grunted again.

Nearing preset coordinates, the vehicle began to slow. A side spur appeared in Carl's mind's-eye map. "Almost there," he said.

The tram swerved onto the spur and they came to a halt. To their right, slumped with unimaginable age and the patient, relentless weathering of micrometeoroids, was the rim of a small, nameless crater.

At the tram's great cruising speed, only minutes separated their stops and they remained suited up. (The slog from the rail siding to a suspect area had yet to be less than an hour.) They unloaded a minimal amount of equipment, entered the doorlock code for the rented tram car, and started toward the nearby crater.

They climbed in silence up the jumbled, sort-of ramp where some of the crater wall had collapsed. They hiked almost halfway around the rim to the lip of an intersecting, somewhat younger crater. *It* was a mere two billion years old. Far around the rim of that second crater, they switched to the rugged rim wall of a third. From it they made their way to a zigzag chain of low rocky hills. At every deep shadow or hint of an opening they surveyed with portable ground-penetrating radar.

And, time and again, they found nothing.

Bounding like kangaroos *across* crater floors, they would have reached their goal in minutes—while leaving, in the eons-deep dust, an unmistakable trail of boot prints. Instead, sticking to the rockiest, most uneven terrain, they spent over an hour reaching the sinuous rille, hundreds of klicks long, that was their goal. They followed the ancient trench until it became roofed over.

Eons ago, a river of magma had flowed here. Where molten rock had drained from its stony conduit, it left behind a natural cavern. Places the tube had subsequently collapsed became valleys. Where the tube penetrated deeply enough beneath the lunar surface, not even the endless hail of meteoroids had brought down the roof.

Every deep lava tube offered a haven from radiation and celestial bombardment—and prying eyes.

Joshua peered into an opening. He said, "Looks like every other lava tube."

"It would," Carl reminded him. "Anything unusual will be deep inside, out of sight."

Portable radar revealed nothing unusual within.

Flashlights showed nothing, either.

After half a klick's hike into the tube without finding anything, they turned back.

"Eleven down," Joshua grumbled.

• • • •

Site twelve was as unnoteworthy. Returning from that trek, leaving their rental vehicle parked on the rail siding, they fit in a much needed meal and a few hours of sleep. Site thirteen showed boot scuffs, several recent bore holes where someone had taken core samples, and the broken tip of a drill bit: an unknown prospector's half-hearted mineral survey.

In the foothills of Montes Carpatus, almost one hundred klicks to the north of Crater Copernicus, nestled candidate site fourteen. There, in permanent shadow, deep inside an ancient lava tube, they encountered a metal bulkhead. Set into that wall was an air lock.

• • • •

Two layers down in the bountiful freezer, excavating steaks and lobster tails, Joshua's gut began rumbling. The camping meals he and Carl had lived on for days tasted like cardboard. Rehydrated, they tasted like soggy cardboard.

"Do you suppose they keep an inventory?" Joshua asked.

"Leave stuff *exactly* as you find it," Carl reminded, busy searching the shelter's other room. So far everything there had looked mundane, too. Life support, power-distribution panel with backup batteries (chiding himself in a stage whisper for not spotting solar panels up above; they had to be out there, somewhere), a pair of

3-D printers, a cabinet/closet, battered furniture—all of it, if sometimes on the antique side, quite ordinary. Rather than uncovering
an ancient alien outpost, it appeared they were merely trespassing.

Joshua lifted out a stack of meal boxes. "This freezer must hold
hundreds of meals. You want me to check them all?"

"For now, just sample—by which I mean X-ray, not eat. Look for
anything out of place. Make sure you get all the way to the bottom."

Before his hands froze, Joshua changed for awhile to checking
out other parts of his assigned room. Beneath the mattress of the
neatly made-up cot. Inside the cabinet. In the single drawer slung
beneath the lone, scarred, lunarcrete table.

"Carl, I found an old pocket computer. And the odd thing? No
wireless interface. The socket for it is empty."

"Human made?"

"Yeah, as far as I can tell. With more capacity than my implant,
but nothing unusual."

"Okay. Keep looking."

Humming to himself, Joshua went back to excavating the freezer.
Until—

"Gotcha!" Carl announced.

"What?"

"Something worth booby-trapping. Come see."

In the back room, Carl had sprung a disguised door. What had
seemed like a wall panel now gaped into the room. Beyond the
opening, extending for at least thirty meters, was a passageway lined
on both sides with enigmatic equipment. Where that equipment
did not block Joshua's view, the walls, floor, and ceiling were a rich,
mottled green. Copper, he surmised. Compared to this tunnel lining, the Statue of Liberty—three centuries weathered—was pristine.

How old *was* this place?

"What's all this?" Joshua asked, camera in hand, panning through
the doorway.

"I have no idea." Ducking his head, Carl stepped into the passage.
"Something worth protecting. The latch was rigged to go *boom*."

He stopped after about five paces. "Huh."

"What?"

"I can quit beating myself up over not finding solar panels. To judge from these coil configurations, this is a fusion reactor. Apart from the coils, though, I don't recall ever seeing a fusor like it. I know I've never seen a unit as compact."

"Intervener?"

"Insufficient information." Carl continued along the passage. Coming to the end, he looked to his left. And flinched.

"What?"

"Remember me mentioning a coffinlike sculpture of Banak's?" *Hiding in plain sight. Sitting in his workshop, just another artsy-fartsy construction in a room full of them. Who would have given it a second thought? I* didn't.

"The one he blew up?"

"And almost me with it." Carl pointed at something recessed behind the last equipment rack. "I don't know whose shelter this is, but they have two empty 'coffins' just like the unit Banak had."

CHAPTER 30

"Carl, thank you for coming in," Helena Strauss said. Her office could have been an executive suite anywhere.

Carl scarcely recognized her as the young woman who had called the intermission in his welcome-to-Earth inquisition. Her tailored suit had been replaced with a typical Loonie jumpsuit. Her hair hung loosely down around her shoulders. On Earth, she had moved gingerly; here, she was as graceful as a lynx. She just seemed at ease, whether from the genial gravity—with which Carl could relate—or because the Armstrong City UPIA complex was her small pond. Or, he dared to hope, because the inquest into Danica's death and the surrounding events had cleared him of wrongdoing.

None of those theories stopped him from wondering why Strauss had been on Earth when Carl had, kind of, met her. Or whether, somehow, his summons here had had something to do with his extracurricular activities. He and Joshua had stayed offline, in theory untraceable, throughout their outing. By the time, approaching Tycho City, he had rejoined the infosphere and retrieved Strauss's message, he hadn't had much time to back-trace for clues he and Joshua might have left to their recent activities. As it was, he had almost been late to his "appointment."

"What can I do for you, Agent Strauss?" he asked.

"Helena." She indicated a chair at the office's oval conference table, and then took a seat herself. "Off the big rock, we're informal. How goes your downtime?"

"Interesting place, the Moon." He would not have volunteered more than that if his purpose *were* a holiday. Gracious manner be damned, Helena had not called him in just to chat—not while dropping *station chief* into her summons—nor had her curt message offered any information. Of course, if the Agency *hadn't* tasked someone to keep tabs on him, he would have been surprised.

"You've been keeping interesting company," she said.

With cameras all over public places on the Moon, he hadn't expected his encounters with Joshua to go unnoticed. He still hoped that their recent excursion remained off the grid. "Is that so?"

"Joshua Matthews. Really? He's the butt of jokes across the Solar System."

"*He* was approachable," Carl improvised, "and I wanted to meet his grandmother. I imagined her take on the Snakes would be interesting. I did get to meet Joyce, but in the main I've been hanging out with Joshua. He turns out to be a nice guy."

"When sober, perhaps." Helena grinned. "Okay, about me asking you in. It's not about the inquest. That's ongoing."

He waited.

"Your reporter buddy has shown up in Saturn system. I know you've been trying to contact her."

Unable to reach Corinne while on his long flight to Earth, he had radioed back to Ariel to have his message relayed through the base's high-powered transmitter. Helena knowing about that indicated the inquest had reached out to Uranus and his erstwhile colleagues. That had been bound to happen; the only question had been how long it would take.

"Is Corinne safe?" he asked.

"She's fine." Leaning forward, Helena folded her arms on the table. "I wouldn't take her silent treatment personally. Best guess is she ignored all contacts rather than acknowledge a stay-away message."

"That sounds like Corinne," he agreed.

The public Corinne. *He* knew that her planned visit to *Discovery*, the starship nearing completion, was mere cover to make her trip to Ariel—to recruit him—less noteworthy. She ought to have been glad to be turned away. Why hadn't she taken the opportunity?

"There was a construction accident aboard *Discovery*," Strauss went on. "Resolved soon enough, without permanent damage, but dramatic. Onsite investigators canceled press access."

"And a journalist was determined to see it anyway? Shocking."

"I suppose not." Strauss straightened. "Consider this update a professional courtesy. Till project security decides what to do with your party-crashing friend—quite likely ordering her back to Earth—she's not being allowed comm privileges. I thought you'd want to know."

"Does courtesy extend to letting me send a message to Corinne?"

"Afraid not."

It hadn't hurt to ask. "I appreciate it, Helena. The update, that is. Don't quote me, but shipping Corinne straight home sounds like a great idea."

Because her pilot looks more and more like an Intervener agent.

Yet again, Carl was tempted. With access to Agency resources, how much more might he learn about the hidden base?

And once again, Robyn's recorded warning—and the implausible coincidence of her assassination and her backups disappearing—silenced him. Security *had* been compromised. Despite media yowling and politicians posturing, the Agency had yet to indicate any progress in their investigation.

For all that, Strauss hadn't had to share the news of Corinne's safe arrival. He was only in her office because the station chief expected a favor in return. "What is it you want to know?"

"Snakes."

"Kind of broad, Helena."

"I've never met one."

"Picture a bipedal puma, scaly rather than furry. It's whippet-thin. It masses just twenty-five kilos or so, and most of that is muscle. The claws come out anytime it gets edgy. Add an upward-pointing third eye. Give it a big chip on its—to you, waist-level—shoulder. Now imagine that, with all three eyes, it's always sizing you up, searching for any weakness or momentary lapse. They call themselves Hunters. Spend ten seconds around one and you'll *know* no other name could be more apt."

"Charming," Helena said. "And you're in a hurry to go back?

Anyway, here's what I know. The Foremost is doing her best to cast you in a bad light. Does she want to be permanently rid of you?"

Of *course* Glithwah wanted to be rid of him. Year after year Carl's deputies came and went, a posting on Ariel being a handy entry in any agent's personnel file. Few—certainly not the latest careerist drone—monitored the Snakes with the diligence *he* had. None had Carl's experience, or his skeptical eye. And now Bruce was, aside from sources and snitches among the civvie human workforce, the lone UPIA asset on Ariel. A scary thought.

"She wants me gone for the best of reasons," Carl said. "I do my job."

Helena's vague, overhead gesture encompassed Earth. "That's the general consensus."

"If you don't mind me asking, how do current affairs on Ariel have anything to do with you?"

"You wouldn't expect them to, would you?" She grinned. "If you want to get ahead in the Agency—not, say, spend your career on a snowball on the outer fringes of nowhere—you volunteer for stuff. Even for the unexciting stuff. Lucky you, I volunteered for your board of inquest. Then *you* chose to wait things out on the Moon."

He shrugged.

"Your former deputy has been vague and less than supportive. Maybe that's opportunism. And maybe not, bringing me to the other reason I asked you here. Check this out."

Carl's implant pinged: a file upload. Recent status updates from Ariel. Purchase orders. Ship arrivals and departures. News gleaned from Ariel's public net. A few ordinary-seeming back-and-forth message exchanges.

"What am I looking for?" he asked.

"You tell me."

"Most of it's in Bruce Wycliffe's style." Carl had plodded through enough stilted, self-important weekly reports to recognize his newly promoted deputy's prose. "Pretty routine."

"And?"

"No embedded duress codes. But you can see that, too."

"So all is well on Ariel?"

"So it would appear." Carl closed his eyes, considering. "I can't tell you why, but these reports feel wrong. What does statistical analysis indicate?"

"The Agency has a more than ample collection of comm with *you* to do such analyses. Not enough pre-handoff samples by Wycliffe."

"It feels wrong," Carl repeated. And lesson learned. If he returned to Ariel, every so often he would delegate his communications with HQ.

His implant held old reports from Bruce, for no better reason than he hadn't taken the time to clear them. He netted copies to Helena. "Have your stats gurus compare the new messages with these."

"Thanks."

Send me back, he almost told her. Because he would bet his pension that Glithwah was up to something. Something *he* might ferret out but that Bruce never would.

Almost. The Interveners worried him more than the Snakes ever had.

"Keep an eye on them," Carl said.

Because he would rather the Agency watch the Snakes than watch *him*.

• • • •

"They must have archives somewhere," Joshua said. *Why lurk, if not to observe and collect data?* "Carl and I searched the hidden facility for computers without finding any. I mean apart from the little pocket model I mentioned, and it wasn't connected to anything. It didn't even have a network interface."

"So what did the pocket comp tell you?" his grandmother asked. She perched, birdlike, on the edge of his sofa. He had dragged it back into the front room of his apartment for her.

"Tell me? Nothing." He grimaced. "Not that I'd know more if we *hadn't* had to leave it behind. Or if I'd had geologic time to work at it. Sorry."

"Don't be. You're good at other things, Josh, or no one would have known to look. Encrypted?"

"Yeah. Carl brought back a memory image. He'll have another crack at it when he has time."

"I wish I'd been there."

He patted Grandma's arm. "If a UPIA spook couldn't break the encryption, I don't suppose you would have."

"Don't patronize me, Josh. Your friend may be a spook, but that doesn't make him a computer whiz. I am."

I'm sure you were, Joshua thought. *But Grandma had retired long ago, and anyway, she had been a manager for most of her career. More computer-savvy than him, sure, but that was a low hurdle. Kind of like stepping over a stripe of paint.*

"You wouldn't have much cared for the hike in," he told her. "To minimize boot prints from the railway, we hiked over some pretty rough terrain."

"There, you've got me." She rocked on the edge of the sofa, head canted, brow furrowed, twisting a hanky. "So what *did* you find?"

He had already shown her on his camera the coffinlike things and the ultra-compact fusion reactor. Now he scrolled to the beginning of the camera's memory for images of the living area. The manual controls seemed archaic, but without shielding he did not dare zap the files to her implant. And to regroup somewhere shielded, or to shield his apartment, risked inviting scrutiny.

Joshua said, "In the front rooms, not a thing you can't find a million places on the Moon. Apart from the location, it'd be without interest."

"And elsewhere?"

"Maybe this." He prodded camera controls to retrieve an image of a nameless, shallow, little crater. Carl's ground-penetrating radar showed that near the Intervener base the lava tube ran, on average, twenty-five meters beneath ground level. Whatever impact had blasted out this dimple had lacked the force to collapse the tube beneath. "See anything interesting?"

"I see a crater. I wouldn't call it interesting."

"Look again."

"Round. Rim walls. Central peak." She took the camera from him and enlarged the holo. "It still looks like a crater."

"Check the scale."

"A little crater, then. So?"

Joshua reclaimed his camera. "That's the problem, or so Carl informs me. Craters this small"—this one measured a scant fifty meters across—"don't form central peaks."

"Meaning?"

"Meaning, he supposes, that if we could get an up-close look without leaving telltale boot prints, we'd find antennas, maybe telescopes, disguised within a false peak."

"Clever, if so. After living awhile on this rock, you no more notice the craters than on Earth you would notice the air you breathe." Grandma stood and stretched. "What about ground-penetrating radar? Did it show anything within the peak?"

"Not the portable unit we'd brought. We're going to go back with better gear."

She looked … wistful.

"Forget it. You couldn't handle the hike."

"I suppose not." She shuffle-glided into the apartment's tiny kitchenette for a glass of ice water. "Hidden instruments. Ordinary living quarters. A pocket comp that might tell Carl something. The hall with those coffin things like the one that almost got him killed on Ariel. Interesting, to say the least."

Joshua realized he had omitted something from his narration. He cycled through several dozen still images. "Then there's this."

Grandma made a noise: mixed "Huh!" and snort and choking on water gone down the wrong way.

"Are you okay?"

"Fine," she managed. She waved off his concern, and slowly her coughing subsided. "You don't recognize these?"

"No. Neither did Carl. Intervener super science, we supposed."

"Except not so super," she said. "More like beads on strings."

"What?"

"Simple. Primitive." She topped off her water glass. "You didn't recognize these as computers because you've never seen anything like them. It's amazing enough that *I* have. You can thank the Snakes."

"How so? These are hardly Snake biochips."

"Could it have been more than eighty years?" Retaking her spot on the sofa's edge, Grandma seemed to be talking to herself. She straightened, and her voice firmed. "The Snake Subterfuge, people call it."

"I *was* going to write an official ICU history, you might remember." *Before the Interveners abducted me, disgraced me, and got me fired.*

"I remember, Josh," she said. "History doesn't always make it into the official files."

"I know this story," he said, stubbornly. "Trapdoors buried deep in the genome of Snake biochip tech. Pashwah"—the Snake's long-time AI agent in the Solar System—"tried to extort the ICU. You and Great-Uncle Kevin talked her out of the attempt."

"Not so much me." Grandma pursed her lips, choosing her words with care. "The thing is, the Snake tech had checked out. It had worked flawlessly through *years* in quarantine before the first biochips were allowed out of the lab."

And into every nook and cranny of the human infosphere, including the neural implants in their brains.

"By the time Pashwah revealed she could hack any biochip she chose, we—not just on Earth, but across the Solar System—were utterly dependent. Kevin didn't *talk* Pashwah out of anything. He extorted her right back. The ICU beamed a warning about the Snakes' deceit to our AI rep in every InterstellarNet system. Not all members had adopted biochips yet. Heck, some still haven't.

"Absent regular coded messages, Kevin explained to Pashwah, Earth's distant agents would release that warning. Throughout the InterstellarNet community, Snakes would never again have sold anything to anyone. Whatever they hoped to coerce from the ICU would've been peanuts by comparison."

Clever, Joshua thought. If Pashwah hadn't backed off, Earth's links to InterstellarNet *would* have crashed. End of coded messages to desist. Warnings released. It surprised him a bit that even so long ago agents had that much flexibility and abstract reasoning. Except—

"Back up, Grandma. The computers were all compromised. How did you encrypt and send the coded messages without Pashwah seeing and blocking them? It had to have been monitoring."

"That's my point. We reverted to museum pieces, pre-biochip." She gestured at the holo still projecting from Joshua's camera. "Electronic, a lot like those."

"The Interveners have interstellar travel, super-compact fusion reactors, and a civilization we *know* dates back at least a half billion years. And you imagine they have computers like museum pieces from, no offense, your youth?"

"So it appears, Josh. So it appears."

CHAPTER 31

Discovery mission: humanity's most ambitious exploratory endeavor.

The starship *Discovery* (see related article), now nearing completion, is the second interstellar-class vessel to be constructed by the United Planets. Like *New Beginnings*, now en route to Alpha Centauri, *Discovery* builds upon the design of the derelict Centaur starship *Harmony* (or, as it was renamed by its Hunter hijackers, *Victorious*).

Where *New Beginnings* is repatriating *Harmony*'s surviving original crew—conveniently, the Centaurs are humanity's closest interstellar neighbors—the *Discovery* mission has more ambitious goals. Vigorous debate over the most suitable destination continued throughout the ship's construction phase.

Advocates of a scientific mission agreed upon Epsilon Indi as their joint recommendation. Epsilon Indi (see related article), about twelve light-years from Earth, observable in the constellation Indus (the Indian), is a K-class star as old as or older than the Sun. Biologists wanted, in particular, to visit Epsilon Indi III. Although III orbits in the middle of Epsilon Indi's Goldilocks zone, the planet shows no indications of life. Climatologists, pointing to III's exceptionally high albedo, asked to explore a world apparently locked in an ice age. Astronomers sought a close look at Epsilon Indi's dim companions, two of the brown dwarf stars nearest to the Solar System.

The prevailing opinion, however, emphasized strengthening relationships with fellow InterstellarNet species. *Discovery*'s maiden mission will therefore be to Tau Ceti (see related article), at a similar distance, although in another direction, and visible in the constellation Cetus (the Whale). Tau Ceti IV is the home world of the hive-mind species commonly referred to as Whales or Mobies.

With departure preparations peaking, the mission office relocated from Earth to Saturn's moon Prometheus, from which project managers can best oversee *Discovery*'s final outfitting, fueling, and crew transfer.

—Internetopedia

• • • •

With a sigh, Corinne ground to a halt outside the dorm room she and Grace had been assigned for their stay—detention being, it would seem, too forthright of a description. *Odyssey*'s tiny cabins would have been more spacious. Jailed for contempt, long ago, for protecting a source, Corinne had had a bigger cell.

To be fair, she did get to roam around much of Prometheus base—just not any of the interesting parts. She was not permitted inside the *Discovery* mission training area, though by wandering the halls and camping out in the mess hall she had managed to waylay some people. A few naval types, mostly low-ranking, all bitter at being stuck here on humdrum patrol duty. To the man and woman they envied colleagues across the Solar System investigating the rash of ship disappearances. (Suspected pirates? Really?) The scientific contingent, the elitist of the elite, pleading they were too busy, never had much to offer. Among the Augmented, a third or more of mission staff, few deigned to interact beyond the minimum requirements of civility. Some encounters had not risen to that level.

The antimatter factory was off-limits, too, as was the local naval command center. Stealthy warships guarded factory and starship. Just how many troops and military vessels were details the authorities would not divulge—no matter that the Snake colony was *far* away.

Not that anyone had asked Corinne, but a light-year would not have been far enough.

Last night it had been the God's-eye-view nightmare again that brought her shuddering awake: the UP's original antimatter plant blown to atoms. An entire *world*, the Jovian moon Himalia, shattered. A civilian population of thousands, slaughtered. *Victorious* escaping with humanity's top scientists and engineers—

And, incidentally, with one utterly terrified reporter.

By day, no matter the nightmares, Corinne found it harder and harder to be fair. Taxpayers across the Solar System had invested a fortune in this expedition. She had urgent matters to attend to on Earth. And she was bored out of her skull, reduced to following local news. On Titan, that meant priority production of antiviral nanites for some flu outbreak, possibly gengineered. On Rhea, the big stories were a high-society wedding and the uptick in a provincial deficit. People on Mimas were agog at their university making it to the final four in the All Saturn System zero-gee polo play-offs.

Sighing again, she reached for the cabin-door latch. She had an hour until the mess hall reopened. Maybe, before dinner, she'd record another vid mail to Denise. Apart from the minutiae of her latest unproductive day, this message would not differ in its essentials from all the others. *I love you. I miss you. I should be there. I'm an idiot.*

And like all those previous vids, the project office would refuse to send this one. She'd still record it. The only thing that Corinne hated more than her regrets and apologies going undelivered was when they went unsaid.

With a final, deeper sigh, she let herself into the cabin.

Grace, stretched out on her cot, opened her eyes. "Melodramatic sound effects aside, you appear to have a silver tongue."

Uh-huh. And a gold-digging uncle back on Earth. Also, Corinne had once been told, big brass *cojones*. "How is that?"

"While you roamed the hallways, Donald With The Ridiculous Sideburns stopped by. He says that, with an escort, you can tour *Discovery* and meet there with some of the crew."

That would be Donald Schnabel: earnest, self-important bureaucrat. Assistant to the deputy to the project manager. Schnabel found no lack of reasons to drop by. Since their arrival, he had invited Grace to dinner at least daily.

"Why the change of heart?"

Because the last Corinne had heard, she would be lucky to avoid formal charges for disregarding traffic control, reckless endangerment, trespassing, loitering, littering, general hooliganism, and aggravated mopery. Maybe someone, remembering that she had arrived in a long-range ship she personally owned (no matter that *Odyssey* was thirty years old), had finally taken her hints about the baying pack of lawyers she could unleash.

"Silver tongue, I tell you." Grace sat up. "Though it might have helped that I agreed to dinner with Donald tonight—aboard *Discovery*."

So much for silver tongues. Well, whatever worked. "I guess you'll be joining us."

"I can be your cameraman." Grace waved off the obvious rejoinder: Corinne had one of the still-exotic A/V-recording implant upgrades to record anything she saw and heard. "If anyone has second thoughts, let 'em have something to confiscate."

A damned good idea. "I suppose we can buy or borrow a camera."

"Or I can fetch mine." Grace batted her eyes. "If I ask nicely, I think Donald will clear me to go aboard *Odyssey*"—impounded as long as their party-crashing continued under review—"for a few minutes to dig a camera out of my locker."

A camera they owned would *look less contrived than having to buy one.* "Go for it. And good job."

"Add it to my tip," Grace said. "Now if you wouldn't mind stepping into the hall for a few minutes, I need to dress for dinner."

• • • •

In the shuttle's view port, minute by minute, the matte-black cylinder grew. And kept on growing. As a habitat molded from a nickel-iron asteroid, it was not all that exceptional.

As a vessel, it was *huge*.

"*Discovery* is the biggest ship ever constructed," Donald With The Ridiculous Sideburns recited. "A klick and a quarter long. About five-eighths klick in diameter. One hundred twenty decks in all, fifty decks devoted to sustaining the onboard ecology."

"That's *amazing*," Grace said, hand resting on Donald's forearm. If she minded that someone else occupied the pilot's seat, she hid it well. "But it seems huge for a crew of … what? A few hundred?"

Donald beamed at Grace's touch. "That's about right. The final crew, including the scientific and diplomatic contingents, is three hundred twelve. As a safety precaution, the ship's carrying capacity is much larger."

Corinne's implant did the math. Volume approaching a cubic kilometer. Aggregated surface area of the decks: eighty-seven square klicks. *Discovery* was twice the size of the ship that haunted Corinne's dreams. Imagining this new ship teeming with Snakes, she shivered. She hoped no one noticed.

Given decent recycling, to indefinitely sustain one adult a habitat needed about four thousand square meters of botanical deck. If fifty botanical decks maintained their full efficiency, this ship could support at least—

"Do I have this right?" Corinne asked, sure that she did. "Capacity of nine *thousand*?"

"More or less," Donald agreed. "As I said, a safety precaution.

If the interstellar drive should break down light-years from home, even if something unforeseen then degrades the shipboard ecology, there's ample margin. Because in that scenario, help might be years in coming."

No one could have missed *this* shudder. Everyone had the decency to pretend.

The cylinder's forward endcap had become a metallic plain, the dots scattered across it revealed as short-range craft similar to the shuttle in which they approached. Lesser dots that emerged had to be spacesuited workers. Just aft of that landing platform/endcap, caverns gaped: hangar bays for the times when the starship's own velocity turned oncoming light and interstellar gas into a hail of lethal radiation.

"Touching down in about two minutes," the pilot announced.

Within five minutes they were through a flexible docking tube, through the main air lock, and in a staging area aboard *Discovery*. The starship was not spinning—that was done only when liquids were being transferred aboard—leaving them, for all practical purposes, in free fall. During the starship's long journey, a steady acceleration or deceleration would hold passengers on the decks.

"You'll want these." Donald handed them magnetic slippers. Looking apologetic, he took clip-on badges from a locker. Where his badge showed a head shot, theirs each bore a bright red V: the scarlet letter for Visitor. Waving a wireless baton over Grace's and Corinne's left arms, he mated each badge to an embedded med/ID chip. "Wear your badge at all times. It's a big ship. We don't want to lose you."

Uh-huh, Corinne thought. A ship-wide security system would be watching them, making certain they did not stray from their escort and that their badges never went far from their arms. However smitten, Donald was following protocol.

"Why bother with badges?" she asked. "Can't you track our med chips?"

Donald's hangdog expression grew yet more contrite. "So people we meet know you're not cleared."

From the security office, they were off to a VIP tour, their glori-fied golf-cart electromagnetically drawn to decks and elevator floors. Tier after tier of farmland, a dozen different crops ripening under artificial sunlight. Warehouses and storage rooms. Hangar bays for the starship's landing craft. Dinner in one of the ship's many mess halls, wherein Corinne gallantly (and to Grace's netted frown) in-sisted upon eating at a separate table. The echoing bridge and, at the opposite end of the starship, the even more cavernous engine room. Crew quarters, labs, and machine shops.

And the accident site. The incident that had made the project office so publicity-shy turned out to have been a bad weld in the heat-exchange system of a secondary fusion reactor. One among an army of welding bots had gotten overlooked in the course of a software upgrade. Stuff happens, Donald assured them. Alas, it was time-consuming to ensure that no other sloppy work like that had gone unnoticed.

Grace appeared fascinated with every aspect of their excursion. Donald doted on Grace.

And Corinne? *She* could not stop imagining—no, remembering!—a ship all too similar to this. A ship coming apart at its seams as Snakes battled the UP marine detachment—and Carl—come to liberate it. A derelict, its stern third blown to dust and gamma rays, hemorrhaging air, water, and bodies, adrift in the cold and dark ....

Only with sheer willpower did Corinne rouse herself to feign interest. She had come billions of klicks so that her leaving Earth would seem less about Ariel; any suggestion now of distraction would defeat the purpose. And so she directed a barrage of questions, banal and obvious as many were, at workers and crew they encountered across the ship.

How do you feel about the upcoming trip? You'll be away for decades; what about the loved ones you're leaving behind? What do you hope to learn? How can you expect to relate to beings as alien as the Mobies?

The questions she *wanted* to ask—are you nuts? aren't you ter-rified?—she kept to herself.

Most answers were as trite as her questions, but between hours of recordings and her after-the-fact commentary, she could cobble together a one-hour documentary. Grace's feminine wiles notwithstanding, they wouldn't have been allowed aboard if their detention were not coming to an end. Editing the raw vid would give Corinne something to do on the slog back to Earth.

. . . .

Only when Grace did her preflight checkout of *Odyssey*, their detention finally over, did she discover that a key photonic component in the fusion-drive controller had gone bad. The design file for printing the part turned out to be corrupted—on Earth, too, when the file was retransmitted.

The two of them were stranded, due to the age of the ship, till a cargo run from the inner system could physically deliver the replacement part.

CHAPTER 32

In Joshua's mind's ear, Tacitus 352 asked, "Are we there yet?"

The AI's tunic- and toga-clad avatar somehow nailed the cadence and nasality of a whining child. Joshua had gone on enough outings with his nephews to know.

"Be happy we're flying," Joshua netted back.

He looked over his shoulder to check yet again on his grandmother. Her eyes were closed, her cheeks drooped, and she had a white-knuckled grip on the armrests of her acceleration couch. Carl was keeping the short hop as gentle as possible, but even a quartergee surge, now and again, was more than Grandma had experienced in, well, Joshua chose not to dwell on that.

As stressful for her as was the flight, hiking to the Intervener base from the maglev tracks would have been impossible. That left flying in. They needed her expertise—and she was adamant that she *would* help. In person.

"Are we there yet?" Tacitus tried again. "I made it from Earth in under two seconds."

As bits streaming between worlds, he would not have experienced even those seconds. But he *had* come, given no more explanation than a chance to join Joshua's "merrie band."

Merrie band. Robin Hood. Robyn Tanaka. Trust an AI to connect dots.

As, at the start of this adventure, Tacitus had helped Joshua to recognize the subtle pattern of Intervener activities against the backdrop of all history and prehistory across eleven solar systems. And, much more than a capable historian, the AI was one of a rare breed: Joshua's true friend.

"Soon," Joshua netted, patting the portable server in which Tacitus now resided. He could not help contrasting this comp with the rack upon rack of alien equipment Grandma insisted together comprised an Intervener computer. If the Interveners didn't have info tech, why not just have their human agents *buy* some?

"On final approach," Carl called. "Let's take a good look around before we land."

From the bridge console, ghostly, a holo projected: the high-res, 3-D rendering of the local terrain to a depth of fifty meters. Here and there the lava tube penetrated too far beneath the surface to be sensed. The Intervener base, lodged in the tube like a pea in a peashooter, almost failed to register in the scan. From orbit, it would not show at all. Inside the anomalous crater above the Intervener base, antennas and telescopes *did* lurk within the (to the ship's radar) obviously sham central peak.

Less than a kilometer from the Intervener base, the lava-tube roof had fallen in. With a deft touch, Carl maneuvered their rented ship through the gap. He sidled the ship about forty meters into the tube, away from eyes in the sky, before setting down.

"Are we done yet?" Tacitus netted, smiling.

Carl toted their first load of equipment, including Tacitus' server, while Joshua helped—as often, carried—his grandmother across the treacherous moonscape. Well before they reached the neighboring lava-tube entrance, the opening that gave access to the Intervener base, all were winded. As Grandma looked around the facility, Carl began unpacking.

Joshua hiked back for another load of their gear. Reentering the lava tube, the Sun at his back, he could not help but notice several large, blackened splotches on the stone floor. These splotches looked no different than the newly scorched patch beneath their ship. Alas, they had no instruments with which to date the previous landings.

In the time Joshua needed to retrieve the remainder of their gear, Carl had erected a portable electromagnetic shield: a Faraday cage. Tacitus' server sat within; for security, they would net to the

AI only while also inside the enclosure.

In the back room, the disguised door panel hung ajar. Cheerful whistling suggested that Grandma was already at work.

In the front room Carl sat perched on the shelter's lone rickety chair, elbows propped on the scarred table, glowering at the portable comp they had found on their first expedition. He had shed his pressure suit. The handgun that had dangled from his suit's utility belt sat alongside the comp.

"Planning to shoot it?" Joshua asked.

"I might as well. I'm still not getting in."

"We just got here."

Carl shoved back the chair. "My implant holds some of the Agency's best crypto software. I'm no whiz, but with these tools I should be able to crack this."

"Unless you're up against an Agency whiz," Joshua said. "In any event, someone skilled enough to get at and wipe Robyn's backups."

"Or an alien with alien algorithms," Grandma called from far back in the corridor.

"You're both *so* encouraging," Carl said.

"What else is going on?" Joshua asked.

"The last I looked, Joyce was puzzling over a keyboard. It was labeled with symbols that meant nothing to either of us. I showed Tacitus a picture of it. The symbols meant nothing to him, either. Now let me work."

Other than children too young for implant surgery, and Humanist Movement dinosaurs who shunned neural implants as impure, did anyone use keyboards? Mulling that over, Joshua went into the back corridor. The green walls were, if anything, more tarnished and textured than he had remembered. Spot welds and caulk dotted the welded seams that joined copper sheets. Several seams and two sheets had patches on patches.

His grandmother knelt on the floor, peering into an equipment rack not noticeably different from any other. Well, perhaps a little different. A deck-of-cards-sized module unplugged from *this* rack was beside her foot. The module was chock-a-block with dice-sized components interconnected with hundreds of metallic interconnects that were actually naked-eye visible.

"Why not just chisel their computer from flint?" he asked.

"Look at these walls. They build to last." She was poking and prodding into a gap—from which the module on the floor had, he inferred, been extracted—with the probes of a multimeter, then jotting notes on a sheet of paper. The enigmatic keyboard sat three racks away on a pullout shelf. "That said, do you remember my comment about your vids? That this equipment was like a museum piece from my youth?"

"Uh-huh." Taking notes on paper was pretty low-tech, too, but you had to make allowances for someone Grandma's age.

A simulated needle jumped on her meter's display. She added a row of digits to her notepaper. "I was too kind. Think IBM 360 mainframe."

"What does that mean?"

She brushed an errant lock of white hair from her forehead. "Big, slow, and energy hogging. But that era's tech got men to the Moon and sufficed for an early antiballistic-missile system."

"Okay …."

She laughed. "Circa 1970. If computing had a Bronze Age, that was it."

At last, a comparison Joshua got. "Can I bring you something? A drink? A snack?" Because until they had new data to work with, he saw no other way to contribute.

"No, thanks. Well, yes. A camera. The one with a laser range-finder."

That was not intuitive. He fetched the camera. Crouching beside Grandma, looking over her shoulder into the gap in the rack, he saw a connector. One by one she was probing its array of metallic leads. Humming now rather than whistling, she took a note after each measurement.

"I have the camera," he told her.

"Bear with me." Finally, setting the meter on the floor, she wrote a bunch more notes. When her scribbling had finished, she reached up. "Okay, camera."

He handed it over.

She took close-ups of the connector, returned the camera, and scooted backward. "I saw a 3-D printer out there. Josh, be a dear, and print me an interface to these specs." She walked him through the details.

He snapped an image of her notes, then uploaded from the camera to his implant. "An interface. What'll it do?"

"Convert between optical and electrical signaling, so that I can connect a pocket comp to this museum piece. With some trial and error, I should be able to read out memory." To his doubtless blank look, she explained, "We think the Interveners have monitored Earth for eons. My guess is that the most common modules store those observations. If so, this"—she nudged the module on the floor beside her—"is a memory unit. I've been characterizing the electrical interface between it and the rack."

"And when the contents read out"—he pointed at the keyboard with its enigmatic symbols—"like that?"

"Have faith." She stretched her arms out and back, joints creaking. "My interface?"

· · · ·

Joshua was unwrapping three meals from their supplies when, from Tacitus' shielded enclosure, the gleeful shout rang out.

"Eureka!" Grandma declared.

She and Tacitus had been cloistered for hours, coy about whatever they did. Some manner of attempt to parse the downloaded data, Joshua supposed, but beyond that he had no clue.

"Come see," she said. "Both of you."

The enclosure was snug for three, but they crowded in.

"We saw the telescope hidden up top," Grandma netted, appending a high-res radar image taken earlier that day of the anomalous crater. "It stood to reason they kept image files."

"Okay," Carl responded.

"The challenge," she went on unperturbed, "is in knowing how to recover the images. I found a recurring lengthy bit pattern I thought might be an end-of-file marker. After that, with Tacitus' help, it was a matter of running candidate files through possible image-encoding schemes and compression algorithms, seeing if any pictures would pop out."

"I'm assuming it worked," Carl netted, "but how?"

"These devices are *primitive*. It seemed worth trying algorithms from early human computing. If an algorithm was obvious to us, maybe it was obvious to them, too. Tacitus was a big help. He can try out algorithms and diddle parameters really fast."

"Tacitus?" Joshua was incredulous. "He's an historian, not a programmer."

"My taking an interest in programming," the AI snapped, "is no less likely than you taking an interest in medicine and your own body."

"Let's focus," Carl netted. "What was the 'Eureka' moment?"

The crater image vanished, and into their consensual meeting space blossomed ...

The beautiful blue-brown-and-white orb was not *quite* Earth. Europe and North America crowded up against one another. Only a narrow channel separated Africa from South America. A landmass to which Joshua could not put any name bulked between Australia and Africa. Annotation along the left edge used characters he had seen on the alien keyboard.

"According to paleogeologic simulations," Tacitus netted, "this image of Earth was captured around 110 million years ago."

CHAPTER 33

In one recovered file after another, the alien archive kept yielding surprises. They found extensive imagery of arrays of chipped stone tools and video of mass demonstrations against genetically modified foods. They saw early English-language outlines for *Frankenstein* and (according to Tacitus) a precursor to humanity's earliest known alphabet.

Oddest of all were the detailed topological and subsurface maps of undersea volcanic ridges. Intervener interest in those seemed inexplicable until, again tapping paleogeologic simulations, Tacitus approximated a date. When mollusks and trilobites had suddenly appeared in Earth's oceans, a half-billion years or so ago, those advances had been revolutionary. Absent a huge surge in calcium (compounds of which, the AI pedantically offered, awakened volcanoes along those ridges would have spewed into the oceans), animals with hard shells and skeletons—like mollusks and trilobites—might never have developed.

And still, Carl marveled, their progress remained halting. Joyce had yet to deduce the Intervener indexing principles. Many clues—the drift of continents, the literally glacial advance and retreat of ice ages, occasional views of night sky—permitted the rough dating of selected images. Whatever the aliens' organizational scheme, it *wasn't* chronological.

With a start, Carl realized they had surfed image files for hours. These glimpses into Earth's ancient past were hypnotic! Neither a techie nor an historian, he could not contribute a thing to the effort beyond alleviating the crowding.

He exited the cramped enclosure, pacing to stretch his legs, looking around. Nothing caught his eye. The two front rooms were as sterile, as devoid of personal touches, as Grace DiMeara's apartment on Earth. That did not mean he hadn't overlooked something.

Methodically he rechecked the rooms without finding as much as a scrap of paper, let alone another hidden compartment. When he sat back at the table for another go at the pocket comp, its encryption continued to mock him.

Carl moved on to the rear corridor. Had the Interveners hidden anything but data back here? Would he spot it if they did? He stared for a while at one of the coffinlike things. In one rim of the person-sized cavity, about waist-high, was a cluster of finger-sized indentations that might be controls. If so, he had no idea how to operate them.

Affixed to the top of the tall hollow was what could be a self-destruct device—an interpretation that might be only painful experience talking. In that device, what he took to be a status LED did not glow. If this was a bomb, it was not armed. He guessed.

He started back up the long corridor, past rack after rack of Intervener electronics. No matter how primitive this computer was, it had to store a lot of data. Joyce continued to skim her trial download, a mere few gigabytes.

He reentered the shielded enclosure. "How much data is in that back corridor?"

Joyce frowned in concentration. "Best estimate? Fifteen petabytes. Of course I can't say how much of that capacity has been put to use."

And they should copy it all. Carl netted, "We'd best change tactics. Stop looking and start downloading."

Joyce countered, "You might want to check out this first."

• • • •

An image of this very room—with the back of a human-looking head. From the wavy, shoulder-length hair, a woman. The scene was in gray scale, so Carl could not discern hair color beyond dark. More of the cryptic alien script along the left edge. A label, logic suggested, maybe a timestamp, only they couldn't read it.

Damn! He netted, "We're going to appear in the surveillance system."

Joyce replied, "Unless we can erase part of the record."

"A gap in the recordings will still show them that someone was here," Joshua netted. "Whoever they are."

"Better that than they know *who* was here," Carl answered. "And maybe they won't find out till their next visit. But it could also be that we triggered an alarm and they're on their way. Let's get out with the data we have, not push our luck."

Joshua netted, "Carl, can you gather up our stuff? I watched Grandma get her trial download. I can copy more while you pack." He paused. "I guess first I should print off more interfaces. Then I can be downloading data into all our comps in parallel."

"Tacitus and I will keep surfing till you're ready," Joyce netted. "If we find a way to cover our tracks, we'll use it."

No one came looking for us after our first visit, Carl reassured himself, cramming instruments, hand tools, and empty meal wrappers into satchels and backpacks. *Probably there had been no alarm, the first time or this. Any transmission from this hidden place would be a security hazard in its own right.*

Was he reduced to hoping for the best? That would be a hell of a thing. He continued packing.

"Carl?" Joyce called aloud. "You need to see this!"

Within the shielded enclosure, Joyce's comp now projected a pressure-suited figure loping down the lava tube. The camera feed from inside the pitch-black tube had to be infrared, though it lacked the telltale greenish cast of human IR sensors. More Intervener high tech, Carl supposed. But the far bigger surprise was behind the helmet visor.

That was—Grace DiMeara!

"Shit!" Carl said with feeling.

"You know her?"

"She's Corinne's pilot."

"That's not why we called you," Tacitus netted. The perhaps-timestamp blinked along the image's left edge. "You know these annotations? Time-sorting enough Earth images according to paleo models let me crack the annotation."

"Like separating year, month, and day fields within a date?" Carl guessed.

"Something of that nature, although the slowest changing field must count something closer to millennia than to years. Having identified that field, reviewing values of lots of time-sorted Earth imagery, I was able to derive the Intervener numbering scheme. They count in octal, if you wondered. Once I could read one field, I could read all the fields."

"So when was *this* image taken?" Carl asked.

"Unclear," Tacitus netted. "We don't yet know their time units. I tried to correlate the changing symbols and images with Earth's day and year, without success. I can tell you a few things. The Earth observations are made on a sampling basis, not continuously, the sampling intervals getting shorter and shorter in modern times. Camera shots from inside this shelter are likewise bursty, but they aren't regularly spaced samples."

"Triggered by motion sensors?" Carl asked.

"It looks that way," Joyce netted.

"And this is the most recent visit, apart from ours?" Carl guessed. As much as he hated the notion of an Intervener agent lurking near *Discovery*—and Corinne—it would mean that no one had visited this base in months. If so, they could take their time snooping around.

"No," Tacitus netted. "It's not even the most recent within this particular memory sample. It *is* a sequence you'll want to see."

Grace's still image came to life. As the viewpoint shifted from camera to camera, she let herself in through the air lock, stripped off her pressure suit, disarmed and opened the hidden panel. By the second her expression became ever more ... blissful.

It gave Carl the creeps.

She hurried down the corridor, indifferent to the alien technology until, at the end of the passageway, she turned and knelt. From the alcove a warm, golden glow washed over her. Her lips moved, but the Agency lip-reading upgrade to Carl's implant could make no sense of her speech.

Whatever she said, she was … worshipful.

The surveillance system, motion sensitive, took no notice of what she saw!

Her devotions continued until—

The golden radiance brightened. Grace tipped up her face into the light. Her already rapturous expression waxed beatific.

The glow abruptly dimmed, and their perspective again shifted. They had a direct view into the alcove at the two coffinlike objects. Obscuring the cavity of the left-hand unit, a translucent field shimmered. An indistinct, man-tall shape tantalized through the luminosity. Atop the "coffin," a red lamp shone. A bomb: armed. Then the lamp blinked off and the glow began to ebb.

The right-hand unit must have begun the process somewhat earlier. In it, the last glimmers of light already ebbed. This vessel, too, held a figure. Its twitching had triggered the cameras.

This alien, they could see.

It had two upper limbs and two lower—and with that, any sense of the familiar ended. The alien had no head, its eyes and ears mounted on stalks that protruded from its shoulders. If shoulder was even the correct term: its arms and legs, like tapered tubes, without visible joints, appeared as boneless as an octopus's tentacles. Each limb ended in a cluster of lesser tentacles.

Apart from a broad, chest-high belt with many dangling pockets, the creature was naked (and if that body exhibited gender, Carl missed the clues). Its torso was a leathery, platinum gray; its limbs, mottled in shading, ranged from taupe to charcoal. Its mouth(s) and nostril(s), if it had such, were not evident. Perhaps they hid beneath the waist-level, fluttering band of fringes. In overall effect, the alien was more medusoid than humanoid—and not of *any* InterstellarNet species.

Stepping from the container—clearly, no coffin—the alien raised an "arm," its "fingers" spread.

Grace prostrated herself.

Tacitus netted, "An Intervener, I presume."

CHAPTER 34

"We should get moving," Carl said. "Can you erase our visit from the surveillance system or not?"

Her lips pursed, Joyce considered. "Maybe," she finally allowed.

"Decide. Every minute we stay risks us getting caught."

"I think so. That's the best I can give you till I try." She flung aside the door flap of the metal-mesh enclosure. "I'll have to work in the back."

"Okay, you do that while I finish packing." He had the enclosure's cover off its framework and had begun to fold the latter sooner than she could shuffle to the back corridor. "And tell Joshua to hurry up."

A few minutes later, as Carl crammed the last of his gear into his backpack, he heard Joyce call, "I have the most recent surveillance video. Do you want to see it?"

"Can you erase back to when we arrived?" Another complication occurred to him. "Oh, and can you deactivate surveillance for a half hour or so, give us time to clear out unnoticed?"

"Yes, to both. I think. You ready for me to try?"

"How are you coming, Joshua?"

"Still copying."

"Why is this taking so long?" Carl asked.

Joyce glanced up. "Not Josh's fault. The Intervener equipment barely creeps along at one gigahertz."

"Ten more minutes," Carl said. "We're already pushing our luck."

He set down his backpack. Other than odds and ends, their gear, including Tacitus' server, was packed and in an untidy heap by the air lock. Apart from getting into pressure suits, Carl saw nothing more to do.

He returned to the back corridor. Joyce sat on the floor, a pocket comp on her lap. A cable with a bulge near one end, like a snake digesting a mouse, drooped from a rack of Intervener electronics to her comp. The holo projecting from the comp showed Carl approaching. He waved. His likeness waved back.

She *had* tapped into the real-time feed.

He said, "Why don't you hold off till Joshua finishes before you try erasing? Whatever you're going to do might interfere with his downloading."

"Okay."

She sat waiting, looking weary, her fingers interlaced. Joshua stood, watching a pocket comp of his own, still copying. Carl stood, watching them.

In Joyce's holo, the motion-sensitive surveillance feed cut to an exterior camera.

Her face unmistakable through a helmet visor, Helena Strauss was bounding down the lava tube.

• • • •

For a moment Carl dared to hope the UPIA was after him. The Agency, when they could, took prisoners. The possibility this was an official op faded as he realized Helena was alone.

That clinched it: she was an Intervener mole—and people who as much as speculated about historical anomalies tended to get killed. How would an Intervener operative take to intruders in their secret facility?

Not well.

"What now?" Joyce asked.

Good question. Bluff? Try to talk their way out of this? That could get them all killed. Take on Helena as she came through the air lock? He'd have the element of surprise. But *she* was born to this gravity, likely combat trained, and many years his junior. The only training he'd done in, well, ages had anticipated fighting meter-tall Snakes in Ariel's pathetic gravity.

Suppose he somehow prevailed? Then they would learn the hard way whether, like Banak, she had a cranial bomb.

Which left what? The air lock offered the only way out.

In the holo, Helena skidded to a halt. She peered down at something off-camera—some bit of detritus or a boot scuff left by one of them?—then whipped a handgun from her holster.

So much for the element of surprise.

The first thing through the air lock was apt to be a flash-bang grenade. That's what *he* would do. They would be helpless when she followed.

"Joshua!" Carl called. "Stop whatever you're doing. Help me shift everything into the back corridor. We've got maybe four minutes till company arrives. Joyce, erase our digital tracks *now*."

On Carl's third trip—pressure suit draped over one arm and helmet in hand; Tacitus' server dangling from his other hand—the world lurched. Suddenly, he weighed a ton!

No, he weighed about what he would on Earth. Either way, the Interveners had some sort of artificial gravity! Somehow he made it across the threshold into the back corridor without dropping anything, set down his load, and latched the panel/door behind him.

"Sorry." Joyce, wide-eyed, sagged from the unaccustomed weight. "I must have done that, erased beyond the end of the memory buffer, clobbered some program."

"You couldn't have known," Carl said. He had more immediate problems. Her diddling with the computer had also killed the surveillance feed.

Helena wouldn't know whether the intruders had come and gone. When she arrived, though, she couldn't help but notice the high gravity. Loonie that she was, *she* would not have turned it up for herself.

Still, they knew Grace had had access to this place. It was possible Helena wouldn't question finding the gravity left at Earth's level.

Uh-huh. And how possible was it Helena wouldn't check here in the back?

"Suit up," Carl ordered. Just maybe, he had a useful idea. Taking

Joshua by the arm, he strode to the far end of the corridor. Together they dragged one of the coffinlike devices from its alcove, taking up the bit of slack in its cables, and turned it to face into the passageway.

Faintly, through the closed panel, Carl heard the cycling of the air lock. "To the front of the corridor," he whispered. "Then down flat on the floor."

Carl crouched behind the mound of their gear. Even from midcorridor the shot would be challenging, but he did not dare try from any nearer. How far had he been from Banak's coffin when it went off? He *had* to hit the detonator. Maybe—it all depended on the explosive—the bullet's impact would trigger a blast.

And maybe they were screwed.

Taking a deep breath, Carl aimed. The red dot of the handgun's laser designator lit his target. He fired.

The end of the corridor vanished in a fireball, smoke and flames sucked backward and out. The gale tugged at him even as the earsplitting roar faded. And something fiery punched into his arm!

"RUN!" he net-texted. His ears, and doubtless theirs, were ringing. He took a moment to slap a patch over the dime-sized, bloodsoaked rent in his suit sleeve. "Out through the back."

Joshua grabbed Tacitus with one hand, half guided, half carried Joyce with the other. Carl helped them scramble over rubble through the hole he had blasted. Then *he* was through, into the lava tube, air whistling from some lesser puncture to his pressure suit. Joshua and Joyce were a few steps ahead.

When the next explosion came, Carl sensed the tremor through his boot soles more than heard anything through the wisps of escaping air or with his still-ringing ears. That had it be Helena blasting open the hinged panel, rendered immovable by the outer room's air pressure.

Perhaps ten meters into the lava tube, Carl went soaring. Sparks erupted from the tunnel floor where, absent the abrupt restoration of lunar gravity, he would have been. Helena, shooting at him.

He was helpless, a floating duck, until he landed. The next shot *would* kill him.

There was no next shot.

When, at last, he settled to the ground, he saw that the lava-tube roof behind them had collapsed.

• • • •

The lava tube ran straight, intact and unobstructed, all the way to where they had hidden their ship. Wearily, they climbed aboard.

Taking a deep, calming breath, willing his hands not to tremble, Carl settled into the pilot's seat.

"Where to?" Joshua asked.

"Hold that thought," Carl said. "Meanwhile, buckle up."

With a bit of altitude, it was obvious. For at least a hundred meters the lava-tube roof, twenty-five meters thick, had come crashing down. The Intervener base was buried, if not crushed.

Helena Strauss would not be walking out of *that*.

Carl turned their ship toward Tycho City. "Let's take you two home."

CHAPTER 35

"Thanks for coming by," Agent McBride said.

Coming by did not begin to describe a no-notice recall to Earth and Agency headquarters, but Carl let the euphemism slide. Rather than a mirrored wall, this room—situated on an upper floor, not the dungeon level of his previous visit—offered two cubist oil paintings, a teak sideboard on spindly legs, and a small refrigerator. He settled deep into the lone hydraulic-assist chair, relieved to have it. He hadn't been offered such amenities at their previous encounter.

"Can I get you something to drink?" McBride continued. "Water? Coffee? Juice?"

Carl said, "What can I do for you, Agent?"

"The Agency is concluding the inquest into Danica Chidambaram's death. To be thorough, do you have anything to add or amend regarding your previous statement?"

"No." It was an answer Carl could as readily have given from the Moon.

"I see." McBride pushed away from the table. "Well, then, I guess that wraps things up."

That's it? "And?"

For an instant of déjà vu, as the door began to swing open, Carl expected Helena Strauss. Rather than the most recent dead woman to weigh on Carl's conscience, the cocky, charismatic figure striding through the door was a man Carl had never met but knew on sight.

Richard Lewis Agnelli: the long-time director of the UPIA.

"No, sit," Agnelli commanded, as Carl struggled to rise from his chair. "You just got here. As for the deaths on Ariel, consider that unfortunate matter closed. You have a provisional reinstatement. How does that sound?"

"Provisional, sir?"

"Don't worry. No matter what I do, the formalities always take way too long." His eyes narrowed. "Or is another shoe waiting to drop?"

Carl was again tempted. He still had Robyn Tanaka's COSMIC ULTRA-encrypted briefing file about the Interveners. He was sitting one-on-one with the chief of the whole damned Agency! Of *course* the man had COSMIC ULTRA capability.

Uh-huh. And that path, if Carl should go down it, led to the death of another Agency operative. Maybe once Tacitus had processed more of the Intervener recordings ....

Or not even then. The Agency director made all appointments to inquests into an agent's death. In Danica's case, Agnelli had assigned an Intervener mole. Had he known? Robyn's message had warned of compromise at the highest levels of the United Planets.

And as always at the oddest moment, the penny dropped. Of *course* the Charleston PD had back-burnered the Joshua Matthews disappearance. All it would have taken was an off-the-record "We can't tell you why, and you can't mention this" contact from someone well-placed within the Agency. Someone like Agnelli?

"No more shoes overhead, sir. Just asking."

McBride, meanwhile, was letting himself out. As the door closed, Carl's implant got a COSMIC ULTRA *ping*.

"We're shielded in this room," Agnelli netted.

"Yes, sir."

Agnelli took a seat at the table. "Twenty years without serious trouble from the Snakes, and *still* you kept requesting more surveillance, more resources, stricter rules. Plenty of people here consider you alarmist."

People such as Carl's immediate boss: conspicuously absent. "Yes, sir," Carl repeated.

"The thing is, my statistics gurus concur with your assessment. Reading between the lines of your former deputy's recent reports, something is not quite right on Ariel. Also, the two freighters that called on Ariel after you left are late in returning."

"Are you sending me back?"

As much as Carl wanted someone watching the Snakes—above all, keeping a skeptical eye on the Foremost—it had to be someone else. But could he decline without raising suspicions? And if he were to object, would Agnelli care?

"Back into what, Carl? That's *my* question. When I do send you back, it may be with shiploads of marines."

"You could send in the marines *now*."

"If it comes to a military occupation, a few weeks delay won't matter. There aren't that many Snakes, and they're stuck on Ariel."

"For the past couple of years," Carl cautiously corrected, "they were allowed to operate some scoop ships." Despite his urgent pleadings. "Harvesting deuterium from Uranus's atmosphere."

"A few scoop ships change nothing. Even if they were stupid enough to grab the overdue freighters. Hell, the Snakes are so rusty they lost their first two ships and crews despite all the training they were provided."

Carl knew when to change the subject. "Then when *do* you anticipate sending me back?"

"You'll tell me when." Agnelli leaned forward, with a flip-of-the-wrist dismissing the topic. "There's something else to discuss. I believe you've met the Armstrong City station chief."

"Helena Strauss," Carl netted. "Yes, she once invited me into her office."

"Well, she's missing without a trace. Nothing's been heard from her for days. No one up there admits to knowing where she might have gone."

"She said nothing to me."

"Agents checked her apartment, of course. They discovered no indications she expected to be away. They scarcely found any sign she lived there."

"I see."

"I wish I did," Agnelli netted. "Are her people covering for her? Are they involved in something *with* her? I need to know. I need an outsider to take a look." Added with a flash of pique, "To judge from the progress we're not making with the Tanaka Astor assassination, I could use a lot of fresh talent."

Nor would they make progress, not with an Intervener-penetrated agency investigating an Intervener murder. He could—

Uh-uh. No way. Getting himself assigned to that investigation would mean someone else looking into Helena's disappearance. Carl couldn't take that risk.

"I understand, sir." *I understand that a person did not get more outside than by spending his past two decades around Uranus.*

"That station needs someone senior—ASAP!—to fill in, to direct the search for Agent Strauss. You want somewhere off Earth to work while assessing the ambiguous situation on Ariel. The Loonie staff might grumble because none of them got the gig, but no one will question your temporary assignment."

"No, sir." And with the resources of a major Agency field office, he might make faster progress on his own investigation. If his new team didn't arrest him ….

"And Carl?"

"Yes, sir?"

"Find Helena Strauss. Whether she's been abducted or killed or has chosen to disappear, something on the Moon is very wrong."

• • • •

Back on the Moon, Carl soon found he had taken on *three* jobs: divination, from a very great distance, of Snake scheming. Guiding, and when necessary, misguiding, the expanding investigation into Helena Strauss's disappearance. Overseeing routine ops of fifty-two agents, almost a third of them AIs, involved in everything from infiltrating gun-runners to battling interplanetary drug cartels, from offering logistical support on pirate hunts (most of the presumed hijacked ships having disappeared far out-system) to investigating a massive, possibly longstanding network penetration on Farside. (If that breach turned out, as Carl half expected, to be illicit AI enhancement, it would be only a Class I violation. Still, any hint of

AI runaway was taken seriously—not that *he* could do much beyond assign AI agents to investigate. It took an AI to catch any AI, much less a rogue.) The silver lining of his massive overload was that no one questioned the crazy long hours he worked—

And that was fortunate. It helped to cover the few hours he squeezed in for his *fourth* job: making sense of the Interveners. Joshua, bless him, had fled the alien base with pocketfuls of down-loaded data.

About a tiny subset of that data, sanitized by Joyce, the unsus-pecting lip-reading linguist camped outside Carl's office was eager to talk.

He motioned her in.

"It's very curious, sir," Faith Horowitz began. She was a recent hire, young and earnest, pretty in a quiet way.

"Close the door and sit," he told her.

"Curious," she repeated. "Where did you get this vid clip?"

"That's need-to-know information."

"And the other side of the conversation?"

That was *really* need-to-know. Joyce had edited out the medu-soid alien, and not merely because of the lack of visible lips to be read. "Sorry."

"Hmm," Faith said.

"I can tell you this much. The woman"—Grace DiMeara—"was ship's pilot on a recent flight to Ariel. As far as anyone knows, she is a native English speaker."

"Well, I can tell *you* this much. Your pilot is a linguist."

"Because she bothered to learn another language?" With neural implants handling routine translations, and AI specialists for hire to translate the obscure languages lesser software could not manage, few people bothered.

"No," Faith said. "Because she learned Basque."

"What's Basque?"

Straightening in her chair, Faith struck a pedantic pose. "The longest surviving pre-Indo-European language of Western Europe. The Basque region straddles the Pyrenees Mountains."

"Take pity on an old spacer."

"The border region between the onetime European nation-states of France and Spain."

He had heard of those. "Thank you. Proceed."

"Linguists classify Basque as an isolate, unrelated to any of the language groups spoken nearby. French and Spanish, for example, are Romance languages, derived from the Vulgar Latin. Basque, in contrast, was—"

"Was?"

"Was. Apart from historians and linguists, I don't know that Basque has been spoken in a century or more. You said native English speaker. Where is the subject from?"

"North America," Carl said. Grace's records—swept up among the records of everyone who had visited Ariel in the past standard year—had provided a succession of addresses across that continent. Carl had Agency people on Earth checking out her former residences. "When not off-world, of course."

"Hmm."

"So: what does our linguist pilot have on her mind?"

"Hard to say." Faith squirmed in her seat. "I'm waiting to hear back from the experts."

"Aren't *you* the expert?"

"On dead languages? I wish. Much less ..."

"Much less *what*, Faith?"

"I've analyzed enough lip, face, and tongue activity to be confident that I've identified the language, but the match nonetheless is inexact. Your pilot isn't speaking *quite* like any extant recording."

"You mean she has a lisp? A speech impediment?" On Ariel, Carl had spent the better part of an hour chatting with Grace. He hadn't heard a trace of either. "Maybe she has an atrocious accent."

Faith hesitated. "Languages change with time. Pronunciations, as well. The thing is, before audio recording any estimate as to the rate of such shifts is quite speculative ..."

Before recording? But Thomas Edison (quick Internetopedia look-up) invented the phonograph cylinder in 1878. More than three centuries ago! "Go ahead. Speculate."

Faith said, "How this could be so, much less why, eludes me—but you asked. In my best professional judgment, your Basque-speaking spaceship pilot speaks a sixteenth-century dialect."

CHAPTER 36

In the time Joshua took to reheat a mug of coffee, Tacitus had been to Earth, shopped, integrated his purchase, and returned to the Moon.

Joshua found it a very long minute.

"*That's* the way to travel." Tacitus netted, announcing his arrival. His avatar, perhaps channeling Mercury, sported winged sandals. "And it seems I'd have been here milliseconds earlier, except for the virus de jour. I got rerouted around two quarantined comsats."

Milliseconds. Poor baby. "You were discreet, I trust," Joshua replied.

"Who is going to question an historian's interest in old languages? And to avoid drawing attention to Basque, I acquired information on a half dozen other extinct European languages. Would you care to chat in Etruscan or Sabine?"

"Maybe later." *Much later.* "How about lip reading?"

"That's trickier." Tacitus straightened his toga. "I understand the physiological basis of speech reading. That's the formal term, you know, not *lip* reading. The problem is, more than one sound may share outward facial and mouth positions, just as the letters 'p' and 'b' do in English. Other sounds are articulated deep within the throat; they don't provide any visual cues. To a speech reader, 'Where there's life, there's hope' *looks* identical to 'where's the lavender soap.'

"Ask me if I can speech read English, and the answer is yes. That's because I understand English idiom, social conventions, and common turns of phrase. I can fill in some gaps and resolve from context many of the aural ambiguities. But spoken Basque? At best, my ability to read *that* will be spotty. And that's apart from issues in translating into English from an old dialect of a dead language."

"And the Interveners?" Joshua asked, sure he knew the answer.

"If they even have lips." Tacitus shrugged. "Suppose we find vids that show them speaking. I still won't understand their physiology. Until we locate audio files and Joyce figures out how Intervener anatomy produces sounds, we're not going to know that side of any conversation."

They had hundreds, if not thousands, of hours of surveillance. Grandma continued to index and organize the purloined archive. Of all that vid, Joshua had spent—obsessed—the longest time on the very first archival sample he had seen: Grace DiMeara awakening two Interveners. Carl had given a snippet from that vid to his expert.

The UPIA expert's eventual, hesitant translation: "Welcome back, my lords."

Joshua linked a segment from that vid. "Can you interpret this?" he asked.

"I *have* interpreted it. While we've chatted, I've already processed almost a hundred hours of surveillance vids. My disclaimers denote experience, not pessimism." Because interacting with a mere human required the merest fraction of an AI's attention. "Here is a vid I think you'll find more interesting."

Joshua needed a second to spot the difference. This time it was Helena Strauss who genuflected before the two alien hibernation pods.

"Okay," Joshua netted. "What does *this* video say?"

"Here is the dubbed version. Remember, we have only one side of the conversation."

In the vid, Helena knelt before the pods, her eyes sparkling with adoration, her lips moving. And Joshua heard (wondering how Tacitus chose the voice qualities): "Bless me with your presence, oh great ones."

Stepping from its pod, an alien raised a "hand," its "fingers" spread. Perhaps it spoke; perhaps its only communication was the gesture.

Helena prostrated herself.

The alien made its way gracefully to a nearby keyboard. It did not walk, exactly, nor did it stride, lope, or glide. The fluid, boneless motion of its lower tentacles failed to match any verb that Joshua could retrieve. Its frenetic keystrokes evoked rapidly scrolling text—in alien characters, undecipherable—on a flat display. Reviewing what had gone on while it slept?

"Is this playback in real time?" Joshua asked, marveling at the flood of text.

"More or less," Tacitus netted. "The vid is just a succession of still images, after all. I've approximated the playback rate from the characteristics of human speech."

Presented to Joshua's mind's eye: more typing on the alien keyboard. Then flashing screens: indecipherable text interspersed with images. Joshua recognized a starship. At the rate the images flashed past, he could not decide which ship. If *Victorious*, before its destruction.

("Terrestrial and lunar broadcasts," Tacitus commented. "And if you wondered, that ship is *Discovery*.")

The second alien exited its alcove. Its sensor stalks tipped forward, suggestive of listening, and then it gestured to Helena to rise.

"Welcome back, my lord," she said.

The first alien turned. Perhaps it spoke, because Helena cringed. "Our people have sinned," she admitted.

("I infer from body language that she spoke in a low voice," Tacitus commented.)

Then, maddeningly, perhaps triggered by the wriggling of fingers/tentacles, the camera zoomed in on just one alien. *Were its motions sign language?* Joshua wondered. *Fidgeting? Some alien mannerism that he could not imagine?*

Whatever the reason, the view remained off Helena and without narration for more than a minute.

When their viewpoint switched back, Helena cowered lower than ever. "We should not wander," she whispered.

To other star systems, Joshua took that.

Their view returned for a long while to the alien.

When Helena reappeared to them, her face was ashen, her eyes downcast. "Do not forsake your children. Give"—pause—"chance to work this out, my lord."

("She was muttering," Tacitus commented. "I can't interpret that bit.")

Several more seconds of the alien silence: eerie.

"The Xool are wise. Let my lords be merciful, too," Helena pleaded.

"Xool?" Joshua asked.

"Not a Basque word, as far as I know," Tacitus netted. "From context, that's the Interveners' name for themselves."

"Be merciful?" *What if they weren't? These beings had shaped the destinies of worlds!* "As in, don't do what?"

Tacitus had no answer.

"Your humble servants will stop the starship," Helena continued. Seconds later, reacting to something not in view, she straightened just a bit. Her voice firmed. "Thank you, my lords."

"Pause," Joshua netted. The playback froze. "There's a sixteenth-century Basque word for starship?"

"That word was in modern English," Tacitus conceded, "nor was it the first instance in the recordings of non-Basque interjections. English tech terms crop up often."

"But why target *Discovery*? It isn't the first."

"True, but *Harmony* become *Victorious* was hijacked, and then it got blown up. As for *New Beginnings*, it's long out of contact."

"Are you suggesting the Xool got to one or both of them?"

"Can you say for certain that they or their saboteurs didn't?"

"No," Joshua admitted.

In the case of *Harmony*, they might never know. As for *New Beginnings*, it would be years reaching comm range of Alpha Centauri. When it did get close enough, any report relayed by the Centaurs would take more years to reach the Solar System.

If it got close enough.

"Enough with the rampant speculation." Because Joshua felt his head was about to explode. "Let's stick closer to the hard data."

Such as that Grace DiMeara appeared in the alien vids and flew Corinne to *Discovery*. Such as that Corinne's regular pilot took ill without warning—just as Joshua had, when the Xool set out to disappear and discredit him.

He shivered. Helena's promise had been unambiguous. *Your humble servants will stop the starship.*

• • • •

Joshua yawned. He rubbed his eyes. His med chip yet again scolded him, this time about twenty-*six* hours without sleep; he banished the nagging from his mind's ear. In the half-full glass by his side the soda had gone flat and tepid, but he swigged it anyway for the caffeine. Another jolt of meds would be two too many.

Perhaps the med chip had a point.

"Where is my grandmother?" he netted Tacitus.

"Gone out for food. Try listening next time."

She should have gone home to sleep! Still, come to think of it, he *was* hungry. Until Grandma returned to his apartment, maybe work would keep his mind off the rumblings of his gut. And if not, maybe he would find *something* else useful.

In days they had gone from too little data to, the case could be made, way too much. The challenge was in winnowing any useful information from all these downloaded petabytes. The major find so far that day, trawling at random, seeking—as yet in vain—for the organizing principle of the archive, was the record of another Grace DiMeara visit to the Xool base. Her purpose that time, as Tacitus' lip reading made clear, was to report to her masters on the Snake Subterfuge.

That was eighty-three years ago! And Grace seemed little changed. Grandma hadn't commented, but he could see it made her feel ancient.

Joshua poked and prodded his latest excerpt of the data. Much was fascinating. Most only mystified him. Nothing answered what he most yearned to know, where the Xool had gone and what their purpose was. And then he stumbled upon—

The mother lode: decade upon decade of intercepted terrestrial and lunar news broadcasts, talking heads speaking straight toward the camera. Well-known events and English screen crawls provided exact Earth dates even when lip reading failed them. Tacitus had already inferred the Xool numbering scheme. Now, matching known dates with Xool annotations, the AI derived the time units implicit in each field of the alien timestamps.

"Dig!" Joshua netted. "Date the earliest record in the archive."

"I already have," Tacitus replied. "Call it 580 million years ago."

• • • •

When Tacitus followed the trail forward they got their biggest surprise.

The surveillance segment showed Grace and Helena together at the Xool base. Whatever the aliens had to convey took a long while, a camera switching to the women only for the occasional obeisance or deferential murmur of acknowledgment. With each reappearance, the women's faces were more grim.

"When, Tacitus?" Joshua asked.

"About six months ago."

In the vid, the last color drained from Grace DiMeara's face. "When will you return, my lords?"

The aliens' answer, maddeningly, was unknowable.

"We shall await your return," Grace said.

"We know what we must do," Helena added. "Have a safe journey home."

Return from where! Joshua wanted to scream at the vid. *Where is home?*

With heads bowed, the women stood by as the Xool wriggled into their vacuum gear. The aliens went out together through their base's air lock. After several hundred meters along the lava tube, they had left the range of cameras.

A half hour later the aliens reappeared to cameras strung along a different expanse of lava tube. Scorch marks dotted the tube floor. A short distance inside, perched upon spidery trusses, sat a flattened ball. Pointy protuberances festooned its bulging waist. By comparison with the aliens, the—whatever—was perhaps ten meters high and fifteen across.

A retreat? A place more comfortable than the human-friendly rooms? Then why the pointy things? Whatever the object was, it had an air lock. The aliens went in. The outer hatch closed—and the timestamp digits jumped.

"About fifteen minutes have passed," Tacitus interpreted.

What motion had triggered the camera? Had the object somehow shifted? Vibrated? Joshua stared, trying to decide—

Until, atop a brilliant column of flame, the Xool *ship* lifted off. In seconds, it had vanished from the camera's sight.

Gone ... home?

CHAPTER 37

Agnelli's meeting was running late.

"The director will be with you in a minute," the perky blond executive assistant told Carl. That would have been a welcome reassurance if he hadn't already heard it five times. And if intel crises were not unscheduled and unscheduleable.

In theory, he could be using the time to organize his thoughts. To an extent, he did. More, he struggled to stay upright in the anteroom chair. Damned Earth gravity.

He would scold himself another time about allowing his exercise regimen to slide.

When, at last, Carl got to enter the inner sanctum, whoever had last seen Agnelli had exited by a rear door. Digital wallpaper showed only Alpine scenery. Agnelli looked harried.

The director was not one for chit-chat. Within a few sentences, including the pro forma question whether Carl would like something to drink and a more sincere offer (that Carl likewise declined) of a mobile hydraulic-assist chair, Agnelli got down to business. Over a COSMIC ULTRA link he netted, "You didn't come all this way just to chew the fat. Did you discover something about Helena Strauss?"

"We continue to turn over rocks."

Because whether from Agency training or Xool, Helena had been a pro at covering her tracks. Her many cover IDs—although neither Carl nor anyone he had assigned to the case believed all had been found—made Helena's disappearance appear planned.

The cover IDs *he* had built for her appeared to trace back to the same computer break-in that had trashed the backup memories of AIs and Augmented, including Robyn Tanaka Astor's. Until this oppressive gravity began compressing his spine, he had appreciated the poetic justice: Intervener sabotage used to mask his penetration of the Intervener conspiracy.

Carl continued, "I came to update you on the situation on Ariel."

"Snakes being Snakes?"

"Amazing, isn't it?" Carl netted back. "The deeper I dig into comm logs, even back to my departure, the surer I am. Bruce Wycliffe"—Carl's erstwhile deputy—"isn't being himself. Glithwah must be up to something."

"Despite pols going on about bygones and new generations, it's the rare person in *this* building who trusts the Snakes." The secure connection broke. Aloud, Agnelli continued, "But there hasn't been a duress code in any of the reports. Correct?"

"Correct," Carl said. "And the regular authentication codes *are* present. I still stand by my conclusion."

Agnelli would connect the dots: the Agency's remaining asset on Ariel had been compromised or coerced.

"And the experts agree?" asked the director.

"*I'm* the expert for Ariel. I'm the expert on Snakes *and* Bruce Wycliffe. Forget that analysts say the variances from earlier messages are statistically inconclusive. Don't ask me to put my finger on specific words or phrases"—because specifics would risk giving those analysts proof he was fudging—"but reading between the lines ...."

"Understood. You've sent your own challenge messages to Ariel?"

"Of course. And received the proper canned response to each one."

"As you would whether or not your man Bruce were compromised." Agnelli frowned. "What's your recommendation? Send in the Navy? Because they're busy hunting and not finding pirates."

"Not yet. I *could* be mistaken."

"And we don't need an inter-world, inter-species incident."

"I'd think not, sir." Carl was counting on that reticence. If the marines *did* go to Ariel, he'd surely be sent with them, and he had other places to be. If the implication of creating grief within the InterstellarNet community hadn't done the trick, he would have mused about how the do-gooder lobby would react to military reoccupation of Ariel. The do-gooders already felt the Ariel population were the victims of collective punishment.

That's what you get when you collectively invade the Solar System.

But for once, the Snakes weren't Carl's biggest worry. Not even close. And at a loss whom at the UPIA he could trust, he had settled on the next best thing: getting out word about the Xool to *everyone*.

Sad to say, he was the worst possible choice for making the announcement. Skeptics—and who wouldn't be?—would see only a disgruntled employee. The Agency would point to Carl's involvement in a fellow agent's death, his recall under a cloud from Ariel, and the weeks he'd spent cooling his heels on administrative leave. Two decades earlier, the Agency had buried his troubled past; they could as easily leak a few details if it served them. (It *would* serve Xool moles he had to assume yet remained inside the Agency.) Meanwhile, cynics outside the Agency could disparage the digital "proof" copied from Xool archives as fabricated with the sophisticated UPIA tools he had at his disposal.

No matter that Corinne sometimes fretted she was a has-been, in her day she had broken huge stories. She was rich, famous, and widely known. The general public would far sooner believe her than some unknown spook with a sketchy background, or an infamous drunk, or the drunk's elderly grandma.

Only Corinne—and with her *Discovery*'s long-range transmitter, at intra-Solar System distances all but impossible to jam—was far, far away.

At least he knew Helena had not lied about Corinne ending up on Prometheus. When, leveraging his temporary authority as station chief, he had reached out to Prometheus, the *Discovery* mission office there had relayed both his message to Corinne and her reply.

In the brief recording Corinne had been allowed to send, gatecrasher that she was, she hadn't say much. The vid clip itself, though? It said lots.

Carl had played that clip, studied it, over and over. Corinne and Grace, seated side by side, drink bulbs in hand, in a noisy dining area. Both seemed healthy. In the curved window wall behind them,

Saturn and its rings served as a spectacular backdrop.

Two men and a woman were visible behind Corinne, seated at another table. When he'd run their images through facial-recognition software, all three showed up in public files as Discovery construction workers. The snippet of their conversation that audio enhancement separated from the background din was innocent, having to do with overtime pay.

But Carl hadn't allow himself truly to believe the vid authentic and Corinne safe until the best analytical tools he had—which were the best tools the Agency had—could find nothing digitally manipulated in the vid clip.

He had to get out there—only apart from mission personnel and naval forces, no one was welcome anywhere near Prometheus. On a chartered ship or a stolen one, Carl arriving in a private capacity would do no good. But if he could get to Prometheus under the apparent imprimatur of the UPIA …

And get the word out before Grace accomplished whatever she had had in mind when a "parts failure" stranded her and Corinne there. *(Your humble servants will stop the starship.)*

The stakes were too damned high!

Agnelli cleared his throat. "I assume you have a recommendation?"

"I do, sir." Carl took a deep breath. "I make a surprise inspection of Ariel, arriving unannounced aboard the fastest, stealthiest courier the Agency has."

"And suppose the Snakes coerce *you*? Suppose they've compromised your man and he reviews or fakes your reports?"

"If you don't hear from me, you'll know to send in the marines. If you get a report purportedly from me, it had better be in new protocols, that we'll define unique to this inspection. Protocols that Bruce can't know."

The words meant: you'll know, one way or another, sooner than they can coerce *me*.

"Okay," Agnelli decided. On one office wall, ship's specs had displaced the digital scenery. "*Hermes* is on standby at Basel

Spaceport. Good enough?"

A top-of-the-line courier. Top-of-the-line Agency stealth gear. Full comms and crypto, too. "That will do," Carl said.

He and Joshua would arrive in the Saturn system, unannounced and unsuspected, aboard an official UPIA vessel, before Carl could be expected at Ariel. On the way he'd work on ways to take Grace into custody that *didn't* give her the option to go out like Banak.

CHAPTER 38

Standing tall, standing proud, Arblen Ems Firh Glithwah, Foremost, bestrode the bridge of her temporary flagship. *Champion*, she had renamed the vessel. Its original name had scarcely befitted the freighter this had once been, much less a mighty Hunter warship. Any objections the ship's erstwhile human crew might have had had ceased to matter.

Glithwah gave her tactical display a glance.

"At full readiness across the fleet," summarized Rashk Pimal, the chief tactical officer. He had to raise his voice above the earnest whispers that emanated from a dozen duty stations.

Twenty-seven icons clustered in the holo, one for each ship of her fleet. The vessels ranged from tiny and agile couriers to huge mining ships. Some carried armed warriors. Others conveyed battalions of combat robots. After the initial two ships, condescendingly bestowed, their reported "loss" much sneered at, her navy had been honorably and cleverly seized. And every ship—however modest its origins, no matter how defenseless in its original form—now bristled with missiles and laser cannons from the clandestine factories on the moon Caliban.

But more precious than armaments, these twenty-seven vessels carried the future of clan Arblen Ems. The entire clan, apart from a few noble volunteers, had squeezed onto these ships. A handful of veterans too old to survive the coming migration had stayed behind on Ariel to maintain the charade of normalcy. To greet—and as necessary, to neutralize—any unannounced visitors. So that the clan could rid itself of United Planets paternalism and rules. So that all could be *free*.

If this fleet prevailed.

Moment by moment, day by day, her gamble looked more promising. As deep into space as passive sensors could peer, not a single enemy vessel was detected. The UP navy had scattered—all according to her plan—across the Solar System. Chasing pirates. Chasing ghosts. Maneuvered off the game board.

Naïfs.

"Recent changes in deployment?" Glithwah probed.

Pimal detailed the latest subtle reconfigurations, the real-time jostlings and rearrangements, and the recoveries from same, inevitable when most crews had trained only on simulators. In the days since departing Ariel, most crews had already shown improvement. He concluded, "Confident, Foremost, of preparedness for battle."

"Excellent," Glithwah said, although she did not expect much of a battle. The clan would have in their favor surprise and local numerical superiority. Not to mention her unsuspected robot army ...

Baring her teeth in joy and anticipation, raising her voice to be heard by everyone across the bridge, Glithwah asked, "And offensive preparations?"

At Pimal's netted directive, the view in the main tactical holo zoomed outward. Far ahead of the main fleet, icon clusters marked three waves of the strike team. The raiders were radar stealthed. Dark as space. Scarcely detectable in infrared—if one were looking straight at them—by the waste heat of their idling reactors. And if, like *Champion*, one's line of sight to the raiders did *not* point straight into the glow of the sun.

If sensors in the Saturn system saw *anything* headed their way, the dim heat signatures of the onrushing forces would be dismissed as the diffuse traces of a spent solar flare.

Before the duty shift ended, the front wave would begin decelerating full-out. Even then, with their fusion drives operating at full capacity, they would be difficult to spot with the sun behind them.

Until it was too late.

． ． ． ．

This nightmare was of the up-close-and-personal variety: of desperate combat, hand to hand, cabin by cabin, deck by deck, for control of *Victorious*. The battle that all sides had lost.

Corinne tossed and turned, flailed and moaned. Time and again she drifted just close enough to consciousness to know that, yet once more, the old ordeal—more vivid than ever—held her in thrall. Time and again, she fell back into the nightmare.

A dozen or so marines, the survivors of a failed rescue attempt. Carl, too: their pilot. Prisoners, Centaur crew and human kidnap victims alike, stressed and stretched beyond endurance. Snakes, warriors and civilians, fighting for *their* lives. Charge and countercharge. Lasers and crowbars, Molotov cocktails and sheer rage.

Chaos.

Klaxons shrieking and alarms strobing. Smoke tickling her nose. The sizzling of laser strikes. The tooth-rattling *boom* of explosions. Shaking. Trembling. Corinne held her pillow over her head, whimpering.

Her eyes flew open as, directly over her head, a siren pulsed and wailed. She didn't recognize the pattern. Make that two patterns, alternating. Grace wasn't in her cot to ask, nor did her friend answer a netted query. The public-safety channel, when Corinne netted in, advised without explanation: Emergency personnel report to duty stations. Everyone else, remain where you are.

She had no assigned duty station, and didn't need one. A reporter's duty station was wherever news happened. Delaying only to strap on magnetic slippers and clip on her ID badge, Corinne was out the door and into the hallway—and almost run over. "What's going—"

Two naval enlisted shot past her, headed, she guessed, for the base main air lock. Seconds later, a rumpled-looking naval lieutenant running in the opposite direction, without slowing, without speaking, shoved her back through her open door.

Flynn, the lieutenant's name was. He liaised between the local naval brass and the civilian project office—and also, with evident disdain, after the restrictions on her had been relaxed, twice with Corinne. Given his mundane duties, neither the military types nor the civvies had any respect for the man. For his perpetual-and-annoying smile, behind Flynn's back many called him Dimples.

He wasn't smiling today.

The sirens wailed again, from a ceiling speaker a scant half meter from her head. Signifying what? She netted to the base public-service database. Of the alternating tone patterns that continued to throb, in the once more empty corridor and in her cabin, only one of the sequences was listed. *Emergency lockdown.*

With her heart pounding, she looked up the navy's alert codes. *Battle stations.*

Habit kicked in, and Corinne set her implant to record. With luck the blaring alarms could be digitally removed later. After a few seconds, blessedly, the klaxons warbled and died.

Dimples had gone off in the direction of the base main control room. Not allowing time for second thoughts, Corinne dashed after him. Here and there along eerily deserted corridors, behind doors just slightly ajar, faces peered out. Most looked terrified.

Me, too.

Faintly, through floor and boots—once, twice, three times—she felt the fierce vibration of a nearby ship launching.

She joined the handful of people queued up to enter the control room. The woman ahead of Corinne turned to glower. "They won't let you in. Authorized personnel only."

"What's going on?"

"Return to your cabin," the woman said. "It's for your own safety."

Safety from what? Beyond the line, past the open door, a big holo display brimmed with icons. Hundreds of tiny blips, all in red, converging. A second swarm, likewise inbound, was emerging around the limb of Saturn. With image enhancement in her implant, she could, just barely, read some of the labels. None of the red blips had accompanying traffic-control icons.

Whoever they were, they were coming in hot. They were decelerating at—six gees!

From a control-room console a warning issued, "… Ships en route to Prometheus, this is Admiral Matsushita of the United Planets Navy. Be advised, you are approaching restricted space. Entrance without authorization is strictly prohibited. Repeat. Unidentified ships en route …"

Corinne kept eying—and recording—the dynamic situation in the big display. The translucent sphere at the center of the holo had to stand for Prometheus. The white cylinder not far off, amid five green blips, had to be *Discovery*.

Another three green blips crept outward from the sphere. Those *had* been launches she'd felt. Gone to protect the starship, she supposed—only her gut insisted they were getting the *hell* away from the antimatter plant on Prometheus.

Titan and Rhea, on opposite sides of the display, each had its own swarm of blips: scattered green dots among many white. She interpreted the color coding as a few naval vessels amid many more civilian ships. Would the navy strip those worlds bare of defenses for the sake of Prometheus—where UP forces would *still* be badly outnumbered?

"… Be advised, you are approaching restricted space. Entrance without authorization is strictly …"

When she and Grace had arrived, disinvited, two naval corvettes had escorted *Odyssey* to its present berth. From that experience, Corinne knew the size of UP corvettes—just as, from research and Donald's guided tour, she understood just how large *Discovery* was. The nearby blips, representing the ships within optical range, were shown to scale. If the onrushing red blips were also to scale? They'd be tiny.

What the hell were they?

The navy's looping broadcast stuttered and stopped. A new message began. "Unidentified ships approaching Prometheus, change course immediately or you will be fired upon. Repeat. Unidentified ships approaching …"

Two more project staff went into the control room, and Corinne found herself at the threshold.

"Ma'am," a hulking marine said icily, squinting at her ID. His badge read *Chang*. "Authorized personnel only. Return to your cabin."

"Flynn, who's attacking?" Corinne called into the control room.

"Get that woman out of here!" someone inside—*not* Flynn— barked. Corinne recognized the raspy voice: Annabeth Miller, *Discovery* project manager. "And close the damned door."

Apart from activities on Prometheus' surface and the project team's squadron of short-range shuttles, this control room didn't *control* anything. Whatever action the naval forces undertook would be run out of the admiral's flagship. There was no reason she *shouldn't* be inside, watching alongside everyone else.

Corinne said, "The public has a right to—"

"*Now*, Sergeant," Miller ordered.

"Yes, sir," Chang said, grabbing her elbow. He out-massed her by at least thirty kilos. "Come on."

"Like it or not," Corinne protested as the sergeant took her in tow, "this is history." Two paces down the hall, she yelled, "Someone from the press needs to *be* there."

Two turns later, almost back to her cabin, the marine skidded to a abrupt halt. "New orders. I'm to bring you back."

"Why?" she asked.

"They didn't say."

Corinne opened the control-room door to find Annabeth Miller slumped against a wall. The woman looked … drained. In the holo, the eight green blips of the local fleet were forming a tight cluster around *Discovery*. The starship's top acceleration was one-third gee. It seemed to Corinne that *Discovery* hadn't even attempted to flee—and so, neither could its defenders.

The leading wave of red blips was closer than ever, still racing straight at them, still decelerating flat-out. The second wave was also plainly converging on Prometheus. A third wave, fewer in number than either of the earlier groups, but individually much larger, had appeared from behind Saturn. These last ships were decelerating at just two gees.

"What happened?" Corinne asked.

"A response."

Corinne took Miller answering her as permission to enter.

A new voice, a synthesized voice, issued from the comm console. "… UP forces near Prometheus, withdraw or be destroyed. We are taking possession of *Discovery* and the moon. Repeat. UP Naval forces near Prometheus, withdraw or be destroyed. We are taking …"

"Our guys are hopelessly outnumbered," Corinne said.

Miller sagged further. "I know."

• • • •

By the minute, the mood inside the control room grew gloomier. "We're being invaded." Corinne struggled to keep the fear from her voice. She was *working*, damn it. "By whom?"

"By what, I think." Miller gestured to an aux display. "By those."

Through the glare of a white-hot fusion drive, even the best digital enhancement could discern little; even a rude outline made Corinne shiver. All angles and tubes, struts and antennae and engine, it offered little to suggest an inhabitable volume. "Robots?"

"Drones." Lt. Flynn swiveled in his seat to look at them. "Battle drones. Those tubes? I'm fairly sure they're missile launchers."

As though cued by the word *missiles*, half of the defending force launched a salvo. Tiny bright dots—like so many gnats—in the holo marked the outbound missiles.

"Are they suicidal?" Miller muttered.

"No," said Flynn, "they're proud. They won't, they *can't* give up without firing a shot."

A counter salvo, twice as large, burst from the front wave of drones.

Their pride is going to get them killed, Corinne thought.

In the display, the encounter of barrage and counter-barrage was a firecracker-like string of soundless explosions. A few UP missiles came through the encounter unscathed—to blink out, moments later.

"What happened?" Miller asked.

"Antimissile lasers," Flynn said. "In a vacuum, without dust or gas to scatter light, the beams are invisible."

Missiles had run the gauntlet going the other way, too. Closing on the paltry few defenders, some of those, too, blinked out. Not all.

"*Orion*," Flynn said in anguish as a green blip flashed, then faded to a dim, washed-out shade. "They took a hit. Their main drive is down."

"Withdraw or be destroyed," the intruders transmitted once again.

The UP warships responded with a fresh salvo, met with another counter salvo. The front wave of red blips, closing fast, deployed into a … Corinne found she lacked the vocabulary. A big, threatening formation, ready to engulf *Discovery* and its guardians.

On most of the drones, decelerated to a near halt, the white-hot fusion exhausts vanished. The … wings? … of the formation would soon meet behind the starship.

"I should *be* with them," Flynn growled.

In a low, discouraged voice, he attempted to explain the tactics, the maneuvers, the thrust and parry of the battle. All that Corinne processed (trusting in her implant to record the details) was that human ships with flesh-and-blood crews would always be outmaneuvered by drones with none. And that the local UP forces, outnumbered as they were, finally had no choice—the three surviving ships, anyway—but to pull back. Admiral Matsushita, in his parting transmission vowed to return.

At battle's end, as one drone constellation took shape around *Discovery* and a second around Prometheus, Flynn still refused to speculate who, if anyone, controlled the drones.

But Corinne thought she knew—hoping desperately that she was mistaken.

· · · ·

Tracing low, tight orbits around Prometheus, stripped of the blinding glare of active fusion drives, the drones, though stealthy and dark, could no longer disguise their nature from surface sensors. No living being could be aboard any of these tiny vessels.

Corinne thought, *Sometimes seeing is worse than imagining.*

But waiting was the worst.

The mute drones overhead were also waiting. On their side, it seemed to be for the final wave of intruders. Those, without doubt, were *human* ships! They approached Prometheus in radio silence.

And then three of the intruders' ships were descending.

Throughout the base and, on the little moon's opposite side, in the hastily shut-down antimatter factory, personnel still huddled wherever the emergency had found them. Miller gave a quick update over the intercom to personnel still huddling wherever the lockdown had found them. She concluded, "For your own safety, remain where you are. Avoid acting in any manner that might be construed as threatening. Cooperate. The navy will be back to help."

Will it? Corinne wondered, as three ships swooped toward a landing.

"This is Corinne Elman," she began, "reporting live from the beleaguered world of Prometheus." She spoke to everyone in the control room, to posterity, and—assuming the navy was relaying—to the Solar System. And so, to Denise.

"Unidentified military forces continue to besiege us. Some are soon to land. As we wait, our fates unclear, we know that the brave men and women of the United Planets navy, outnumbered and outgunned, did their best to—"

"Where's Dimples?" someone asked in a stage whisper.

"Stepped out," another answered. "Ten minutes ago, maybe?"

"Their best to defend us and the mission," Corinne continued doggedly. "After heavy losses they—"

With the battle lost, the control-room main display now cycled among the base's several outside cameras. From fiery sparks in the sky, descending, Corinne's view flipped to the Prometheus "spaceport": a bulldozed plain pocked with scorch marks. And on the periphery, amid a jumble of boulders—

A figure in a spacesuit, aiming a short tube.

"Jesus, that's *Flynn* out there," Miller said.

The control-room window overlooked the spaceport. As Corinne turned to see, yellow-orange fire burst from his tube. And then, almost too fast to take in:

—Flame, streaking skyward, vanishing into the white-hot seething exhaust of a descending freighter.

—Countless laser blasts, lancing downward from ships and orbiting drones, rendered manifest in sudden eruptions of gas, dust, and steam.

—And, above Flynn's glowing, rapidly dissipating, vaporous remains, where his missile had struck ... an enormous fireball.

• • • •

Laser pistols in hand, snarling, two armored Snake soldiers strode into the control room.

Corinne felt her eyes go round. This couldn't *be*! She *must* still be dreaming.

Glithwah strode in after the soldiers, her glittering eyes taking in a scene of shock and dejection. "Who is in charge?" she demanded.

Annabeth Miller squared her shoulders. "I am the project manager here."

Glithwah pointed to wreckage glowing outside the window. "That was unwise. Brave, but foolish."

Flynn couldn't *not* act. Nor, Corinne realized, could she stand fearfully at the back of the crowd. Whatever happened, happened. She stepped forward. "No, Foremost, it is your leaving Ariel that was foolish."

Glithwah blinked. "This *is* an unexpected surprise. Today must be your lucky day."

"What do you mean?" Corinne asked.

"I mean," the Snake said, "I have quite the scoop for you."

THE XOOL RESISTANCE

CHAPTER 39

With her eyes closed, Grace DiMeara would have known the mess hall was dangerously overcrowded. Had she covered her ears—against the widespread murmuring, the sobbing children, the roar of an HVAC system unequal to the heat given off by so many close-packed bodies—she would still have known. The miasma of sweat and fear was that thick.

But Grace was not about to close her eyes. Because a panicked stampede seemed all too probable. Because, in eerie silence, their jailors, one posted at every door, ceaselessly scanned the room.

And because the stakes were far, far higher than her own insignificant life.

"It'll be okay," Donald With The Ridiculous Sideburns whispered to her. Only rather than the pest who had hit on her daily these past weeks on Prometheus, rather than the self-important assistant to the deputy to the project manager, Donald had become, as far as anyone in the room knew, the person in charge—

Apart from their captors, that was.

"How, okay?" she countered, fighting back a shiver.

As though reading her mind, Donald glanced toward the crumpled bodies of the three men who had rushed a guard. One had wrestled a gun from it. Had, at pointblank range, emptied a full clip into it. Ricochets took down the shooter, the slugs bouncing without effect off the armored robot. In a trice, it had gutted its other assailants.

Donald's gaze flicked again, this time toward the window wall.

Saturn dominated the view, its rings, seen edge on, cutting a brilliant slash across the sky. By planet light, widely scattered wreckage, some of it still glowing a sullen red-orange, cast long, inky shadows across the landing field. And seemingly wherever Grace looked, glints and sparkles—the firefly-like flashes of distant fusion drives—marked the intricate dance of Snake and United Planets ships. Where sparkles converged, perhaps there were skirmishes.

Donald said, "There are good guys out there, too."

The operative word being *too*. Again, Grace shivered. How in the name of her lords had the local Snakes obtained a battle fleet?

And again, Donald seemed to read her thoughts. "They had the advantage of surprise."

You think? Not to mention killer-robot swarms—tech that no one in the whole frigging Solar System was supposed to have. Sharing the mess hall with just a few such bots made her skin crawl.

"Uh-huh," she said. "And now they have the advantage of hostages."

In the kitchen, an argument had broken out. "I'd better go arbitrate." Donald insinuated his way through the milling throng toward the disturbance, urging everyone to remain calm, squeezing past tables shoved together and chairs stacked high to clear space.

All around, snatches of conversation emerged from and dissolved back into the background din. Even the speculations were circumspect, the questions people *wanted* to ask unsuitable for uttering aloud. As for mind-to-mind links, those were impossible. Every attempt at a link, even with heads touching, dissolved into meaningless static. Befitting their status as prisoners, RF suppressors had been deployed to jam neural implants.

And so, few dared ask: how long did the Snakes intend to stay? Would they, as in their past outrage, make their run for interstellar space holding hostages? How would the United Planets navy react, and how soon—

And what level of casualties among the hostages would the navy consider acceptable?

An elderly woman, lean and hollow-cheeked, her coarse gray hair close-cropped, marched up. She wore the cold and distant stare so typical of an Augmented. Many among the starship's crew were such human/AI hybrids.

Abominations, every one.

Grace had met this woman while touring *Discovery*. One of the astrobiologists? Without access to her implant, Grace could not recall. As for a name, she had no idea.

The woman said, "You were speaking with Mr. Schnabel. What does he know about—"

"No more than you or I know," Grace interrupted.

And what she knew was nada, not even where her roommate was. An hour before the world had been turned upside down, Grace had taken her insomnia—after all her scheming, all her efforts, all her bold words, she had yet to fulfill her commitment to her lords—for a meandering, mind-clearing walk down empty, nightshift halls. Slowly pulling the cabin door shut behind her, Grace had had her last glimpse of Corinne.

Where was Corinne now? At best, being held with the base's senior execs, also unaccounted for. Grace preferred not to consider at worst.

"But Mr. Schnabel must have told you—" the woman said, stopping abruptly as, at the front of the mess hall, the sentry bot snapped to attention with guns raised.

The robot stood at least two meters tall. With its four legs and two arms, the chassis suggested a classical centaur, while its lone eye seemed cyclopean. But what mythological figure had ever held vigil with the metronomic sweep of a laser beam?

Just as the doors opened, ceiling lights faded. The Snake home world orbited a red-dwarf sun, and the aliens liked things dim. She recalled that most of Ariel colony had been on the gloomy side, too.

More robots entered, with guns at the ready, followed by a Snake in an utterly unornamented uniform. Make that *the* Snake: Firh Glithwah, Foremost of the Snakes interned on Saturn's moon, Ariel. Only how many Snakes, if any, remained on Ariel?

People crammed into the mess hall had already backed away from the sentry bot and its carnage. Now everyone recoiled farther from the entrance. Between the overcrowding and the fetid, muggy air, Grace found it difficult to breathe. The rotten-eggs taint that clung to Snakes did not help.

The clamor of moments ago faded into silence.

Glithwah was tall for a Snake, and that made her a bit over a meter tall. She massed, perhaps, twenty-five kilos. Still, she dominated the room. Maybe it was the knowledge that she held the power of life and death over everyone here.

Glithwah gestured at tattered corpses on the floor. "I regret the loss of life," she said, her voice pitched well into the soprano range.

"Then stop causing it," growled someone anonymously deep within the crowd.

"Then cease your futile resistance," the Foremost rejoined, her English flawless. "*We* are in charge here. Make no mistake. Hope the UP naval forces nearby make no such blunders."

Donald pressed to the front of the crowd. "What is the endgame here?"

Glithwah licked her lips: a Snake smile. "We depart aboard the starship, of course."

"With us as hostages?" Donald asked.

"Only in a manner of speaking," she answered cryptically. "If you would have us gone, you can speed the process."

"How is that?"

"This settlement stocks many valuable supplies. As the clan's ships have other priorities"—and she inclined her head toward the dance of fleets beyond the window—"we thought to avail ourselves of your shuttles. The sooner we transfer those additional supplies aboard *Discovery*, the sooner we'll be on our way. Who are your pilots?"

"Not a chance," Donald answered, to cheers. "You'll have to loot us without our help."

As Grace interpreted Glithwah's words, the accursed Snakes were improvising after one magnificently brave and foolish soul had destroyed their cargo ship. Well, the sad truth was, she needed to improvise, too.

"*I'm* a pilot," Grace called out.

Donald shot her a dirty look, then turned back toward Glithwah. "That woman is a visitor. She isn't qualified to fly our shuttles."

"Come closer," Glithwah ordered.

Grace made her way forward.

Glithwah studied Grace's face. "I've seen you before, in surveillance records on Ariel. What is your name? What are you doing here?"

"Grace DiMeara. I flew Corinne Elman from Earth to Ariel, then here."

"A short-range shuttle ought not to challenge you." Glithwah crooked a finger at her. "You'll do. Come with me."

"Traitor," a man hissed as Grace stepped out of the crowd.

I'm doing this for all of you, Grace thought. *Because, if you only knew, Snakes pilfering supplies are the least of your problems.*

• • • •

Robots loaded while Grace did preflight checkout on a shuttle's cramped, two-person bridge. Aboard *Discovery*, other robots would unload.

The Snake robots she had seen would not fit on the bridge—and having witnessed three men try to take on a robot, her plan, such as it was, depended on that. And if not on the bridge, she wouldn't have a robot minder aboard at all. Anywhere but the bridge, a robot would only take up precious cargo space.

Grace *had* half expected to share the bridge with an armed Snake. She had steeled herself to attack it. Dial up the bridge lights. Take it by surprise and half-blinded. With her longer reach and twice the body mass, Grace felt confident she could take it.

Perhaps Glithwah had done the same calculation.

Whatever the reason, Grace would fly the hop to *Discovery* solo—ever in the sights of Snake warships and drones. If she were dumb enough to make a run for it, she'd get a missile up her ass.

She was counting on that, too.

"Loading complete," an English-speaking Snake traffic controller radioed. He(?) dictated a flight plan. The Snakes followed familiar standards—not unexpected, because their ships looked human-built.

However the Snakes had sunk their claws into those ships, it had happened a while ago. No way could a Snake fly an unmodified human ship. Language issues aside, the tiny aliens had tiny hands. "Do not deviate."

"Copy that." A few taps on her console shut the cargo hatch and released the boarding tube. She gave the tube a few seconds to retract across the little moon's cracked and cratered surface. "Shuttle six, departing for *Discovery.*"

"Acknowledged."

As soon as she cleared the low-orbiting combat drones, she flipped on autopilot. She had about ten minutes to work unsupervised.

• • • •

Discovery loomed in the shuttle view port before Grace could even half finish surveying drawers and lockers on the bridge for anything useful.

"The biggest ship ever constructed," Donald had once boasted, as though by shuffling requisitions and duty rosters he had made a contribution. He had been escorting Corinne and Grace to a tour of the starship. "A klick and a quarter long. About five-eighths klick in diameter. One hundred twenty decks in all, fifty decks devoted to sustaining the onboard ecology."

To judge from the ships offloading, room and eco-capacity for a lot of Snakes. A freighter, small only in comparison to *Discovery*, filled one of the starship's three hangar bays. Another vessel, too large to dock, held station nearby. As Grace watched, a cargo lighter cast off from the larger freighter, vectored toward the starship. Drone swarms parted to let the lighter through.

Grace's radio crackled. "Shuttle six, hold at ten kilometers."

"Copy that," she said, wondering how many drones had her shuttle in their crosshairs. As if she could inflict any damage by ramming this behemoth. It would be like a bug hitting a windshield. But she had to do *something*.

She watched the lighter settle into a hangar bay.

"Shuttle six, proceed to hangar bay three, behind *Discovery* from your current position. Do not exceed fifty kph on approach." Left unsaid: or else drones would take her out. "For your own safety, remain inside your shuttle at all times."

"Copy."

She had hangar bay three to herself. Aft of her shuttle, the massive bay door remained open into space. Two robots ferried crates from the shuttle; a third, guns in hands, kept watch. So, she assumed, did the slowly panning camera mounted above the air lock that led aboard *Discovery*. Her shuttle's external cameras saw just the one.

The robots did their job quickly. Five minutes after docking, with quick bursts from the shuttle's compressed-nitrogen attitude jets, she lifted the emptied shuttle, then spun it to face outward. With slightly longer gas bursts, she eased out of the hangar bay. Once well clear she lit the main drive, heading back to Prometheus for another load.

En route to her next delivery, she completed her inventory. She had solvents, cleaning agents, lubricants, and several gas cylinders for an oxyacetylene utility torch. She had flare guns and a box of cartridges. Scavenged from her pressure suit, she had a helmet radio to adapt as a trigger. As robots offloaded the shuttle for the second time, she fine-tuned her plans.

On her third inbound flight, she completed her preparations.

• • • •

You're a reporter, Corinne kept telling herself. *You're a reporter and this is news*. She couldn't manage to care. She did not foresee ever being allowed to leave this ship, ever seeing Denise again.

In *Discovery's* cavernous and echoing bridge, only Corinne sat—and not by choice. She had been bound into a crew chair. About fifty more chairs stood empty, or had been unbolted and stacked, outsized for the Snakes busy all around her. Most were technicians, laboring at, or inside, consoles, retrofitting the hardware for clan speak, stubby arms, and tiny hands. Other Snakes stood watch.

High-pitched voices squealed in Corinne's ears. Through a translator AI—that the Snakes provided a translator and let her listen to
bridge chatter only reinforced her fears Glithwah intended *never* to
let her go!—Corinne tried, and failed, to follow even a small part
of the action. Beyond that the Snakes' takeover was running a bit
ahead of schedule ....

Extending from deck to overhead, arrayed all around the vast
circumference of the bridge, giant displays added to her mental
overload. From cameras in the hangar bays: the ceaseless transfers
aboard of Snakes and their supplies. In telescope views and tactical
displays: United Planets warships, and the robotic drone swarms
that kept the would-be rescuers at a distance. Relayed from cameras
on Prometheus: the weary faces, devoid of hope, of hundreds of
hostages. She tried, and failed, to spot Grace in the crowd.

Glithwah, who had departed on an undisclosed errand, came
loping onto the bridge, her magnetic sandals clanging on the deck.
With Corinne bound to a chair, they were almost eye to eye. "Enjoying the view?" the Snake mocked.

As best her bonds permitted, Corinne shrugged.

"And yet you find my people so interesting," Glithwah continued. "Like clockwork you've shown up on Ariel, every five years on
the anniversary of our setback. To gloat. To profit."

Your *defeat!* Corinne ached to correct, but she didn't trust her
voice not to quaver. And to judge by events unfolding all around,
setback was the more accurate term.

"Be happy," Glithwah said. "This may be your biggest story yet."

Having kidnapping her, the Snake meant to let her go? Corinne
felt the first stirrings of hope—to have them crushed as Glithwah
licked her lips.

The Snake said, "This ship carries a very powerful transmitter."

Corinne looked away. On one of the many bridge displays, a
shuttle swooped in for a landing. Two robots stood by, ready to
unload. A third—

Corinne inclined her head. "Why is an armed guard in that
hangar bay?"

"As a precaution against stupidity."

As the shuttle's cargo hatch opened, bots went to work. Corinne had to imagine the boom and clang of magnetized feet snapping to the bay's metal deck. Stars shone behind the shuttle, through the hangar bay's gaping outer doors. Something shiny streaked by: an armed drone, she presumed.

"Let's hope your friend Grace isn't stupid," Glithwah continued.

"Grace? Why?"

"She is piloting that shuttle."

Why would Grace …?

Near the shuttle's bow, the crew air lock began cycling open.

Glithwah gave a high-pitched snarl that the AI translated as, "Remind the human pilot to remain inside her ship."

That warning, presumably, was radioed to the shuttle, even as the guard robot, with guns raised, stomped closer. By now, the shuttle air lock was half open.

Flame erupted from the lock, engulfing the robot. Small objects sailed out through the billowing smoke. There were muzzle flashes and more fireballs, all the more startling for the eerie silence. Apart from the scattered bursts of light, black smoke hid everything from the camera.

Did the thick smoke blind the bots, too?

Glithwah shouted.

"Put a squad into that hangar bay *now!*" the translator offered.

"Not possible," one of the bridge crew said. "The air lock onto the hangar bay is jammed. An explosion must have—"

"Unimportant," Glithwah cut him off. "Seal the emergency bulkheads on that deck. Cut through the hatches. Blow up the lock, if necessary."

"At once, Foremost."

On the hangar deck, out of the rapidly dissipating smoke, something loomed. It rose. It pivoted. And then, for an instant, before the image dissolved in static, Corinne saw—

Fierce, blue-white light: the exhaust of the shuttle's fusion drive! Hotter than the surface of the Sun, it would be melting everything and everyone it touched.

On a tactical display, the icon of a ship burst from *Discovery*. The shuttle: accelerating like mad. Making a run for it.

"Go, Grace! Go!" Corinne shouted, her eyes tearing.

"Destroy it," Glithwah ordered.

The shuttle, caught in the pitiless stare of a telescope, popped onto a wall display. The little ship's fusion drive blazed. Faster and faster the shuttle fled—

Two missiles, faster still, burst into the telescope's field of view.

"Foremost, hail the shuttle," Corinne pleaded. "Warn Grace to turn back."

"She made her choice."

The shuttle zigged and zagged, bobbed and weaved. The missiles, reacting to every maneuver, were closing fast. Closing ... closing ... closing ...

When this fireball cleared, the telescope display showed... nothing.

CHAPTER 40

In an eventful life, using more names than he could easily remember, Carl had been many things. Asteroid miner. Killer, if only in self defense. Fugitive from the mob. Rent-a-pilot. Commando. Jailor. Spy. To that list he had recently added felon, and when his theft of *Hermes* was discovered, he could expect to add prisoner.

That the fate of the galaxy might rest on his theft remaining secret for another few days did nothing to encourage sleep.

Not that sleep seemed possible anyway. Since leaving the Moon, Joshua, in the courier ship's lone passenger seat, had carped about the unending two gees. That was understandable enough. But most of the nattering was Joshua arguing with Carl's second passenger. Tacitus, snug in his portable server, could not have cared less about the acceleration. And with petabytes of Xool archive to explore, there was no possibility those two would run out of topics about which to squabble.

When they took a break from Xool mysteries, it was only to debate matters possibly even more obscure. Were King Arthur or Robin Hood actual people, or purely myth? Carl had heard of more than a few lost colonies, but none was named Roanoke. He gathered that it got lost centuries before space travel. And as for their latest snit ...

"It was *clearly* a religious site," Joshua said.

"A burial site, I'll concede," Tacitus replied through his server's loudspeaker.

"That's no concession, considering all the graves nearby. If it were only a burial site, why also construct it to predict solstices and equinoxes? Why put up all those megaliths at all?"

"Bah," Tacitus said. "How does predicting the solstice establish a tie to religion? The structure could as well be a solar observatory."

Stonehenge, Carl decided. He had seen the ancient stone circle months earlier, among the dozens of earthly sites he'd toured to draw attention away from his stopover in New York. Not that breaking into Grace DiMeara's apartment had told him anything ....

"Huh," Joshua countered, "I could as well argue that maybe it was only incidentally a burial site. From the archives I've reviewed, a significant proportion of the interred bodies exhibit deformities. It could just as easily be a pilgrimage site, an early Lourdes, and the graves the resting places of those who failed to find their miracle cures."

Lourdes? Neolithic solar observatories? Carl said, "You two sound like an old married couple." *An old married academic couple, in any case.*

"He could do worse," Tacitus said.

Joshua ignored them both.

By the time his friends turned to possible origins of the Atlantis myth, Carl all but tuned them out. He considered, yet again, insisting that they squabble by net—but being alone with his own thoughts would not help him sleep, either. Taking what comfort he could from their arcane banter, he counted the hours till Saturn.

Until a klaxon wailed.

"The ship's okay," Carl said, slapping the Acknowledge button. "That's a comm alert."

He hadn't said: *we're* okay. Because in all likelihood, they weren't.

No one should know where they were. And yet, the alert text flashing on his console indicated a TOP SECRET message. It told him the authorities had found them. It told him he had failed. Whatever the unopened message's precise wording, it had to mean Go DIRECTLY TO JAIL. DO NOT PASS GO.

Only the communiqué, when Carl read it, indicated something quite different.

• • • •

As improbable as it seemed, matters had gotten worse.

"We picked up a broadcast," Carl told his passengers. "*Hermes* hasn't been spotted, but we need to respond."

And that meant revealing themselves.

"Why?" Joshua asked. "I mean, you had reasons to be pushing my brain out the back of my skull. Reaching Prometheus unannounced and unexpected. Exploiting your Agency credentials there to commandeer the starship's big transmitter. Exposing the Xool so universally that their presence can no longer be suppressed. That *is* the plan, isn't it?"

And in the process safeguarding the starship and its crew from the Xool—only all that had been overcome by events.

"Was," Carl said. "Was the plan. The broadcast we picked up is a general UP naval recall."

Joshua frowned. "Recall from where?"

"All over. Much of the navy is scattered across the outer Solar System, chasing pirates."

"And *why* is there a recall?" Tacitus asked.

Carl said, "Snakes showed up in force in the Saturn system. They overwhelmed and scattered the naval detachment stationed there, then seized *Discovery*."

The odd thing was, the news didn't surprise him. Not really. Because he so distrusted Glithwah? That was a part of it, surely, but there had to be more to it. Because Corinne was nearby, and it would be just her karma to get caught up in a second Snake hijacking? Maybe it would've been that, too, had he believed in karma. Because, with vessels going missing all over the outer Solar System, the problem didn't extend to Saturn system? Maybe.

The other odd thing was, the takeover had happened a day earlier. Why no naval recall till now? Because the brass had expected to resolve matters with its resources at hand? Or because they hadn't decided how to spin the fiasco? TOP SECRET orders notwithstanding, no one could redeploy that many ships without the situation getting noticed.

Maybe the news had leaked already.

Carl aimed *Hermes'* primary antenna at Saturn. And from that direction, the transmission preempting or overpowering commercial broadcasts, he saw—

Corinne Elman, her face ashen.

. . . .

The military around Saturn bounced Carl along the chain of command for more than three hours before, at last, putting him through on a secure comm link to the local admiral. Three hours was more than long enough to confirm Carl's *bona fides* with authorities on Earth. He doubted that was a coincidence.

"Make it short," Admiral Akihiro Matsushita snapped by way of greeting. He had a pencil-thin mustache and close-set eyes like two black marbles. "We have a situation here."

"With which you'll want my help," Carl snapped back. *Hermes* was two light-minutes from Saturn, decelerating furiously, and that made real-time conversation—barely—possible. "I'll venture to guess you won't find another Snake expert within a billion klicks of here."

Joshua, in the other seat, leaned to his right, just out of camera view. Matsushita preferred vid to a VR link, and Carl wasn't ready to explain having uncleared, unauthorized passengers aboard the UPIA courier.

Matsushita said, "I fought the Snakes in the *last* war."

Two decades earlier. The admiral looked to be about fifty. That would have made him a junior officer back then.

"And I spent most of the past twenty years on Ariel."

"Why, exactly, are you here?" Matsushita countered. "Agnelli"— that would be Richard Lewis Agnelli, the long-time director of the UPIA—"said you were on your way back to Ariel."

In the opposite direction, in other words. Far, *far* away.

"Be glad I suspected the Snakes might be up to something."

However disingenuous that statement, it was more credible, not to mention simpler, than the truth. Circumstances had retroactively converted Carl's misappropriation of the courier from theft to brilliant insight. Call that the atom-thin silver lining to this fiasco. As for the implication to be drawn from his subterfuge that he suspected a mole within the Agency, it was true enough—if not in the way Matsushita would take it. "It's why I'm most of the way to you."

"Lucky us," Matsushita said.

"Over the years, the Foremost and I played a lot of b'tok. You're familiar with b'tok?"

"A strategy game. The Snake equivalent to chess."

Close enough. "My point, Admiral, is that I have an understanding of how Glithwah thinks."

"And how often did you win at b'tok?"

"That's not the point." Which meant never, and Matsushita, from his smirk, knew it. "This recent piracy? Pure Glithwah. Scatter the opposition and assemble a free navy in one operation."

"What with you being the expert, why didn't you see this attack coming?"

The gibe came of frustration, at least in part, and Carl didn't react. "And the drone swarms? The robot soldiers? You know them?"

"All too well."

"By now, your engineers must have examined some. The bots and drones use Boater technology, don't they?"

"We've studied a few," Tanaka said, "all shot to pieces. Barring a lucky hit, they self-destruct to avoid capture. So far, about all the experts have agreed on is that this isn't any familiar tech. I'll give you that one."

"That problem I saw coming," Carl exaggerated.

Because without establishing credibility, he wouldn't be allowed to *do* anything. Military types didn't think much of his kind, considered spies loose cannons. They would keep him close. To pick his brain, they'd say, when their true goal would be to stop him from meddling.

And there were things, important things, he must get done.

He *had* suspected Ariel colony of money laundering for illegal and untraceable tech purchases over InterstellarNet. But to buy what? He'd never been quite certain. Glithwah's repeated requests that she be allowed to import advanced robotics might have been misdirection.

But in hindsight? With twenty thousand Snakes, children and ancients included, facing off against humanity's billions? Of *course* Glithwah had wanted war bots. And if she was to be reliant on bots, they would outclass anything she expected them to encounter. That meant Boater robotics—a technology that human authorities continued to ban.

"All right, expert," Matsushita said. "What's your advice?"

"That I meet with Glithwah. Determine what she wants."

"She wants *Discovery*—and she's grabbed it. Apart from that, she wants a clean getaway."

"Let me share how Glithwah thinks," Carl began, channeling his many defeats. "She plays b'tok by indirection. It's a rare maneuver that advances just one of her objectives. It's a rarer maneuver, until the mid-game, that poses any obvious threat. By the time a pattern emerges, by the time the purpose of her maneuvering becomes clear, it's almost always too late to react. In the unusual event that something takes her by surprise, she adapts quickly."

"Uh-huh." Matsushita looked less than impressed. "Once you arrive, rendezvous with the flagship. When I have time, we'll talk."

"Wait." Because Carl couldn't permit himself to be sidelined. He needed to earn the admiral's trust—fast. It was well and good to *say* he understood Glithwah …

"What the Foremost wants is to get away with *Discovery*. Without pursuit, because she's brought along the entire clan. Without further engagement, further loss of life, on either side."

"As I've already said. And as Glithwah's pet spokeswoman has told the worlds."

"Bear with me," Carl said.

Defending Corinne—once more a Snake prisoner?—would not further his case. It was time for his many games of b'tok, all those hours spent one-on-one with Glithwah, to pay off.

The Snakes' original foray into the Solar System had ended in disaster all around. Thousands of humans killed. Hundreds of Snakes, including the then Foremost. For the clan's survivors, internment on bleak little Ariel.

What would *this* Foremost do differently?

"Glithwah wants your assets neutralized, Admiral. She wants the rest of the navy kept spread all over. If she allows the UP to concentrate its resources, she's done. The Snakes would be outnumbered hundreds to one.

"I'll make a few predictions. Most hostages aren't aboard *Discovery*, where they'd justify a pursuit; they're elsewhere. Still on Prometheus, I'll guess. So Glithwah is streaming real-time vid, not expecting you to take her word for things."

Matsushita scowled. "Most mission staff are being held in the base mess hall, in view of public-safety cams the Snakes have left up and broadcasting. There's no audio, and bits of the video are being blurred to prevent lip reading. Due to the severe crowding, we haven't gotten an accurate headcount or made a lot of facial matches. Senior mission leadership and two captured marines are being held in another room. Current thinking is they've been separated lest they try to organize resistance." The scowl deepened. "As it is, a few of the hostages, braver than smart, attempted to take on a bot. It tore them to pieces."

Ugh. "And how many hostages aboard *Discovery* itself?"

"Just the reporter, as far as we know. Crew and workers were relocated to Prometheus. If Elman is being held against her will, she hasn't said. She may just think she's chasing another Pulitzer."

Corinne did not have to say: Carl had seen the fear in her eyes. She had almost died as a Snake prisoner, aboard their *last* hijacked starship.

"She owns a ship, right?" Carl asked, trying to sounded casual. "What about her pilot?"

"Grace DiMeara. We saw her escorted from the mess hall. We don't know why or to where."

Carl said, "I predict the hostages will remain on Prometheus, under robotic guard, till *Discovery* is far away. And lest you contemplate pursuing the clan anyway, Glithwah will reveal—maybe she already has—more robots and drones positioned to threaten the antimatter plant. If your ships make a move toward Prometheus or the starship, she promises the drones will blow the factory." And with it, the hostages. When Snakes destabilized the antimatter factory on Himalia, that blast shattered the whole frigging *world*. "How am I doing?"

The next four minutes would be interminable. Within one minute, Carl's mind resumed its churning. Everything he had heard about the Snake incursion, every ploy he had extrapolated, seemed like Glithwah. Sort of. Brilliant, to be sure. Flawlessly executed. But not sufficiently … overwhelming. Another shoe still waited to drop.

"Another prediction," Carl radioed into the lengthening silence. "Having dispersed the UP navy across the Solar System, Glithwah will have a plan to keep those ships far from *Discovery*." He rubbed his chin, pondering. Glithwah was not one to leave clan mates behind. "It'll be drones pre-positioned to threaten soft targets elsewhere."

And something else, some yet deeper ploy, because Glithwah never relied on a single line of attack. What more she might undertake refused to make itself clear.

Only virtual reality could accommodate the complexities of b'tok, and their last few encounters remained stored in Carl's neural implant. At many times actual speed, he replayed games in his mind, studied her attacks. They were indirect, multipronged, subtle.

But there was something else about her game play. Some other attribute. Her actions were precise. They let nothing go to waste. They were very … what was the word …?

Surgical.

"Admiral," Carl radioed. "I assume most vessels captured earlier by the Snakes had crews. My bet is most are still alive. The reinforcements on which you're counting will no sooner set out for Saturn than the SOS calls will begin. Survivors abandoned far and wide across the Solar System, their robotic captors just departed. Desperate men and women, without resources, in urgent need of rescue."

Minutes later, mid disdainful dismissal of Carl's earliest predictions as patently obvious, Matsushita blinked. "Two such contacts have come in so far today," he said. "Listen."

"Mayday, Mayday," the message began. "This is Lyle Logan, captain of the *Betty*. My ship was one among many captured by Snakes. Fourteen of us are marooned on a Kuiper Belt object. Apart from eyeballs, we have no instruments to ascertain our location. Our Snake guards and their robots evacuated awhile ago, but until today this transmitter I'm using was inaccessible, in a vault secured by a time lock. We have remaining maybe two weeks of oh-two, less food, and ..."

Matsushita killed the playback. "They left their message looping as a homing beacon. The other message sounds as dire."

Carl waited.

"Okay," Matsushita added. "I'm authorizing you to open a channel with the Snakes. If they'll talk with you, go for it. Learn what you can—but don't commit to anything before clearing it first with me."

"And if the Foremost agrees to meet face to face?"

"If you go in, you may not come out."

"Risk is always part of the job," Carl said.

The next pause extended long past what mere light-speed delay could explain, and for much of the wait Matsushita's mic was muted and his camera frozen. Until—

Matsushita said, "If you get the go-ahead, we'll allow *Hermes* through our perimeter."

CHAPTER 41

Glithwah responded within ten minutes to Carl's hail.

No checking in with or second-guessing by remote authorities *here*. No stalling. Instead, he supposed, although the Foremost's body language gave no sign of it, there was curiosity.

"I had imagined myself rid of you, Warden," Glithwah said after their first, formal exchange of greetings. Her fluent English rendered his former title ironic. "Yet here you are, almost in time for your presence to matter."

"I'm a better strategist than I let on," he lied. That his plans had converged with Glithwah's was coincidence. That or, as he was coming to believe, his subconscious was the strategist.

"And yet you lacked the confidence in your deductions to have alerted authorities here."

Their conversation was in the clear, and the navy would be listening. Matsushita had already commented on Carl's nonwarning. "We have serious matters to discuss, Foremost."

"There is only one secure way," she said.

Her technicians would have recovered crypto software from computers both on Prometheus and aboard *Discovery*. Whatever UP algorithm he agreed to use she must assume contained a backdoor. If he had stolen any clan encryption algorithm back on Ariel, she knew he wouldn't admit it—and that the UP navy would already be eavesdropping with it.

"Agreed. I'll need a few minutes to prepare." He broke the link.

"Prepare?" Joshua asked.

"To be boarded." With a few keystrokes, Carl set free a highly specific Trojan from its quarantine in *Hermes'* main computer. "First I must destroy all the Agency crypto software aboard."

The same Trojan would introduce a backdoor into *Discovery's* computers, if the Snakes were careless enough. Carl did not foresee that happening.

"The Foremost will come aboard to talk? It'll be snug."

Carl shook his head.

Joshua sighed. "And here I supposed things were already interesting."

• • • •

The midsized shuttle dispatched from the starship was clearly of human design. On the shuttle's final approach, Carl read its tail number. A listing in his implant confirmed this was among the disappeared ships—it already seemed like something out of a bygone era—that the UPIA had struggled so long and ineffectually to locate. With a few precise puffs of compressed gas from its forward attitude jets, the shuttle came to a smooth stop, nose to nose with *Hermes* and separated by perhaps two meters. Pilot and copilot, visible through the cockpit canopy, were Snakes, and good at their jobs.

Carl studied the dance of distant sun glints—constellation upon constellation of armed drones, patrolling around the starship—while, slowly, a docking tunnel reached out from the shuttle. With a thump, the mating collar met *Hermes'* hull. Lights blinked on his console as the tube sealed around his air lock.

"And if this goes badly?" Joshua asked.

"Your grandmother knows all we do about the Xool." And what a crushing burden that would be, were he and Joshua not to return. "Let's see to it that this doesn't go badly."

A warrior soon came floating from *Hermes'* air lock, steeped in the stench of Snake ecosystems. Rotten eggs, just-lit matches, and other sulfurous odors to which Carl had never put a name, gave him an instant headache. He found sealed packets of nostril filters in the bridge first-aid kit and handed one set to Joshua. "These will help."

What else had he overlooked?

The Snake, meanwhile, scarcely blinked at encountering an

undeclared passenger. Carl knew her: Firh Koban, a young cousin of Glithwah's. Back on Ariel, Koban had piloted the settlement's first scoop ship—reported lost with all hands.

From a pocket of her uniform she removed a hypo spray.

Carl nodded, and she gave him the injection. "Neural suppressor," he explained to Joshua. It was meant to preclude wireless conspiring or eavesdropping, here or on the starship.

Joshua submitted, flinching as the spray stung his neck.

"Onto the other ship," Koban ordered Joshua. Her marginal English retained the implicit-verb flavor of clan speak. "No baggage," she added as he grabbed the handle of the portable server by his feet.

"It's not baggage, it's an AI," Carl explained, "and I'll need it." Because if they were to leave the server unattended, Snake technicians *would* poke around in it. And then Carl's hastily modified Trojan, retargeted to erase Xool files, would wipe a big chunk of Tacitus' memories.

Just for an instant, Koban's eyes glazed. Mind to mind, she would be consulting with her superiors. "A moment."

Not until Carl yanked the network-interface biochip and double-wrapped the server box in metal-mesh sheets was Joshua permitted to bring Tacitus. The AI, if it took offence, kept its speaker shut.

As Koban inspected the bridge, engine room, and tiny shower/toilet/galley for bombs, Carl watched through external cameras as two pressure-suited and tethered Snakes examined *Hermes* from the outside. The scrutiny unfolded in silence, coordinated, he presumed, through neural implants.

Satisfied at last, Koban sat, looking, in the human-sized passenger chair, like a particularly lethal doll. As soon as the exterior inspection finished and the shuttle had retracted its docking tube, she gestured at the bridge console. "To hangar bay three."

A traffic controller aboard *Discovery* directed Carl's approach. Saturn's light gave the huge vessel a jaundiced cast. The starship appeared unharmed by its seizure and any initial skirmishing.

Discovery was in freefall; Carl flicked on magnetic coupling to pin the tiny courier to the hangar deck. A shuttle, presumably carrying

Joshua, swooped in seconds later. The great exterior hangar doors closed behind them. Through the cockpit canopy, Carl heard the whoosh of air refilling the hangar bay.

"What now?" he asked.

"Out," Koban directed.

"Okay." Carl slipped magnetic slippers over his boots, popped his seat harness, and exited his ship. Surrounded by Snakes, still clutching Tacitus' server, Joshua was emerging from the shuttle. He also wore a pair of magnetic slippers.

A dozen or more thick metal plates had been welded to the deck, the overhead, and the nearest bulkhead. Pitting and ripples—melted metal, recongealed?—were all around. Scorches surrounded the air lock that led into the ship proper. Walking closer, his slippers clanking, eying hasty welds, Carl wondered why the entire air lock had been hastily replaced.

"What the hell happened here?" Joshua asked, joining Carl.

The shuttle crew, all armed, fell in around them.

"That's not clear," Carl said.

Something had gone wrong: battle damage, by the looks of it. Why disclose that?

As the lesser of two risks, he decided. So that if he had smuggled a bomb aboard, a possibility Glithwah could not dismiss, the blast would spare a second hangar bay.

"Inside," Koban directed.

"And what then?" Joshua asked.

"A long walk."

Beyond the air lock, they gained two additional escorts. Carl could imagine either bot dismembering any mere human. They walked, then rode a cargo elevator forward five decks, then walked a bit farther. Some corridors were empty. More were lined with pallets and crates secured to the deck with ropes and nets. Yet other corridors teemed, the armed warriors outnumbered by weary, shuffling families of Snake refugees clutching their few belongings.

The starship was *huge*; it could not have been a coincidence when Corinne emerged from a side corridor. Her face was drawn and her clothes were rumpled. Though she had aged in the few months since Carl had last seen her, she appeared unharmed.

The way her eyes widened, she hadn't expected to see at least one of them. She had been summoned by Glithwah, Carl supposed, this "chance" encounter captured by a hallway camera.

"Are you all right?" he asked.

Corinne smiled wanly. "Considering."

Written notices in clan speak had been taped everywhere, sometimes, but not always, obscuring the permanent English and Mandarin wall signs. They came to a halt outside massive double doors labeled Captain's Ready Room. It would be Glithwah's office now.

"Your place here," Koban directed Carl. "Proximity with him," she ordered one of the bots. "The rest of you," she gestured, "with me."

Joshua and Corinne exchanged worried looks.

"It'll be fine," Carl assured them. He hoped Joshua remembered to be discreet.

Koban's eyes glazed for a moment as she netted a report of their arrival. Then, with Corinne, Joshua, and Tacitus in tow, Snake and robot escorts continued down the corridor.

"Enter," a familiar soprano voice called from inside.

Carl let himself in, his robot escort following. With a soft, metallic clank and the hum of electric motors, the bot assumed a watchful stance in the nearest corner.

The Foremost stood behind a massive oaken desk, on a platform of some sort. Boxes where everywhere, whether her possessions coming in or those of the unlucky human captain going out. Bulkhead displays slowly cycled through earthly panoramas.

"Welcome aboard *Invincible*," Glithwah greeted him.

Because *Discovery* was too humble a name for a Snake ship. "Hello, Foremost."

Glithwah took two clear drink bulbs from the refrigerated drawer in the desk. "Vodka, Warden? The man who had expected to sit at this desk had a fondness for the stuff."

"Sure." Carl caught the bulb lobbed toward him, took an

appreciative sip. "If ever that title fit me, the day is long past."

"For whatever it is worth, Warden, throughout your tenure you inconvenienced our preparations. Far more, certainly, than did your successor."

Was he expected to appreciate the compliment? "And yet not nearly enough, it would appear." Carl took another swallow. "About him. How is Bruce doing? May I see him?"

"He was healthy, though not happy, when we left him," Glithwah said. "On Ariel."

"And still unhappy, I would surmise." After being physically or psychologically abused enough to have cooperated.

"He would have been no happier had we brought him." Glithwah stood taller, signaling that the social niceties had come to an end. "Warden, you have traveled far for no purpose. Nothing will dissuade me from departing with this vessel. Did you somehow imagine otherwise?"

"We should talk," Carl said.

CHAPTER 42

Spacious, well-furnished, and comfortable, the suite of rooms was nonetheless a prison. Had Joshua not already realized, he would have needed only to glimpse the wary expression on Corinne's face, or to recall the fearsome robot sentry posted outside the suite's entrance.

They had so much to talk about—but back aboard *Hermes*, before the Snakes docked, Carl had said to assume at all times that they would be bugged. If only he and Corinne could net!

"Come here often?" Joshua improvised. He had to say *something* casual, something to draw attention from the warning he must give her. Soon.

"Why not? You've come all this way, too."

He patted the server box, still wrapped in metal mesh. "Blame Tacitus."

"Hi," the AI said.

This conversation was so strained that even Snakes must soon take notice. Setting down Tacitus, Joshua gave Corinne a big hug. Lips to her ear, he whispered, "Join me on the sofa. Whisper and we can compare notes. Tacitus will talk for the three of us, synthing all our voices."

Tousled curls brushing his cheek, Joshua felt her nod.

"Boy, it feels good to stretch my legs," he said, sitting on the sofa. "That courier ship we came on was teensy." *Teensy* was a codeword for Tacitus.

"And I'm glad to have someone new to talk with." Tacitus began on cue. "I've become fascinated with the Lubell case." Corinne had first made a name for herself covering the gruesome murders, never solved. "I have a theory to bounce off you."

Tacitus (speaking for itself *and* "Corinne," with the occasional

274

bored aside from "Joshua,") launched into dialogue less strained than anything the flesh-and-blood parties had managed.

"What are you *doing* here?" Corinne whispered.

"You're in danger." He had to choke back the inappropriate laugh that struggled to be free. "I mean besides from the Snakes. We set out from the Moon before we knew about them. From Grace DiMeara."

Corinne winced. "How do you even know that name? For that matter, how do you know *Carl*, much less how did you connect up with him?"

"He was recalled to Earth while you were en route to Prometheus." That innocuous *was recalled* subsumed a lot, but Joshua had no idea how long they would go unsupervised. "Back when you were on Ariel, recruiting Carl, you mentioned the Matthews conundrum and a disgraced historian. He put two and two together, tracked me down."

There was much to catch her up on. Speaking quickly, synopsizing like mad, he tried to hit the highlights: the quest for the alien lunar base. The clunky alien computers and recovery of most of their database. Glimpses in that archive of meddling with Earth history for eons before the first human. He barely touched upon Helena's untimely arrival and their brush with disaster. The Xool heading home. Even to hit the highlights was daunting.

"What does any of this have to do with Grace?" Corinne interrupted.

"She's a Xool agent. Interveners, you would call them. Surveillance vids show her visiting their lunar facility."

"Grace is *dead*," Corinne said, the word seeming to catch in her throat. "Killed trying to escape. The Snakes blew up her shuttle. I was on the bridge when it happened. I *saw* it."

All data pointed to Grace having poisoned Corinne's regular pilot to get herself to *Discovery*. In order, somehow, to stop the starship. Joshua just could not see how running away from the starship could fit into Grace's plans. Then again, a Snake takeover would not have been in her plans, either.

But within the Ariel settlement—to which Grace had gained

entry by piloting for Corinne—Carl had uncovered another Xool mole. A Snake mole. Dolmar Banak and Grace had met on Ariel. Banak might have told Grace about the imminent clan jailbreak ....

"And so the case can be made," Tacitus was pontificating, "that the DNA evidence exhibited markers for post-arrest tampering by gengineering. If so, then—"

The AI had been going on, in three distinct voices, for a while. Ten minutes was Joshua's best guess. With his implant chemically disabled, how was a person to keep track?

"You said the aliens went home," Corinne whispered. "Where's home?"

Maybe the answer hid somewhere in the recovered database. His grandmother had hunted endlessly for it. On the grueling flight here, he and Tacitus had searched their copy, too. If the archive included a star map of any kind, it had eluded everyone.

"No idea," he admitted. At the next lull in Tacitus' little drama, Joshua injected, "Whoa, partner. Enough ancient history."

Whoa was another cue.

"Then what *should* we talk about?" Tacitus asked.

"Something else. Anything else. Or maybe"—and Joshua stood abruptly—"nothing else. I'd like to see more of this ship."

"Are we allowed?" Tacitus asked.

"Are we?" Joshua asked Corinne.

She tipped her head, thinking. "I've had all but free rein. With an escort, I don't see why not."

"Good," Joshua said. "Lead on, starting with the sick bay. I have one *bitch* of a headache."

"You need nose filters."

"Done, but not till after I'd gotten a good whiff."

"Sorry." Corinne shrugged. "I don't notice it anymore."

He hoped not to be aboard long enough to adapt. That wish begged the question how Carl fared with the Foremost ....

"Till then ...," Joshua hinted.

She led him (and Tacitus, his server awkward but weightless in free fall) on a serpentine route. If their path had any logic, Joshua failed to grasp it. Perhaps she was testing for limits. If so, it was a successful experiment, because their escort, thumping along behind them, raised no objections. Apart from the children, Snakes in the halls ignored them. Passing the ready room, Joshua heard nothing through the doors. It could mean effective soundproofing. It could mean that Carl and the Foremost had gone elsewhere, perhaps on their own tour. It could mean nothing. It could mean that, his head throbbing, Joshua was overlooking something.

"About sick bay?" he prompted.

"Almost there."

Sick bay turned out to be wild understatement. The medical facility, when they came to it, was more of an ER and high-tech storehouse than a pill dispensary. "What do you suggest?" he asked.

It wasn't Corinne who responded.

"I am Galen," a disembodied voice declared from an overhead speaker. "What is the nature of your medical need?"

Of course: a medical AI. This ship must be rife with AIs.

"Something for a headache," Joshua said.

He submitted to scans. Nothing in the pharmacological inventory targeted this particular headache. (Naturally. *Discovery* was not meant to teem with ambulatory sulfur sources.) As the AI directed a medicinal synthesizer, Joshua glanced around. Even for an ER, the range of equipment impressed him. Then again, this ship was built for decades of self-sufficiency.)

"I came for a pill," Joshua grumbled after a few minutes. "I don't need you to grow me a new kidney."

"But it could," Corinne said. She ran splayed fingers of both hands through her hair. "Or new legs, for that matter. Become ill enough, or have a serious enough accident, and it can upload you."

"Backups." *That's why there was so much hardware.* "How many of the ... original crew"—Joshua almost slipped and said *real crew*, a label apt to irritate whatever Snakes were eavesdropping—"are Augmented?"

"About a third."

"Your medication is ready," Galen announced. On one of the

synthesizers, a status lamp flashed green. "If I can be of further service, do not hesitate to ask. I can provide a full gamut of preventative and therapeutic services to all crew."

Two Snake children shot past the sick-bay door, bouncing off corridor walls, floor, and ceiling. High-soprano shrieks stabbed right through his head.

One of Galen's robotic arms reached over an operating table to offer him a drink bulb.

Washing down his pill, Joshua thought: *Galen, you may be in for bigger challenges than you anticipate.*

"Ready to continue?" Corinne asked.

"Sure," Joshua said. He just wished he knew if he was a tourist or an immigrant.

The answer to that depended on Carl—and Glithwah.

CHAPTER 43

Carl gazed across the cluttered expanse of the captain's ready room. "I need assurances the hostages will be freed, unharmed."

Glithwah licked her lips: a smile. "That is a decision for others to make. Matsushita, for one. More than most humans, you think strategically. You have some appreciation for how I reason. I expect you to provide your admiral with wise counsel."

"Suppose this ship is allowed to depart. Suppose the navy does not pursue. Then what?"

"Then the hostages on Prometheus *will* go free, unharmed." Licked lips. "I would advise everyone to steer clear of our rearguard as they withdraw."

No doubt that rearguard would be automated. Matsushita had mentioned self-destruct behavior by robots and drones. "Understood," Carl said.

"I thought you might."

"All hostages," Carl persisted. "The leadership group you're holding separately, too."

"Agreed."

"And the civilian pilot removed from mess hall." *Especially* her. Carl had spent much of the jaunt from Earth imagining ways to capture Grace. If he could knock her out before she triggered her cranial bomb ...."

"That won't be possible," Glithwah said. "She foolishly attempted an escape."

"That's unfortunate." Carl kept his face expressionless—he hoped. "And it brings me to a core matter. How do we know that after you've withdrawn the hostages *will* be let go?"

"Can you trust me?" Once more, she licked her lips. "Set aside trust, Warden. Consider the clan's best interests. Do you suppose I would give the UP justification for a revenge pursuit?"

More justification, she meant. Over the past several years, the investment to build and provision this starship had exceeded the annual GDP of most *worlds*. But Glithwah was likely correct. After this latest incident, how much of the public would consider their taxes well spent if they rid the Solar System, once and for all, of Snakes? At least if human casualties were held to a minimum.

He said, "That's not proof."

Glithwah did not deign to answer.

"And where will you go?"

She didn't respond to that, either.

"Agreed. I don't need to know that," Carl said. "You can't blame me for being curious."

Whether from old clan rivalries or for control of the starship's technologies, any return to the home system must kick off the war to end all Snake wars. If his many defeats at b'tok had taught him anything, it was this: a frontal assault would be Glithwah's last choice. She wouldn't head straight home, wouldn't take on those rival clans, wouldn't put her entire clan at risk—not for as long as she had other options. And plenty of fallow solar systems were within *Discovery's* cruising range ....

"But I digress," Carl said. More than his curiosity was at stake. "To continue, facilities on Prometheus are to be left unharmed. All facilities."

"That is my intention. No needless casualties or damage." Glithwah leaned over the desk, her eyes narrowed, almost staring. "We will vacate the antimatter factory last of all."

Leaving even freed hostages imperiled till they could be evacuated *far* from the moon.

"To be clear, I'm also speaking of the hostages you hold outside the Saturn system."

"What do you mean?" Her eyes glittered, testing him.

"On Ariel, to begin. And the crews, wherever you interned them, of all the ships you captured. And your unsuspecting hostages, wherever *they* are. I'm sure you've deployed drones widely, just in case you find you need the UP navy further distracted."

"Very perceptive, Warden. Your hours at b'tok were not entirely misspent."

He thought, *don't gloat, damn you.* But why wouldn't she? He was, after all, negotiating surrender terms. Matsushita would be furious. "Same conditions? No pursuit?"

"Same conditions," she agreed.

Carl stood. He had yet to mention the hostage most on his mind. "That's what I needed to know. We'll meet with Admiral Matsushita and discuss specifics. Timelines. Ship movements. Force separations."

"We?"

"We. I include Joshua Matthews, Tacitus, and Corinne Elman."

"You and I had not discussed the woman." Needlelike talons slid from Glithwah's fingertips. "She is a reporter. These events are historic. Our odyssey will be historic."

"All hostages go free," Carl said. "Give me this one hostage now as a show of good faith."

"Ms. Elman is my guest."

"She is your prisoner," Carl said flatly. "I saw it in her eyes. I know her that well."

"No."

"That's it? Simply: no? After everything you've accomplished, after all the preparation"—*after proving me a fool!*—"you would wager the clan's future over a single hostage?" *Can you be that pissed off at her reporting, over the years, of the clan's defeat?*

"And you?" Glithwah shot back. "You would wager the lives of thousands for your friend? You would see another antimatter plant, another world, blown to gravel? Perhaps you would. Admiral Matsushita will not."

"Think about it," Carl said. "For everyone's sake."

The robot guard clanked across the room to loom over Carl. "Come with me," it said.

"I will consider your suggestion," Glithwah said. "Briefly. You should consider mine."

. . . .

On *Invincible's* echoing bridge, the crew attended with laser-like focus to their duties. Glithwah stood among them: studying tactical displays, gauging crew demeanor, absorbing overall status. The campaign had evolved as expected, the few deviations minor and of little consequence. All but a handful of the clan's ships had completed offloading their passengers and cargoes. Onboard supplies had been supplemented from stockpiles on Prometheus, despite the loss of a freighter and the DiMeara woman's treachery. The warships designated to fly escort as *Invincible* withdrew had completed their refueling. UP ships within sensor range had been taught to keep their distance. All proceeded within the parameters of the plan. Pimal, in short, had matters under control.

It was the seemingly harmless anomalies that gnawed at Glithwah, chief among them Carl Rowland showing up. His arrival, here and now—like encountering Corinne on Prometheus, a bonus bit of revenge—felt too coincidental.

Suppose Carl *had* suspected a clan breakout to seize the starship. Wouldn't the local UP forces have been forewarned? Why did he care about one foolish pilot, and why had he tried so hard to disguise his interest? Why was he not negotiating harder? Why was he not negotiating at all, other than for the damned reporter's release?

In war, as in b'tok, defeat most often came from the attack you did not see coming.

"All prisoners to my ready room," she netted, storming off the bridge.

When the robots had shepherded them all in, she said, "You have been less than honest with me."

"I don't know what you mean," Carl said.

"I think you do." Glithwah bared her teeth. "And you should also know that my time and patience are limited."

With fleeting glances and all but imperceptible nods, the humans consulted about … something. Whether to be more forthcoming, she assumed.

"Okay," Carl said. "Send the bots elsewhere. Convince me this room isn't bugged and that you're as off the grid as we."

Did the warden suppose her become drunk with success? Insane? Why else, in time of war, would she agree to be alone and incommunicado with a cunning enemy agent of three times her mass?

At her netted command, the big robots herded the prisoners toward the door. "You will not enjoy your stay here," she promised.

"Banak had allies," Carl hissed.

"Halt!" Glithwah ordered.

CHAPTER 44

Bound tightly to her chair (again!), the chair bolted to the deck, to the atonal and arrhythmic droning that Snakes considered music, Corinne pondered a spectrum analyzer through its clear, shrink-wrapped covering. The controls and labels were human. The dust film on the plastic suggested months undisturbed inside some musty storeroom.

Carl, helpless in his own chair, was also studying the device. The safeguards for this private conversation had been his suggestions. "Turn it on."

A writhing, fat-and-fuzzy-caterpillar-like band popped onto the display. Did it signify a broad-spectrum jammer? Corinne had no idea. Her implant, drenched in suppressive neurotransmitters, had had nothing to offer her but static *before* the so-called jammer came on.

All must have been satisfactory, because Carl nodded his approval.

Glithwah, laser pistol in hand, massive desk separating her from the rest of them, settled into her own chair. "About Banak."

And Carl talked and talked. And talked. Of Banak reinventing himself, generation after generation, to disguise having far exceeded his reasonable lifespan. Of technology in Banak's studio on Ariel matching devices in the clandestine alien base on the Moon. Of Joshua's abduction, Robyn Tanaka Astor's assassination, the corruption of Astor's recent memories, and infiltration of the UPIA itself. Of the conspiracy the Xool labored so hard to hide: eons spent steering developments on Earth and the other InterstellarNet home worlds. Of solemn oaths to stop the very starship they were on.

Carl tried to keep his presentation to an overview, but Glithwah, again and again, drew him into details.

"Stop us?" Glithwah once more interrupted. "Grace DiMeara tried, and the damage was minimal. You saw it in hangar bay three. Your Xool, or at least their agents, do not seem so formidable."

"Minimal?" Tacitus said. The mesh enclosure it had worn lest it tap local wireless networks also shielded its server from the jammer. "About 450 million years ago, Earth went through its second-largest mass extinction."

"The Ordovician-Silurian Extinction," Joshua interjected, pedantically.

"I *know* that," Tacitus said. "It wiped out about half the multicellular species in Earth's oceans." Interrupting one another, the two historians launched into competing speculations of the cause, or causes, of the massive die-off. Quarreling like an old married couple, Corinne decided.

Sharper than any knife, fiercer than any laser, the guilt pierced her. She had been off Earth for *months*. When she had had the opportunity to send messages home, all too often she'd found reasons not to. Then—as though somehow it mattered—she'd filled her implant with recordings that Denise, it became clearer and clearer, was never going to see.

And Corinne felt even guiltier admitting: the past few months, chasing aliens and conspiracies, had been … exhilarating. If she were to be honest, she hadn't felt as alive in *years*.

Glithwah didn't let the bickering pair get far. "I fail to see the relevance."

"K'vith had an ice age about the same time," Tacitus said. "No, more than an ice age. A total snowball phase, the continents wiped clean of life."

A dangerous growl sounded deep in Glithwah's throat. Was it from anger or impatience? "Why do these things? What can these Xool hope to gain?"

That had been Corinne's question, too. She'd never come up with an answer. Neither, when she'd had the chance, had Robyn.

"I don't know," Joshua admitted. "But it's no coincidence that things—catastrophes—like this befell K'vith, Earth, and almost a dozen other worlds at about the same time. And at other times, too."

"And from mass extinctions your Xool switched to telling ghost stories? To influencing interstellar trade?"

"It's all true," Carl insisted. "We have proof."

Glithwah double-blinked: Snake condescension. Or maybe it was skepticism. Without Walt's knowledge of Snake body language, she couldn't decide. "You have a clever story, nothing more. Why don't you—"

"We've been inside a Xool facility," Joshua reminded.

"So you say. Conveniently, your evidence is more than a billion kilometers distant—and buried beneath tonnes of rock."

"We have proof *here*," Carl said. "In Tacitus' files."

Another double-blink. "Warden, you disappoint me. No matter how inventive this tale, you can't expect me to network with your AI. Suppose you explain why you really came?"

"The Xool *are* why I came," Carl said.

"What has any of this to do with your friend here?" Glithwah asked.

Did it have *something to do with me?* Corinne frowned, stymied. It could not be anything she had contributed to the conversation. She had been out of the picture since Ariel—except, of course, for traveling billions of klicks alone with a Xool mole. As for that, she had been oblivious.

"It has everything to do with Corinne," Carl said. "I don't know who I can trust. Not my agency, clearly. Telling the wrong people will just get us killed."

"So suddenly you trust *me*?" Glithwah asked. "Even now?"

"I trust that Banak chose not to let you take him alive. Since you're not a Xool mole, I have to hope you'll listen."

"You have yet to explain how this relates to the woman."

Carl said, "I've explained why I don't dare tell just anyone. Instead, to expose these Xool, I plan to tell *everyone*. Except it won't be me telling."

Finally, Corinne understood. "It will be me."

"When we set out," Carl said, "*Discovery* was in UP hands. I planned to play the Agency card, grab time on this ship's big transmitter. Between your worlds-wide audience and that radio, we'd spread the word to so many planets and moons, asteroids and Kuiper Belt objects, it could never be suppressed, no matter *how* deeply Interveners have penetrated Earth's comm networks." He stared at Glithwah. "We still can, Foremost. We must."

"Give it up." Glithwah stood. "I have work to do. You have withdrawal terms to finalize with your admiral. Robots will escort you back to your ship."

Me, too? Corinne dared to hope.

"Wait!" Carl said. "Just entertain the possibility I'm telling the truth. You had questions about Banak, even before he blew his head off. Right? So let me bring Corinne. I need her."

"Even entertaining the possibility, the last thing I'd help with is public disclosure. That these Xool don't suspect you know of them is your sole advantage." Another double blink. "But of course I don't believe any of this."

"What if you had proof?" Corinne asked. "What if you had a Xool agent?"

"Proof." Yet another double blink. "This wouldn't happen to be the saboteur you and I both saw blown to dust and gas?"

Grace hadn't just happened to end up on Prometheus, any more than she happened to move to New York, to hang around till she met Corinne. Any more than she had happened to be available when Corinne happened to need a substitute pilot. When some mundane weld giving way on *Discovery* had led the mission office to cancel press invitations, it had been Grace—playing Corinne's ego like a violin—who convinced her to drop out of comms and show up anyway. And it had been Grace, this time playing Donald With The Ridiculous Sideburns like a fiddle, who had gotten Corinne—and herself—a guided tour of this very ship.

Having gotten back aboard this ship, would Grace have run amok and gotten herself blown out of the sky? Uh-uh. No way.

"No," Corinne said, "it's the saboteur who remains aboard this ship. The saboteur who only wanted you to think she was dead. And I know how to find her."

CHAPTER 45

Bruised and bloody, her clothes in tatters, almost mad from the stress of avoiding thousands of Snakes, Grace doggedly shoved a bulging knapsack before her through *Discovery*'s labyrinthine network of ventilation ducts. The only illumination was what seeped through widely separated vents. Without gravity her sweat did not drip; instead, whenever she brushed against the ductwork, accumulated moisture dissolved more of the ubiquitous filth into yet another dollop of slimy paste. Only air, and perhaps the occasional cleaning bot, was intended ever to move through the ducts, so there was no reason to burnish every seam. Every few meters some screw tip or metal edge, hidden by gloom and muck, would snag her rags or inflict another wound on hand or knee or scalp. Every hundred meters or so she stopped to override control circuits, whether to interrupt the slice-and-dice whirl of some giant fan or to manually open a damper.

The circuit bypasses, at least, were straightforward, because until the Snakes arrived this had been a civilian mission. Within the ducts, she had yet to encounter a single security sensor. It was not a vulnerability she could expect the Foremost to tolerate for long.

She gave her knapsack another shove, slit yet another finger scrambling after it. Dodging killer robots was supposed to have been the difficult part of this plan. But her dash across the hangar bay, though scary, had proven anticlimactic, the smoke and heat of her improvised explosives having blinded cameras and IR sensors alike. Within seconds she had been through the hangar-bay air lock. Within two minutes, tops, she had made her way deep inside *Discovery*, decks away from her point of entry. By then the lash of the shuttle's fusion-drive exhaust would have melted the air lock to slag. Any notion of an intruder should be unimaginable.

Shove. Wriggle. Another meter forward. Another painful whack on a many-times-bruised knee. Shove. Wriggle. Shove. Rip. Free snagged knapsack. Shove.

"Soon," she mouthed to herself. It had become her mantra. "Soon."

Because one way or another, this would *all end soon.*

This ship stocked almost unbelievable quantities of fertilizer. No one would miss what she had appropriated, a little each from a dozen separate farm decks. Volatile hydrocarbons were scarcer, but between solvents and lubricants she had accumulated enough for her purposes. (Among the tasks she had underestimated: liberating enough containers to transport all those chemicals.) The fertilizer/hydrocarbon mix was not a high explosive, but that just meant she needed more.

A few tonnes of the stuff, in the right places, should more than do the trick.

And it all *stank*. She couldn't transfer the explosives—especially not through air ducts!—without first hermetically sealing each load. And without scrubbing herself raw before every single trip (holding her breath for however many immersions it took, in remote ponds restrained by taut rubber sheets), so that *she* would not stink.

No matter how much she scrubbed and scraped, the stench never left her nostrils.

For the umpteenth time her knapsack strove to go its own way, the wrong way, where a feeder duct split. As weightless as everything else, and as she herself, her cargoes nonetheless had inertia. She had the screamingly sore muscles, smashed fingers, and (though she couldn't prove it without a med scanner) the torn ligaments to prove it. Gritting her teeth, Grace tugged loose her knapsack and started it moving along the correct branch.

More than supplies and rude sanitary facilities, the farm decks provided food. No one would miss the fruits and vegetables she scavenged, never enough from any single plant to be noticeable. The way her body craved *more*, no matter how much she ate, had to say something about the need—in her mind, if not her belly—for protein.

She wouldn't be hungry much longer.

Unlatching a vent cover, she wriggled into a between-decks crawlspace just forward of the engine room. This stash of explosives, one among many, must mass close to a tonne, and the mere sight of it reminded every muscle in her body to protest.

She removed a detonator from her knapsack, positioned the device among the sealed bags and jars of explosive, then gathered her strength to move on. For detonators, as with everything else, she had had to improvise. As a high-impact shock device to set off the bulk explosive, she had a bottle of acetylene from a welding torch. A radio-controlled irrigation valve—modified to overload and spark—would first release the gas into the air and then ignite the mix.

Not even tonnes of explosives could destroy a ship this large, but that was all right. Her bombs needed only to destabilize the magnetic fields that isolated and contained *Discovery*'s antimatter fuel. Just for an instant. Once the slightest trace of antimatter escaped to make contact with normal matter ...

She checked her work, tied shut her knapsack, and wriggled back into a duct branch. Place a few more detonators and she would be done. Thank the lords, because she was *so* tired.

For only a moment, Grace let her eyes close.

• • • •

With a shudder, Grace came alert. She had no time to sleep! She stretched—or tried to, anyway.

Lights came on all around her.

"You used me," Corinne said.

Grace ignored the accusation, ignored her inexplicable nausea, to survey her surroundings. She was alone in an orchard, seated in a metal chair, the chair chained to sturdy trees. The trees would have been out of reach even if her wrists had not been taped to the chair's arms and her ankles to the chair's front legs.

The trees (apple?) were in full bloom, and bees flitted about. No one was within sight, either Snake or human. Apart from trees, chair, and the grassy field/deck beneath her feet, the only things nearby were an ordinary pocket comp and what might be a medical scanner. Duct tape kept both devices from floating away on an errant draft.

"And now you're trying to kill me," Corinne continued, her voice emanating from the comp.

Streaming video showed four faces: Corinne; Glithwah, the Foremost; Carl somebody, the warden on Ariel; and—Grace ransacked her memory to put a name to the final face, which she recognized from old reports—Joshua Matthews. She had no idea how, when, or why the two men had come aboard.

Grace's isolation suggested her captors knew of her cranial bomb. What else did they know?

"Not so," Grace said, her face turned toward the comp, addressing only the second indictment. "It's not my doing that you are aboard."

Damn it, she had been *so* close. In another half hour she'd have been done. Nothing would have remained of this ship but gamma rays and glowing gas.

Her interrogators' next question must be: why did she want to destroy the ship. Only it wasn't.

Carl said, "Why do the Xool want this ship stopped?"

Grace's heart thudded. *How could he know of the lords?* She had failed to stop this ship, and the lords' wrath against humanity would doubtless be harsh, but she was sworn to die before betraying their secrets. She focused her mind on the autodestruct sequence and—

Static, nothing more.

"While you were still under the gas," Carl said, "I gave you a hypo of neural suppressant. That's why your implant is offline. From that flash of dismay you just showed, more than your implant is refusing to work."

Her lords, when first she had begun to serve, had honored and entrusted her with a cyanide capsule and the hollow molar in which to hide it. For centuries after, merely to die when captured would have been enough.

No more. Not when, even in death, secrets might be gleaned from her neural implant. For the time had come when human adults who remained unnetworked were marginalized, drew unwelcome attention. As abhorrent as her lords found neural interfaces, they required their human servants to be so equipped. Immediately after Grace had had her neural interface implanted, a lord had replaced the suicide pill with a more robust failsafe.

The bomb within her skull that refused to arm.

Her captors would have X-rayed her while she was under, confirming their suspicions that there indeed was a bomb. Would have convinced themselves that the device was inoperable—at least for as long as they objected to repainting an operating theater with her gray matter. *Damn their thoroughness!*

"How did you find me?" Grace asked.

A security sensor she had failed to spot? Maybe. Or, by sheer bad luck, someone had come upon her buried pressure suit and begun a search. How hardly mattered, other than as an excuse with which to stall.

"Biometrics," Corinne said. "Remember our tour of this ship?"

Grace thought back. Donald With The Ridiculous Sideburns. The short flight from Prometheus. Donald's apologetic insistence after their shuttle had docked that his guests wear visitor badges. Visitor badges electronically mated to their medical ID chips. Since that day, she had been registered with the starship's security system—and of everyone aboard, no one but Corinne would have known that.

And so they had located her in the ducts and then gassed her. Grace still felt woozy.

"In the interest of efficiency," Carl said, "I'll share a little of what we know. The Xool have been around for ages. They're more than a little strange-looking: headless, with sensor stalks protruding from their shoulders; tentacles for arms and legs; a band of fringes at their waists. They *had*"—he paused, emphasizing the verb tense—"a secret base on the Moon, within a lava tube, in the foothills of Montes Carpatus. Their trusted servants, like you and Helena Strauss, meet with them to make reports and receive your orders."

Helena exposed, too! What had her friend let slip? Because it was inconceivable that she would reveal this much by choice.

"What are you *talking* about?" Grace asked.

"We're trying to save time," Carl reminded her. "Had you noticed the medical scanner at your feet? We're monitoring it remotely. When I named the Xool, your heart rate jumped. Your brain scan lit up like a Christmas tree. The readouts spiked again when I mentioned the lunar base. You know exactly what I'm talking about."

She bit her lip rather than say more.

"The Xool don't want humans 'wandering,' and so Helena made them a promise." Carl smiled unpleasantly. " 'Your humble servants will stop the starship.' And here we found you, stockpiling explosives. Humble servant."

"You don't get it!" Grace blurted out. Her lords, when angered, could do … anything. And they had made their desires clear. "It's for your own good."

"Then help us understand," Carl said.

She could not stop the questioning. She could not make her body not react. But if they had had confidence their chemicals would keep her from triggering her bomb, they would be *here*, not on a vid link. Maybe, their concerns were valid. Maybe, if she could string them along for a while …

"What do you want to know?" she asked.

"How is 'not wandering' in our best interest?" Carl asked.

"The Xool have a vision for humanity." A vision they did not share. Except for some *shalt nots*, Grace little more understood her lords' vision than she had when, long ago, as a young orphan, elderly servants had taken her in. "Leaving the Solar System isn't a part of that."

"What is?" Carl asked.

"I am not at liberty to say."

"Do I need to know this undisclosed vision?" Pensively, Carl rubbed his chin. "Of course. I need to know because the Xool are so damned powerful. They have wondrous technologies—setting aside that they have the most pathetic computers in eleven solar systems. I need to know because they're insistent upon achieving their vision. So here's the essential question, Grace. What will the Xool do if we go off script?"

In truth, she also marveled at the lords' cumbersome computers. More than once she had offered—nay, pleaded—to equip their lunar facility with decent hardware. For her own use, if not theirs. Apart from permission, finally, to bring in the lowest-end of personal comps, hobbled by removal of its wireless chip, her argument had accomplished nothing.

"What will they do? I don't think you want to find out."

"The thing is," Carl said, "the UP no longer controls this vessel. For the next few years, at a minimum, the Foremost has stopped humans from roaming. You knew that before sneaking aboard. Kudos on that stunt, by the way. I'm impressed. So why destroy this ship *now?*"

A query to her implant evoked less static than just after she had awakened. Days running on desperation and adrenaline might well turn up a person's metabolism. She might be burning off the suppressant faster than her captors expected. If she could continue a little longer without revealing anything critical ...

"It is because my lords have a distinct vision for each InterstellarNet species. Trafficking among them is contrary to those visions."

Corinne sniffed. "What is InterstellarNet *but* trafficking among species?"

And so it was. Grace and Helena and other servants had done their best to strangle interstellar communications in its cradle. In other solar systems, other servants had also made the attempt. Their efforts had seldom worked, either.

On Grace's next attempt, the static within her skull was clearly fading. Just a little while longer and she could end the threat to the lords that was ... herself. She was revealing too much. She *knew* it, and still she couldn't seem to stop. A residual effect of the knockout gas? Something more than suppressant in that hypo?

"Do not mistake the lords' leniency in one instance with license to defy them." She only paraphrased an answer she had been given, in a very different context, early in her service. "The present situation is more serious."

"I would have words with your 'lords,' " the Foremost said.

"First you'll have to find them," Grace said.

"They went home to chat," Carl said offhandedly, "so just point us to their home."

A chill ran down Grace's spine. How did he *know* so much? She began to doubt Helena, to fear Helena had betrayed the lords. If not her friend, then one of the lords' servants on Earth.

Grace said, "That's information you'll never get from me, because I don't know."

"Because they don't trust you to know," the Foremost said, "and yet you serve them. Have you no self-respect?"

"I serve the greatest minds in the galaxy!" Grace shot back. "I am honored to do so."

"Let's talk about that," Carl said.

• • • •

It was, Joshua thought, *like watching a tennis match—only instead of a tennis ball, they whacked about the fate of worlds.*

One subtext after another soared over his head. There were meanings within meanings, wheels within wheels. Like peeling an onion. Like matryoshka dolls. He wasn't useful here. Hell, he couldn't even pick and stick with one metaphor.

But there was another way he could help: a way he did not expect would be well received. A way that, once the notion had occurred to him, he couldn't get out of his mind. A way that both terrified and beckoned to him.

Joshua covered the mic with a hand. "I'm going to sick bay."

"Still have that headache?" Corinne asked. "Sorry."

Carl brushed aside the hand. "Be right back." He froze the camera and muted the mic. "*Now*, Joshua? Seriously?"

"Now," Joshua said—hunched over, eyes downcast, doing his

best to look pathetic. "Trust me. I need to leave." *If not for any reason I'm willing to share. Call it the Plan B that I'm afraid we'll need—and that I'm* more *afraid I'd be too easily talked out of.* "You can't say I've contributed a damn thing to the interrogation, or that I'm likely to."

"We have to keep pushing," Carl said, "While Grace is rattled and still punchy from the knockout gas."

"Right," Joshua said. "*You* do."

Corinne turned toward Carl. "Tacitus can handle whatever historical esoterica come up."

"Well ...," Joshua said. "He'll remember the way to sick bay from the tour you gave us."

"I'll bring you," Corinne said.

Joshua shook his head once, wincing at pretended pain. "You know Grace. No one else here does. If she acts out of character, no one but you will catch it."

"I agree that Corinne belongs here," Glithwah said. The Snake's attitude toward his friend had changed since Corinne had given them Grace. "I'll summon a robot to guide Joshua."

"No need." Joshua patted the server at his feet.

Carl said, "It's bad enough that we have to trust a comm link from here. Let's not risk someone sneaking a bug into this room on a robot."

"Someone. Another mole, you mean." Glithwah licked her lips. "When did you become the more suspicious one? You might yet, someday, best me at b'tok."

For an instant, the Snake's attention was elsewhere. "All right, Joshua, take Tacitus. I've netted authorization. You're cleared to move about unescorted on this deck. I hope you feel better soon."

"Thank you." Joshua grabbed the server handle and shuffled toward the ready-room door.

"What was that about?" Tacitus asked once the door closed behind them. "The infirmary is a three-minute walk ... if you dawdle. You'll make all of two turns getting there. And I remember signs on the walls. With big, bold letters. Even through this damned mesh I could read them."

"Quiet," Joshua said.

Two Snakes in magnetized sandals came clomping toward them. Neither gave Joshua a second glance.

He let them pass before asking, "You think you know me?"

"I think I do."

Joshua turned to his left. At the first cross-corridor, he turned right. "Let's find out."

He had a proposal to make, *proposal* being an especially apt word. As for the nature of the proposal, desperate times called for desperate measures.

"Let's find out," he repeated.

• • • •

"Thank you," the warden said. Rattling her. Needling her.

Grace stared daggers at the med scanner at her feet. When she lied, the device caught her. When she refused to speak, brain patterns disclosed what she recognized, what alarmed her, what had gone wide of the mark. All Carl had to do was speculate … whether he guessed right or wrong, he learned.

She tried yet again to end it all. She failed, but the interference seemed less staticky than earlier.

"Let's recap, shall we?" Carl continued. He did, and the extent of his forbidden knowledge was appalling. "That's the what. But why do the Xool meddle?"

She spat. Like *where do the Xool come from?* and *how did they recruit you?* this latest sally was a question without a simple answer. She defied anyone to read the answer from her mind, no matter how sophisticated the med scanner.

Unlike yes-or-no questions. With each of those, her thoughts gave something away.

Star by star, Carl asked whether the Xool home was warmed by *this* nearby sun. When he ran out of suns with proper names, he had the pocket comp project a star chart. Then he grilled her about dozens more stars identified only by cryptic survey codes.

"I don't know," she answered, truthfully, every time.

"New topic," Glithwah finally said. "Let's talk about Dolmar Banak."

At *that* name, synapses must have fired like mad. Grace did not bother to feign ignorance of the Snake servant.

Glithwah leaned toward the camera. "Did you know Banak before your recent trip to Ariel? No. Did you know *about* Banak before your recent trip? Yes. Because a Xool told you? No. Because a fellow human agent of the Xool told you? No. Because Banak or another Hunter agent of the Xool had contacted *you*? No."

Grace thought, *good luck sorting out her connection with Banak by playing twenty questions.*

Corinne took a try. "On our flight to Ariel, you mentioned hoping to buy a sculpture without middlemen or shipping costs. Had you recognized Xool technology in some news report about him?"

A documentary, to be precise. Grace kept her mouth shut, for all the good that did.

"The hibernation capsule in the back room of his studio." Carl said. "The 'sculpture' that looked like an open coffin. You saw it on some vid and knew that only another Xool agent would have it. Right?"

The way Corinne's eyes went round, the damned scanner must have blazed like the freaking Star of Bethlehem.

Did her interrogators use *hibernation* as convenient shorthand, or did they understand that within the devices, time actually slowed? Did they even suspect that through the wonder of such a device, her service had extended across more than five centuries?

And how did *that* line of thought show up in a brain scan?

• • • •

"That's how it is, Admiral," Carl concluded his report. Glithwah would have bugged the stateroom he had been given, but—Carl hoped—the crypto within his implant, now that *his* dose of suppressant had worn off, remained secure. "Approach this starship and its escorts, or attempt to impede their departure, and hostages will die."

Matsushita's avatar stared back impassively. It appeared against a starry backdrop, giving no hints aboard which warship, and where on that ship, its owner was located. Comm delay implied a location three light-seconds distant, but the direction and apparent distance might be disguised by relay buoys.

The admiral asked, "When do the Snakes intend to depart?"

"They won't tell me," Carl said, "but foot traffic in the corridors and elevators, from the civilians settling in, seems to have peaked. My guess is they'll be ready in another day or so."

Because no mere eons-old alien conspiracy could make Glithwah lose focus on liberating her clan.

"Foot traffic in the corridors and elevators. So much for rapport and deep insights from playing b'tok together."

"Nor has my coming aboard hurt anything, Admiral. How are the hostages?"

"To judge by the video streaming from Prometheus, exhausted and overcrowded, but unharmed. Nothing we can sense from afar contradicts that. As for the interned crews abandoned in the outer system, help has reached the closest groups. They're okay."

All clean and precise—just as Glithwah played b'tok. "That's good news, Admiral."

"And the reporter? Is she free to leave?"

Was she? Carl didn't know. "For now, she expects to stay."

"Unacceptable. Bring her back with you."

"When I'm done," Carl said, wondering if he could keep that promise. "I'm not ready to give up here." Because bigger issues were at stake than Matsushita could know.

And because Joshua—by the time Corinne had thought to wonder about his continuing absence and gone to check on him—was in no condition to be moved.

What the hell *had Joshua been thinking?*

• • • •

In slow motion, as in some B horror vid, time passed. Or maybe time only seemed to pass; with her implant suppressed, Grace had nothing with which to gauge time's passage but a growing thirst and the pressure in her bladder. On the comp's projected image, inquisitors came and went. She wondered what those comings and goings meant, and which were real and which computer legerdemain.

But an end finally came to her interrogation, during which robots brought and chained down a three-meter-square cell. Except for its padded bars, the enclosure was featureless. One bot gave her another hypo of suppressant, ripped off the tape that bound her to the chair, and shepherded her into the cage. A second bot, holding a Taser, stood guard even after the deadbolt slammed home with a definitive, metallic clang.

Once she was locked inside, the first bot provided diapers, drink bulbs and foil-wrapped emergency rations, and a many-times-folded thin paper sheet. If her captors intended the modesty drape to seem a considerate touch, she was not fooled. Of *course* she was under continuous observation. The bots doubtless carried millimeter-wave radars that rendered her effectively naked.

Soon after, the overhead dimmed: simulated night for the orchard. As best she could, Grace slept.

• • • •

Too soon, the motorized *whirr* of a robot woke Grace. She saw it had slipped more food packets and water bulbs through the bars of the cage. Ignoring it all, she tried to trigger the bomb in her head. Nothing happened.

A comp was still taped to the ground near her cage. The projected holo showed Carl, Corinne, and the Foremost.

Corinne asked, "Why inflict the Frankenstein myth on humanity?"

"I don't know," Grace said. That hadn't been her project, though she could take credit for Jekyll and Hyde.

"A lie. To discourage our development of biotech?"

"I don't know."

Corinne smiled humorlessly. "Yes, you do. Is that why the Xool gave a similar myth to the Centaurs?"

"I don't know." And this time Grace truly didn't. It was rare enough that her lords explained their purposes on Earth.

"Why not also impose that myth on the Hunters?"

"I don't know."

"Was the novel *Superminds* unleashed on the Hunters to encourage their development of neural implants?"

"I don't *know*."

On and on the questions came. Grace stopped answering, although her silence seldom made any difference. Her thoughts betrayed her, revealing secrets through the damnable scanner.

But once more, the static in her head seemed to be fading. And as with every perceptible decrease she reminded herself that standard neural suppressors had never anticipated her self-destruct device. Certainly, her tormentors believed that. As long as *they* refused to share a room with her, *she* would cling to the hope their wariness had justification. That sooner or later, they would miscalculate the necessary timing for a re-dose.

Damn it, they had *to!*

After a while Carl changed subjects. "Did you abduct Joshua? No. Do you know the people who did? Yes. Were any of them Xool agents? Yes. All of them? Yes. Was he abducted and returned drunk and ill to discredit the Matthews conundrum?"

No verdict announced this time. Because Grace was guessing what this "Matthews conundrum" was?

"An ambiguous answer because it was an ambiguous question?" Carl mused. "Yes. Okay, let's try this. Joshua observed that the local interstellar neighborhood has several intelligent species in radio contact, while beyond our cosmic corner there is silence. With that clarified: was he abducted and returned drunk and puking to discredit that line of inquiry?"

Grace willed herself not to react, willed herself to *die*. Both times she failed.

"Excellent," Carl said. "Now we're getting somewhere. And are the Xool responsible for that interstellar anomaly? Yes."

"Think about that," Grace said. "I mean, really *think*. Try to comprehend their power. You and I are fleas. Less than fleas. Totally insignificant. When my lords first came to Earth, the land was barren. Sponges were high on the food chain. That's more than you are meant to know—and it should make you tremble in awe.

"They made us. They molded us. Everything we humans are, everything we have accomplished, we owe to them."

Carl said, "And when we presume to think for ourselves, they kill us. Or on their behalf, agents like *you* kill us."

"No!" Grace said. "Well, sometimes. When it is necessary. When we have no other way to keep forbidden knowledge from people. As you pointed out, we didn't kill Joshua Matthews."

"No, you just ruined his life," Corinne said.

"Forbidden knowledge." Carl was not to be deflected. "Subjects that we are not told—except, perhaps, in the most oblique ways, like *Frankenstein*—are forbidden."

Why couldn't they see? Grace wondered. *Any more overt identification only gave the taboo matters credence and cachet.*

"We keep you from blasphemy." From the scowl on Carl's face, the scanner must have confirmed Grace's unshakeable conviction. "So forget about interstellar travel. My lords will *not* allow you to spoil projects underway for eons."

So listen, *damn it! I am trying to* save *lives! I'm as human as you.*

She tried her bomb again. Nothing. But not much static, either.

"What projects?" Carl asked. "What are the Xool trying to accomplish here? How would our travel to another star spoil anything?"

"I don't know."

"Guess," he prompted.

Could they possibly believe she had never tried? "I don't know."

Carl glared at her. "And if we don't play along?"

Armageddon? Her lords were adamant. "For your sake, for

humanity's sake, destroy this ship and forget about my lords."

"And why should *I* care," the Foremost asked, "about humanity's sake?"

"Do you imagine Snakes are any less insignificant?" Grace snapped.

"They underestimate us at their peril," the Foremost said.

The static in Grace's head dipped a bit further. "And you underestimate me."

Regretting only that she could do no more for those she served, Grace triggered her bomb.

CHAPTER 46

In the clamorous expanse of the starship's main dining hall, at the one remaining table of human proportions, Corinne nursed a drink bulb of hot coffee. If she concentrated, she could sometimes separate the voices of individual Snakes from the babble. If she cared, the language module newly downloaded to her neural implant would translate. The few times she bothered, all she got for her trouble were random pleasantries and family squabbles.

She told herself that commonplace banter was a good portent. She told herself that Joshua, last seen with his head planted up a truly scary medical gizmo, would—eventually!—come out of it okay. She told herself Denise was all too accustomed to her long absences. She told herself Carl's tardiness for breakfast meant nothing. She told herself that the memory would fade of a head turning before her eyes into a sleet of blood, gray matter, and bone shards, that she would move past the headless, tattered corpse afloat in its padded cell.

Corinne told herself many things, none of which she believed.

Fifteen minutes late, Carl came into the dining hall. She waved till she caught his eye. He nodded, then gestured to a coffee urn.

With his own drink bulb, he joined her at her table. "Didn't sleep well?" he asked.

"You know how it is." That was a simpler explanation than bolting awake, her heart pounding, the few times she had somehow dozed off. Cage bars bowed out ... the echoing blast ... the gristle and gore spattering and splatting on the camera lens ...

She doubted Grace's exploding skull would *ever* leave her dreams.

"Yeah." He took a sip, made a face. "Sulfur garnish does nothing for the coffee."

"When we get out, I'll buy you coffee anywhere you want. Hell,

I'll throw in breakfast." *Because Glithwah knew the stakes now. She had to let them go. Didn't she?* "I'm assuming you've settled matters with the Foremost. When do I go on air?"

A high-pitched yammer blared over the PA system. It was in clan speak, and she did not bother to have the announcement translated. A concurrent mind's ear *ping* suggested a ship-wide notice had been posted. She ignored it, too.

"About that." With his free hand, Carl took hers. "You *don't* go on the air. And we don't go home, either."

"So despite everything we've revealed to Glithwah, we're prisoners." Confirmation of her worst fears came almost as a relief. "The navy will be okay with that?"

"I'm a UPIA agent, and that's unambiguous. You showed up at Prometheus despite having had your authorization revoked, and Glithwah can claim you're a spy. If the navy's hands weren't already tied by her holding so many more hostages, you and I would still be stuck. Spies are expendable."

"Joshua is no spy!" Not that he was in any condition to leave.

Carl shrugged. "No one else knows he's with me, though his grandmother may guess."

The PA reawakened, this time sounding a shrill, warbling tone. The electric horn cut off, followed by short Snake words spoken in a quick cadence. As sudden pressure—gentle at first, but building and building—pressed her into her chair, she knew the words had been a countdown.

They were on their way ... where?

Another *ping* rang in her mind's ear, but this one was coded COSMIC ULTRA.

Carl gave her hand a squeeze. "Bottom line?" he netted. His avatar exhibited none of the original's patent weariness. "Don't think of us as prisoners, but more like honored guests who can't leave.

"Glithwah has worked for years to free her clan. Not even the Xool and their minions will dissuade her. Quite the opposite, in fact: since the Xool don't want humans 'wandering,' Glithwah would be a fool not to scram before the Xool find a way to destroy this ship."

And Glithwah was nobody's fool.

"I get it. She can break away while keeping us." Corinne chewed on that notion for awhile. "But why hold us? And why not let me broadcast?"

"She has good reasons." In the real world, Carl managed a brief, crooked smile. "At least once you've played enough b'tok."

"My big plan, not knowing who to trust, was to use this ship's big transmitter and your celebrity to get out word about the Xool." Okay, he'd come to accept that he had had other motivations. Rescuing her. Keeping the starship from Glithwah, even before knowing it needed rescue. He had failed at both, and saw no gain in admitting either. "Bypass their hidden agents, their moles in government, their penetrations of our networks. Make *everyone* aware. Get *everyone* focused on the problem of rooting them out. Spread the news beyond any possibility of suppression. Take back control of human destiny."

"It still sounds like a plan," she netted.

"The thing is ..."

"What?"

"Something Grace said: 'My lords will *not* allow you to spoil projects underway for eons.' It's a decent bet that unmasking the Xool after all their efforts at secrecy won't further their projects."

Corinne sighed. "And Glithwah cares what happens on Earth?"

"Assume the Xool take action against Earth and Earth-settled worlds. They might go after anyone else who could have heard."

Such as the clan of Snakes fleeing the scene, Corinne completed the thought.

Carl went on, "Whatever else I may think of Glithwah, I can't see her as a fan of genocide. Though she doesn't admit it, maybe she's protecting us from ourselves."

In the physical world, Snakes were abandoning their tiny tables, streaming from the dining hall. *Headed for duty posts,* Corinne wondered, *or just seeking more comfortable places to take the acceleration?*

"Okay," she netted. "So Glithwah doesn't let me broadcast. Why not let us go? Given the bigger picture, keeping me prisoner just seems petty. And what did Joshua ever do to her?"

"Suppose she lets us off the ship. How does she know we won't find another megaphone somewhere?" Carl laughed bitterly. "That's if someone like Grace doesn't kill us first. I should be flattered Glithwah worries we might survive to talk."

Corinne slumped in her chair, and the still-building acceleration was only the least part of it. "So we're off to … where? The Snake home system?"

Carl gave her hand a squeeze. "I'm told we have years before we need to know where."

. . . .

Examine any isolated part of a meat brain, and it is glacially slow. But meat brains overall are not slow. Consider the entirety of a meat brain—its billons of neurons, its trillions of synapses—and you discover evolution's clever solution: massive parallelism.

Although in fairness, Joshua had to concede, *all that parallelism might be a clever solution of the Xool.*

Biochips compact and low-powered enough to tuck within the crannies of a meat brain were slow, too. But stimulate the brain to create enough new synapses and the biochip/brain interface also became massively parallel. Thus interconnected, brain and biochips spoke—exchanging data, information, knowledge, wisdom, even insight—at prodigious rates.

But not without training. Not without probing every niche and nuance of those trillions of synapses, and of Tacitus' uploaded memories besides.

Not without re-experiencing and re-imagining *everything*.

The majesty of the tides. The textures of distant nebulae. Centuries of Yorkshire property records, curiously evocative. The rustle of grass in the breeze, the mathematics of a Beethoven sonata, and the mouth shape of every word Joshua had ever heard spoken. The taste of every food imaginable, in unimaginable combinations.

All that took time. Weeks, typically, and two months were not unheard of, because neurons could not be rushed. Per the real-time clock that was the merest fraction of the functionality of just one of the chips newly embedded in his brain, he and Tacitus were but two days into the process.

When they *had* completed their synthesis, would they find Corinne and Carl still aboard? Joshua hoped not, but supposed otherwise. He could see no reason Glithwah would ever let them go. He expected Carl saw that, too. Either way—or even if his friends *could* go, but his inability to leave made them choose to stay—in the bigger picture, them ending up aboard mattered not a whit. *Something* had to be done about the Xool, and it meant taking the confrontation to them. This was the only available starship, and Glithwah would never give it back.

After everything he had been through, he *would* see this to its end. Whatever it took.

"Integration is proceeding nicely," Galen netted.

"Glad to hear it," Joshua said back. In theory, anyway; what he *heard* come out of his mouth was an inarticulate gurgle. Was that because the new him couldn't yet produce speech, or couldn't properly interpret the sounds? Indeterminate. All he knew for certain was that within his skull, rewiring proceeded.

And from deep within the maelstrom of neural rewiring, in kaleidoscopic glimpses of everything he and Tacitus had ever experienced, patterns beckoned ....

CHAPTER 47

The hostages on Prometheus had been freed, the last castaways rescued from Ariel and Caliban and even scattered Kuiper Belt objects. The last UP navy vessel, its fuel reserves exhausted, had stopped shadowing the departing Snakes and turned for home. The last clan escort ship had docked on *Discovery*. To stern, the Sun was but one bright light among many.

As for the red dwarf sun dead ahead, its sullen glow scarcely registered in a telescope. Their destination would be invisible to the naked eye for years.

· · · ·

An expectant hush came over *Invincible*'s bridge. On the main tactical display—blurry with distance, subtly distorted by five cascades of photomultipliers—a knobby mass of ice and rock grew moment by moment. The image was being repeated on displays across the ship.

"Status?" Glithwah asked aloud.

Carl's implant translated the terse request. Anyone aboard could as easily monitor operations by implant, and at much greater depth than spoken words permitted. Only this was not about immersion in details, but rather some kind of shared experience for everyone.

Apart from a brusque summons, minutes earlier, Glithwah hadn't shared squat with *him*.

"Yes, Foremost." Pimal, the clan's chief tactical officer, straightened in his chair. "*Hermes* on final approach. Radar lock on target. Impact forecast as per schedule."

Hermes? Impact?

"Excellent," Glithwah answered. "Latest characterization of target?"

"As per earlier determinations," Pimal said. "Comparable in mass to *Invincible*. Typical cometary-belt object."

"Excellent. Authorization for completion."

At Carl's side, Corinne was riveted to the telescopic close-up of the Oort Cloud object. "Billions of years it's been out here, alone and untouched. What happens to it now?"

"It gets touched," Carl guessed.

"Do you perceive the point?" Glithwah asked, switching to English. "We have a couple of minutes."

The b'tok master tests her protégé? Carl took in a deep breath, then exhaled sharply. "Let's see. To begin with, *Hermes* is perhaps the fastest ship you have."

Where sky peeked around the rim of the distant snowball, the star field matched what he recalled of their view ahead. Images saved in his implant agreed. So *Hermes* had been sent racing ahead to some random snowball along their course. Why bother?

With nothing coming to mind, he looked around for inspiration. He saw Snakes at their duty stations. Instrument consoles, none revealing anything amiss. Tactical displays, none showing pursuit. Other displays, showing star fields.

A different star field than provided backdrop for the featured snowball.

"When did we change course?" he asked Glithwah.

"Two days ago," she told Carl. "You are on the right track."

Three days ago, by his best guess, they had departed the range of UP naval sensors.

Hermes continuing along their former course. A snowball comparable in mass to this ship. Impact, Pimal had said.

"You're faking our destruction," Carl said.

"How?" Glithwah asked calmly.

He took that as confirmation. So must have Corinne, from the way she paled.

On the main display, the snowball loomed ever larger. *Hermes* was almost upon it.

So: *Hermes* hits the snowball, like a bullet smacking into a wall. There would be debris, sure, and maybe a brief flash. But would anyone deeper in the Solar System even notice?

"You put antimatter canisters aboard," Carl guessed.

Glithwah didn't comment.

Once more, from the top. Ship smacks much larger snowball. Ship comes to a sudden stop, flattened. Everything inside ship crumples, too—including the canisters that isolated the antimatter. The merest instant after the electromagnets in the canisters fail, some of the antimatter makes contact with normal matter, and—

Boom!

"Gamma rays," Carl said. Because gamma rays of very specific wavelengths were the hallmark of matter/antimatter explosions. "*That's* what will get people's attention. And when they turn telescopes toward the source of the pulse, they'll see plenty of glowing gas and dust."

Glithwah licked her lips, as if daring him to imply more.

"Ten seconds until impact," Pimal alerted them. "Switchover to *Invincible*'s telescope."

The snowball image became a dim point, more ordinary than ever—only in a moment, for just a moment, it would become (if you could see gamma rays) the brightest thing around.

"Three ... two ... one ..."

Flash!

The visible spark from the impact soon faded.

"Very good," Glithwah announced with a raised voice.

The bridge crew responded with a roar of approval. But at Carl's side, Corinne was fighting back tears.

"What is it?" he asked her.

"Denise will think I'm dead. Blown up. Vaporized. Splattered across space."

"Perhaps that's a mercy," Carl said softly. "We're never coming back."

Shaking her head, at a loss for words, Corinne sank into herself.

"So, why, Carl?" Glithwah asked. "What do we gain by sacrificing your fine little ship?"

Spies aren't allowed feelings, he told himself. In that bitter reflection he found his answer. "No one is going to believe *Invincible* just happened to blow up."

"No, they won't," Glithwah agreed.

"My former colleagues at the UPIA will suppose I somehow did it." He thought some more. "And any Xool or Xool agents left back in the Solar System will think Grace pulled it off."

"Let us hope so," Glithwah said. "The Xool don't want us wandering."

"Then it's over. Years from now, light-years from here, you'll colonize someplace no one will ever come looking for you."

Leaving humanity in their billions, across the Solar System, to fend for themselves.

"At best, it's over for *now*," Glithwah said. "Radio chatter in our new solar system will eventually betray our presence. Nothing can truly be over till we have had a heart-to-heart conversation with the Xool. But for that to happen, first we must find them."

"That's all right," a familiar-yet-changed voice said. *Joshua!* He stood at the main hatch onto the bridge. "Ir know where we can find them."

. . . .

Joshua/Tacitus felt all eyes boring into them. Joshua explained, "*Ir* is the Augmented first person."

"Never mind grammar," Corinne said. "You gave us a fright. How are you feeling?"

At the same time, more to the point, Carl asked, "Where?"

At the same time Glithwah demanded, "Humans to my ready room, *now*."

"Ir am fine," Tacitus told Corinne. Health-maintenance software provided by Galen was already tweaking and tuning their hormone levels, orchestrating isometric exercises, recommending optimiza-

Edward M. Lerner

tions for their next nutritional intake, growing cranial stubble out to proper hair. "Foremost, to call mir human is not exactly correct."

"Walk," Glithwah growled.

They walked.

As soon as the ready-room doors closed, Tacitus took over. "Where? It has been right in front of us all along, though it would be best to have the mole confirm."

Corinne averted her eyes. "Grace killed herself."

No matter, then, Tacitus thought. And also, *what else had happened while he had been out of the loop.*

"Ir am sorry," Joshua said. "Despite everything, Ir know you considered her as a friend."

"Where?" Carl tried again.

"A star more or less as bright as Sol," Joshua began, laying the groundwork. "We know the illumination levels at the lunar base. We saw Xool and their agents were equally comfortable in Earth-like room lighting. The illumination did not change when gravity bumped to what we surmised was Xool-normal. That all suggests their native world orbits an F-, G-, or K-class star."

Glithwah said, "Narrowing our choices to, more or less, a quarter of the stars in the galaxy. Billions of suns. How is that helpful?"

"We'll get there," Joshua said.

"A little faster, please," Carl said. "And *how* do you know? Was the location in a part of the Xool database the rest of us hadn't yet searched?"

"Nothing so overt," Tacitus answered.

"Don't be smug," Joshua netted to his other half. "Or coy. Carl's only human."

"Then you explain," Tacitus netted back.

Joshua said, "The Xool project, whatever it is, involves nearby solar systems. If light-speed is a limit, that argues for the Xool themselves being nearby. As do the surveillance vids we've seen. Grace and Helena expected to be around for the return of 'their lords.' "

"These beings shape worlds," Carl said. "Their tech must far exceed ours. Light speed might *not* be a limit for them."

Tacitus said, "Light speed is almost certainly a limit for them, too. You have to picture their experiment in deep time. The few stars that comprise InterstellarNet are neighbors *now*. Relative to the Sun, Barnard's Star"—native system of the Snakes—"is the fastest moving star. Barnard's is passing by at about ninety kilometers per second."

"Deep time," Carl echoed. "Hmm. The experiment began ...?"

"The first discernable synchronization among the InterstellarNet worlds happened around the time of our Cambrian Explosion," Joshua offered. "Call it 550 million years ago."

"One and a half *million* light years?" Corinne said. "Barnard's and Sol were that far apart when the experiment began?"

"Your multiplication is correct," Tacitus said. Her implant's multiplication, more likely. "However ..."

"Please excuse my sarcastic and socially inept other half," Joshua said, reclaiming his vocal cords. "Still, Tacitus is correct that linear extrapolation doesn't apply. Had InterstellarNet stars ever been so far apart, they would not have had as much as a galaxy in common. Since the Cambrian Explosion, our Sun has more than twice circled the Milky Way's core. Other stars follow their own orbits around that core.

"But at a more basic level, Corinne, you are correct. When, ages ago, the Xool began their project, they chose stars that were widely separated. Stars that would, however, converge."

"And then diverge?" Glithwah asked.

"For beings who plan in eons? Yes." Joshua paused, let the others take that in. "And that perspective makes our era, in which the InterstellarNet solar systems *are* neighbors, all the more anomalous."

Glithwah said, "Our stars converge just as our civilizations achieve advanced technologies. That's can't be a coincidence."

"Advanced technology?" Joshua said. "That's less than clear. The Xool might not consider what we've accomplished"—*apart from computers*—"in any way noteworthy. What Ir doubt is coincidental is that as these stars converged, the Xool intervened more and more often."

Carl grimaced. "I've lost the thread somewhere. And I'm still waiting for the *where*."

"Fair enough," Joshua said. "It's a very tangled thread. Why choose solar systems that will converge?" When no one ventured a guess, he offered his own. "Because there's a desire, perhaps a need, to compare notes across those solar systems at a particular point in the project. And because at least at this stage of the project, light speed as a limit *does* matter."

"Suggesting the Xool world is close," Corinne said. "Only there are what, about forty stars within twenty light-years of Sol?"

"When you count binaries and triples as a single star," Tacitus agreed, "and if you ignore brown dwarfs and free-floating planetary mass objects. But your twenty light-years are arbitrary. The farther out you look, the higher the count goes."

"Guys," Carl said, "I promise to admire your brilliance later. Where *are* the Xool?"

"We're almost there," Joshua said. "Ir needed first to establish that they must have a presence nearby. Corinne, when you and I first met, everyone else believed I was a hopeless drunk, a failure, a loser, slinking home after a weeks-long binge. You stuck with me. Why?"

"Why do *you* change the subject?" Glithwah asked.

"Ir am not." Joshua said. "Corrine?"

She chewed her lip, as if thinking back. "Your assets went untouched the entire time you were missing. The only ones who came forward claiming to have information, going after your family's reward, were obvious cranks and con men. The police never found any trace of you."

"Maybe at first that's what sold you. It surely didn't keep you convinced."

"I suppose not." Corinne smiled wanly. "Fine. You tell me why."

"Because," Joshua said, "my disappearance fit a pattern. Bad things happened to historians who shared my curiosity, who might bring attention to the anomaly of InterstellarNet in an otherwise silent galaxy. It was the pattern you couldn't explain away."

Corinne nodded. "Nor could Robyn Tanaka explain it away."

Once pointed in the right direction, no Augmented *could* miss such an obvious pattern—and getting involved had gotten her/them killed. But if humanity was to survive, an Augmented had had to get involved again.

As now one was.

You're welcome," Tacitus netted.

Joshua continued, "There is a silent solar system, its sun of spectral class K, located well within the InterstellarNet bubble. A star that is speeding by almost as quickly as Barnard's. And bad things happen, in statistically significant numbers, to *astronomers* who study it."

"Enough!" Carl said. "Just name it."

"*You* can name it. What nearby solar system is of unique scientific interest, was the consensus choice across the *Discovery* mission team, and yet politicians overruled it as a destination?"

Just for a moment, everyone's eyes glazed—diving into the ship's library, following Joshua's hints.

"Epsilon Indi," Carl said.

"Epsilon Indi," Joshua agreed.

CHAPTER 48

Clan governance was not democratic, not exactly, but it involved consultation.

Abandon everything achieved on Ariel over twenty long years? Stake everyone's lives on war against the United Planets? Those hard choices had been debated.

Choose a particular nameless, unexceptional star? Commit generations to come to building a new civilization there? Those choices also had been debated.

And whether to cast aside those decisions, to risk the freedom obtained against such daunting odds, to boldly go seeking out the Xool? Whether to roll the dice yet again with the lives of the clan? *That* must be thoroughly debated, as well.

And it was.

And was approved, by acclamation.

Aware that while they might run, they could not hide.

• • • •

Unblinking, unforgiving, stars like specks of diamond dotted the planetarium dome. When Carl turned his head, an absence of stars, like some silhouette-shaped dark nebula, revealed Corinne. He guessed she was contemplating the way forward. Studying the unexceptional orange-white spark that was Epsilon Indi. Almost twelve light-years distant ....

"Thirty years," he said.

"A long wait for answers," she said. "A long while not even knowing if they'll deign to speak with us, if we'll *get* answers."

Or if they'll squash us like bugs, offended by our temerity. "That it is."

"I shouldn't complain. Glithwah isn't."

And Glithwah would *never* have answers. If she were to become the oldest Hunter—other than a Xool agent—who had ever lived, still old age must claim her before *Invincible* would reach its destination.

Whereas he, Corinne, and Joshua would merely be old.

"Glithwah is exceptional," Carl said.

Corinne broke the awkward, lengthening silence. "And if the Xool don't appreciate our showing up?"

"We'll reason with them."

"Tricky that, when not even Joshua has any inkling what they want."

"*We* have thirty years to prepare," Carl countered. "*They* don't know we're coming."

"Uh-huh. And maybe they've anticipated for ages that someone would come."

He mulled over whether a particular conversation with Glithwah was in confidence, deciding it was more in the nature of a prophecy. And more like a curse. "Glithwah predicts *I'll* reason with them."

"Not Joshua and Tacitus?"

"No one argues that they're smart," Carl said. Smarter by far than *him*. "No one doubts they'll be involved, but smart and strategic are very different concepts."

Especially from the perspective of a b'tok master.

Minutes ticked by. The unblinking stars (or was it the unblinking gaze of imagined Xool?) continued to unnerve him.

With a netted command he could have sent meteors streaking overhead. He could have stretched a comet—its head ablaze, its tail shimmering—across the dome. He could have evoked the well-remembered majesty of Uranus in Ariel's sky, or Earth as he had admired it from the Moon, or the stark beauty of a tumbling asteroid.

He made none of those changes, letting that pitiless, cosmic stare instruct him.

"*Me*," he said. Days after, Glithwah's prediction still felt unreal. "Reason with *them*."

"If Glithwah said it, she's probably right."

"That's what worries me." Carl laughed, just to show he was kidding.

If only he were. Because Glithwah did tend to be right. And because he had witnessed how she had "reasoned" with the United Planets to take control of a starship.

To prepare for his encounter with the Xool, Carl foresaw a great deal of b'tok in his future ...

WAR AGAINST THE XOOL

CHAPTER 49

Ceding fine-motor control to his other half, Joshua observed yet another calibration. Over the past thirty years, sometimes from boredom, as often with an eye to mundane practicality, he and Tacitus had acquired many new skills. Not that, so far, today's exercise gave proof of any skill, for this fine-tuning had accomplished no more, if instruments were to be believed, than their previous five tweaks or, for that matter, the wholesale swap-out of components.

And as much as Joshua would have liked to blame his pressure suit and its bulky gloves, he doubted sausage fingers were the underlying problem here.

"Nothing," he summarized.

"Nothing?" Carl echoed. He waited nearby, twice tethered to a catwalk. Exit *Invincible*'s main hull—no matter if only by centimeters, where not even the slightest bit of sky could be seen—and safety protocol demanded a suited-up buddy.

"Could Carl *be* any more literal?" Tacitus netted. "Quaint, limited, Mark I humans—"

"Built you," Joshua interrupted. Aloud, he said, "Nothing modulated, to be precise. Solar RF noise and Jupiter RF noise come through loud and clear."

"As before your adjustments?"

"As before," Joshua said.

He reclaimed control over his right arm, scratching an itch on his right thigh as best he could through the sturdy fabric of his pressure suit. The itch, as though provoked by his ineffectual efforts, sidled toward his knee. The tip of his nose, beyond reach within his helmet, began to itch, too.

"What's left to try?" Carl asked.

"Ir am thinking." While trying not to channel an ant trapped between nested bowls. Hangar bay two's concave roof, underfoot, and the convex underside of the antenna, looming overhead, both seemed enormous.

"Because," Tacitus reminded gratuitously, "they are. The antenna dish is 599.4 meters in diameter and 101.95 meters deep."

"Well," Joshua retorted, "if you're of a mind to be precise, don't call the attenna a dish."

Because the minutest irregularities within a unitary structure would degrade the antenna's focus. Instead, plainly visible from the instrumentation node at which they labored, the antenna was comprised of many small panels. ("10,448," Tacitus offered. "Just to be precise.") The minuscule gaps among so many discrete panels were what kept this enclosed workspace in vacuum.

Still no bright ideas. Joshua kept looking around, daring inspiration to strike.

He stood in a forest of plasteel pylons. The pylons supported a complex latticework that in turn supported thousands of servomotors ("10,448," Tacitus re-netted), one motor to anchor and individually position each panel. Work lights and his helmet lamps glimmered off pylons, motors, and panel backs. Hidden from his sight, suspended far above the dish, hung an instrument platform massing almost a thousand tonnes. Everything on that platform, including its ultrasensitive receiver elements, had checked out flawless, too.

For a wonder, Tacitus did not recite the platform's mass to fifteen decimal places. Instead his friend teased: "Above?"

Because, for the nonce, *Invincible* was in freefall.

The dish trembled, if only a little, whenever the main drive ran. Had the instrument platform been deployed before now, tremors would have jiggled its suspension cables, too. Even the residual quivers that got past multistage shock absorbers would have spoiled the dish's capacity to aim across interstellar distances.

"Don't be difficult," Joshua netted back. "*Above* is a valid synonym for *overhead.*"

"You're certain about our pointing?" Carl interrupted, oblivious to their internal dialogue.

In Joshua's mind's eye, the spark that was Sol was centered in the crosshairs of a netted image from the ship's optical sighting telescope. "Yes, Ir am certain. If things weren't aligned, the dish wouldn't be picking up solar RF."

"Then why not manmade RF, too?"

That was the big question, of course. No one had any reason to beam signals toward Epsilon Indi, but it should not have mattered. This was an InterstellarNet-class transceiver. The chatter back home among three planets, dozens of moons, hundreds of asteroids, and however many thousands of ships ("Do *not* quibble with my numbers, Tacitus, because whatever database you access is thirty years out of date") should have merged into an unmistakable background roar. Hell, the Leos had detected humanity from the RF murmurs of mid-twentieth-century Earth. Using vacuum tubes.

"If Ir knew …"

"Yeah, yeah," Carl said, "you'd have told me, if not already have fixed the problem. Speculate."

"Something Ir haven't yet thought to check. Something not formally a part of the transceiver, or of this dish, but that nonetheless interacts with one or both of them."

"Something knocked out of kilter back when Grace blasted her way aboard," Carl interpreted glumly. "Only I felt certain we'd found and fixed all those problems."

A not unreasonable expectation, Joshua agreed. This *was* their second go at diagnosis and tweaking. Their first go had come years before, at turnover, when the Foremost had permitted them a brief listen—and when they had failed to detect even the broad-spectrum radio noise that every active star emits. That silence had proven to be merely an alignment problem.

"Either that," Joshua said, "or our earlier repairs were incomplete, or we must separately remediate the effects of more years of engine vibrations."

"What sort of something might it be? I don't suppose you would care to hazard a guess."

"It do not."

But even less did he/they care to give voice to what they most feared: that the Xool or their agents had, once more … intervened. If the solar system *ahead* had emitted any modulated RF, that inference might have been inescapable. But Epsilon Indi, now little more than ten light-hours removed, seemed as devoid of artificially produced radio emissions as the home system, 11.8 light-years in their wake.

If the Epsilon Indi system was empty of Xool, could they rely upon any of the reasoning that had led them here?

"Leaving what?" Tacitus challenged. "Some weird software defect? Undetected irregularities in power generation or transmission with the improbable effect of disguising only modulated RF signals?"

"If I knew what," Joshua thought wearily, "I would have already—"

Ping! The change in Carl's facial expression suggested he, too, had gotten a priority interrupt. A summons from the Foremost.

• • • •

Interstellar drive: more formally, the T'Fru long-range drive, after T'Fru Lei, the Centaur physicist whose theory of gravitation underpins the technology. (See related article, T'Fru theory of gravitation, an extension to Einsteinian general relativity.)

A T'Fru drive propels a spaceship by manipulating the gravitational field: the local curvature of space-time itself. The drive, because it does not rely upon expelling reaction mass, is an efficient— and, to date, the only—practical means of travel among the stars.

T'Fru drive technology can, in concept, operate anywhere, but practical considerations limit its use to interstellar domains. Any perturbation to the artificially reshaped gravitational field will contort nearby space-time and, in the process, tear the vessel to shreds. Between stars, where space-time is all but flat, occasional passing gravitational waves necessitate complex, real-time rebalancing. Within a solar system, the motion of planets and moons in their orbits continuously alters the local curvature of space-time; there, the dynamic rebalancing required to stabilize a T'Fru drive remains unachievable.

Circumstantial evidence suggests that the interstellar drive of a lifeboat, activated within the Jupiter system, triggered the destruction in 2165 of the first United Planets antimatter factory, and with it the moon, Himalia. (See related article, Himalia Incident.)

—*Internetopedia*

• • • •

In speckles and splotches and interlocking whorls—the terrestrial greens vivid, almost psychedelic, against K'vithian black—a field stretched out around Corinne. At this stage of the voyage, apart from one small sector of one deck (and this was not the deck), soy and corn were weeds. She did not need an agronomist's input to deduce matters had gone awry.

Bottom line: a couple of gene-tweaked terrestrial super crops had run amok. The question was, why? The crops themselves? Maybe. It might also be a side effect of some gene-tweaked bacterial symbiote of the crop, or a program bug in some nanite pesticide, or a new, mutated crop disease. In the course of this interminable voyage, she had seen them all.

And just as likely, some mundane environmental parameter had drifted out of tolerance. Any minor glitch with irrigation or artificial sunlight or soil pH could weaken whatever K'vithian crop had been sowed here, opening the way for invasive species.

Boring.

Corinne shifted her stance just a bit. In zero gee, separated from the metal of the deck by twenty or so centimeters of compacted soil, the maneuver required skill and attention to detail, at least if she planned to avoid setting herself adrift or taking divots. She wiggled one boot, disengaging its curved cleats. When the boot lifted free she replanted it a little to her right, and then repeated the process with her other boot.

Someone who *was* an agronomist, speaking in a tiresome soprano singsong, stood nearby. Likely he was answering all Corinne's as yet unvoiced questions. The gaggle of students here to observe (but instead fidgeting in the manner of human teens) might benefit from the details. She was content to let the words wash over her. One more biotech, or nanotech, or eco, or whatever mishap scarcely qualified as news.

She remained a journalist because, well, what else did she have to do?

At their journey's start, that decision had shocked Glithwah.

"But why?" Glithwah had asked.

"When you kidnapped me, you promised"—with a sneer—" 'quite the scoop.' "

"That was before," Glithwah had objected. Before learning about the Xool. Before departing for Epsilon Indi. "You are a guest."

"Whom you did not allow to leave or broadcast," Corinne had completed.

"For good reasons. Be honest. You wouldn't have wanted to be anywhere else."

Except home. Except with Denise. "Still leaving me to find a reason for getting up every morning."

And if the main project to which Corinne had set herself—unmasking Xool agents among the Hunters—had gone nowhere, well, she had reported on such events as did occur. Even when that meant the umpteenth so *very* serious (but do not worry, it's certain to be contained) outbreak of this or that. The last excitement, eight interminable years ago, had been a damaged robot gone berserk. She had to admit: the custom-programmed nanites that took *it* down had been more than a little cool.

A starship, it had turned out, was but a small town in extreme isolation. Throughout thirty years of the Hunter equivalents to PTA bake sales, Kiwanis breakfasts, and what amounted to municipal elections, the occasional enviro-glitch counted as big news.

"You're recording this spiel, right?" Corinne netted to Hank.

When Corinne first toured this vessel, the primary shipboard artificial intelligence had called itself Henry Hudson. Days later—on a renamed vessel, under new, alien management—the AI had gone informal. Maybe it had done so to downplay its eponym's fate: cast adrift, never to be seen again, by the mutinous crew of the original *Discovery*. When Snakes had seized their first starship, they lobotomized its Centaur-built shipboard AI.

Funny thing, Corinne thought. *Those were Snakes. These are Hunters.*

"I am recording," Hank agreed.

"And the short, non-pedagogical version?"

"Balancing two biospheres is hard. Wry amusement that one of humanity's talents turned out to be the hardiness of their gengineered crops. The latest remedial nanites incorporate enhanced environmental sensing. These new nanites will mutate symbiotic bacteria, helping or weakening each plant appropriately to each field."

"How does that work?" Corinne asked.

"By sensing concentrations of biochemical markers in the soil. The new nanites adapt their behavior to favor the preponderant crop and selectively weaken any invasive species."

Improved nanites had to beat flamethrowers, which had at one time been the response to this sort of outbreak. Still, how much cleverer was this fix than the last however many fixes? Once again she wondered: *did today's little ceremony rise to the level of news?* Either way, this would have to do if nothing more interesting came along soon ....

With a flourish, still talking, the agronomist decanted his new batch of nanites. The act of decanting: that could be seen. The nanites said to be released: they, of course, could not.

The nanites' actual release would be through the underground irrigation system, applied directly to the roots. The purported aerial release, however, was more visual. Also entirely symbolic, while the ship remained at zero gee. No one had wanted to postpone the crop treatment while the listen-back-home interlude ran late.

Begging the question: what *was* taking Joshua and Carl so long?

Corinne dutifully captured vid in her implant's memory of the anticlimactic staged nanite release. She recorded the mask-wearing demonstrators circling the field in protest of the release. Just in case nothing more newsworthy turned up.

The staying power of Xool-sponsored fairy tales amused her.

"Corinne," Hank netted.

"Yes?"

"The Foremost has called a staff meeting. At four, ship's time. Your participation is requested."

At four? That scarcely left time for decontamination, absent which she would not be permitted off this deck. "Give my apologies here, please, and confirm for me. Oh, and stay linked for the meeting."

"Of course."

In magnetic boots and a fresh outfit, Corinne made it to the Foremost's ready room with only minutes to spare. She found the place packed. Carl, looking haggard, and Joshua/Tacitus were there, too. Carl had saved her a chair, and Corinne nodded her thanks.

"What's this about?" she netted.

Carl shrugged.

When they had first come aboard, this ready room, apart from unpacked boxes, had been pristine. Over the decades everything had become worn. Faded. Tattered. A few years into the flight Glith-wah had given up on replacing the wall displays. Sulfur dioxide in Hunters' breath dissolved into any trace of water condensation, the sulfurous acid thus produced pitting and etching surfaces until displays became useless. Whatever imagery everyone needed to consult could be accessed in consensual space.

It was all just … old.

As was she—not to mention frail, fragile, and readily exhausted. As was Carl. Joshua, not so much, as Tacitus supervised endless exercise, neural and hormonal biofeedback loops, and swarms of nanomeds and nanosensors. That discipline, or the repeated gene tweaking, worked: Joshua, who was eighty-five, did not look a day over seventy-five. Nor, any longer, entirely human. He/they were skeletal and somehow freakishly intense.

A distracted expression showed that Joshua/Tacitus were away in the infosphere, or in netted conversation, or both. They managed to net-text her a terse, "HI."

The Foremost swept into the room. Cluth Timoq was tall for a Hunter, broad of chest, and erect of bearing. His gaze was intelligent and confident. His knowledge of affairs aboard his vessel was encyclopedic. He was, in a word, imposing.

Timoq's stiff posture as he sat told Corinne this was no time to indulge the failings of age. Sweeping his gaze around the long oval table, he announced, "It is time to complete our journey. What remains to be done?"

That was not exactly what he said, of course. Few among the oldest Hunters remembered a human language, if ever they had learned one. Of those born on this ship, none learned anything but clan speak. Why would they? English was a language of their ancient, made-thorough-fools-of oppressors. And what would be the purpose? Even Joshua, no matter the joyless regimen on which Tacitus kept him, must eventually succumb to age. Uploaded, he would no more care about language choice than Tacitus.

And so, the three of them had mastered clan speak. If Corinne had never learned to think like a Hunter—taking comfort that not

even Carl claimed full success in doing that—she had become profi-
cient enough to no longer notice the implied-verb syntax or stumble
over their units of measurement. When, rarely these past few years,
she encountered an unfamiliar word or expression, dictionaries in
her implant handled it. As for expressing herself, well, she had been
born one pair of vocal cords shy for clan speak. Every cabin and few
meters of corridor had a public-address loudspeaker in its ceiling;
when she had something to offer aloud, she netted the words to
the closest speaker. *It* never suffered from her laryngeal deficiencies.

Among the least of his many mid-voyage gene tweaks, Joshua
had grown extra vocal cords and now spoke fluent clan speak. The
few tweaks Corinne had had done upped her tolerance of the ubiquitous sulfur compounds.

Little of which was reminiscence, exactly, because so little about
the voyage merited nostalgia. Still, the wandering of her thoughts
seemed a harmless enough indulgence. In responding to the Foremost's leading question, most of his officers, one by one, going
around the long table, merely murmured their readiness.

"On your command, Foremost," Rashk Folhaut, the navigator,
concluded the survey.

The Foremost turned to Joshua, "Can you secure the big antenna
within the shift?"

"It will take two shifts. After we finish here, of course. But is that
appropriate? Ir find the silence in our home systems anomalous."

"No, worrisome," Corinne murmured. If not anyone else, their
failure so far to detect home's radio chatter worried *her*.

"Poor reception does not equal an anomaly," If Hrak Jomar, the
chief science officer, had heard and translated her sotto voce correction, he ignored her. "We hear only natural background noise from
other InterstellarNet systems, too."

"And *that* doesn't concern you?" Carl asked.

"Having only an inferior transceiver bothers me," Jomar shot
back. "Luckily, we have no need of interstellar communications."

"Jomar, you will send technicians to assist," Timoq directed,
ending the discussion. "Joshua, you will have one shift."

Looking around the room, reading Hunter faces, Corinne saw no evidence of doubt.

But Carl frowned. "Foremost."

"Yes, Carl?"

"In my opinion, for now we should remain far from the star. As one more rock in the cometary belt, we can observe unobtrusively. There is much that we don't yet know."

"Such as?" Timoq asked.

Such as, Corinne thought, *the perils to which I doubt you give credence.* But she sat in this meeting only by custom and sufferance. Glithwah, before she stepped down, had established the precedent: on critical matters, the humans had unique perspectives worth hearing out. Timoq might disagree, and Corinne would bet anything that he did, but the clan still honored, even revered, the leader who had led them to freedom.

Or if she was of a mind to be honest with herself, that's why *she* was tolerated. Carl, for many years at the top of the shipboard b'tok ladder, had through strategic genius earned his place in the clan councils. Joshua/Tacitus had earned their place by their brilliance at, well, most everything else. After thirty years together, not a few Hunters remained intimidated by the very notion of Augmentation.

Maybe Timoq will heed them.

Carl pressed on. "Such as the deployment of the Xool. Their capabilities. Their intentions."

Several among Timoq's staff studiously looked away. Of those who did not, many had disdain in their eyes.

And maybe not.

"Somewhere there were Xool," Timoq conceded magnanimously. "From afar, their presence in this solar system was a plausible inference. From afar. From *here* we could not have failed to have detected an occupied world. We will proceed to colonize."

"We need supplies," Firh Koban interrupted.

Was the old pirate—not a figure of speech—changing the subject, Corinne wondered, *or subtly backing Carl?*

Glithwah's cousin had been a pilot and a warrior, a veteran of the secret campaign to capture human ships and build a navy. She had led the troops who stormed this starship. Now Koban, no longer young, managed the starship's logistics. She would have made a good tactical officer—if the clan still had one.

Glithwah, while she still led, had kept a tactical officer on her senior staff. She had held combat drills, encouraged b'tok tournaments, seen to it that young Hunters trained in the old ways. But even in Glithwah's time, the chief science officer had become her critical aide. Yes, another Xool agent might be aboard or a Xool vessel might somehow intercept them in the vast emptiness of interstellar space. The *certain* dangers of this epic voyage were ecological.

As, just before this meeting, Corinne had seen yet again.

Three Hunters, given their diminutive stature, required no more food, water, or air than a single human—but on the day Koban's troops seized *Invincible*, it became home to more than twenty thousand Hunters. Specialists had to deal with sulfur compounds degrading the terrestrial biosphere that kept everyone breathing. They had to rework fertilizers, lighting, and irrigation systems, deck by deck, to the needs of specific K'vithian crops. With the ecosphere straining even from the start, demographic specialists and economists micromanaged who could have children when and for what careers those children would train. Tactical officer became a ceremonial post, even as everyone curried favor with the chief science officer.

Five years out from Ariel, Timoq, then a young chief science officer, had succeeded as Foremost. Glithwah had devoted the remainder of her life to mentoring—when, in the face of Timoq's disdain, she found disciples—in the art of b'tok. Ten years from Ariel, soon after Glithwah passed away, Timoq without ceremony suspended the position of tactical officer.

The ship-wide memorial netcast for Glithwah was among the hardest things Corinne had ever had to do. One made friends under the strangest circumstances ....

Once again, Corinne had found herself woolgathering. She let Hank catch her up.

"What supplies?" Timoq asked.

"Top off our water tanks. Distill deuterium. Distill oxygen. Gather metals and trace elements for life support."

"Can we not obtain those supplies from inner-system worlds?" Timoq asked.

"Doubtless, Foremost," Koban agreed, "but until we have resupplied, we are not optimally prepared."

"We wouldn't want to meet anyone until our resupply is complete," Carl said.

"Ah, you *are* still with us." Timoq licked his lips in a Hunter smile. "I thought perhaps you were busy at b'tok. And why would we expect to meet anyone?"

Joshua leaned forward. "For all the reasons that led us to Epsilon Indi."

"Except there are no adversaries here." Timoq stood. "There is no one at all."

Joshua stood, too, towering over everyone, forehead furrowed, but it was Tacitus' intonation that rang out. "Then how do we explain the third planet's appearance?"

"Sit," Timoq commanded. Joshua did. "Jomar?"

The science officer summoned an image into the meeting's consensual space. Even at full magnification, the planet deep in the habitable zone manifested only as a brilliant white dot. "This appearance? A world locked in an ice age, just as astronomers surmised before we first set out. Inconvenient for us, but perhaps why the Xool, if they ever occupied this system, have left."

"The planet reflects too much sunlight even for an all-ice surface," Tacitus said.

Jomar sneered, "You would have us hide from shininess?"

"*I*," Carl said, "would have us retain the element of surprise. Suppose Xool are in this solar system. To resupply out here, we would enter a distant orbit using the T'Fru drive. To go much deeper in the system means switching over to fusion drive and shouting out our presence."

Lest the random tug of some random Kuiper Belt object destabilize the interstellar drive and blow them to atoms. Corinne was not the only person around the table to shiver.

"To be clearer," Timoq said, "we are done, unless someone has something *new* to offer. Something other than wild speculation."

"This is new," Hank offered through a ceiling speaker. "The third planet has gone behind its sun."

"So?" Timoq asked.

"From this distance," Hank said, "my sensors cannot dependably separate direct sunlight from the far dimmer light reflected by the close-in planets. While III passes behind the star, its reflected light does not reach us. Barring questions, I will omit the details, but from the slight drop in illumination I can infer much about III's atmospheric composition."

"And we will determine much more from closer," Timoq said. "Dismissed, everyone."

"No."

Even Corinne felt the word's intensity. As for the Hunters, as one they flinched.

Once, long ago, Robyn Tanaka Astor had done something similar to Corinne and Joshua, some kind of Augmented trick. She/they had given her/their voice a special timbre, subtle harmonics—something—that slipped past the conscious mind, that demanded attention. That grabbed a mere human by the figurative lapels and *shook*.

So Joshua/Tacitus had mastered enough Hunter psychology to shake them—and chosen this moment, of all moments, to reveal the power.

Claws slid to their full extension from Timoq's hands. "Explain yourself."

"My pardon, Foremost," Tacitus said. "This matter is critical. The significance of the latest observation is that the third planet has no atmosphere."

"Impossible," Jomar snapped. "So near to the star, ice cover cannot persist without an atmosphere. Ice would melt. Melt water would boil off in the vacuum as vapor. Ultraviolet light would split the vapor. The planet is too small to hold onto free hydrogen, but it would retain the oxygen."

"Making it all the more puzzling," Tacitus said, "that this supposedly icebound planet lacks an atmosphere."

Timoq turned toward his science officer.

"Is this true?"

Jomar's eyes glazed as he retrieved the latest observations from the ship's databanks. His eyes cleared and he bowed his head. "Foremost, it is so."

Carl asked, "Can anyone suggest *natural* causes by which III appears as it does?"

No one did.

Timoq said, "*Invincible* will divert to a distant orbit while a scouting mission investigates."

"I will see at once to the planning," Jomar said.

"A *tactical* mission," Timoq clarified. He looked straight at Carl. "And I ask you, as tactical officer, to lead it."

"It will be my honor, Foremost."

Inwardly, Corinne smiled. Her evening netcast would offer real news after all.

CHAPTER 50

Excalibur's bridge displays showed … the incomprehensible.

The planet become known as Xool World loomed larger, but was no less improbable, than when studied from afar. It projected virtually no magnetic field; its surface, thus unprotected, endured a vicious bombardment of cosmic rays and solar wind. It offered about as much topographical interest as a cue ball—and was more perfectly spherical than one. Its dayside gleamed, an all but ideal mirror, like Epsilon Indi's little brother—except for in ultraviolet wavelengths which, inexplicably, it drank up. Its nightside, glinting starlight, was as featureless.

Xool World *did* have an atmosphere, it turned out, but those wispy hints of gas proved as baffling as everything else about the planet. The occasional molecule would travel for kilometers before encountering another. A satellite circling this world would have geologic time before its orbit decayed.

As for satellites, Xool World had three. Two close-in moons were identical: about fifteen klicks across, as perfectly spherical and reflective as the planet. They shared an orbit, at *just* the right altitude, hanging *just* above the terminator line, that both moons experienced perpetual sunlight. Around any normal planet—the tug of its gravity subtly varying over land and ocean, over mountains and plains—such perfect orbital synchronicity could never persist. And each mirrored moon had, for an object its size, an inexplicably low mass.

The final satellite was about one-fourth Moon-sized. A gray, stony, cratered body orbiting much further out, at a distance averaging about sixty thousand kilometers, *it* was utterly and refreshingly normal. This world being the exception (and to the puzzlement of the literal-minded Hunters), Carl dubbed it Blue Moon. And although he would have distrusted any inference drawn only from those two anomalous inner satellites, Blue Moon confirmed *something* familiar: Xool World possessed a mass comparable to Earth's. These moons would not have had these orbits otherwise.

Unless Xool artificial gravity was at work here, too.

Nor did the planet, as aberrant as it appeared, reveal any hint of intelligent occupants. No radio waves, apart from reflected solar noise, came from its surface. No energy emissions of any kind could be detected. Aside from scattered reflections of starlight and Blue Moon light, no glimmer of illumination interrupted the nightside gloom.

And so, *Excalibur* and its three escorts coasted in for a closer look. They flew stealthed and, making their final approach from the daylight side, hidden in the sun's glare. Stealthy drones following that course had sped past Xool World unmolested. And if something should entice him to brake for a more lingering look? Until he was right on top of them, the white-hot exhaust of fusion drives should then likewise be washed out by the sun behind them.

He was following Glithwah's playbook from the capture of the starship.

The bridge crew calmly went about their duties as Carl observed, waiting for some cosmic shoe to drop. Yet again he found his fingers clutching the padded arms of his acceleration couch; yet again, he willed his hands to relax. No matter how much he wanted to fly, as commander of Task Force Mashkith he had higher priorities.

No matter who flew *Excalibur*, she was his ship, and she was a beauty. Thirty years parked and sealed on a hangar deck had left his flagship pristine. Before setting out, telling himself the modification was mere prudence, he had had the copilot's station retrofit to human needs.

Joshua, somehow, dozed in the bridge's remaining human couch; Tacitus, who never slept, remained on call. If anything new were detected, Tacitus would rouse Joshua. At fifty thousand klicks from the planet, with or without novelty, Carl would wake his friend.

With six million klicks to go, it seemed Joshua would enjoy a nice nap.

Carl spent the approach second-, third-, and fourth-guessing himself. How should one drop in, uninvited, on a wise and secretive—and manipulative—elder race? Announcing oneself openly might be safest, just as showing up at all might prove disastrous. A stealthy period of study might arm him with vital knowledge, but getting caught lurking might unleash Xool wrath.

Five million klicks.

There was no way to know, and there would be no second chances. The clan—if not the entirety of the InterstellarNet community—required a master strategist. When they needed Glithwah, all they had was her antiquated protégé.

Three million klicks.

And yet maybe all this worrying was for nothing. The planet gave no sign it had ever known life.

One million klicks, and Carl's doubts, like the world ahead, remained featureless and foreboding.

Five hundred thousand klicks. The most precise measurements yet, and still he saw no chink in Xool World's baffling uniformity.

And still, Tacitus pondered. Joshua softly snored.

But as the distance closed to one hundred thousand klicks—

"Infrared contact," Rashk Motar announced from the primary sensor console. Like many of the officers Carl had handpicked for this foray, Motar regularly ranked high on the b'tok ladder. Twice, he had almost beat Carl. "Designation Bogey One."

Joshua straightened in his chair, instantly awake.

In the main tactical display, an unidentified-ship icon now blinked between Xool World and its largest satellite.

"Visual?" Carl asked.

"On screen," Motar said.

The holo showed a flattened ball, with pointy protuberances around its bulging waist. Just like the ship two Xool had flown from *the* Moon.

"Open all channels," Carl ordered. "Tacitus, translate to Basque. This is the exploration vessel *Excalibur*. Unidentified vessel on approach to the nearby planet, please respond. Repeat, please respond."

In the long-range image, the Xool ship's drive exhaust grew longer and hotter.

"Bogey One stepped up its acceleration to almost two gees," Motar said.

Carl tried again. "Unidentified vessel, we wish only to talk. Request you assume orbit around the planet. Please respond."

"No response," Motar said.

Could it be that the Xool didn't use radio? "Try our comm laser, dialed *way* down."

"Still nothing," Motar reported.

"I can intercept," radioed Gral Tofot. He was young; cocky, too, if that wasn't redundant in describing a fighter pilot. Tofot's experience, aside from the few training jaunts in the cometary belt, had all come in simulation. As was unfortunately true of all Carl's pilots ....

On the encrypted command channel, Carl responded, "Negative, *Sting*. All ships, maintain course and speed."

Instead, out the main bridge view port, Carl saw the one-person fighter dart away. "Lieutenant, return to formation. That's an order."

Sting peeled off, accelerating at three gees.

Crap. "Unidentified Xool vessel, we have sent an escort. We will join you in orbit for consultations."

"No response," Motar said again. "*Sting* is overtaking."

Weapons release was no way to open discussions, not even firing on one of his own. Carl hadn't identified *Excalibur* as an exploration vessel on a whim! Bottling his anger, Carl radioed, "Lieutenant, maintain a separation of at least hundred klicks."

"Copy that," Tofot radioed.

For long minutes, Carl could only watch. As *Sting* closed the gap, the Xool ship killed its drive.

"Bogey One maneuvering," Motar reported. "Flipping over. Drive is back on, decelerating."

But the Xool ship was not going for orbit insertion. Unless Bogey

One had capabilities yet to be demonstrated, it was on a grazing collision course with the planet.

Sting adjusted its course, too, tapped its brakes, still closing on the Xool ship.

"Break off, *Sting*," Carl radioed. "Leave Bogey One some space."

Sting kept closing.

At just over six klicks per second, Bogey One met the enigmatic mirrored surface—and disappeared.

"A mirage!" Tofot radioed. "I knew it!"

"*I* don't," Tacitus said.

"*Sting*, break off at once," Carl said. "A drone will check things out."

"Can't … hear *Excali* … Breaking up."

"Cut the crap, Lieutenant," Carl snapped. "Pull up, *now*. Full emergency power."

"Five seconds to entry," Motar said.

Five seconds later, on the edge of the otherwise flawless orb that was Xool World, a fireball erupted.

CHAPTER 51

In an instant, *Sting*'s remains vanished. Almost before Carl noticed its disappearance, the glow reemerged on the planet's opposite side—racing across the visible face, blurring with motion almost into a stripe—and vanished *again*. Xool World spun at an unimaginable pace! An eye-blink or so later, the glow reappeared. Fainter with each return, all visible trace of the crash soon vanished. The drones he dispatched detected nothing instructive.

As for whoever or whatever held dominion over Xool World, they regarded the pursuit, the crash, and Carl's subsequent broadcasts with equal indifference.

A drone accelerated to match the inexplicable planetary spin and sent down to the crash site sensed what might be *Sting*'s diffuse, atomized remains—if the observations were to be believed. Telemetry of the drone's internal state became inconsistent, then nonsensical, until, approaching the mirrored surface, unknown forces tore the drone apart.

Carl recorded an account and sent it onward. Allowing for *Invincible*'s hopefully anonymous remoteness deep within the cometary belt, the ping-ponging of his message through a cascade of stealthed relay buoys lest hostiles backtrack his transmission, and light-speed delay, he could not expect a response for almost a day. Any comment the Foremost might have to offer was apt to be overcome by events before its arrival.

By another circuitous route, Carl sent a detailed tactical report to Firh Koban, whom he given acting command of the stealthy (hopefully) main force, Task Force Glithwah, coasting at the discreet (hopefully) distance from the planet of about five million klicks. Koban's only reply was a curt acknowledgment. Corinne, aboard Koban's flagship, determined to cover the biggest story of the eon,

343

netted back a slew of questions that Carl could not have begun to answer even if he had had the time.

"Find out where that ship came from," Carl ordered the bridge crew. "Start by surveying Blue Moon." Recalling the Xool vessel's white-hot exhaust, he added, "Check the surface for hotspots."

But drones inserted into close orbits around Blue Moon found neither electromagnetic emissions nor hotspots.

He had *seen* fusion-drive flame with his own eyes, not that a ship on that little world need take off at full throttle. Had launch heat already dispersed across the sun-baked surface? Perhaps. Had the ship been loitering in space, between planet and moon, hidden from his view? Also possible. Or, just maybe, the ship had launched from somewhere out of sight: a hidden Xool base on the forever planet-facing side of *this* moon, too.

"Search for lava tubes open to the surface," Carl directed.

"Yes, sir," Motar said.

"Way ahead of you," Joshua said, popping up a holo globe sprinkled with red circles. "The cross section of that Xool ship left only a few possibilities, two of them snug fits."

Dispatch landing parties to all five locations? Doable. On the other hand .... "The Xool lunar base had a fusion reactor," Carl said. "Let's scan for neutrino fluxes."

Two hours later, low-orbiting drones had triangulated the position of an intense neutrino source. In a close-up holo, Carl studied the nearby terrain. Walking distance from both gaping entrances to one of the candidate lava tubes. A scattering of craters. A shallow, zigzagging crevasse. An arc of space-weathered low hills.

Joshua jabbed a finger into the holo. "This crater is about a klick across, too small to have formed a central peak."

Except that, as in the anomalous crater near the hidden lunar facility, this crater *had* a central peak.

Almost certainly, a Xool base lurked close by.

• • • •

Hails to Blue Moon also went unanswered.

At the target site, the sun had just set. Daylight would have been nice, but Carl refused to wait twenty hours until dawn. After a drone landing had established *this* surface was as harmless as it appeared, *Excalibur* set down near a mouth of the lava tube.

"Motar, you have the conn and command of the task force," Carl said, suiting up. "Also your ROE"—rules of engagement—"if anything should happen."

"Yes, sir. No firing unless fired upon."

"And no aggressive pursuits," Carl reminded. "Disable rather than destroy, when practical." *Because war was not the goal here. Dialogue was.*

"Sir." His officer hesitated. "We don't know what's out there. Better I go and you remain aboard in command."

Carl shook his head. "I've seen a Xool base. I've met their agents."

"Unaware they were agents," Joshua netted. "And almost getting yourself killed."

"Not helpful," Carl netted back. Aloud he said, "But I acknowledge the uncertainties. That's why I'm going alone."

"Yes, sir," Motar said. Long, disapproving pause. "I have the conn."

With four robot escorts (armed, although not blatantly so), Carl left *Excalibur.* Any embodiment of Boater robotech was scary. Overlay Hunter tactical algorithms and you got highly efficient killing machines. None of which kept his heart from pounding in his chest.

A surface-skimming drone flyover had seen a queue of ships down a lava-tube opening. So many vessels: call that one more data point to suggest, if not yet prove, that this solar system was important to the Xool. He dispatched two of his robots to that tube opening, tasking them to keep watch. Two stayed by his side.

Approaching the second entrance, virtual gauges twitched in his mind's eye. "I'm picking up faint RF noise."

"You no longer have meters of rock between you and whatever is down that tunnel," Joshua said.

And that was true enough.

"Wait here," Carl netted to his remaining escort bots. Alone and unarmed seemed the way to make contact. To those waiting anxiously on the bridge of *Excalibur* he added, "So far I have the place to myself. I'm going in."

"Copy that," Joshua said.

Two strides into the passageway overhead lighting switched on, whether automatically or through Xool intervention Carl could not tell. He clicked off his helmet's work lamps. Four strides into the tube, he felt heavier than on the surface. With each step his weight grew.

Every several paces he feigned a stumble, catching himself with an arm outthrust to a tunnel wall. Anyone watching might blame his clumsiness on the shifting gravity, and not notice the trail of tiny RF repeaters he left stuck to the wall.

Nothing on the barren surface or in the tunnel appeared threatening. Of course not long ago a whole *planet* had turned out to be lethal, and he hadn't foreseen that. Instinct insisted this hidden base, too, had unseen defenses, that it guarded itself and the planet.

Why might an untouchable planet need further defenses? Even speculation eluded him.

The air lock that gave access to the Xool lunar base had been of human manufacture; the control panel of this air lock subtly differed. It hardly mattered. Air locks were critical safety equipment, intended to be obvious in their use. The outer hatch stood open, suggesting he was expected. Carl stepped inside the lock. Before he had touched anything but the metal floor, the hatch closed behind him.

When the inner hatch cycled open, four aliens, arrayed in a shallow arc, stood facing him.

• • • •

Carl extended his arms, palms turned upward. Empty hands: the supposed universal gesture of peaceful intentions. Ideally the symbolism would prove more universal than had hands.

Ideally no one here felt like exploding its brains.

He stood at an end of a tunnel-like construction, its walls arcing over to form the high ceiling. Horseshoe archways set about every five meters suggested division into rooms. The nearest room, scattered with ottomans of varying heights, struck him as a foyer or social space; the chamber beyond the first archway, crowded with consoles and large displays, seemed more of a control center. What he could see of the room beyond that was row upon row of open, on-end coffins. Walls, floor, and ceiling: wherever he had an unobstructed view, surfaces showed a richly textured copper patina, like the hideaway at the rear of the Xool lunar base.

And, as at the lunar base, the copper sheathing was much patched, its seams rife with spot welds and caulk strips. If anything, this facility evidenced more repairs. Was this place older than the lunar base? More heavily used? Or was the wear from simple metal fatigue, as Tacitus had predicted? Blue Moon, orbiting so close to Xool World, endured ferocious tidal flexing.

Whatever had damaged the copper lining, at millimeter wavelengths every caulked seam and patched hole became an impromptu slot antenna. Despite the metal enclosure all around, a helmet-sensor readout netted to his mind's eye showed passable connectivity, daisy-chaining from neural implant to helmet radio to the series of repeaters deployed outside the air lock and on to the robots standing guard at the lava-tube mouth.

Chalk up one for our side.

"You getting this?" he netted to *Excalibur*.

"Ir am," Joshua netted back. "Your greeters look familiar."

True enough: the waiting Xool might have stepped from the lunar-base vids. The aliens were bipedal yet medusoid—and headless, their eyes and ears on telescoping stalks that protruded from the shoulders. Chest-high, many-pocketed utility belts, the only clothing they wore, carried patches that might mean anything, but that made Carl muse about insignia of rank. Tools or instruments (or weapons?) dangled from belt loops.

Stalk extensions aside, the aliens varied little in height from one another or from Carl. They differed more with respect to iris color, in swirls of yellow and green, in irregularities of their waist-level fringe bands, in stockiness, and, most of all, in the mottled gray-on-gray patterns of their leathery skin.

Four Xool had met Carl and several more were visible, standing at consoles, in the next room, but the extent of the facility—and the many ships hangared outside—suggested many more aliens somewhere nearby. Deeper within the complex, he supposed.

"Translate for me," Carl netted to Joshua, glad he didn't have to rely on the scraps of Basque his implant could manage. "Begin with this: I come from the planet called Earth."

A portable speaker hung from a clip at the waist of Carl's pressure suit; in Joshua's voice, the speaker said … something.

To Carl's right a Xool responded, its voice also originating from waist level. A mouth must lie behind that band of fleshy fringes. This Xool's eyes were predominantly jade green, the insignia on its belt a square of royal blue.

"That likewise was in Basque," Joshua netted. "He, she, or it said, 'Understood. We are familiar with Earth and humans.' "

"He," Carl decided. "As a pronoun of convenience, until we learn otherwise."

"Fine, he. As an unrelated observation: Ir don't know the extent to which their skin markings vary. Mottling patterns might repeat among them as often as hair colors recur among humans. That said, Tacitus believes 'he' could be someone we've seen in the lunar vids."

Carl had inferred as much from getting his answer in Basque. He netted, "Tell them that others traveling with me are Hunters, native to the Barnard's Star system." Joshua, via the wireless speaker, translated that, too.

"If you speak English, that would be more convenient," Blue

Square said in English, speaking with a curious, sibilant lilt. "And by the way, our air is safe for humans. For Hunters as well, although they would find it flat from the lack of sulfur compounds."

Pressure-suit readouts had indicated as much. Before removing his helmet, its transceiver left switched on, Carl netted, "No more speaking through the loudspeaker. Let them believe software in my helmet handled the Basque translations. They may not realize I have a connection to the outside."

"Understood," Joshua netted. "But ask: why not Basque?"

Carl passed along the question.

"We found it effective," Blue Square said, "to recruit our servants from among orphans in an isolated, oppressed subculture. More recent servants favor the old language out of respect."

Respect? As Carl remembered the lunar vids, the attitude of agents was reverential. That made Basque a liturgical language. Did the aliens encourage that worship?

Blue Square continued, "If any of our human servants survive. Your arrival here might suggest otherwise."

"Some are gone," Carl admitted. "They have the disconcerting habit of blowing themselves to pieces rather than talk." Or of falling silent because tons of rock had fallen on their head. After all these years, Helena's death still haunted him.

"Enough trivialities," Blue Square said. "You should not be here."

"So we have heard. 'Humans aren't meant to wander.' Why is that?"

"A moment." Blue Square and his colleagues launched into a lengthy exchange.

Their clipped intonations, sometimes guttural, sometimes sibilant, could mean anything. They went on (and on), for far longer than any moment.

In the artificial gravity, gear and pressure suit grew heavy. Carl wished someone would invite him to sit, but no one did. Maybe the ottoman-like things weren't seats. Maybe Xool didn't sit. He set his helmet on the floor and continued to wait. As the hiatus dragged on, Carl updated Motar for relay to Koban and Timoq. Mostly that involved uploading snippets of aural and optical recordings from his implant, annotated with his impressions.

As the Xool kept talking among themselves, Carl, with an inward sigh, chose an ottoman and sat.

• • • •

Squirming with boredom in his couch on *Excalibur*'s tiny bridge, Joshua netted, "This is like watching paint dry."

"I'll have to take your word as to the simile," Tacitus came back, "but I'll go along with waiting here being a waste of our time. I'd like to see—but you already know."

How could I not? Joshua thought to himself. Aloud, he said, "Motar?"

The Hunter turned.

Joshua gestured around the cramped, overcrowded room. "Would you mind us going to our cabin?"

"That's fine. I'll net you when something happens."

"Excellent. Ir will be examining that curious central peak outside." He/they stood to take leave of the bridge.

"What?" Motar said. "You can't go outside."

"And why not? You can reach mir as easily on the surface as aboard this ship, as Ir can as easily net from there with Carl."

"You are needed here on *Excalibur*."

"No, Ir am needed on comm. Ir will remain on comm."

"And if the Xool should—"

"Should *what?*" Joshua interrupted. "What reason is there to suppose we're safe *anywhere* on this world?"

To which sally Motar had no immediate answer.

The acting captain would simply order any of the Hunter crew to remain—and they would jump to. But Joshua? He/they weren't crew exactly, and he/they—more so, the idea of Augmentation—still intimidated the hell out of many Hunters. Certainly, it intimidated this one.

"So Ir will be in touch," Joshua concluded, headed for the

pressure-suit lockers.

"You'll take along a guard," Motar said. Insisted. Asserted himself.

"That's unnecessary," Joshua said. "To do what? Shoot the hidden telescope Ir expect to find?"

"You will take an escort, or not go at all," Motar growled.

"Fine," Joshua said. He had intended from the start to bring a tech, but that had to seem like Motar's idea. "Hrak Votan, perhaps. She can at least make herself useful."

"Fine," Motar said, having established his authority. "You'll remain in touch throughout."

"Of course." And as the alien chatter, still unintelligible, droned on from the Xool base, Joshua took leave of the bridge.

· · · ·

After almost twenty minutes, Carl cleared his throat. "Why don't we start over? My name is Carl Rowland, and you may call me Carl. I am an agent"—at least, he chose to see himself that way—"of the United Planets Intelligence Agency. I also represent the Foremost of Hunter clan Arblen Ems."

Blue Square said, "Just a moment more, Carl."

As the cryptic sidebar continued, Joshua netted, "Do these guys imagine you're not recording? With enough speech samples and interleaved English for context, correlation will give us a start at translation."

The Xool might not perceive the risk. Language translation with primitive computers like those found in the Xool lunar base would take geologic time. Of course the Xool executed plans that stretched across geologic time, a perspective that rendered them more alien than their tentacles or the lack of heads.

"They don't care if we know what they're saying," Tacitus offered. "To judge from whatever they've wrapped around Xool World, we're as backward in physics and engineering as they are with computers."

That was Carl's theory, too. The Xool figured they could squash uninvited guests like bugs. They were probably right.

The rasping, hissing consultation finally ended amid much bobbing of eye stalks. Did the mannerism denote agreement? Disdain? Laughter?

Blue Square edged a few centimeters closer. "I am Iroa Ene Leiahoma, leader of the Xool assigned to the human solar system. Consider me our spokesperson. You may call me Ene."

"Ene, I am pleased to meet you." *Pleased was the politic term*, Carl thought, *if also an exaggeration. Negotiation called for tact.* "We're here for a purpose."

"Your intentions are immaterial," Ene said, "just as your presence in this solar system is unacceptable. For your own safety, you will leave at once."

I don't think so, Carl thought. *Not without answers.* "Ene, your people have intervened in countless lives. We don't understand why. What do you expect of us?"

The four Xool once again compared notes. Ene said, "Only that you fulfill your destiny."

"And what is that destiny?" Carl asked.

"If we knew," Ene said, "we need not to have undertaken so much."

"Do jellyfish *have* destinies?" Carl asked. "They were the advanced life forms on Earth when your people became involved."

"True," Ene said, "we have long been engaged in this project. It is all the more reason why you must not interfere."

"Project," Carl echoed, struggling to hold level his tone of voice. "That's what we are to you? A science project?"

"An important project. You can be proud."

"If we knew the nature of the undertaking, we might be proud. Perhaps, with mutual understanding, we would agree to leave this solar system."

"Do you mean any of that?" Joshua netted.

It was the first comment for quite a while from Joshua or Tacitus; Carl supposed the two had found some more productive line of inquiry. That *start at translation* Joshua had hinted at would come in handy.

"No," Carl netted back, "and hence 'might' and 'perhaps.' But it's strategic to dangle the possibility. I'm trying to open negotiations. Because what I want—what I believe we *all* want—is for the meddling to end. To be left alone. To have the opportunity, from here on out, to chart our own destiny."

"That will require more than talk."

The inner door of the Xool air lock opened—and Joshua stepped through! He removed his helmet.

Ene, his eyestalks tipped forward, studied Joshua. He said, "Dr. Matthews, I presume."

CHAPTER 52

Matthews conundrum: a variation upon the discredited Fermi Paradox (see related entry). In an age before contact with interstellar neighbors, twentieth-century physicist and Nobelist Enrico Fermi asked about (then only theoretical) alien intelligences, "Where are they?" Well into the modern era, historian Joshua Matthews (see related entry) asked why the detectable alien intelligences all clustered among neighboring solar systems, thus able to establish InterstellarNet, amid a larger galactic silence.

Apart from Matthews, no credentialed figure ascribed any significance beyond random chance to the spatial grouping of known intelligences. Matthews's evident substance abuse and subsequent disappearance discredited him and further relegated his speculations to fringe status.

Following the onset of the Great Seclusion (see related entry), some scholars have controversially speculated that both astronomical-scale enigmas might in some way be related.

Few proponents of such linkage advance an explanation for either phenomenon. Joyce Matthews (see related entry), grandmother of Joshua and a onetime secretary-general of the

Interstellar Commerce Union, released a data archive she attributes to a theretofore unrevealed, non-InterstellarNet, alien species named the Xool. The senior Matthews asserts Xool involvement underlies the conundrum—an hypothesis dismissed by authorities.

Under the crisis conditions of the Great Seclusion, her efforts to raise funds to excavate a purported Xool facility have been without success.

—Internetopedia, Lunar edition

• • • •

"Ir am, in part, Joshua Matthews," Joshua said.

Ene's eyestalks retracted jerkily by half their length. "You are an Augmented?"

"Ir am."

"We find your kind ... interesting."

If eyestalks set to twitching were reflexive, then "interesting" would seem seriously understated. Joshua thought, *and that's one more data point to ponder.*

"Joshua," Carl netted, "you're not supposed to be here."

"Hence Ir did not ask." Joshua followed that netted utterance with the close-up of a solar system, its worlds mere dots. In several cases, dots he found disturbingly bright. Aloud, he said, "Do you know what else is interesting, Ene? The large optical telescope"—far more powerful than any instrument *Invincible* carried—"hidden in a nearby crater."

Joshua had had to aim the telescope via manual overrides, stymied by the still-cryptic symbols on its control console. But that could change. Even as he had operated the telescope by hand, data—an event log or program trace, he supposed—had streamed from the console to a nearby storage unit. And not merely to the

Xool memory device ....

An interface cable printed aboard *Excalibur*, like the unit his grandmother had designed for tapping computers at the Xool lunar base, had accommodated the local gear. Thirty years later, the Xool used the same electronic connectors and signaling protocols. He needn't have made Votan lug a 3-D printer to the observatory.

So: he had downloaded everything. When they could spare the time, Tacitus would correlate log entries with the observations set up by hand. Meanwhile, they had left Votan onsite to begin digging through the data.

But all that was detail with which Carl would lack patience and about which Ene was best kept in ignorance.

In the shared solar-system image, Joshua set one pixel blinking. He said, "Carl, do you remember how Epsilon Indi III appeared to astronomers back home?"

Carl nodded.

"The image Ir sent you *is* home," Joshua said.

"You're showing me *the* Solar System? *Earth* is become like"— Carl gestured overhead—"Xool World?"

"Like Xool World," Joshua agreed, and then ceded shared vocal cords to Tacitus. "Just like that. The Moon, too, and Mars. Ir saw hints that some Jovian moons are likewise altered. Being far more distant from the Sun, they are too dim to be certain. K'vith has also changed."

Ene said, "Across InterstellarNet, people are fulfilling their destiny."

His eyes narrowed, Carl said, "It's time, Ene, for you to explain *exactly* what that means."

"It is time," Ene countered, "to discuss the Matthews conundrum."

• • • •

"Life is common throughout the galaxy," Ene said. "Complex multicellular life is not. Intelligent life is scarcer still."

"Except in this neighborhood," Joshua said.

Ene's fringe tendrils wriggled. (*Laughter*, Joshua wondered, *or agitation?*) "We will come to your conundrum, Dr. Matthews. Please, be patient."

Carl cleared his throat. "And how do the Xool know these things?"

"We listened," Ene said, "and heard no one. We looked, and observed no one. The implications were so disturbing that we went searching."

"Throughout the galaxy," Carl said, sounding skeptical.

"Yes," Ene said.

"Throughout the galaxy," Joshua repeated. At the outset of this adventure, neither he nor Tacitus had had more than a layman's grasp of science. After the long voyage occupied by study, they knew a great deal more about, among several topics, physics. Nothing they had learned led them to doubt Einstein. And the galaxy, with its billions of stars, was a disk-shaped structure about 100 thousand light-years in diameter. "Have your people repealed the light-speed limit?"

"No," Ene said.

Joshua said, "Then this will be a story too long to stand through." He joined Carl on one of the low ottomans.

"Indeed." Ene added something in his own language that sent his companions gliding away, before claiming a nearby seat for himself. "If you brought refreshments, feel free to eat. We will provide water."

Carl leaned forward. "When does this story begin?"

"In Earth terms, about six hundred million years ago." Ene sank into an ottoman; his tentacle-legs deflated. "Xool biological and computer technologies lag behind recent human levels, but our physical sciences are further advanced. It was our physics that enabled everything we will discuss.

"In brief, we have the technology to slow the passage of time.

Crew on our off-world missions scarcely aged. Applying the technology on a larger scale, scarcely twenty years have elapsed on our home world."

"Twenty years," Carl repeated. "In which to manage 600 *million* years of galaxy-spanning machinations? That sounds impossibly ambitious."

"It was decided," Ene said, his tendrils fluttering, as though no further explanation were needed.

But Joshua scarcely heard that exchange. He remembered all too well the ride he had once unwittingly taken in a Xool agent's "cab." For him, less than an hour had gone by; for the world, a month had passed. The disappearance that he could never explain, that no one could explain, had ruined him. The old rage boiled up—

Only to wash away in a surge of serotonin.

"This isn't the time," Tacitus told his other half.

Aloud, Tacitus speculated, "A unified field theory?" To Carl, he explained, "The reconciliation of gravity with the other forces of nature, such as electromagnetism. A unified field theory would be an extension to Einsteinian general relativity and T'Fru gravitation. A unified theory may also underpin their technology for artificial gravity."

Carl nodded. "Thanks."

Ene said, "Just so. Humanity's incomplete notions of relativity permit time dilation by traveling at near-light speeds and in proximity to very large masses. The more complete theory offers more elegant means to the same end."

The Xool dropped tantalizing hints, more metaphor than math, until Carl interrupted. "Big picture? A boundary of slowed time is what surrounds the planet. Correct?"

"In simplified terms, yes," Ene said.

"We watched a ship pass through the barrier," Joshua said. On behalf of Tacitus, he asked, "Was it equipped to penetrate, to dynamically match the changing rate of time's flow?"

"Nothing so straightforward," Ene said, "but you are essentially correct."

"And do all your ships—"

"But *why?*" Carl interrupted. ("Yes, I'm changing the subject," he netted to Joshua. "We want to learn about their capabilities, but without showing interest.") "Let's suppose I believe the Xool could take a time-out from the rest of the galaxy. Why would you?"

"From an abundance of caution," Ene said. "We knew that we lived on an unexceptional planet orbiting an unexceptional star, at the outskirts of one galaxy among billions. That our species should be unique was implausible—and yet the silence of the sky suggested we were alone. We needed to know: was our situation, somehow, exceptional, or was catastrophe in our future? Because our best minds foresaw in emerging technologies all too many pathways to our own extinction."

"Nuclear war?" Carl asked.

"As one among the possibilities," Ene said.

A Xool approached carrying a tray with a carafe and three stemmed goblets. Condensation beaded the carafe; drips zigzagged down its side. He set the tray on an unoccupied ottoman, waggled his fringes as though gesturing, and departed.

"Ice water," Ene explained, decanting some for Carl and Joshua, and more for himself, with deliberation and precise motions suggestive of a Japanese tea ritual. Guiding a goblet beneath the ragged band of fringe, Ene offered them a glimpse of vertical lips and massive, many-cusped teeth.

Even after Ene downed half his serving, Joshua left his own goblet, untouched, sitting on the ottoman. Carl did, too. It seemed unlikely Ene would try to drug them, and less likely still that Blue Moon would stock human-specific drugs that their nanites wouldn't handle, but why take the chance? If they got thirsty, helmet reservoirs would suffice.

Votan, whom Tacitus had left poking into the computer console at the Xool telescope, chose that moment to call. Entrusting Ene's recitation to Joshua and implant memory, Tacitus accepted the link. In clan speak, he netted, "What news, Votan?"

"Preliminary analysis of log file complete. Its composition: runtime trace of program execution. Its consequence: determination of

Xool computer instruction set."

Tacitus detected a touch of gloating in Votan's report. In hours, she had cracked a problem that had thwarted him for three decades. Of course in all those years, *he* had had only a random memory dump. *She* had a physical Xool computer to examine, and with it an execution trace to match against known activity, and all the analytical tools he had coded over the years against just such an opportunity as this.

"Upload of sample?" Tacitus requested.

The technician netted over two files: raw data from the run-time trace and an annotated version. Beyond determining the Xool computer's instruction set, she had also made a healthy start toward reverse engineering its operating-system protocols.

Here and there, scanning the files, Tacitus encountered instruction sequences that must invoke networking services. Evidently, the observatory computer was cabled into the Xool base. That was hardly surprising.

An intrusion alarm seemed like the sort of thing that might interrupt Ene's recitation. Had Votan resisted the temptation to probe the Xool network—or had she broken in, unobserved?

"Level of security?" Tacitus asked.

"Defenses laughable, as from the dawn of computing. No biometrics and only 256-bit encryption of passwords. No effective intrusion detection. No AI or even elementary heuristics for virus discovery, just pattern matching. Software-only firewall, with the same vulnerabilities as the operating system. For all of it, implementation amateurish and open to hack."

Amateurish? Perhaps. More likely, all Xool programming was typical of early-stage computing. The mystery remained why, having options, the Xool hadn't upgraded their primitive technology. Grace and Helena could have equipped the Xool lunar base with decent computer gear. Ene, or one like him, must have prohibited all but a low-end pocket comp.

Or, microseconds of contemplation suggested, not a mystery. Add imported tech to the mix, and then what? Such meager defenses as Votan had described would never see coming—and could not cope with, if they did—modern adaptive, learning malware.

On occasion *modern* did not denote *progress.*

"Further analysis," Tacitus directed Votan. "With utmost discretion. Also derivation of Xool network map, if possible."

"Tacitus," Carl's avatar interrupted. "Are we getting anything new here? I sense Ene is stalling us."

Tacitus scanned recent memories. If Ene could be believed, the Xool might well have explored the galaxy. Sublight speeds were no obstacle—if the crew, in time-slowing modules, ceased to experience the passage of time. If the Xool populace, in their world-encasing field, opted out of the passing ages.

Two very large ifs.

"New information, yes," he netted. "Amid much repetition and circumlocution, to be sure. Despite speaking fluent English, Ene may not reason like us. Maybe he is stalling, but Xool—or just Ene—might favor giving many examples. He could simply be wordy or nervous. He might be required to consult often with his non-English-speaking colleagues."

"But you might find *this* interesting," and Tacitus gave a quick summary on Votan's probing of the observatory's computer.

"Keep me posted on her progress," Carl netted. "But don't let Votan try anything that might reveal her probing."

Reclaiming shared vocal cords, Tacitus broke into the saga about the era of Xool exploration. "A few million years were ample to search the galaxy. Whatever you found"—and Tacitus was beginning to have his suspicions—"caused you to initiate another project. So: what did you conclude?"

An eyestalk pivoted toward Joshua/Tacitus. "Intelligent species arise. Not often, but it does happen. Across the galaxy and the ages, we've encountered scarcely a hundred examples. They developed technology. And then … they self destructed."

"From computer technology run amok," Tacitus said. "That's what you feared. That's why Xool use only the most elementary computing, little more than number crunching." *And why your computer technology is so static.*

"Once a society collapses," Ene said, "it is difficult to ascertain root causes. The evidence falls prey to rust and decay, to weathering and willful destruction. And after collapse begins, who knows? Transportation networks might fail and, if endless listening to your broadcasts properly instructed me in your idioms, for the want of a nail, a civilization is lost. Production of all kinds might stop. Any disruption might leave a civilization without the energy to produce the energy with which to sustain itself."

"That's your big lesson?" Carl said bitterly. "Things may break, so don't use tech? Obviously, you don't believe that. You control time and gravity. You have a fleet of starships. And anyway, what the *hell* does any of this have to do with plunging InterstellarNet worlds into slow time?"

Eyestalk twitching, in the mannerism that, by correlation and inference, Tacitus had concluded denoted fear or dismay. *The most agitated so far*, Joshua decided.

"There is more," Ene said, recovering. "After enough archeology and painstaking reconstructions, a pattern emerged. Amid the ruins, across every fallen civilization, we never once glimpsed technology advanced much beyond our own. The warnings of our brightest minds, and of our worst nightmares, seemed prescient. We stood— no, we yet stand—on the brink of self destruction.

"Once, in all our explorations, we almost witnessed the crisis. If we could have *seen* what went wrong, maybe we would have learned what, precisely, to avoid. But the galaxy is a big place, the emergence of intelligence rare, and the works of civilization ephemeral. We might search for eons and never find ourselves in the right place at the right time."

Carl tipped his head, considering. "It wouldn't be just one thing, would it?"

"We supposed not," Ene agreed. "As our explorations continued, we *knew* not. We came upon worlds that had been, for the lack of a better word, devoured, their surfaces become some seething, homogeneous mass. Any probe sent to such worlds was eaten, too."

"Gray goo," Carl said. "Nanotech failure."

"Or nanotech warfare." This time, Ene's eyestalks retracted by almost their entire length before, gradually, returning to their usual extension. "On other worlds impossibly vibrant, primitive life choked the ruins of vanished civilizations. Our biologists had had recent progress in genetics, deciphering a mechanism akin to your DNA. Almost certainly, on these worlds genetic engineering had slipped out of control. Yet elsewhere we encountered worlds populated by robots, devoid of life beyond the microbial. Eeriest of all"—that characterization punctuated with yet more eyestalk tremors—"was the planet we found ... abandoned. Vacant buildings and unattended fields. In the cities, weeds just beginning to encroach. Nowhere, any sign of violence. Nowhere, bodies. Nowhere, answers of any kind."

"You were there?" Carl asked.

"I took part in several expeditions," Ene said. "Yes, I saw that deserted world."

"Had they transcended to some higher plane of existence?" Carl asked. "Become something beyond our understanding?"

"That is the concept from your literature." The twitching grew more agitated than ever. As though involuntarily, eyes swiveled to stare at Joshua/Tacitus. "Or, perhaps, newly suicided."

A nanotech plague more discriminate than gray goo, Tacitus guessed. *One that devoured only animal life*—at which idea, it was Joshua who twitched.

"So technology not much different than Xool level looked dangerous," Carl summarized. "What does that have to do with us?"

"Altogether too much," Joshua said, "Ene means technology little different from InterstellarNet standards."

CHAPTER 53

It was, to borrow a favored phrase of Corinne's, like drinking from a fire hose.

No, Carl decided, worse. To steal sips from the revelatory flood did not begin to suffice. Somehow, he had to take in *everything*. Somehow, he had to put all this knowledge to good use. The Xool, notwithstanding Ene's loquacity, were not friends to humanity or Hunters or anyone else.

Carl uploaded another status update, ending, "I can't help but believe we're being stalled."

Aboard *Excalibur*, Motar still had the conn. It only seemed as if they had been inside the Xool base for days. Motar asked, "Stall? For what purpose?"

"I don't know," Carl admitted. Since he had left *Excalibur*, on Xool World less than the blink of an eye had passed—assuming Ene's tale were true. "What's happening on your end?"

"Hi-res mapping of Blue Moon, compiled as we get imagery from orbiting drones. More craters too small to form central peaks nonetheless have them. We've spotted nine fakes so far, in a narrow band along Blue Moon's equator, more or less evenly spaced."

"Corresponding to other underground bases?"

"Unclear," Motar netted. "The nearby fake peak is by far the largest, and it's the only one near a lava-tube opening. I'd like to land *Durendal* to inspect another."

The suggestion made perfect sense, but a second ship on the ground, vulnerable, made Carl uneasy.

"If you haven't figured out the anomalies once the survey is complete, ask me again. Stay alert. Make certain Task Force Mash-kith"—the three surviving ships of it—"is ready for action."

"Will do. *Excalibur*, out."

"One more thing." Carl summarized the effort, begun at Joshua's request, to penetrate the Xool observatory's computer. "Keep watch on that, too."

"I've already heard from Votan. She has identified many of the Xool operating-system functions and feels she'll be able to compromise it. Once she has attack code to load, she proposes to force a reboot."

"No!" Carl directed. "Absolutely not. Do *not* allow her to do anything the Xool might notice."

"Not to worry." Motar's avatar licked his lips. "That's what I told her."

"Good call. Contact team, out."

"*Excalibur*, out."

What else, meanwhile, amid his circumlocutions, had Ene revealed? What did the rising Xool chatter in the back rooms signify? "What'd I miss?" he netted Joshua/Tacitus. "The short version."

A piercing, mind's-ear tone preempted any response. The moment the alarm stopped, Motar netted, "The inner moons are *gone*, somehow replaced by fleets. And they're headed—"

Carl's radio link to *Excalibur* went dead.

• • • •

It *had* been a stall.

"What's going on?" Carl demanded.

Ene ignored him as three Xool rushed into the room. Their belts held holsters.

"Ir still can't translate." Joshua netted as the Xool spoke. That the two of them could still net meant they weren't being jammed, at least not inside the base. What had severed the link to the outside? "What do you think is happening?"

"You got Motar's alert, I guess."

"Ir did."

What did he think? He did not have much to go on. As Carl

tried to wrap his brain around moons morphing into fleets, the room trembled. It wasn't one continuous event, either, but several distinct shocks.

How likely was a meteor shower just as two moons pulled their magic trick and his comm cut out? Not very. Especially meteoroids large enough to shake the floor a good thirty meters belowground. Ship launches or missile strikes seemed far more probable.

Reflexively, he tried to reach Motar and *Excalibur*. Still nothing.

Too late, Carl deduced what hid in those sham peaks. He netted, "There are disguised facilities all around this moon. Sensor clusters. Eyes for defensive systems."

Because when you're masking your very presence, you don't deploy satellites.

Carl took a step toward the Xool. "Why attack us? We've done nothing but *talk*."

"Be silent," Ene said. "You should not have come."

Not believing it, Carl told himself one of those shocks had been *Excalibur* getting away. Motar would not sit still to get pounded, would never go down without a fight. Not the way *he* played b'tok.

"End this while you still can," Carl said.

With perfect timing, the room shuddered. Dust rained from the ceiling. From places deeper within the base Carl heard the yowling of Xool, and thuds, and a din like glass shattering and fabric ripping.

Joshua said, "Way to go, *Excalibur*."

At Ene's rasped command, two Xool unholstered their weapons. In English, he ordered, "Silence, both of you. Hands together."

Joshua held out his arms so that a Xool could slip something like plasticuffs around his wrists. When Carl's turn came to be bound, the grazing touch of a tentacle against his skin felt hot and gecko-pad sticky.

"You don't want to do this," Carl said. The Xool attending to him (call him Red Circle, for the insignia on his belt) gave the cuffs a final yank. The strap bit into Carl's arms. "We don't need to be enemies."

"You may speak when spoken to," Ene snapped.

"Our turn to be reverent?" Joshua netted.

"Not going to happen," Carl netted. He tried a different tack with Ene. "Halt the attacks, or battle bots will tear this place apart."

The base shook again. In the control room, two display units leapt off the wall and shattered on the floor.

"I doubt it." Ene said. "The lava-tube opening through which you entered is now deep in slow time."

Inaccessible, and with the robots trapped inside. *There's* where the comm link had failed.

Carl said, "Call off the attack, Ene. We've done nothing to harm you."

"Your presence here is unacceptable."

"Uninvited," Carl said, "nothing more."

"Unacceptable," Ene repeated.

Joshua netted, "Why are we still alive?"

"He's not done talking with us," Carl netted.

From here on out, the conversation was apt to be unpleasant. It was as obvious as why Ene had permitted the two of them into the base: hoping to keep Task Force Mashkith sidelined until the Xool attack.

The floor trembled again. Battle debris or errant missiles?

"Why haven't they wrapped themselves in slow time?" Joshua netted. "Save themselves from attack?"

Because they can't, Carl decided. This facility was the Xool command-and-control center. Without it, they couldn't wage the battle already underway.

"You're in deep shit, Ene," Carl declared.

Then he was on the floor, his ears ringing. His upper lip was split and his nose askew. The tang of copper filled his mouth. Red Circle loomed over him, arm-tentacle raised for another blow. The weapon in his coiled grasp dripped crimson. At Ene's command, with one last threatening gesture, Red Circle backed off.

I'm way too old for this, Carl thought.

Ene said, "Enough impudence. I know your capabilities. The ships chased away could not have brought you to this star. Where is your primary vessel?"

Carl sat up and spat blood. He gestured with bound hands at the nearest pile of debris. "Chased? I don't think so."

"The starship," Ene repeated. "Where is it?"

Carl ignored the question. "The two close moons, wrapped, like the planet, in slow time? They weren't moons. Had I thought about their negligible mass, I'd have understood sooner. You needed fleets ready to defend the planet if anyone showed up. Their crews could no more wait out eons in real time than you, or the Xool below on the planet. So the fleets stayed in orbit, wrapped in slow time, oblivious to events. And if anything should take down your primitive computers ...."

As though on cue, lights flickered. The floor rippled. A shock-wave lifted Carl, Joshua, and every Xool in sight, sending everyone flying.

Carl bounced off a wall and twice off the floor, bruised from head to toe, before tumbling to a stop. Nothing felt broken. Sitting up, he nixed the painkillers his med nanites had already started to synth. This was no time for drug-dulled thoughts.

"Everyone okay?" he netted.

"Barely," Tacitus netted. Joshua remained sprawled on his back. "What *was* that?"

"My guess? Motar realized this base is the primary target."

"With us inside?" Joshua asked.

Clearly. "Do the math, Joshua. How many ships the size of what we've seen will fit inside a fifteen-klick-wide sphere? Now picture that many ships coming down our throats. Because at about two gees, it's only a forty-or-so minute flight. Motar intends to take out this base before they all arrive."

Another shock, the strongest yet, sent Carl flying. More dust rained down. Sirens wailed: loss-of-pressure alarms, judging from Xool rushing to slap patches on the walls.

Levering himself up off the floor, his right arm screamed with pain as broken-bone ends grated. He managed to sit using only stomach muscles. Through clenched jaws he asked, "Do you seriously expect to survive till your ships can get here?"

Ene, seemingly uninjured, stood. "You have three ships. We have hundreds coming. If need be, this facility will be rebuilt."

Motar would have signaled Task Force Glithwah, requesting support. Depending how hard Koban pushed it, how much she decided to slow down before they swept past, reinforcements could be here in as little as three hours.

Carl said, "Despite a tunnel filled with ships and silos with missiles you're the one getting pounded."

Another blow struck, tossing them like dice in a cup. Carl landed on the broken arm; for a moment, he blacked out. He swam out of the darkness to find Joshua crumpled, chest slowly rising and falling, oozing from a jagged cut along the scalp line. ("We'll be okay, Tacitus netted.) Red Circle, bleeding purple, lay inert in a second heap.

This time, Carl did not override his implant's guidance to his med nanites. The fog of pain ebbed.

And in his mind's ear, over the insistent beeping that denoted unopened urgent messages—where the *hell* had they come from?—a voice demanded, "Should I proceed?"

It was Votan!

"Sitrep," Carl netted, after adding Tacitus to the link. Because if anyone had ever needed a situation report, it was they.

"Yes, sir. *Excalibur* is overhead. *Durendal* and *Joyeuse* remain in orbit. The last I saw both seemed fine. Many drones do, too."

"Blue Moon drones, or the drones we left orbiting the planet?"

"Blue Moon. I don't know about the other."

"And the battle?"

"It's over."

"If the battle is over, why are we taking this pounding?"

Motar joined the link. "So that we could consult. If you and Joshua hadn't been inside, I would have nuked the area and had done with it."

In a netted terrain image, near a mirrored, slow-time, curved surface, a new crater had appeared. In and around that pit, almost directly over Carl's head, dust and debris had yet to settle. Twenty meters deep, he guesstimated the hole. Meters more rock would have been pounded to gravel—porous to shortwave RF—above cracks and crevices penetrating deeper still into bedrock.

"Ir appreciate your restraint," Tacitus offered.

Motar netted, "Two-hundred-plus ships are about to descend on us. Even after the pounding we've taken, we could handle twenty or so—these guys have terrible reaction times; they can't track targets, identity decoys, or evade ordnance worth mentioning—but not hundreds. Given the rate of fire their railguns can sustain, they're dangerous even firing just dumb projectiles. We'll retrieve Votan before we pull out, but what can we do about you two?"

"Show me the tactical situation," Carl netted.

In consensual space, a 3-D graphic displaced the battle-scarred terrain. Red sparks swarmed above Xool World, still shrouded in slow time. As many again red sparks were en route to Blue Moon, harried (or so it seemed) by tiny blue dots: Hunter drones that had been monitoring the planet. In the vicinity of Blue Moon itself, only blue sparks appeared: the three vessels of Task Force Mashkith and drones. They had lost *lots* of drones. Task Force Glithwah, still hours away, merited only a flag along an edge of the graphic.

"What happened to the local Xool ships?" Carl asked. "And didn't I feel missile launches?"

The tactical graphic gave way to a new terrain image, panned back from the first. The second lava-tube entrance had collapsed. Wreckage lay strewn across a new, still dust-shrouded crater. "Just the one ship made it out before we closed the door," Motar netted. "But on its way down, that ship took out your last two infantry robots."

"And Xool surface weapons?" Carl asked. "Any apart from the railguns you mentioned?"

"Silo-based missiles," Motar netted. "Easily swatted, given a little warning. Some drones went down, though, in the initial surprise. We've taken out the silos we've spotted."

"Okay," Carl netted, "Grab Votan and make a dash for it. The Xool ships on their way have built up speed. You need a head start."

"And you?" Motar asked.

"We aren't going anywhere," Carl netted.

After the last strike, Ene had shouted. It must have been a call for assistance, because the five Xool hustling into the room had tended to Red Circle. As they trundled Red Circle from the room on a gurney, Ene seemed to remember his prisoners. "The starship."

Joshua was unconscious. *Maybe*, Carl thought, letting his eyes fall shut, *he, too, could appear out of it.* He slumped—with care, trying not to jostle the broken arm. Ene would have ample time later to abuse them.

"I can crash the computers here," Votan netted from the surface. "Force a reboot, maybe rolling reboots. The details are in messages I've sent you. I've been working on the code; I'll need maybe five minutes to finish. Ten minutes, tops."

Motar netted, "You don't have five minutes. *Excalibur* will set down in two, as near as we can get to the observatory. A minute after, we go. Whether or not you're aboard."

"Then leave me," Votan netted. "You can't spare the time to retrieve me anyway and I have to strike back. Somehow. Pick me up when you return for the commander."

Except, Carl thought, *there won't be any coming back.* The obvious tactical move was dropping one of the nukes Motar still held in reserve. Take out the command-and-control center.

"If you could disable all their computers, that'd be one thing," Carl netted. "Bringing down the observatory computers for a short while isn't worth your life. Run like hell for *Excalibur*. That's an order, soldier."

"The computers here are all I can hurt," Votan netted. "Sorry."

Tacitus netted, "But with Votan's help, Ir can do much more."

CHAPTER 54

Keeping the metaphor to himself, Joshua found the situation too much like an octopus juggling chainsaws:

—Ene and Carl verbally sparring. Emergency patching, of walls and fellow Xool alike, had preempted Ene for awhile, but now he was back.

—Control-room chatter from which, given only the occasional phrase that emerged from the background din, and the few words Tacitus had maybe translated, Joshua intuited only enough to add to his confusion.

—Tacitus' urgent netting back-and-forth with Votan.

All as hundreds of ships pursued the three battered survivors of Task Force Mashkith, and while Joshua, still feigning oblivion, strove not to react to anything.

For the first time since meeting Carl, Joshua thought, *maybe I should have learned b'tok.* The discipline in massive multitasking, especially with Tacitus preoccupied, would have been useful.

"The starship," Ene said. "Tell me where the starship is, and we'll attend to your friend."

"Who is fine," Joshua net-texted.

"*I'm* about to pass out," Carl told Ene. "You want answers? Remove these cuffs. Let me get at my first-aid kit."

"The starship." Ene said again. "Where is it?"

"My arm is broken," Carl countered. "I need meds from my kit. More than that, I need to see to Joshua."

"After you give me something," Ene said.

"How much longer?" Carl netted.

"A few minutes," Joshua texted back. Texting took fewer CPU cycles than simulated speech, and just then Tacitus needed every cycle they could get. "CALL IT FIVE."

"WHAT'S TAKING SO LONG?" Carl answered, taking Joshua's hint this time. "NEVER MIND. MY KNOWING WON'T HELP. DISTRACTING YOUR OTHER HALF CERTAINLY WON'T."

Did Carl imagine this was easy? Working at the machine-code level, all zeroes and ones, Votan had isolated the binary representations of most instructions, some operating-system calls, and network services. She had crafted, still toiling in binary, the most elementary of viruses. So far, Tacitus had spotted three reasons why Votan's virus would not have worked on the Xool computer.

Fortunately, biochips ran rings around neurons, human *and* Hunter.

"This process can get very disagreeable," Ene eventually said. "Answer my questions."

"I've heard only the one question," Carl said. "If you have another, try me. Maybe that'll be something I can answer."

"The *starship*," Ene rasped.

"READY," Tacitus texted.

"THAT'S FORTUNATE," Carl texted. "IT'S ALMOST SHOW TIME."

Joshua opened his eyes and, with a groan, sat up. "What did Ir miss?"

"How are you feeling?" Carl asked.

"Groggy," Joshua lied. "The worse for wear. Ir could use water." That Ir will not actually drink.

"Ene? Some water? Ene? Ene?" Carl asked.

But Ene was not heeding. His eye and ear stalks had swiveled toward the control room, where, amid swelling chatter, Joshua heard words that might mean *enemy ships*.

"Something wrong?" Carl asked.

"No! Tell me about—"

"Those fusions drives that just lit up?" Carl offered. "Of *course* you've not seen that fleet till now. Those ships had been coasting, stealthed. And now ..."

Ene turned to shout something to the control room.

Several Xool converged on the largest of the consoles. The alien seated there shouted back. In that long, sibilant response, Joshua heard words he believed meant *messages sent*.

He ceded their vocal cords. Tacitus deserved to be the one to announce, "It's done."

"Done." Ene echoed. "What is done?" With the din in the control room swelling into a yet louder, somehow agonized, cacophony, he demanded, "*What* have you done?"

"You don't know?" Carl asked.

Carl's head wobbled as Ene lashed his face—left, right, left—with a ropy arm/tentacle.

"What have you done?" Ene repeated.

"Do you remember that observatory on the surface?" Tacitus asked. "And the computer in it? Well, Ir did."

Ene turned toward Joshua, arm/tentacle raised threateningly.

"In the early days of human computing," Carl said, blood dripping from his nose, "malicious software took days to exploit vulnerabilities across networks. Within decades, that latency came down to minutes. Now, a minute is a long time."

A Xool dashed in from the control room. Purple Octagon. He and Ene had a heated, inexplicable exchange.

"What have you done?" Ene voice had taken on a sibilant edge that seemed, somehow, ominous. "Explain, *now*."

"Done?" As Tacitus spoke with his usual flat delivery, Joshua fashioned their face into a sneer. "Ir created a state-of-the-art, learning, evolving, self-replicating, memory-resident worm. While *you* …"

"We?" Ene prompted.

Joshua took over. "*You* opened a comm channel to your hundreds of ships—and thereby turned them into so many clay pigeons."

• • • •

Ene did not understand skeet shooting or the finer points of worm design. He did not quite get how Xool twentieth-century software was helpless before twenty-second-century malware. But that ships gone silent had begun reconnecting over emergency, audio-only, analog radio channels, that every ship to make contact reported itself blind and defenseless? *That*, Ene got.

Since the cyber attack, per Carl's implant, three minutes had passed. Three frantic minutes that had surely instructed the Xool neither rebooting nor rollback to backup files would resolve their problems.

"You have twelve minutes to convince me not to launch smart missiles at your ships," Carl told Ene. "Smart missiles will *not* miss."

There was a quick exchange in Xoolish, and then Purple Octagon snipped their cuffs.

"Thanks," Carl said. "I told you before: your people and ours don't need to fight. But if you choose war, it'll be over soon."

"What do you want?" Ene asked.

Glithwah, bless her heart, had been right all those years ago. He *would* get to reason with the Xool.

"To start, confidence-building measures. You release the tunnel entrance from slow time." Releasing two infantry bots. Carl let Ene work through that implication for himself. "The ships in planetary orbit return at once to your home world." Per Motar's latest tactical download, that entailed half the opposition. "The remainder break off pursuit, head home as quickly as they are able."

Ene and Purple Octagon consulted. Around Purple's midsection, the fringe band writhed agitatedly.

"Shall I take a look at your arm?" Joshua netted.

"It can wait," Carl netted back. "Ask again in twelve minutes."

"Unacceptable," Ene said. "Those ships would endanger every network at home."

"Destroy their onboard computers," Carl countered.

"In twelve minutes?"

"Closer now to eleven. Jettison them. Take axes to them. Set them afire. I don't care how."

More animated consultation.

"And in exchange? What do we get?" Ene asked.

"The lives of everyone aboard those ships." Perhaps not everyone, Carl admitted to himself. Reentry without computers would be tricky. It still gave those crews better odds than as bull's eyes in a shooting gallery. "And, we resume discussions. Aboard my ship. On more of an equals with equals basis."

Louder than ever, Purple and Ene conferred.

"Nine minutes," Carl interrupted.

Purple and Ene kept talking. Other activity ground to a halt, the Xool in the control room turning eyes and ears toward the debate.

How many ships and crews must die to make his point? "Five minutes."

With two minutes remaining, as Joshua, unhindered, returned with a water pitcher and glasses, the Xool deliberations reached a crescendo. Purple strode toward the control room.

"Very well," Ene said. "We will order all ships home."

CHAPTER 55

Ene and Purple Octagon, the latter now revealed to be named Lua, settled into the least claustrophobic cabin—Carl's own—aboard *Excalibur*. They, too, had had a challenging day. Before talks resumed, it was best that both sides take the time to process everything that had transpired. Because they had nothing but time. On the planet below, Carl estimated, the Xool had had perhaps seconds to consider the sudden and helter-skelter descent of their crippled fleets.

Shuffling along the main corridor, enjoying low-gee, he took Motar's report in person. Without decent computers, Xool ships were outclassed. Without smart weapons, they were hard-pressed to hit anything. Maybe that was why, when they *did* hit something, often they kept on hitting it. The only Hunter losses that day had been among drones, in almost every case units stationed in close orbit, with little warning to dodge or defend themselves.

What Carl did not get was why the outward-sweeping Xool ships had *maintained* a barrage aft, or why, in doing so, they switched armaments from missiles to railguns. Whatever the reason, the Xool tore to shreds any disabled drones near their planet. No one he had asked had offered a theory, either.

Motar finished, and Carl, still shuffling along the main corridor, netted through to Koban. Together they reviewed Task Force Glithwah's deployments as some ships shepherded home Xool stragglers and the rest mounted patrols. With those details attended to, Carl peeked through robotic eyes at affairs, on and underground, here on Blue Moon.

He yawned, telling himself he could always bunk with Joshua. If the day's adrenaline surges and caffeine megadoses ever faded. If the opportunity for sleep ever again presented itself. If the throbbing in his nose and arm—both set by Joshua, *Excalibur's* medical resources being minimal—and from assorted bruises, ever receded sufficiently to allow sleep. If the din of repairs to *Excalibur's* Swiss-cheesed hull ever diminished. If the infernal itching beneath his cast let up.

For that last, he kept reminding himself, the end was in sight. A day at most. Bless the nanites. If Xool had had bones to break and require knitting, maybe they would have felt differently about nanotech.

In the comfort of the copilot's acceleration couch, to the familiar background chatter of the bridge crew, Carl reclined, closed his eyes, and began organizing a report for the Foremost.

Before drifting off to sleep ....

• • • •

Show time, Carl thought.

The wardroom was not much of a meeting venue, but *Excalibur* could offer nothing better. He and Joshua sat across from their "guests" at the lone remaining human- (and Xool-) height table. Koban, whom Carl had invited to attend, had demurred, preferring to remain on patrol. That decision left Corinne, also invited, seething with curiosity and frustration, trapped aboard *Fearsome*—a scant few thousand klicks distant—until Koban reconsidered or arranged other transportation for her.

Remembering the padded, backless furniture at the Xool base, Carl had had a crewman find pillows to cushion rigid plasteel seats. Recalling Xool hospitality—before the beatings had begun—Carl asked, "Cold water, anyone?"

Joshua, not waiting for answers, stood and got four drink bulbs from the refrigerator.

"Shall we begin?" Carl suggested.

The two Xool consulted.

"Why are we here?" Ene asked.

"To stop a war," Carl said.

More consultation.

"Has it not already stopped?" Ene asked.

"A skirmish ended," Carl said. "To end the war, many worlds must be released from slow time."

Further consultation.

"What you ask cannot be," Ene finally offered.

"That's a difficult position for us to understand," Carl said. *And an impossible outcome for us to accept.*

Amid yet more Xool consultation, Joshua netted, "On another subject, Ir believe Lua understands clan speak. On the walk from their cabin, he appeared attentive to hallway gossip."

"Uh-huh," Carl netted. "And it was at my request that there was audible gossip to be overheard rather than netting. It stood to reason our second guest would be Ene's companion from the Moon or a colleague who'd spent ages monitoring K'vith. My money was on the latter." Before the failed power grab that drove Arblen Ems into exile, they had been among the Great Clans. Any Xool tasked to watch K'vith was apt to have learned clan speak. "Ene and Lua will search for any opportunity to drive a wedge between us and the Hunters. Let's keep to ourselves what we suspect."

After a long Xool sidebar, Ene came up only with, "What do you propose?"

Carl took a sip from his drink bulb. "Explain why you won't release our worlds."

"I cannot," Ene said.

"You can't explain, or you can't release our worlds?"

"Either."

Carl said, "You *won't* explain. That's different."

"Very well," Ene said. "I lack the authority."

Carl stood, stretching muscles already become tense. "*I'm* giving you the authority."

"A moment." Ene and Lua held yet another long conversation. "I ... we will not. No one on this world will. Our families are below."

Hostages? Carl wondered. Maybe that was being too anthropomorphic. Obedience to policy could be a matter of family honor, or some yet more esoteric behavior he could not hope to anticipate.

"Then contact the proper authorities on the home world," Carl said.

"I cannot," Ene said.

Because the worm had somehow disabled the base radio, Carl supposed. "You can use this ship's radio."

"You cannot either," Ene said.

"This once," Tacitus netted, "I don't think the obstacle is recalcitrance. Remember, Xool World is a mirror. Apart from UV, it reflects virtually all electromagnetic waves across the spectrum. That includes radio waves."

"How about a UV laser?" Carl netted, although he wasn't optimistic. If the Xool could communicate by laser between moon and planet, they would not have sent a ship to report intruders. And then *Sting* would not have chased that courier to its doom.

"Insufficient information," Tacitus netted.

"Ene," Carl said, "I understand why radio is problematical, but the slow-time field seems to respond differently to ultraviolet. Can we speak by UV laser with authorities on the planet?"

"A moment." Ene and Lua caucused. "Solar ultraviolet is absorbed to amplify the field. Ultraviolet does not reach the surface."

Carl said, "I've heard more than enough about what we can't do. Take us to the planet."

"Nor is that allowed," Ene said.

"Too bad," Carl snapped. "Find a way."

Or else, his words implied. Or else, what? We talk until you're convinced? How long would that take—if it even worked? Torture? Distaste aside, torture might not work—and Ene, like his human agents, could have his own suicide bomb.

Carl's gut churned. By his leniency toward the fleeing Xool crews—by taking those defenseless ships off the board—had he squandered his only leverage?

"Or else," Joshua said, breaking a lengthening silence, "we can begin throwing rocks."

"What the hell?" Carl netted.

"Look at them," Tacitus netted. The two Xool were, suddenly, in urgent consultation. "They don't much care for that idea."

"So only I'm in the dark? Explain, please."

"You had wondered about Xool ships pounding drones near the planet even after they were disabled. After analyzing the records, Ir have yet to see Xool ships stop firing until one of two things happened. One, the drone has been reduced to small pieces. That's the typical case. Two, the drone, or a big piece of it, has been batted away."

"Knocked out of orbit?" Carl netted.

"Perhaps not in the sense you mean. Bumped up to escape velocity."

"But *Sting* came apart when it impacted the slow-time field."

"That doesn't mean nothing punched through, or that the field wasn't in some way disrupted. Think conservation of energy."

Ene waggled an arm tentacle for their attention. "What do you mean, throw rocks?"

"Just what you think," Tacitus said. "Ir believe that, over the eons, someone diverted asteroids and comets that would otherwise have hit the planet. That preventing such impacts was a primary function of your nearby base and its ships. But give us a moment to consult."

"No, I'm ready," Carl said.

Conservation of energy—of a kind. Any external strike upon a slow-time field would somehow be compressed into the much briefer interval within, effectively intensifying the blow. The field might absorb minor impacts, but—judging by the dedication with which the Xool ships continued to target quite small infalling debris; judging from how they had sent railgun slugs, never more massive missiles, back toward the planetary field—any such protection could work only to a point. And the compression factor multiplying the effects must be up in the millions ....

That *Sting* might have struck a blow at the Xool buoyed Carl's spirits.

Carl locked eyes with Ene. "Your choice. You can bring us to speak with your leaders. Or, we can lob stones until you change your minds."

"No, you won't," Ene said. "Disturbing and redirecting the orbits of big asteroids will take years."

Carl strode to the table, staring down at the Xool. "Not to anyone inside."

His sensor stalks slumped, Ene said, simply, "We shall comply."

CHAPTER 56

An army of robots took weeks to salvage an intact Xool ship from deep inside the collapsed lava tube. After that much anticipation, passage through the planet's slow-time barrier was anticlimactic. One moment the squished sphere of the Xool ship hurtled toward its reflection; the next moment the ship was through. Below, an Earth-like world stretched before them, swaddled in blue sky and fluffy white clouds. It looked heartbreakingly normal until, glancing upward, Corinne took notice of the starless black heavens.

Pinched by a tight harness, brushing shoulders in one of the four jump seats shoehorned in along the aft bridge bulkhead, she could not *wait* to set down. Lord, but she was sick and tired of ships.

Joshua sat to her right. Carl sat to her left; seated to his left, arrived in-system by courier ship only the day before, just for this excursion, was the Foremost. Straight ahead, in the pilot and copilot seats, were Ene and Lua. Except for brief interactions with traffic control and one cryptic radioed notification, both Xool were silent.

("A code phrase," Tacitus netted apologetically about the notification, "without a meaningful direct translation. Perhaps it's only 'warning, manual landing.'"

"Or recommending a declaration of DEFCON 1?" Carl netted back.

Tacitus' avatar just shrugged.)

Were the Xool happy to be home? Anxious about bringing interlopers through the barrier? Corinne wished she could better read their body language.

As the ship plunged into the atmosphere, she heard the first faint keening of reentry. Sky glimpsed through the view port took on a tinge of darkest blue. Starlight did not penetrate the barrier, but sunlight, somehow, did.

"Weird," Carl muttered, as outside the Xool ship the noise of reentry swelled.

"What?" she asked.

"Artificial cabin gravity. My eyes and experience insist we're pulling several gees, but I don't feel it. This is like a video game, not flying."

"But it's impressive technology," Tacitus offered.

"No argument here," Carl said.

The sky paled, and the panorama beneath started to flatten. Breaking through thin, wispy clouds, Corinne saw a patchwork quilt of greens: farmland, she supposed. They flew over a lake, its surface densely rippled, like corduroy. A weird wind, she decided. But what were those dark, roiling columns in the distance?

"Ene?" she said. "Ahead, about thirty and sixty degrees to your left. Are those fires?"

"Examples of your handiwork," Ene rasped. "Crash sites. Scarcely four minutes have passed on Horua"—the proper name for Xool World—"since you people arrived. Less, for the ships reentering, many with battle damage, none with working computers."

"Do *not* apologize," Carl netted. "They attacked us. Rather than order those ships home, we could have blown every one from the sky."

Leaving what to say? Corinne wondered. *Acknowledgment that they, too, were flying seat of the pants, without a working computer?* Because to have helped Ene's compatriots scrub the worm from this ship's computers would have taught them how to restore all their ships.

Tacitus broke the awkward silence. "Four minutes here to a month outside. That means a slowdown ratio of only about ten thousand to one."

"Things would have been sped up," Ene said, "upon the notification of your arrival."

"So authorities here could better monitor the battle?" Tacitus asked.

"If need be," Ene said.

"How about we stop distracting the pilot?" Carl suggested.

And so, in uneasy silence—Corinne wondering all the while if *this* ship would drill into the ground, if she and her friends were about to become the latest column of smoke and dust—they swooped to a landing at an eerily idle spaceport.

A long, sleek, ground-effect vehicle awaited them on the runway. All six from the ship climbed into the back. As gritty industrial cityscape sped past, Corinne wondered how there had been time to order a limo for them. Hadn't it been only minutes?

The Foremost had had the same thought. Corinne understood Timoq's question, and she sensed Lua did, too. But Ene, as far as she knew, did not know clan speak.

Tacitus could handle translations among English, clan speak, and, for the lack of a better term, Xoolish. Hearing everything two or three times had gotten old, so Corinne activated her implant's latest software upgrade. It buffered non-English speech long enough for Tacitus to signal whether he would net a mind's ear translation. If the signal did not come, her auditory cortex, none the wiser, received the speech just a few syllables delayed. In general, he would translate and, compared to the Xool, she would gain some quiet thinking time with every verbal exchange.

"Be honored," came Lua's answer in translation. "This vehicle is usually reserved for her Excellency, the Chief Administrator."

Was coddling heads of state universal? Corinne wondered. "I suppose we are being brought to her."

It was not a question, so maybe the absence of a response wasn't entirely rude.

With escort vehicles ahead and behind, light bars flashing, they glided past a sprawling manufacturing center, a warehouse district, and a chemical complex. Tenement buildings, bland and blocky, separated industrial zones.

The escort cars, like their transport, had tinted windows. Corinne tried to put her finger on what about the tableau nagged at her. That honchos rode ridiculously sized vehicles in ostentatious motorcades, just like on Earth? That the Xool were *that* similar to humans? For a moment the resemblance felt like a piece of the puzzle—until she remembered who had had a hand, or tentacle, anyway, in shaping Earth's cultures. Rather than Xool acting like humans, maybe humans mimicked the Xool. She found that a depressing inference—and yet not what continued to bother her.

So what was? Something outside the limo. Something about the long lines of traffic pulled onto the shoulders to clear the way for the racing convoy.

Trucks, hundreds of them, with Xool aboard! How quaint and unproductive to expend labor driving around cargoes! And given the Xool's simple computers, such inefficiency would not be limited to hauling freight. Countless mundane and dangerous tasks on this world would get done by living workers, or not at all.

She netted, "So the discovery of the millennium is that Xool live in Dickensian squalor?"

"More like the drab tedium of Stalinist realism," Joshua netted.

"I haven't read either," Carl netted.

"You wouldn't enjoy Stalin," Joshua predicted.

Industrial and commercial districts gave way to office parks and residential neighborhoods. Those, in turn, yielded to ever more of the grandiose ostentation Corinne suspected must characterize capital cities everywhere.

"We're almost there, aren't we?" she asked aloud.

"We are," Ene said, his fringe band fluttering.

Corinne was willing to bet this time she *did* read body language: agitation.

• • • •

Carl was not surprised when, near the imposing entrance of an epically large and ugly edifice, Ene and Lua were ushered away. Of course, the Chief Administrator would hear her people's report before meeting with the alien interlopers. But soon enough, armed guards led Carl, Joshua, Corinne, and Timoq down a long, high hallway lined with statuary to a conference room that was all swirled neon colors and plush scarlet furniture. The rear wall, all glass, overlooked an open-air promenade along whose mauve, mossy lawn ornate monuments and heroic statues stretched into the distance.

Nine Xool occupied ottomans on three sides of a padded rectangular table: four on one long side, four on the opposite side, and one at the far end. Ene and Lua perched on ottomans against a side wall, without a table. A smaller table and four ottomans near the door showed the visitors where to sit—though Timoq, to see and be seen, stood on his. Both tables and the spare ottoman beside Ene offered goblets and a carafe of water.

The Xool on Blue Moon all had gray-on-gray mottling patterns and stocky torsos. Of the Xool around the table many were of similar appearance, but four—among them, the lone Xool seated at the head of the table—were slender and had green-on-gray mottling. And the Chief Administrator, they had been told, was "she."

Were the off-world Xool all males?

At the head of the main table, the Xool straightened. She spoke and Tacitus' netted translation announced, "I am Wataninui Wue Tihotiho, Chief Administrator. These are my advisers."

In parallel text, Tacitus netted: Do you want a distinctive voice for each aide?

Counting Wue, Ene, Lua, and themselves, they already used eight voices. Carl didn't relish trying to keep straight eight others, especially representing nameless, faceless Xool.

Carl texted: For me, lump the aides (if any speak) into a common voice. But remember which aide says what, in case it matters later.)

As mind's-ear audio to all his team, Carl added, "Now, our protocol explanation."

Tacitus, hissing and rasping, with simultaneous netted translations, gave a short prepared statement that he would both articulate the views of, and silently translate for, his companions.

At the main table, sensor stalks twitched on two of the advisers. The Chief Administrator did not visibly react.

One by one, each voiced distinctively by Tacitus, the visitors made their introductions:

"Cluth Timoq, Foremost of clan Arblen Ems."

"Corinne Elman, media representative of Earth."

"Joshua Matthews and"—with a change in timbre—"Tacitus. Both of Earth."

"Carl Rowland, representative of the United Planets."

Wue spoke. "You should not have come. Having come, you should not threaten us."

"*You* should not have played God," Carl responded. "Release our people from slow time. Or show us how."

Perhaps no one spoke so bluntly to the Chief Administrator. She took her time just to respond, "No."

Carl tried again. "Help us to understand. Explain how we came to this point, why you shaped developments on our home worlds."

"No," Wue repeated.

"Then I'll tell *you*." Carl had wrestled with this puzzle since Ene's first, grudging admissions, and the evidence supported just two theories. He would start—dearly hoping it was correct—with the possibility that might prove comparatively benign. "You set out to fashion the companion intelligences your explorers could never find. And you have! You're *not* alone anymore. So why attack us when we come to talk? Why lock away humans and Hunters at home?"

"Because," Wue said, "you mistake our purpose."

CHAPTER 57

Joshua texted: I TOLD YOU SO.

To which Carl answered: I'M NOT SURPRISED, JUST DISAPPOINT-ED. YOU WANT TO TAKE IT?

Joshua said, "Humans, Hunters, every species in InterstellarNet: we're guinea pigs. The Xool spent 550 million years—to them, less than two decades—'configuring' their experiments. Culturing Petri dishes. Watching to see which samples run amok, and how."

To which Wue said ... nothing.

"Eleven Petri dishes," Carl said. Because InterstellarNet had eleven members.

"It would suspect more," Joshua said. "We found no record of genetically engineered organisms in their lunar base. To drive and shape evolution, to encourage intelligence to emerge, they would have relied on the blunt instrument of planetary-scale disasters. Who's to say some interventions weren't too disastrous?"

"Ene!" Corinne burst out in English. "You threw the rock that doomed the dinosaurs?"

With a jerk, Ene's eyestalks retracted to a third of their usual length. "That was an *accident*," he insisted. "We had sensors through-out the solar system, ceaselessly scanning for dangerous rocks. This rock came plunging in from way above the ecliptic. By the time the asteroid's orbit was characterized and the computers decided to release us from slow time, it was too late to stop."

Carl couldn't decide how he felt about that. No, he could decide: he was conflicted. Suppose Ene lied. Suppose he and his friends, for whatever reason, hadn't liked the idea of dinos evolving to sentience, and so they had permitted that big rock to strike. Maybe they had pitched the dinosaur-killer themselves. Either way, it would be just one more atrocity among many others—and a turning point for life on Earth, absent which neither he, nor Joshua, nor Corinne would exist to take umbrage. In a way, maybe he should be a tad grateful. But the larger part of him wanted to take Ene's protestation as more evidence that the Xool had their blind spots.

Carl found he could be skeptical, encouraged, and a tad appreciative all at once.

Ene's outburst invited a rebuke from Wue.

Carl said, "If not by hurling rocks, how *did* the Xool drive evolution?"

With a supple gesture, Wue indicated one of her advisers.

"Yes, Excellency." Turning eyestalks toward Carl, the adviser said, "Each of the experiments has been equipped with an array of time-slowing generators. Arrays were activated, as needed, to synchronize progress across the various worlds. Also as needed, the slow-time field is detuned to accelerate evolution by means of ecological stresses."

"Detuned," Carl said. "I don't get that."

"What they've failed to volunteer," Tacitus said, "it that the field enwrapping the planet must do more than reduce the passage of time. Slow time by half and that's like doubling the intensity of sunlight. Minus, of course, the narrow band of ultraviolet siphoned off to power the field generator."

"Give me a moment," Carl said.

Nothing about the Xool merited an *of course*. What did he truly understand? Apart from a bit of UV, Xool World reflected almost all the sunlight that reached it. Time on the planet was slowed by a huge factor—at present ten thousand to one, Ene had indicated on the flight down—while energy from Epsilon Indi streamed undiminished. If something did not reflect almost all the inbound sunlight, everyone and everything inside the slow-time field would incinerate.

Set the field to *reflect* a hair too much sunlight, and bring on an ice age. Set the field to *admit* a hair too much sunlight, and suffer instant global warming. Nor would the effect alter just temperature. Ice ages locked away a world's fresh water in glaciers, bringing on drought. Warm eras melted icecaps and flooded continents.

And nothing in any world's geological record would even hint at the underlying cause.

Carl denied himself the indulgence of feeling sick at heart. He said, "And now Earth looks like Xool World, very reflective, because its time-slowing field is back on."

"Correct," the Chief Administrator acknowledged. "And elsewhere in your solar system where we suspected you might eventually colonize. Arrays of slow-time generators were pre-deployed on all such worlds, just in case."

And if those fields had been detuned, if home worlds across InterstellarNet were being frozen or incinerated, how likely was Wue to disclose that? About as likely as she was to acknowledge the thousands, perhaps millions, who must have died, starved, when the barriers went up. Asteroid bases, mining ships, orbital stations, Lagrange habitats: all relied upon trade with the Earth and the major colonized worlds.

Carl tamped down his anger. This was no time to lose self-control.

Wue continued, "Our best minds and our explorers concurred: it is the nature of certain technologies to grow exponentially and, upon reaching some critical state, careen out of control. Technologies of mass destruction, every one. Genetically engineered organisms outcompeting the natural ones. Nanites outcompeting life itself, replicating without bounds. One AI designing a smarter AI designing a smarter AI until normal minds can't hope to compete."

"Is she calling mir abnormal?" Tacitus texted. "Ir think Ir am insulted."

"Take offense on your own time," Carl texted back.

"Ir won't say that Ir agree." Joshua said, pausing to scratch his nose. "But while Ir can understand caution with AI, you avoid more than that. Every aspect of your computing technology—Ir am just being honest—is quite elementary. Why?"

Wue turned toward an adviser. (Of their consultation, Tacitus netted, "It appears they have a second language. I can't translate this, at least not yet.")

The adviser said, "It may be the case that the sole path to artificial intelligence is purposeful programming. What if programming is but one path among many? What if, as in biology, intelligence can emerge unguided from networks of sufficient complexity? We dare not take that risk."

"But Ene or one of his minions *knows* modern human-level computer science," Joshua countered. "To destroy multiple copies of Robyn Tanaka Astor's memory backups, to erase what she had learned of your interventions, someone with talent had to hack into some of the securest computing centers on Earth."

This time, Ene awaited permission to respond. "Not I. Just a few of our indigenous servants were directed to acquire those skills. It was necessary. Without such expertise, servants could not monitor your people's process. Of course we did not permit the servants to bring such dangerous technology into our—"

"*Damn* you!" Corinne blurted out. " 'Monitor the *process?*' You and your 'servants' *killed* Robyn Tanaka, my friend. You killed how many others?"

Ene's eyestalks twitched. "Without us, there would have been no Robyn Tanaka—nor any of you, either. Without us, advanced life on Earth might still be jellyfish and algae mats."

"And that justified experimenting on your children?" Carl said. "You gave us matches as toys to see what would happen?"

"Matches," Ene echoed. "Our children. You object that I taught your early ancestors to use fire? Do you likewise suppose your lives would have been better had we not introduced agriculture, and your intellectual development richer without the idea of the alphabet?

"But no, I infer you speak metaphorically. To extend your metaphor, humans devised their own matches. In recent centuries, when we intervened, it was to take away some matches, different sorts of matches, on every world."

"Beginning," Tacitus netted, "with basic physics. Ir blame the Xool for our lack of a unified field theory, for an absence of progress dating back to Einstein himself. They would not risk humans developing the technology to penetrate their slow-time fields."

Carl said, "Leaving us with only our Xool-sanctioned matches, to see if with those alone we would burn down our house."

"Enough!" Wue said. "Any conflagration that your people sets will be their doing, not ours. However the experiment concludes, we will have been instructed by your experience."

Carl asked, "Are we supposed to take comfort in that?"

"That is immaterial," Wue said.

Immaterial!? Carl had to change topics before he strangled Wue with her own tentacle. "Explain the mechanics to us. Your people have spent eons preparing other worlds for just this moment. What happens now, exactly?"

Wue gestured to Ene, squirming on his ottoman. "We watch. Because technology's crisis appears to be a runaway phenomenon, we slow down events the better to observe and contrast them."

Slow down events: as in activating the time-retarding field. Joshua had spotted Earth's encapsulating field by telescope. That left the observation portion of the Xool experiment. "Only you're not watching. You're light-years removed just when everything might be coming together."

"What transpires at the critical juncture is … unpredictable," Ene said.

The Foremost broke his long silence. "Dangerous, you mean. Not nearly so dangerous as meddling with the destiny of Hunters! You are about to learn—"

"Stop!" Carl texted to Tacitus, cutting off the translation. To everyone, Carl sent, "Tactics are *my* job, remember? It's not yet the time for threats."

Carl said, "I'm missing something. Who is left to observe? Your native agents?" The people who had once abducted Joshua remained at large.

"And instruments," Ene said.

"Instruments on Earth, for example," Carl said. "To do what?"

"Excuse me." Ene grasped a water glass. "To record news reports."

"Supposing your instruments survive," Carl said, "A gray-goo incident might eat them."

"Indeed." Ene's eyestalks went through another twitch/retract/extend cycle. "Our off-world probes periodically streak through the upper atmosphere. Servants and ground-based instruments, for as long as they are able, upload reports to the probes."

Probes built with Xool super-science, able to penetrate the slow-time field. Those probes must transmit back. Carl asked, "And what are you hearing about Earth?"

Ene again swiveled an eyestalk toward the Chief Administrator, seeking permission. "On Earth, for now, time's flow has slowed by a mere factor of one hundred. Only a few months have passed. It's apparently too soon to transmit anything." Ene paused for another sip. "If we *had* heard, it would have meant a crisis."

Corinne said, "So humanity hasn't dissolved into gray goo, or been devoured by super bugs, or ascended to some alternate plane of existence."

"Most likely not," Ene agreed. "As of twelve years ago, anyway. In the galactic time frame, that is."

"But suppose nothing goes wrong?" Carl asked Ene. "Suppose Earth keeps its technology under control?"

Ene shifted on his ottoman. Loath to answer?

"It won't," Wuc said.

"Suppose it does," Carl persevered.

Wue said, "Then we will know how, too. We will have learned something important."

Carl's hands had become fists; he willed them to relax. "And then you'll deactivate the slow-time field, declare the experiment at an end? You'll permit us to rejoin the galaxy?"

Wue's eyestalks stiffened: a mannerism they had not yet seen. "A hundred tragedies show that won't happen. These worlds must remain isolated."

"And if a world doesn't self-destruct?" Carl persisted.

Wue said, "Any who survive the crisis will have surpassed us in unknowable ways. We will maintain quarantine until our solar system is safely away."

"How many years is *that*?" Carl demanded.

"I doubt he means years," Joshua said, "at least not from our perspective."

"Dr. Matthews is correct," Wue said. "But do not worry. In a few million years, our solar systems will have sufficiently diverged."

Carl's mind raced. "In a few million years, the Xool will rule the galaxy—or have vanished themselves. Either way, you won't let us out."

Tacitus added, "And if they slow time further? In what would seem only a few years, the Sun would grow old, swell into a red giant, and swallow the Earth."

"This is unacceptable," Carl said. "You *will* release everyone from your experiments."

"No." Wue stood, and her advisers stood with her. "And because you don't get to decide, you will have to accept it."

CHAPTER 58

"Are you finally convinced," the Foremost netted, "these Xool are the enemy?"

Carl took a moment to reflect. To be enemies implied a sense of, if not parity, at least similarity. Absent that, *enemy* seemed the wrong term. The Xool, having raised other species practically from the primordial ooze, might be incapable of seeing anything more than, as Joshua had put it, Petri dishes.

And dismissed the semantics as irrelevant. To the billions trapped on Earth, K'vith, and elsewhere, that would be a distinction without a difference.

Carl netted, "Agreed." They all knew what that meant.

The Xool World slowdown, according to Ene, was presently ten thousand to one. Actions set in motion outside the barrier were coming to fruition sooner than Carl had intended; in view of the Chief Administrator's intransigence, that might be for the best.

"When will the show start?" Carl netted to Tacitus.

Because Tacitus, by the calculations he performed, was their timekeeper. In preparation for this encounter Joshua had had a gravimeter implanted. Changes in strength and direction of Blue Moon's tidal tug revealed the passage of time outside the slow-time field.

"Five minutes local, give or take," Tacitus netted. "The measurable effect isn't as strong as Ir had hoped."

"*Sit*, Wue," Carl said. "We're not finished."

Ene trembled. Because he feared blame for his charges' impertinence?

"Who here understands b'tok?" Carl asked. "No one? Lua, after watching Hunters for so long, you must know something of the game. Explain."

Without an implant, without decent computers, no Xool could play b'tok, but it hardly mattered. Carl was running out the clock.

When Lua's halting explanation proved less than complete, Timoq stepped in. "B'tok is our premier means of teaching strategy. More than a simulation of combat dynamics ..."

The five-minute countdown Carl had set in his implant reached zero. Nothing happened. *Give or take*, he reminded himself.

"The thing is," Carl interrupted, "a key component of b'tok is logistics. The more resources an adversary controls, and the longer that adversary is undisturbed to develop and exploit its resources, the greater their advantage. For a time, I suffered from the misconception that dynamic favored the Xool. Ironically, the time-dilation technology that made possible your scheme is also your greatest weakness."

And as though on cue—

Flash!

Far brighter than the sun, a fireball erupted over the capital city.

Tacitus could not translate Wue's shout or the advisers' cringing responses. A demand for answers and many excuses, Carl guessed, as other aides rushed into the room to report.

"The thing is," Carl continued, trusting Joshua/Tacitus to project their voice over the Xool babble, "you abandoned the resources of the galaxy. You denied yourself even the resources of this solar system. Without automation, or biotech, or nanotech, you can't even take full advantage of this single planet's resources. And as much you as slow down time, that's how much faster our people on the outside can out-produce you. So long story short—"

A sonic boom, long and loud, rattled the hall. Here, the window held, but even through walls and closed doors, the shattering of glass was unmistakable.

"Twenty-three seconds," Tacitus announced. "Call it seventy kilometers away."

"Dramatic," Corinne netted, "but a little too close for comfort."

Because Koban could not see through the field, she could only throw asteroids at random. From her perspective, there would have been only a brief flare-up as the rock penetrated the field. In her timeframe, another rock wouldn't strike for more than a year. Here, unless the Xool dialed back time yet further, the next blow would come within the hour.

As a great roar rolled on and on, Carl hoped the next rock didn't come any closer.

He strode up to Wue. "Each rock will be bigger than the last. Soon enough, the strikes will cease to be airbursts. Are you prepared yet to negotiate?"

• • • •

"This is quite simple," Carl explained when the meeting resumed. "Until I call off the operation"—physically impossible unless the slow-time field went away, or they were permitted to leave—"redirected asteroids will keep falling. And the longer I'm out of touch, the bigger and more often those rocks will strike."

"You can as easily drop asteroids on us if we returned to real time," an adviser countered. "Better that we slow down time further."

"To give yourselves all the time in the world." Carl laughed, wondering if Tacitus could convey the sarcasm. "Oh, but you're bluffing. Because the slower you allow time to move here, the more you would amplify the intensity of whatever strikes. Nor are your worries limited to the rocks sent on purpose. No one is left to look for or deflect *anything* anymore."

"We will discuss this," Wue said.

"Here is my free advice," Carl said. "Talk fast."

Switching to the second, unfamiliar language, the Xool debated. After a few minutes, one left the room. To dial back time, Carl guessed.

"Will they decide?" Corinne netted. "*Can* they decide? We're dealing with an entire world so fearful that it shut itself away. How do we convince so many to change their minds?"

"We won't have to," Carl netted.

If history repeated itself. If Joshua/Tacitus were, once again, correct ....

• • • •

Zheng He: fifteenth century admiral, explorer, diplomat, and trader of Ming-era imperial China. In a series of seven voyages spanning 1405 to 1433, Zheng He exerted Chinese influence across the South China Sea and the Indian Ocean. His fleet explored and traded along the coast of India, around the Arabian Peninsula, and south along the eastern coast of Africa at least to the modern port of Mombasa. Inconclusive evidence suggests Zheng He's fleet explored yet farther, rounding the Cape of Good Hope to discover the Atlantic Ocean.

Within a century of these voyages, China had turned inward. The Emperor banned all overseas trade; to sail from China in a multi-masted ship became a capital offense. Records of Zheng He's travels were suppressed and in large measure destroyed. And so the onetime preeminent maritime power of the East fell prey to navies sailing from Europe ....

—*Internetopedia*

• • • •

"Joshua," Carl netted to the group, "explain it to everyone." In a private text he added, BUT KEEP IT BRIEF.

"Consider the state of this world," Joshua netted. "An entire civilization, many millions, more likely billions, of people cut off—by conscious action, by means of technology—from the galaxy. A civilization that has so far suppressed at least a half dozen technologies that developed on InterstellarNet worlds.

"Was this quarantine entered into by common agreement, or some democratic choice? Conceivably, but Ir doubt it. And if that were the case? That era soon passed into totalitarian rule.

"Only by totalitarian rule could the Xool enforce a worldwide ban on AI and genetic engineering, on robotics and nanotech. Only an all-powerful government, after mastering interstellar travel, could withhold from its people even the resource wealth of their own solar system. Only through constant, intrusive surveillance and by wielding absolute control over everyone and everything could a government impoverished by those decisions expropriate the vast resources to explore the galaxy, to build and staff a defensive fleet just in case, and to shape *our* worlds. And like the Chinese turning away from the world, that means dictatorship."

So much for brief. "What Joshua means," Carl netted, "is we need only to convince Wue."

And with that thought, another penny dropped. Since Ene's earliest admissions, Carl had struggled to wrap his head around shoehorning this epic, incredible undertaking into twenty years subjective. Even to try? That was, well, crazy.

But demanding that everything happen within the lifetime of a dictator? *That* made sense to him. So, in that context, did hostage-taking. So did permitting only one gender off-world, lest expedition-ary teams abandon the dictator's project and set up shop for and by themselves on some fallow world.

The second asteroid strike—on some distant part of the world, evidently, but revealed by the scurrying arrival of aides—seemed to agitate, but not accelerate the Xool deliberations.

Carl strutted to their end of the room. "The longer you wait, the worse things will get."

"Enough! Wue said. (Did she direct her pique at Carl or at her own squabbling advisers? Perhaps both.) "Suppose ten years pass outside. A hundred years. We will absorb whatever damage we must from your indiscriminate bombardment. You are few and we are many, and in that time we will construct an indomitable fleet. Then—if you have not already destroyed yourselves—we will obliterate you."

"Here's the thing," Carl said. "The lesson of b'tok: victory favors those with the time to amass resources. By your choice, time is on our side. While you spend a day building a fleet, we'll have spent a thousand days, or a hundred thousand, or a million, improving ours. And even today, because of our computers, our warships and weapons are superior.

"Meanwhile, our engineers and scientists are examining the slow-time personnel capsules and the starships we seized on the moon overhead. Will enlightenment come after ten years? A hundred? A thousand? Who can say? But I know they *will* master your technology, no matter how much you've hobbled our past development. They *will* find a way to release our worlds from slow time—and for you, it will have been in the blink of an eye."

"And then they'll hunt you down here," the Foremost growled from across the room.

Carl continued, "And if all that should fail? You will still lose. As we speak, robots are manufacturing robots and battle drones. Those will build more, and they yet more." In factories the Xool would *never* find, even if they emerged to look. Throughout the years Glithwah had plotted the clan's escape from Ariel, Carl had little suspected, much less succeeded in locating, her robot factory. "If you hope *ever* to exit slow time ..."

Wue and advisers caucused again. Whatever suggestion one might offer, whatever objection another might raise, Wue seemed quick to interrupt.

"Impatience," Joshua netted. "The prelude to decision."

Wue emerged from her cluster of advisers and aides. She said, "This is the choice you would give those who nurtured you. Death by bombardment? Or suicide by one of the self-destructive plagues your kind has always unleashed?"

"Disaster is certain," Carl said, "in only one of those scenarios. Choose wisely."

Wue slumped. "You cannot imagine the horrors my people have encountered across the galaxy. This choice is no choice."

Corinne cleared her throat. "Except that, Chief Administrator, matters *don't* need to end badly."

THE ELMAN SOLUTION

CHAPTER 59

Great Seclusion: the isolation from the rest of the Solar System, behind impenetrable force fields, of Earth, the Moon, Mars, Mercury, and several other settled worlds. Gravitational influences imply these worlds continue to exist. If so, Earth may have all but ceased spinning; outside its barrier, Earth's magnetic field has dropped to one percent of its former value. Conditions inside are otherwise unknown. That the barriers reflect virtually all incident solar energy bodes ill for the continuation of life on the worlds rendered inaccessible.

Observers have detected no change to the force fields since their onset, without warning, in 2186.

Barriers appeared around all affected worlds at essentially the same time. In the years following, with allowances for light-speed delays, astronomers determined that the home world (at a minimum) of every InterstellarNet member species has become similarly mirrored and that the phenomenon struck everywhere at once.

Whether the Great Seclusion is a natural phenomenon or was brought about by party or parties (and technologies) unknown remained a matter of conjecture until the approach to the Solar System, in 2246, of the starship *Amends* ....

—*Internetopedia (Belt Edition)*

• • • •

"See you on the other side."

Her brave words had not ceased to echo in Corinne's thoughts, any more than had the unfortunate sensation of backing into a coffin, when the shimmering field closed her in—and disappeared.

Hell, she had barely had time to blink.

"Now *this* is the way to travel," Joshua declared from an enclosure beside hers. "Not even one second subjective time."

As she contemplated that, Carl and Ene moved from their slow-time boxes to the pilot and copilot seats on *Amends*'s compact bridge. They busied themselves with the Xool ship's instruments.

"Where are we?" she asked.

"About eight billions klicks from the Sun." Carl turned, grinning. "The radio chatter is unmistakable. Moons of Saturn, Uranus, Neptune, countless asteroids and Kuiper Belt objects. There's still a civilization here."

"Then I should get to work," Corinne said.

Carl said. "This far out, I doubt anyone has spotted us. You can take your time."

Fifty-one years ago—eighty-one years, as far as her soon-to-be audience was concerned—she had scooped every media outlet in the Solar System by revealing a United Planets secret: the imminent arrival of a Hunter starship. Now *she* approached aboard an alien starship, to recount an epic tale eons in the making. By comparison, the incursion of the Hunters had been a trivial item of gossip. Maybe she could take her time before broadcasting; she didn't want to. She couldn't bear to. "Whenever the gear is ready."

Ene gestured at his console to indicate the camera, then vacated his seat. "You can transmit now."

Corinne sat. She squared her shoulders and took a deep breath. At Carl's nod of encouragement, she began. "This is Corinne Elman, reporting live from the Oort Cloud, aboard the Xool starship *Amends*. People of the Solar System, it is our mission to release the trapped worlds from their isolation ...."

• • • •

Another day, Joyce Matthews told herself wearily. Another go at convincing the authorities, and anyone who might influence the authorities, and anyone with money, of the urgent need to dig for answers at the buried Xool base. Alas, all that the establishment could see—all that anyone ever saw—was a collapsed lava tube, kilometers from nowhere, deep in the foothills of Montes Carpatus. In the eighth month of the emergency, few people would hear out, much less entertain diverting scarce resources to investigate, some crone's wild conspiracy theories.

Before tilting yet again at windmills, she would complete her other, likely more productive, daily routine: four shuffling circuits of the grassy central glade of the Tycho City Arboretum. The park had always been crowded, visitors drawn to the great dome and the view overhead as much as for these lovely woods.

But no longer.

Avoidance. Joyce got that. Sky without Sun or Earth or stars only rubbed a person's face in the horror of their plight. And so, as so many days since the ... whatever, she had the park almost to herself.

Completing a lap, winded, her knees aching and her implant exhorting her to rest, she ground to a halt. Settling onto a park bench, peering upward, she wondered yet again what the citizens of Earth, studying their sky, saw—if anything. Perhaps they were also cut off. Perhaps they, too struggled, severed without warning from the resources and markets of other worlds. Perhaps they—

A fiery spark arced across the sky. A ship! But from where? And how?

Joyce linked to the traffic-control channel. The woman seemed almost familiar, like someone who looked like someone Joyce had once known. But that was not quite right, either. Maybe the woman resembled someone Joyce had once seen on the 3-V. She tried, and failed, to match a name to the voice and face.

"… Starship *Amends*," the woman was saying, "People of the Moon, it is our mission to release the trapped worlds from their isolation …."

And in the background, standing behind the almost recognized woman? Looking gaunt, looking decades older than Joyce remembered—

Wasn't that man, somehow, *Joshua*?

• • • •

With hands clasped, eyes closed in concentration, head canted, Richard Lewis Agnelli took everything in.

Had Corinne ever contemplated meeting the legendary director of the UPIA, she would not have pictured it like this. Not at the summons of the chief spook himself, or in his private office. Not in the company of old friends. Not as an intel source herself. Least of all, not too distracted to focus.

Because her mind raced and her guts tied themselves in knots, knowing where she must go next. To the home she scarcely remembered. To Denise, whom she could never forget. To Denise, whom she had given up hope of ever seeing again, to whom, over the years, she had professed her love and regrets in untold thousands of undeliverable messages. To Denise, who—until that very morning, when *Amends* had taken down Earth's slow-time barrier—must have believed Corinne dead.

Carl spoke. Joshua/Tacitus spoke. Agnelli mused about how much Ene might yet reveal if his UP bosses weren't sticklers for ambassadorial prerogatives. Carl spoke some more. Corinne, when prompted, maybe contributed a little.

"Interesting." Agnelli's eyes opened. "You're carried off by the Snakes aboard a hijacked starship. You fake its destruction, only to return a few months later, aboard *another* starship, with an unknown type of alien—and those aren't even the exotic elements of the tale."

"I suppose not," Carl said.

"Right," Agnelli said. "So: the relative positions of the planets indicate sixty years and a bit have passed. The few surviving agents in the Belt, with whom I'd lost contact, insist sixty years have passed. But you know what convinces me I've been in a time warp? You, Carl. In the not quite eight months since you last sat in this office, you've become older than Methuselah. And still I only believe you're you, DNA match and resemblance notwithstanding, because you have a COSMIC ULTRA implant."

Corinne managed a smile. "Could have been worse. We skipped the last thirty years."

"And where did you all leave *Discovery*, or *Invincible*, whatever you want to call it, not to mention 20 thousand thieving Snakes?"

"Through whose help we've liberated 35 billion people in this solar system alone," Joshua commented.

"And whom I couldn't have stopped from keeping the ship," Carl said.

"Had you wished to," Agnelli said. "I doubt you did."

"Short answer, sir?" Carl said. "I don't know where Timoq took *Invincible* and most of the clan. I can't tell what I don't know."

"Because this Timoq, their new Foremost, figures the UP might hold a grudge."

Carl shrugged. "Do you blame him? As you say, for you it's been only months."

As it had been only months for Denise. How would she react to someone become so ancient? *Someone she surely believed lost in the feigned destruction of* Discovery? *Someone once mourned and perhaps moved past?*

There was a soft tapping at the door. "Come in," Agnelli called. A steward entered, pushing a cart; he set out coffee service and left.

"Most of the clan, you said." Agnelli sipped coffee, considering. "The rest went off in Xool starships, just as you returned here, to liberate other InterstellarNet worlds?"

"Most, anyway," Carl said, "expecting to report back that the hidden slow-time generators *could* be turned off. Should they report otherwise, the few Hunters who stayed behind in the Epsilon Indi system will let the rocks keep falling."

"And that brings me to the big question," Agnelli said. "Your Xool friends expected us to self-destruct. Hell, they created us just so they could watch, then they locked us away so the watching would be safe. The Matthews conundrum, and all that. Then, eons and eons later, changing their minds, they taught you how to let everyone out. I have to ask. Why?"

"You mean apart from the ever bigger rocks that were raining down upon their heads?" Carl said.

"And apart from the robotic hordes we had begun to build?" Tacitus added.

"Because the Matthews conundrum, it turns out, has an Elman solution," Joshua said, turning toward Corinne.

"Well, Ms. Elman?" Agnelli prompted.

"A plague, Wue called us," Corinne began. "No, it's what she called our technologies. Nanotech, AI, gengineering. Plagues that had eradicated entire civilizations. Plagues to be feared, to be contained at any cost—before some rogue Xool scientist, working in secrecy, unleashed the apocalypse. Plagues scary beyond self-inflicted poverty, beyond hiding from time itself. Plagues that, given the lesson of their galactic explorations, ought to terrify *us*, too.

"And knowing all that, I asked myself: why aren't *I* scared?"

"Here's what I decided. For thirty years, we lived in one small, overcrowded habitat. We brought with us not one, not two, but maybe every technology dreaded by the Xool. Artificial intelligences, both human and Hunter. Minds linked with implanted Hunter biochips. Competing biospheres enhanced with Wolf gengineering. Centaur nanotech and Boater robotics." She patted Joshua on the arm. "Not least of all, an Augmented.

"Did life aboard *Invincible* always go smoothly? Hardly! Biospheres skirmished field by field, farm deck by farm deck. We had gray-goo incidents, and software gone awry, and wild robots. But the undeniable fact was … we kept it together. Hunter programs would stymie a human program gone rogue. Crops of both kinds evolved and adapted and evolved again. Nanites tamed genetically modified organisms become too successful and, the once, a berserker robot."

"Meaning?" Agnelli prompted.

"Meaning," said Tacitus, "that the Xool, unknowingly and un-intentionally, did more than breed test strains of plague. Perhaps any one of these technologies *is* fatal. But together? The synergistic interaction of—"

"Meaning," Corinne interrupted firmly, "that while any one of these technologies might become a plague, another tech might offer the cure. And that because no one can suppress technology *forever*, the only hope for the Xool is to emerge from their self-imposed quarantine and become part of a community.

"As long as they fear plagues, InterstellarNet offers their only chance to get vaccinated."

"And the Xool bought that?" Agnelli asked. "They were terrified of the technologies lurking nearby."

"Convinced?" Corinne shook her head. "I wouldn't put it that way. I'd say, rather, we left the Xool without any choice."

"And *I'd* say," Tacitus said, "that having opened a Pandora's box, all that was left to them was Hope."

• • • •

Amid the bustle and din of the Basel Spaceport main concourse, the friends stood silent. Parting after so very long together, what could one say?

Corinne could barely interpret the staticky announcement, "This is the final boarding call for Tycho City." Netted, the words would have been crystal clear—but to net would mean switching on her implant, and to do that would mean knowing each time Denise tried to reach out. Or, worse, that Denise *wasn't* trying.

Good news or bad, Corinne intended to hear it in person.

"That's our flight," Carl said unnecessarily.

They hugged, then Carl stepped aside, and she and Joshua hugged. She blinked and blinked, holding back the tears, before asking herself: why bother?

At the yawning doorway to the boarding tube through which Joshua had disappeared, Carl paused. "Remember the Elman solution," he called out. "We're all in this together."

And then Carl, too, was gone.

We're all in this together. Squaring her shoulders, hoping Carl was right, Corinne strode down the concourse to catch her own flight home.

Afterword

The InterstellarNet saga began, with *InterstellarNet: Origins*, in musings about the viability and technical underpinnings of a multi-species society loosely bound by radio communications. The community's alien members *had* to live nearby (astronomically speaking), because even a one-way radio transmission to the closest solar system takes more than four years.

For story purposes, at the least, such (relative) proximity is a manageable problem. SF authors have considerable leeway in how we build universes. It's one of the perks of the job. We can posit high-tech alien neighbors.

What about meeting face (or whatever) to face?

For as long as mainstream physics continues to insist that light sets the universal speed limit, travel even among neighboring star systems will be daunting—but doable. And so, in *InterstellarNet: New Order*, I exploited the proximity of InterstellarNet's members to step up the inter-species conflicts with the beginnings of (slower than light) travel among community members.

That made *two* novels in which I had conveniently ignored the Bandersnatch in the room.[1] Oh, I'm not alone in doing so. Plenty of science fiction conveniently assumes alien civilizations in close proximity to one another and in control of nearly identical (read: competitive) levels of science and technology. Even with an FTL warp drive, I suspect the *Star Trek* franchise would crumble absent such handy competitors close at, well, hand.

Authorial convenience notwithstanding, such proximity flies in the face of an ever-lengthening Great Silence. In *InterstellarNet:*

---

1. Think Lewis Carroll or Larry Niven. Your choice.

Enigma, I like to think I came up with a new explanation.

Yes, indeed: the opportunity to build universes *is* a neat perk.

Edward M. Lerner
March, 2015

Behind the Scenes

Did you flip forward out of curiosity, not having yet finished the novel? Then I implore you: avert your eyes! There be mega spoilers ahead!

Do you savor stories for awhile after completing them? Do you enjoy teasing out loose ends, solving for yourself any little puzzles, theorizing about the unexplained details, extrapolating from glimpsed bits of backdrop? You, too, will want to delay reading this section.

But if you're ready to learn more about the Xool, their plans, and their capabilities, if you wonder about the implications and limitations of Xool technology, this is the place.

(What if this background material proves esoteric for your taste? Then, channeling the Great and Terrible Oz, pay no attention to the science behind the curtain. Skip this section and enjoy the novel on its own.)

The Time-Slowing Field

The technologies to slow time and produce artificial gravity exploit knowledge far beyond present-day human science; we don't know why they work. But just knowing that such technologies *do* (somehow) work, they offer—as the Xool discovered—many fascinating and useful applications.

Let's consider circumstances on Horua (aka, Xool World) while it's enclosed in a time-slowing field that's set to a parameter we'll call X. During the timeframe of the story, X has a value minimally in the thousands, and often much larger.

Incident sunlight: beyond the field, the sun emits energy at its accustomed rate. Horua, its size and orbit unchanged, intercepts as much sunlight as ever. As each second passes within the field, X seconds-worth of solar energy arrive. Slow time by a factor of two, for example, and for each second experienced on the planet *two* seconds-worth of sunlight arrive. Hence: the slow-time field must reflect incident light in rough proportion to X, lest everyone inside the field roast.

Why only rough proportion? Because some energy, in the form of ultraviolet light, is siphoned off to power the field itself.[1] And, as discussed below, the fraction of light permitted through the field must be fine-tuned to adjust for several factors.

Magnetic field: Earth's magnetic field, which extends tens of thousands of kilometers into space, deflects solar wind and cosmic rays, protecting terrestrial life from what would otherwise be an unending stream of deadly radiation. This magnetic field is believed to arise from the circulation of molten iron deep inside the planetary core. Horua once had a significant magnetic field that protected life there—but as seen from outside the slow-time barrier, that protection has greatly diminished. If an external observer could observe the planet within, Horua's spin would be seen to have slowed by a factor of X. The magnetic field measured outside the field decreases accordingly.

What now protects Horuan life from celestial radiation? The slow-time field itself. Solar wind and cosmic rays—and small meteors—are stopped in their tracks by the vast deceleration caused by encountering the time dilation.

Angular momentum: much like energy and momentum, angular momentum is always conserved. For Horua's spin to slow by a factor of X, *something* must spin faster. That something is the slow-time field. The field doesn't exhibit mass in the familiar sense—but mass is just a form of energy. Energy fields can and do spin.

(What if the field hadn't absorbed the angular momentum lost by Horua? Then the planet's angular momentum would have transferred to Horua's satellite—flinging Blue Moon out of its orbit.)

---

1. UV *partially* powers the field. We'll get to the other power source.

Any object, whether a spaceship or an asteroid, that enters the slow-time region will surrender angular momentum abruptly to the slow-time field. We're familiar with the unpleasantness of suddenly losing ordinary/linear momentum—as when, for example, our car hits a tree. Suddenly losing angular momentum is just as undesirable.

In brief: Don't try to penetrate the barrier without a Xool counteracting-field generator.

Tides: Einstein's theory of general relativity indicates that an object (say, a planet) distorts the contour of space-time in proportion to that object's mass. The resulting curvature of space-time then influences the motion of other objects (say, a planet's moons). We call that influence gravity. Time doesn't enter into the picture.

Horua's mass being unchanged by the slow-time field, Blue Moon's orbital parameters—including its forty-hour orbit around Horua—are unchanged. An observer on Horua's surface doesn't see beyond the field (more upcoming about that), so he doesn't see Blue Moon in the sky. He *does*, however, experience the gravitational tug, and hence the motion, of Blue Moon.

Surviving the tides: Anyway, an observer on the surface *would* witness Blue Moon zipping past if the complications doesn't destroy the planet beneath him. Tidal energies, like solar energies, are multiplied by X. For a slowdown factor of, say, 100,000 (X's value when Carl and company arrive), Blue Moon will zip around the planet in little more than a *second*. But the pounding of coastal ecosystems turns out to be the least of the Xool's problems with the tides ....

Water seeks its own level; when tides rise high above average sea level, it's clear that energy is involved. Nor do the tides effect only large bodies of water—the crust itself flexes. We don't notice the crust flexing (although subtle instruments can measure it) because rock, being strong, moves far less under tidal influence than does water. Even so, tidal flexing pumps heat into the crust. Crank X high enough, and all that flexing will melt the crust.

What's a clever Xool to do? Apply his second super technology: gravity control.

The Xool deploy an array of gravity generators in Horua's crust and oceans. Pulses of artificial gravity synched to the time-slowing factor X offset the too-rapid tides.[2] Yet other gravity generators, deployed in the oceans, throb on a forty-hour cycle (as measured by a surface clock) to emulate Blue Moon's normal tides.[3]

Such workarounds never compensate perfectly, of course. That's why, as Corinne and company swoop to a landing on Horua, she spots densely packed standing waves on a lake (but misattributes the waves to a freak wind).[4] That's why, from within the slow-time field, Joshua's instruments can still detect, and estimate the passage of outside time by, Blue Moon rushing past.

Solar tides: A sun's gravitational pull plus a planet's rotation about its axis give rise to the solar-tide cycle. With Horua's rotation slowed by a factor of X, the solar tides the planet experiences likewise slow to a crawl. The Xool emulate normal solar tides (as, we have seen, they emulate Blue Moon normal tides) by the deployment of yet other gravity generators.

Seasons: Earth's seasons are the result of the planet's axial tilt. The hemisphere whose pole is tipped toward the sun receives more intense sunlight than the hemisphere whose pole is tipped away. That

---

2. The synching of gravity generators with time-slowing generators involves only a simple analog control loop—no advanced digital computers required. The tide-induced geothermal power drawn by the slow-time and gravity generators is another input to deciding what tiny fraction of sunlight should penetrate slow time.

3. How strong, on average, are Blue Moon's normal tides? About the same as Earth's lunar tides. Blue Moon's lesser volume, hence its mass, offset the tidal effects of its closer-in orbit.

4. Standing water waves, what hydrologists call seiches, occasionally occur on earthly lakes and oceans—even in swimming pools. Wind of just the proper strength and direction can cause seiches, as can seismic events.

Earth follows an elliptical orbit, at slightly different distances from the sun at different times of year, has only minor climate effects.[5]

On Horua, wrapped within slow time, matters are more complicated. As measured by an inside-the-field clock, one trip around the sun lasts X years. Seasons would be correspondingly prolonged, to the detriment of crops and other plant life—unless the light/energy permitted to penetrate the field is dynamically adjusted to emulate the traditional seasons.

The sun and stars: with Horua's rotation slowed by a factor of X, the progress of sun and stars across the sky decreases correspondingly. Only 1/X of the sunlight is permitted to penetrate the field, while X seconds (outside) correspond to each second inside. The effects offset; net sunlight intensity inside the field is unchanged.

Thus Horua's sun *could* shine in the sky as brightly as ever—if sunup to sundown were permitted to last an average of X/2 days by internal-clock measure. For X values in the thousands or millions, a sun so slowly creeping across the sky would bake one hemisphere and freeze the opposite hemisphere. On the planet's dark side, photosynthesizing plant life, and much other life dependent on the plants (say, anything that eats plants), wouldn't survive the years-long night. Between the all but perpetually hot and cold sides, horrendous storms would beset the twilit bands.

Instead, the field must redistribute the fraction of light that is allowed to penetrate. Half the field's inner surface is kept dark, the other half light. Recall that the field is spinning much more rapidly than Horua, having absorbed angular momentum from the planet; hence, the field generators must modulate lighting very rapidly. The dayside sky diffuses light toward the planet from all directions; for safety's sake, the night-side sky emits a faint background glow.

Night and day: a day, in the sense of one complete rotation of

---

5. If the Earth's location along its orbit caused the seasons, then northern and southern hemispheres would experience their summers (and winters) together, not half a year apart.

the Earth about its axis, is fixed in length.[6] The daylight/dark split, however, varies with the season and latitude. Anyone living north of the Arctic Circle enjoys (if that's the correct verb) midnight sun during part of summer and (surely in this case *enjoy* must be interpreted ironically) round-the-clock darkness during part of winter. The duration of daylight is a biological cue to which many organisms respond, from plants inferring a change in seasons to, in humans, seasonal affective disorder.

Horua, too, has axial tilt. Once in slow time, the dayside illumination (i.e., the diffuse sky glow discussed earlier) must be adjusted by latitude according to the emulated season. Get the emulation wrong, and that's one more way in which to mess up the environment.

The climate: to emulate the diurnal and seasonal cycles for which Horuan life evolved, real-time control of sky glow must adjust for: the planet's spin, the field's spin, the planet's axial tilt, the planet's position along its elliptical orbit, the instantaneous value of X, and, at various points across the globe, the latitude. Over millions of years, the star itself slowly grows hotter; the fraction of sunlight allowed through must also adjust for that effect.

The emulation is less than perfect, and the ecosphere suffers for it, because the Xool, by intent, have only primitive computing with which to run models and control the field generators. Even if the emulation were otherwise perfect, the diffuse nature of the illumination would still adversely impact any phototropic, sun-seeking species (such as terrestrial sunflowers, which turn to track the sun across the sky). As much as the social disincentives of a dictatorship, degradation of the ecosphere is why Carl and company encounter a seedy, rundown economy. Twenty years (inside) are far too short a time for the ecosphere to have adapted.

---

6. Well, almost fixed. Over the eons, Earth's rotation has slowed down slightly for complicated reasons having to do with tides and angular-momentum coupling between Earth and Moon. In recent times, Earth's day has been lengthening at the rate of about 2 milliseconds per century.

A virtue from a vice: on Horua, the limited fidelity of emulated diurnal and seasonal cycles is problematical. On other worlds? It can be a tool. There's nothing like an ice age or a sudden jump in global temperatures to stir the evolutionary pot. More on that to come …

Xool Starships

For all their physical-science prowess, the Xool don't have inter-stellar-drive technology superior to what Centaurs invented and humans use.[7] In part that's for the lack of incentive. Xool travelers cross interstellar space in slow time; the folks back home, awaiting the reports of explorers or the results of the Grand Experiment, are likewise in slow time.

But if the Xool *could* accelerate their ships to near-light speed … they wouldn't dare. A starship needs time to see and swerve from the path of any space junk it encounters; at near-light speed, there would be virtually no warning. If they did detect something on a collision course, without decent computers they'd be too slow to plot course changes.

That said, Xool ships have their pluses. Human ships must sustain a life-friendly biosphere for years on end, recycling *everything*. Xool ships, with their crews normally in slow time, dispense with the cost, bulk, and complexities of sophisticated, closed-loop life-support systems. When a Xool crew emerges into real time, they have artificial-gravity technology to offset the unpleasantness of acceleration and, while in orbit or otherwise coasting, of free-fall conditions.

The Grand Experiment

Simply put, the Xool set out to evolve and nurture intelligences in many solar systems, steering each group's cultural development so

---

7. The T'fru interstellar drive is a significant topic in its own right. If you're curious, see *InterstellarNet: New Order*.

that the ultimate consequences of particular distrusted technologies could be observed.

In practice, there is nothing simple about it.

Evolution and climate: the Xool fear genetic engineering, so gene-tweaking isn't a tool in their toolbox. Instead, over and over, they stress ecosystems to force evolution. To operate the slow-time field around a planet and *not* stress its environment would have been difficult.

On Horua, as we've seen, the Xool permit through the slow-time field—to the extent their primitive computers can manage it—such fractions of sunlight as correspond to what the various regions of the planet would naturally receive. On the experimental worlds, the Xool sometimes dial up or down, whether globally or regionally, the amount of sunlight getting through. Aggregate illumination is a straightforward control knob for Joshua to explain—unlike, for example, how the Xool can also muck about with the emulated seasons and tides.

Experiment overview, phase 1 (in theory): the experimenters cause a thermal climate shock, wait out in slow time a few million years of evolutionary recovery, emerge for a quick look-see, then repeat as needed. If evolution on a planet hasn't progressed according to their schedule, they dial up time dilation and squeeze in extra cycles. If on one planet evolution progresses too quickly, the Xool need only slow down time there, but without further stresses, to maintain that world on the common schedule.

Experiment overview, phase 1 (in practice): the observer teams find themselves always rushed. The longer they spend in real time— whether reworking a planetary environment, assessing the effects of the latest induced stresses, speculating how emergent phyla might further develop, or doing upkeep on their own facilities—the more they age with respect to the families left behind on Horua. Generations of experimentation would be appropriate—except that the dictator on Horua is determined to see the project finished within her lifetime.

As one visible token of the observers' perpetual state of haste, the copper walls (electromagnetic shielding) of their hidden bases receive only the minimum patching that keeps them air-tight and more-or-less functional.

Experiment overview, phase 2 (in theory): Episodic forced evolution under Xool control continues until the very end of the process, when modern humans (or, on other worlds, other intelligent life) has emerged. Had the sky vanished during historical times, someone would have noticed!

In this final stage of the experiment, the time-slowing generators (and related tide-mitigating gravity generators) remain off. The Xool indoctrinate and rely upon their native agents to steer civilizations and technological developments—sometimes encouraging, sometimes (by planting Frankenstein-like myths) discouraging a technology. Throughout this phase, until the experiment's final years, the native agents have the benefit of Xool technology advanced beyond human norms.

Having used time dilation when/as needed to keep their scattered "Petri dishes" on schedule, the Xool complete their experiment by again putting Earth (and the other worlds) in slow time. That shift to slow time serves two purposes: (1) more opportunity to observe and (2) protection from the (presumed) technological contagion within. The supervising Xool set a timer to trigger the slow-time field, then head for home.

Automated Xool ships periodically swoop inside the barrier for updates from native agents and snippets of local news broadcasts. That information is then beamed back to the home system. By observing technological crises in detail, the Xool will learn whether and how the various technologies that have long been suppressed on Horua may be allowed to advance.

Thereafter, test worlds will be held safely in slow time "for a few million years" until they and Horua have moved far apart. If need be—because, say, a Berserker robot plague developed—a planet can be maintained indefinitely in quarantine.

Technologies: apart from physics, the Xool do all they can to keep their technology behind what has become cutting-edge Interstellar-Net technology. The ultimate purpose of their experiment, after all, is to preview if and how specific scary technologies lead to disaster. Hence, the Xool encourage, say, genetic engineering on one world, nanotech on another, and artificial intelligence on a third.

Choosing stars (in theory): even in possession of slow-time technology, efficiency is a virtue. The Xool prefer to experiment on worlds close to one another and Horua. Alas, rather than stay put, stars revolve around the galactic core and (most often to a lesser degree) have their orbits perturbed by passing encounters with nearby stars and star clusters. Over the duration of one turn around the galaxy (at Earth's distance from the core, an excursion of roughly 200 million years), even passing encounters may cause once neighboring stars to diverge.

Over the course of the Xool experiment, Horua's sun will complete almost three revolutions around the galactic core. They don't much mind their "Petri dishes" diverging mid-experiment, when little is happening beyond prodding evolution. They do want their experimental worlds to be near Horua and one another once intelligences emerge. Observer teams can then efficiently compare notes. Home-world authorities can take reports from all solar systems at more or less the same time.

Choosing stars (in practice): The orbit of a planet in a solar system depends mostly on the far more massive star, and comparatively little on other planets. In the same way, the orbits of stars depend mostly on the overall mass distribution of their galaxy (more so on dark matter than on the visible kind). Thus the Xool, even with their primitive computers, can approximate stars' orbits, to help them choose solar systems that will converge with Horua at experiment's end. Sometimes, the approximation suffices—as happens with the solar systems that comprise the InterstellarNet community. When the approximations fail, experimental worlds end up scattered along much of the galaxy's Orion spiral arm.

Experiment overview, phase 2 (in practice): the Xool developed without intelligent neighbors with whom to communicate. The emergence across several convergent solar systems of InterstellarNet takes the Xool by surprise. The resulting technology swaps among neighbors is, from the Xool perspective, cross-contamination of the Petri dishes. In eleven solar systems, rates of technological progress suddenly accelerate beyond what the Xool anticipated or know how to control—leading to improvisations like Joshua Matthews's kidnapping.

As InterstellarNet matures, the far-flung Xool observer teams find their ability to coordinate—among one another, and with the home world—seriously hampered. Across light-years, the tightest radio beam diverges to wider than a solar system. Hence, with InterstellarNet members all operating interstellar-grade radio transceivers, Xool agents in neighboring systems dare not risk detection by coordinating via telecom.

So: at experiment's end, the Xool observers are reduced to coordinating slowly, by interstellar travel. They eventually decide to quarantine all the InterstellarNet worlds, with all quarantines to be activated simultaneously. Synchronized quarantines avoid the unpredictable impact on the experiment of one InterstellarNet member observing that something unprecedented has befallen its neighbors.8

The Xool's grand scheme is likewise disrupted by the Centaurs' success in building the first InterstellarNet-community starship. Coordination with Horua (about twelve light-years from Earth) involves decades of travel; for safety's sake, earlier than first planned, the Chief Administrator decrees they must raise the slow-time bar-

---

8. The Xool pre-positioned/hid slow-time and gravity generators wherever in a solar system colonization seemed most likely. Thus, the Moon and Mars entered quarantine when Earth did—but scattered communities on asteroids and smaller moons remain in real time.

The Xool have been left to gamble that those remnants of civilization will be too hard-pressed to further develop dangerous technologies.

riers and begin the quarantines. The observer teams transmit time-delayed startup codes, delaying the barrier activations while they put some distance between themselves and the Solar System. Any human ships and colonies left outside slow time would not treat kindly an unrecognized vessel spotted fleeing the scene ....

Beyond InterstellarNet: the Grand Experiment originally encompasses many solar systems. Heavy "handed" Xool meddling mucks up some ecologies so severely that the observers abandon these worlds as lost causes. Staff from these worlds then move on to reinforce the observer teams where things are proceeding better, until—once ubiquitous broadcasting and networks make monitoring easy—most Xool returned home.

Scattered worlds, approaching their technological crises somewhat ahead of the clustered InterstellarNet community, have, locked behind slow-time barriers, been seen to fall into a gray-goo, AI runaway, robot apocalypse, or other nightmare. Such collapses have only further committed the Chief Administrator to her experiment: the Xool are learning—while reconfirming that these technologies are as dangerous as she has always feared.

Of clocks and dating: Why doesn't anyone detect past diddling with time's passage? Hasn't Earth become curiously younger than, say, Mars?

The short answers: accurately determining a planet's age is hard, and not so that anyone can tell.

Our planet is ever being reshaped by erosion, volcanism, plate tectonics, and the occasional asteroid strike. Other solid worlds in the Solar System experience (or once did) many of the same age-obscuring processes. The planets and major moons thus do not exhibit—nor are they expected to—surface features as old as the solar system.

How then do we ascertain the age of our planet? Very indirectly. First, the ages of meteors are estimated from an analysis of radioactive-decay products (of very-long-half-life isotopes of lead) within those meteors. Earth's age is then estimated using models of planet formation and the calculated age of the oldest meteors.

To estimate the Sun's age, believed to be about 4.6 billion years, is likewise indirect. It entails models of both fusion processes and the circulation of fusion byproducts from the solar core, where fusion takes place, to the observable solar surface, as well as inferences about the primordial composition of the dust-and-gas cloud from which the star formed.

If Earth spent the occasional few millions of years in slow time, the age discrepancy between Earth and Sun would not be obvious. If a discrepancy were noticed, it could easily be dismissed as a glitch in one of the models.

What's next?

As retirement on Earth loses its (pun intended) novelty, it will occur to Carl to wonder about other worlds, hundreds or more light-years distant, once also part of the Xool experiment. With slow-time technology, all such worlds become eminently reachable.

Each journey would take—though it would seem only an instant—many centuries. If any civilizations Out There have survived, perhaps they, too, can be set free. Someone should look into that.

Someone like Carl?

But that's a story for another occasion ....

InterstellarNet History: Key Milestones
The Earth-centric Perspective

1958   Leos (of the Lalande 21185 system) detect Earth's radio emissions. The faint signals are not at first recognized as evidence of intelligence.

2002   Earth receives Leos' radioed reply (transmitted in 1994). Humanity responds under United Nations auspices, opening an era of interstellar barter in intellectual property.

2003   The UN begins a program of radio beamcasts to other stars, in search of other intelligent neighbors.

2006   Onset of the three-year-long Lalande Implosion: the collapse of petroleum-based portions of Earth's economy. The adoption of advanced fuel-cell technology, deduced from clues within the 2002 Leo message, triggers the crash.[9]

2010   The "Protocol on Interstellar Technology Commerce" takes effect. The international treaty creates a new UN agency, the Interstellar Commerce Union, to oversee Earth's radio-based commerce with extraterrestrial species.

2012   The Centaurs (of the Alpha Centauri A system) contact Earth by radio, the first of many ET species to answer Earth's exploratory messages.

2031   A permanent lunar settlement is established. Colonies and research bases begin to spread across the solar system.

2041   Europan gambit: an interplanetary megacorp impersonates an ET species native to Jupiter's moon Europa, attempting to circumvent ICU refusal to import Centaur nanotechnology.

---

9. The fuel cells, exploiting a revolutionary new catalyst, draw power from almost any fluid hydrocarbon, including natural gas and alcohol. After 2007, few new automobiles use internal combustion.

2050 Transmissions disclosing Centaur nanotech reach the Solar System.

2052 The ICU proposes a secure e-commerce mechanism that gradually becomes the flexible basis of a more sophisticated interstellar trading community.

2055 The United Planets Charter is ratified; the UP succeeds the United Nations.

2061 An artificial intelligence is received from the Centaurs; the AI trade agent is successfully installed and confined by the ICU. Other AI agents follow, as more distant species receive, accept, and respond to Earth's 2052 proposal.

2072 The AI trade agent to Earth of the Hunters (colloquially, the Snakes, of the Barnard's Star system) announces a computing technology far in advance of human photonics. The debate whether to license incompletely understood alien biocomputers roils human society and interplanetary politics. A deal for the tech is not consummated until 2076.

2084 Human and Wolf (from the Wolf 359 system) authorities acknowledge their near parity in technology, paving the way for lightly regulated interstellar commerce among private parties. The practice spreads as InterstellarNet fosters technological convergence.

2102 Snake Subterfuge: the attempt, very nearly successful, to extort a fortune from humanity. The exploit involved trapdoors long hidden in the now ubiquitous—but still incompletely understood—Hunter/Snake biocomputing technology.

2110 The asylum request of the Centaur trade agent precipitates an artificial-intelligence emancipation movement across human space. Granting of the agent's request sours relations between humans and Centaurs.

2112 The AI emancipation amendment to the UP charter is ratified.

2125   The habitat-sized Centaur starship *Harmony*, the first starship built within the InterstellarNet community, sets off in secrecy for Barnard's Star.

2126   A former Secretary-General of the Interstellar Commerce Union nearly succeeds in subverting InterstellarNet trade mechanisms by illegally cloning the AI trade agent from Tau Ceti.

2145   *Harmony*, its Centaur crew in cold sleep, reaches the fringes of the Barnard's Star system. The starship is captured by a fugitive Hunter clan. Lacking the technology to mass-produce antimatter, "their" starship at this point carrying antimatter fuel for only its planned return voyage, clan Arblen Ems undertakes a desperate journey.

2165   The Hunter starship *Victorious* (actually *Harmony*, its Centaur crew imprisoned) reaches the Solar System. In the conflict that breaks out: the UP antimatter factory is destroyed (the "Himalia Incident"); *Victorious* is pursued, boarded, and also destroyed; the rescued Centaur crew are resettled in the Australian Outback; the Hunter survivors are interned on the Uranian moon, Ariel.

2178   The UP-built starship *New Beginnings* sets off for Alpha Centauri to repatriate those Centaurs young enough for another interstellar trek.

2180   The UP begins construction of a new starship, *Discovery*.

2185   Joshua Matthews is named historian of the Interstellar Commerce Union, *Discovery* nears completion, and the story opens …

Dramatis Personae

Terrestrials

Richard Lewis Agnelli: Director, United Planets Intelligence Agency (UPIA)

Denise Chang: Wife of Corinne Elman

Danica Chidambaram: UPIA covert agent

Grace DiMeara: Freelance pilot employed by Corinne Elman

Corinne Elman: Reporter; detainee during the Hunter raid on the Solar System

Lyle Logan: Pilot; repairman for robotic mining ships

Joshua Matthews: Historian; former employee of the Interstellar Commerce Union (ICU), an agency of the United Planets

Joyce Matthews: Retired secretary-general, and formerly the chief technical officer, of the ICU; grandmother of Joshua Matthews

Akihiro Matsushita: Admiral, commanding UP naval forces in the Saturn system

Carl Rowland: Warden and UPIA station chief at the Hunter internment colony on Ariel; long ago, under an alias, free-lance pilot for Corinne Elman

Donald Schnabel: Assistant to the deputy project manager, *Discovery* mission office

Helena Strauss: UPIA station chief on the Moon

Robyn Tanaka Astor: ICU secretary-general; an Augmented (human/artificial-intelligence (AI) hybrid)

Astor 2215: AI; later, a partial backup of Robyn Tanaka Astor

Tacitus 352: Historian; Joshua Matthew's colleague; an AI

Bruce Wycliffe: Deputy UPIA station chief on Ariel; assistant to Carl Rowland

Centaurs

K'tra Ko ka: Coordinator (ka) of the Centaur colony in Australia

T'Gwat Fru: Historian in the Centaur colony

Hunters

Dolmar Banak: Sculptor and craftsman

Rashk Folhaut: Navigator (Timoq era)

Firh Glithwah: Foremost of clan Arblen Ems; leader of the Hunter colony on Ariel

Hrak Jomar: Chief science officer (Timoq era)

Firh Koban: Logistical officer / pilot / Glithwah's cousin

Loshtof: AI; Glithwah's translator

Cluth Monar: Glithwah's aide

Rashk Motar: Engineering officer aboard *Excalibur* (Timoq era)

Pashwah: Trade agent representing the Great Clans; Earth-resident; an AI

Rashk Pimal: Glithwah's tactical officer and chief aide

Cluth Timoq: Foremost of clan Arblen Ems as successor to Glithwah; biologist

Gral Tofot: Fighter pilot (Timoq era)

Hrak Votan: Crewman aboard *Excalibur*; computing specialist (Timoq era)

Xool

Iroa Ene Leiahoma (Ene): Leader of Xool observers in the Solar System

Atufea Lua Duruza (Lua): Leader of Xool observers in the Barnard's Star system (the Hunters' home)

Wataninui Wue Tihotiho (Wue): Chief Administrator (dictator) of the Xool

About the Author

EDWARD M. LERNER worked in high tech and aerospace for thirty years, as everything from engineer to senior vice president, for much of that time writing science fiction as a hobby. Since 2004 he has written full-time.

His novels range from near-future tech-nothrillers, like *Small Miracles* and *Energized*, to traditional SF, like the InterstellarNet novels, to (collaborating with Larry Niven) the space-opera epic Fleet of Worlds series of *Ringworld* companion novels.

Ed's short fiction has appeared in anthologies, collections, and many of the usual SF magazines. He also writes the occasional nonfiction technology article.

Lerner lives in Virginia with his wife, Ruth.

His website is **www.edwardmlerner.com**.

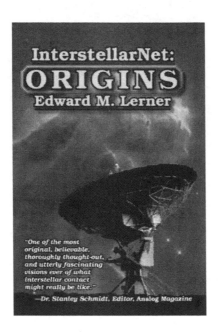

InterstellarNet: Origins
When the First Call from the Stars Comes, Do We Even Dare to Answer?

Life changes for everyone in general—and for physicist Dean Matthews in particular—when astronomers detect a radio signal from a nearby star. First Contact forces humanity to face hard questions, and do it fast. Every answer spawns new questions. Every solution sets in motion a new and more daunting crisis to challenge Dean, his family—and an expanding number of interstellar civilizations—for generations to come.

"One of the most original, believable, thoroughly thought-out, and utterly fascinating visions ever of what interstellar contact might really be like."

—Dr. Stanley Schmidt, Editor, Analog Magazine

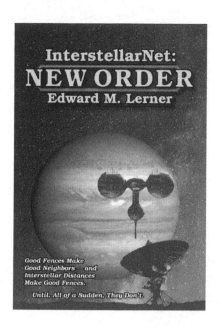

InterstellarNet: New Order
Good fences, said the poet, make good neighbors ...
and interstellar distances made very good fences.
Or so we thought ....

Earth and its interstellar neighbors have been in radio contact for a
century and a half. A vigorous commerce in intellectual property has
accelerated technical progress for all the species involved. Ideas, riding
on radio waves, routinely cross interstellar space—almost like neighbors
chatting over the interstellar back fence. But there is a way over, or under,
or around, almost any fence. Sooner or later, when we least expect it, the
neighbors, friendly or otherwise, are going to pay a call.... *InterstellarNet:
New Order* chronicles the startling events of *Second* Contact, upfront
and personal, as humanity discovers that meeting aliens face to face is
very different—and a lot more dangerous—than sending and receiving
messages.

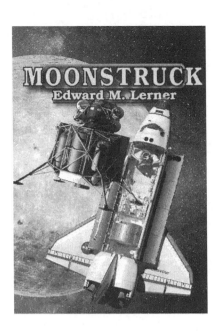

Moonstruck
Will our first contact with aliens be the dawn of a new tomorrow—or the last act in human history?

The moon has suddenly acquired its own satellite: a two-mile-across starship that represents a hitherto unsuspected Galactic Commonwealth.

The F'thk, a vaguely centaur-like member species for whom Earth's ecology is hospitable, have been sent to evaluate humanity for prospective membership. The F'thk are overtly friendly but very private—"Information is a trade good" could almost be their mantra. The Galactics' arrival may signify the start of a glorious new era, or it may presage the cataclysmic end of human civilization. Which outcome do the aliens really desire ... and what will they do if humanity refuses to play its assigned role?

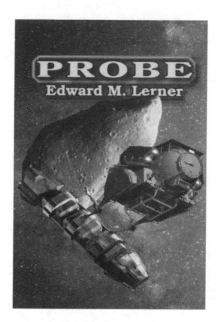

Probe
What if First Contact doesn't come the way we expect it?

Bob Hanson, the chief scientist of a major aerospace corporation, has made an incredible discovery: a wrecked alien spacecraft adrift in the Asteroid Belt. The military enthusiastically embraces an investigation of the extraterrestrials, remarkably indifferent to the inconsistencies that begin to appear. But Hanson keeps digging ... and finds much more than he had ever bargained for. Are aliens manipulating events on Earth? Did unscrupulous corporate executives invent the aliens in search of giga-buck government contracts? Has the Pentagon fabricated an alien menace for its own purposes? Or is the truth something *really* unimaginable?

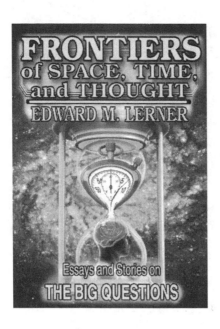

Frontiers of Space, Time, and Thought

This volume brings together more than a dozen of Edward M. Lerner's most engaging short stories to take the reader on a grand tour of Big Ideas: from virtual reality to artificial intelligence to homicidal time-traveling grandchildren to troubled aliens wondering if *they* are alone. But truth can be stranger than fiction—and Lerner's fact articles have pride of place in this collection, posing some Really Big Questions. How can we protect Earth from asteroids? What will commercialized spaceflight be like in the post-shuttle era? What will privacy (or the lack thereof) mean in the Internet age? Lerner lays out the why, where, and (perhaps the) how of faster-than-light travel, and the challenges of communicating with alien species. Expanded and updated with the latest information, and with full references and links to further reading, these essays will take you to and beyond the *Frontiers of Space, Time, and Thought*.

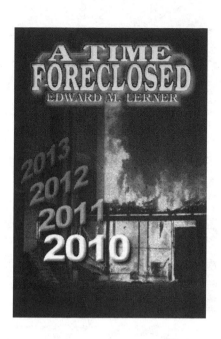

A Time Foreclosed
Where are all the time travelers?

If it is possible to move between past and future, shouldn't someone from somewhen in all the infinite reaches of the future have visited by now? The good news is, there are answers to those questions. But then, there's the bad news....What if a man could go forward in time to learn about the future—and then backwards in time to correct a dreadful mistake? But what if going back in time was, in and of itself, the most terrible mistake possible?Could things really be that bad? A life's journey that started off bending—and breaking—a few real estate laws couldn't really wind up ending life as we know it? That would have to be impossible. Or would it? Previously published as "Time Out," this mind-bending story will keep readers guessing until the final page. Includes the bonus story "Grandpa?"—one of Edward M. Lerner's most popular tales.

FoxAcre Press

Made in the USA
Lexington, KY
17 December 2016